I0694497

Butterfly

VAMPIRE GUILD CHRONICLES

BY KATIE GABBERT DOWNEY

Printed in the United States of America

Content guidance: This story explores themes of sexuality, romance, friendship, vigilante justice, and mental health struggles. It contains explicit sexual content and graphic depictions of violence and is only suitable for readers 18 years and up.

Paperback ISBN: 978-1-971025-01-8
Hardcover ISBN: 978-1-971025-02-5
eBook ISBN: 978-1-971025-00-1

Editor and book designer: Cooper Downey

For my vet med girlies who'd like to dish out some vigilante
justice

"Let yourself be silently drawn by the strange pull of what you really love. It will not lead you astray."

—Rumi

CONTENTS

CHAPTER ONE

"How in the hell is he able to keep finding me?" I mumble to myself as a stab of pain through my abdomen makes me double over. "He could compete in the Hide and Seek World Championship."

Beneath the silver crescent moon shining brightly in the night sky, I watch as the man walks cautiously along the beach towards me. The waves of the restless ocean pound the sand, obliterating the quick and steady sounds of his footsteps. The wind whips his shoulder length blond hair back from his face with each gust. He walks much faster than a normal person with a fluid feline predatory grace that is entrancing.

With each step closer, the encompassing pain in my body eases. The fire and burning that is consuming my body from within which has immobilized me to this spot, recedes like the waves from the shore. His face is slowly becoming more recognizable in the moonlight as he draws closer. Cool, steely blue-grey eyes fix on me, his mouth tight and brows furrow as he tries to decipher if I am about to flee. Leaning back into my chair, I give him a reassuring smile—he has won this round, and I did not plan on running any farther. There is nowhere really that I want to go anymore, and the easing of the pain in my body is welcome after the last few torturous days. Being in constant searing pain is extremely exhausting and I can feel every cell in my body invigorate with every step closer he takes.

"It took you three days to find me this time," I tease as he draws closer. I look at his face and try to gauge what he is feeling.

He nods, holding his body tightly, as if anticipating me bolting from him. His lips are held in a tight line as he studies me, his eyes roaming over my entire body. The heat of his gaze stirs a longing in my chest. He is hard to resist—even now…after everything that I've learned.

The tension between us grows, but the changing sensation in my body keeps me from speaking. He sits down next to me, his body so close to mine that instead of the pulsing easing of pain, the pulse slowly starts to change to pleasure. The pulsing gets stronger, throbbing harder and harder. I close my eyes and lean forward, trying to steady myself. Sharp residual pain pulses down my limbs and pleasure pulses back up them. It feels like I am tearing apart on a cellular level. He leans over to me and gently touches my hand, running his thumb against the inside of my palm, and I gasp. A new pleasure begins to circle there as he traces a spiral from the middle of my palm radiating out to my fingers. I open my eyes and glance around at the beachside hotel that I had finally stopped at and found refuge, verifying that we are still alone on the beach.

The lounge chairs we are sitting on are positioned along the beach facing the ocean and remain empty. The waves crash louder now as the wind gusts around us. We are still the only people out at this time of night. I feel a powerful pull of my body towards him, and I resist it. The magical connection pulses and pulls me towards him. Our physical separation had been stretched to its limit, and I know I had gotten close to our destruction while running, but I had wanted to make a point. I wanted him to feel something uncomfortable, and I had been willing to let myself suffer to ensure that.

The magic between us pulls at us like we are two magnets trying to bridge the gap between our two bodies. I fight against it and hook my legs around the legs of the lounger and sit firmly in my chair, fighting the urge to touch him more as my body begins to vibrate ever so slowly towards him. Stubborn as ever, I wait for him to initiate the next phase. Although I had stopped running, I still wasn't done fighting.

He slowly sweeps his shoulder length blond hair out of his face and looks at me quietly. His face is as unreadable as stone as he observes me. It is impossible to tell what he is feeling when he looks at me like this, and it is so very frustrating. Turning my head from him I look back out at the ocean. It had been a peaceful evening beside the sea, and I was going to miss the beauty of the water tomorrow. Gently, I feel him pull my hand into his and encircle it with his other hand. I involuntarily sigh with relief. Fighting the need to touch him is exhausting and I am out of energy to do so any longer. I knew it was time for me to give in, but I didn't enjoy it.

"It was much too long this time," he says softly with a hint of sadness in his voice. His voice is like liquid velvet as it pours out of his mouth. I would recognize it anywhere.

He closes his eyes and bows his head, gripping my hand tighter. My hand burns as a flow of energy surges between us, making my entire body vibrate. I let out a strangled moan, looking at him while trying to hide my fear—this hurts much worse than last time. His eyes meet mine, turning lighter blue in color, but he holds on tightly to my hand as I try to pull away from him, not wanting to feel the burning any longer. It feels like my hand is stuck in an electrical socket, my survival instinct is triggered, and I needed to escape this sensation. The flow of energy surging between us stings more than it ever has before. The separation between us the last few days has affected our connection greatly. When we were close, the channel was open and the energy flowed painlessly between us, but the longer we were apart, the more the channel had started to close, which meant that this time the channel had to reopen. The ache from that process is unbearable.

"Do you feel that? Is it hurting you as much as it is hurting me?" I gasp, flinching as a surge of pain hits me. I continue to try to yank my hand back from him, but he holds tighter. I knew if he released me, he would just have to grab me back up again to open the channel, so I am thankful he holds on—but the pain is horrendous. We must hold together until the channel is fully open again.

"Yes," he says evenly, and I wonder how he is able to withstand it. He is giving me no indication that he is in as much pain as I am.

I moan loudly as the energy gives one final surge and then dissipates. I slump in my chair in relief. It had felt as if there were millions of tiny pieces of glass burrowing through my skin and I contemplate never running away again—the pain is getting more intense with every attempt. I look at Brigham with tears in my eyes, and his eyes reveal the concern he has for me. I give him a weak smile, and he starts rubbing the palm of my hand. His caress helps and the pain begins to alleviate faster. I sigh and laugh at myself. I don't breathe anymore, sadly. There is no need now that I am a vampire. Sighing and inhaling were no longer necessary, but I cannot seem to stop. I was always punctuating my responses with this dramatic gesture. It was a very human habit to emphasize emotion with breath and hard to break the habit. My affection for this wasn't unique, as I had witnessed other vampires huffing and sighing as well, so at least I wasn't alone in this.

The flow of energy stops pulsing between us, and Brigham lays my hand back into my lap. I am glad it is over with. That was intense, and I wasn't sure how much longer I could have withstood the pain.

"It hurt quite a bit this time," I muse, looking at my hand. It throbs and aches only slightly now. Under the moonlight my skin shone silver. I had been pale as a human and now as a vampire I was even paler.

"You say that as if you are proud," he says with an edge to his voice. I turn to him in surprise and flash him a guilty smile.

"I suppose I am a little," I admit. It was quite rebellious to run away from him. No one had ever done something like that before, or at least that is what my best friend Anton had told me.

Brigham's eyebrows knit together, and he turns away from me and runs his hands through his hair. His reaction surprises me—usually he is much more stoic to my insolent responses. I must have really angered him, and that fact sends a thrill through me. Immature as it is for me to be excited about getting a negative response from Brigham, I just couldn't seem to help myself. I am still pretty pissed at him about this whole thing, and I feel betrayed. I had trusted him, and he wasn't honest with me.

Brigham stares out at the ocean for a few moments, and his features soften back into his usual stoney facade, his skin shining like moonstone and my eyes trace the curve of his jaw to his high cheekbones. I had forgotten how handsome he was in the moonlight, and I admire him for a moment. He catches my gaze and gives me a disapproving look. Another emotional response! *This is so exciting!*

"I can't admire you now?" I ask innocently.

Brigham ignores my question. "Did you have to hurt Brandon so badly when you left?" he asks, turning his body towards me quickly. His face is still stoney, but his eyes blaze changing to midnight blue betraying his calm facade.

I look at him in embarrassment and cringe. The incident Brigham was referring to was my least favorite so far as an immortal. "He wouldn't get out of my way," I say softly. Brandon was the human bodyguard Brigham had assigned to me to watch me when he was attending to business matters. Unfortunately, Brandon and I had a difference of opinion about where I was allowed to go and that didn't end well for him.

"It's his job to protect you," he says firmly. His hands tighten into fists, and I cannot help but stare at them for a moment. Why was he so mad? *I was the one who should be mad!*

"He made me feel like I was a prisoner on your orders," I accuse, jabbing a finger into his chest. Even with my vampire strength, Brigham was formidable and I hardly made a dent into his skin. "What exactly is he protecting me from?" I huff angerly. I am already getting annoyed by this conversation. Maybe I will run away again, after all.

"Yourself," Brigham says darkly. Was he serious right now? *God, he could be so patronizing!* Does he even realize what he sounds like?

"Myself, you say, huh?" I spit, grinding my teeth in frustration, trying to fight the urge to attack him like a deranged alley cat. *Did he really believe that?* Was that really true? A month ago, I would have believed Brigham's words, but now I'm not as certain. I know I am a newly made vampire, but I can take care of myself. I have proven that numerous times.

Although, hurting Brandon was not my finest moment and I did agree that going off by myself to the ocean wasn't the safest action to take, given I am still learning about this new body and its limits. I had been feeling increasingly reckless with my life since I was turned, and angry, but fuck him. It is still my life and if I wanted to fuck it up, so be it. I understood that Brigham's protectiveness was a remnant of a sense of gallantry from the time when he was born, but he was overdoing it. This protectiveness is outdated and irritating. In most respects I think he'd adapted well to modern society. He wore the right clothes, drove the right car, talked using current vernacular, and had a knack for business, but his protectiveness towards me seemed excessive—even for a boyfriend.

"Butterfly—" Brigham starts, but I cut him off.

"Do you really believe that? Is Brandon really protecting me from myself? I think he is protecting you more than me. I think it's more about your peace of mind than anything else," I seethe, unable to leash my anger any longer. Brigham sighs heavily in defeat. *WOW!* I had never heard Brigham sigh like that before! I must be hitting his buttons tonight! *Good!*

"Maybe you are right," he says quietly and looks out at the ocean. The dark blue waves move like a lover's body against the sheets, rising and falling in a graceful dance. It is hard to not get aroused watching them. "It's beautiful here," he whispers and reaches for my hand. He leaves it hanging in the air and I stare at it, unsure what to do next.

"That's why I picked it. I thought it would be a nice backdrop to my death scene," I say dryly, hoping to get another emotional response. His head snaps back at me sharply. *That worked!*

"Did you really think I'd let you die?" he asks, raising his voice. He takes my hand aggressively and holds it tightly, staring at me intently.

"No," I say, shaking my head sadly. "I knew it was a fantasy."

"Yet you tried."

I nod. "Yes, I tried." I really didn't want to die, that was never my intent. I was only acting out. Brigham had hurt me, and I hadn't forgiven him yet.

"You're my immortal beloved," he says tenderly, as he rubs a circle against my palm. A carnal jolt of energy surges into me that is not only due to our connection.

"Don't call me that," I whisper. It embarrasses me when Brigham calls me by such silly, lovey-dovey nicknames. I had never been in a relationship where you called each other sweetheart, honey, or babe. Honestly, it weirds me out a little when I hear people talk like that. "You know I hate it." Immortal beloved seemed so dramatic and final, couldn't he just call me his girlfriend?

"But that's what you are."

"No, there's still time to change that," I say. I wasn't trying to be cruel—I was just stating a fact…okay, maybe I was trying to be a little cruel. *ARGH!* I can't seem to release this anger I had towards him right now. *I am still so pissed!*

"Very little time left," he says, and I can hear the anguish in his voice.

I sigh loudly. "Yes, very little," I admit. I look at Brigham and he gives me the slightest of smiles. A flicker of muscle twitch really, but it is enough for me to know he cared. I was glad he came to the ocean to be with me. "Is Brandon okay? I was planning on healing him when you brought me back."

"He's healed, but he doesn't want to be your bodyguard anymore."

"I don't blame him—I wouldn't want to either after what I did to his arm."

Images of the broken bone protruding through Brandon's shirt flash in my mind and I shake my head, trying to dislodge the image. I really hadn't meant to hurt him as badly as I did—my strength is still a bit new to me, and I am still learning how to control it. Humans are so fragile now and breakable. I was trying to get by him, but he was trying to stop me, and I had not realized how hard I had thrown him. Brandon could be a bit brash at times, but he was an okay guy, and he didn't deserve to get hurt doing his job. I am not happy with myself for losing control. Maybe Brigham is right—I probably did need to be watched over, at least around humans—but it is still insulting.

"We could come back to this place sometime if you like," Brigham says, gesturing towards the ocean. I look out at the dark water and listen to the waves hitting the shore. I did love it here. Being next to the ocean made my current problems seem smaller.

"Maybe…" I say noncommittally. I am not sure what I wanted to do right now and planning anything in the future left me with a pit in my stomach.

"Why are you fighting my love so much now?" Brigham asks sadly. My head snaps back at him. I had not realized that that was what he thought I was doing.

"I am not fighting your love. You know I love you, but I thought I was getting something else in this life."

"What did you think you were getting?"

"Freedom."

Brigham holds my gaze, and no expression shows on his face. My irritation grows. Why does he not understand why I am so mad?

"I'm getting vampire bodyguards this time. I can't let you keep hurting humans."

I turn away from him in disgust, letting go of his hand. "That's probably for the best."

I close my eyes, trying to escape for a moment. Tears start to well in my eyes, but I fight the emotion back. My tears were so gross and bloody now, and I look scary as hell after I cry. A large wind rolls off the ocean and blows my hair off my shoulders. I loved the wind. There was something so chaotic and powerful about it, so uncontainable and raw. Where did it start and where did it go? The answer was anywhere and everywhere. That's how I wanted to be—like the wind.

"Did you feel it—this morning?" I ask, keeping my eyes closed. "The unraveling." Brigham shifts towards me, his knees grazing my legs, causing me to open my eyes. There is a darkness in his face that I don't understand.

"Yes…" he says, and he pulls me into his arms. I stiffen in his hold but let him slide me into his lap, as he grips me tightly to his chest. "I felt you slipping from me, it was the scariest feeling I have ever had since becoming a vampire. It made me feel mortal and vulnerable like a human."

It had felt like a slow fade on my end, not a rapid slip or slide—like I was a copper coil slowly unwinding. The ache had steadily grown over the three days, but I knew Brigham was on my trail when I awoke in the evening. The ache wasn't as sharp as it had been when I'd retired. Since I am a new vampire, I still had the need for sleep—so that had slowed my escape.

"It was interesting, wasn't it?" Again, I feel Brigham tighten his arms around me, his sandalwood scent engulfing me. I am surprised at this reaction from him. I know he cares for me, but was my possible end really going to have that large of an impact on his life?

"I didn't much care for it," Brigham says slowly. There was a slight rumble to his voice—almost a growl, and I am starting to understand it as anger that had crept into his answer. Was he mad at me or how my action made him feel? I didn't know, but it is fascinating and something I would have to investigate further.

"So very interesting," I say, unable to hide my curiosity about it.

I lean back into him, letting his scent and touch soothe me. As mad as I am at him, it still feels so good to be close to him. I love the way I feel safe and loved in his arms.

I close my eyes and listen to the waves crashing against the beach. Brigham gently brushes his fingers against my face. They are cold but it isn't a frigid coldness—I can feel a warmth from them that had nothing to do with temperature. I open my eyes slowly and look at his face looking down at me. There is an intensity there that is unsettling. I could feel my gravity pull towards him as he pulls me in with his eyes. There is no chance for me to get away and I didn't really want that anyway. Running away had been a test, another silly experiment concocted from my crazy scientist brain. Brigham looks at me deeply, trying to read me.

Questions always distract him, so I ask, "Has this been the longest a master and a new vampire have been apart?"

Brigham's gaze doesn't leave my face, and he leans down and kisses my neck. "No, I knew of one newly made vampire who stayed away from her sire for five days."

His hand grips the back of my head and pulls me in closer as he leaves a trail of kisses down from my neck towards my breast. He knew how to work my body as well as I did him and he wasn't going to play fair right now. He must not want to discuss the sire connection and that realization only makes me want to know more. His kisses deepen as he moves from my chest back up the other side of my neck, nipping and licking at my skin. I moan with need. This man sure knows how to get me worked up!

Brigham pulls his hand away from me slightly and my mind breaks free from all the lusty feelings. I sit up quickly from him trying to increase the distance between us so I can formulate a coherent thought. "Five days!" I say breathlessly, shaking my head. Brigham nods gravely. I wonder how well he had known the newly made vampire. Why did they try to escape their sire? Were they forced to become vampires? It was against the Vampire Guild's code to turn someone against their will, but the story made me worry that it might be happening.

"Five days, but I'm not letting you go that long." Brigham's mouth sets in a hard line. So subtle were the hints of his emotions.

"I know," I say, waving my hand dismissively and rolling my eyes at him. It had been difficult enough to be away for three—five was an impossible feat. The wind blows harder around us, and large white crests roll in the distance, tumbling hard against each other. "But that's something, isn't it! Making it so long! *WOW! Five days!*"

"You're trying my patience," Brigham says with an edge to his voice. "I do not know why you find that so fascinating."

"I know you are upset with me, but I wanted to know what would happen if we were apart—I needed to know for myself."

"If you would have taken my word for it, it would have caused us a lot less pain."

"Yes, but I didn't feel I could trust your word," I say quietly. The truth in that statement hangs thickly in the air between us.

Brigham shifts uncomfortably and says, "I *love* you. How do you not understand that?" There was the slightest inflection in his voice when he said the word love, so slight that a human would not have heard the tone difference.

I cock my head to the side and give him a sweet smile. "I know that." I did know that—I did feel that from him. He made me a vampire after all. That wasn't a small gesture.

"Are you going to try and run away again?" he asks with the tiniest bit of anxiety seeping into his voice. Brigham's scale of emotion was so diminished compared to my own that it was hard for me to judge the emotional equivalents. What set me off on an emotional rampage barely registered with him. I wasn't the most observant or discriminating person and I wasn't convinced I was going to be able to crack Brigham's code of conduct.

"Probably…" I tease. I bite my lower lip and shoot him a naughty smile. "You know how I like experimenting."

"Even when you know you are hurting me?" he asks, baring his teeth at me. I groan in frustration. Brigham isn't going to take my bait and let this go.

"I don't know what I am going to do right now," I answer as I try and push off him, but he clamps down hard on my legs, keeping me in his lap. I growl and consider attacking him. I am not a cruel person by nature, but I can't seem to stop myself from thinking about running away from him.

"Do not run! We need to talk about this!" he says through clenched teeth. "Why do you keep running away?"

I struggle against his arms, trying to escape him, but the strength of them feels like iron bars locking me into him. *"Because you are an ass!"* I yell.

Brigham turns his head slightly down towards me with confusion flashing across his face. "Why do you say that?"

"This life isn't what I expected," I say honestly and then cringe slightly. I sound like a sullen teenager, and I didn't like it.

"I don't understand." Brigham shakes his head and his eyes look wild. "You're a powerful, rich, beautiful, and immortal vampire. What more do you need?"

"Freedom."

"You keep saying that! No one is free. Someone is always bound or tied to someone else."

"Not me, I used to be free when I was human." It seemed like that was forever ago, but really it was only weeks.

"You're still free."

"Not after the new moon phase begins. Once the sire connection is complete, you'll be in control. You'll be able to read my thoughts and control my body at any time." This is why I am so mad, Brigham hadn't told me this little tidbit before he turned me.

"I'm not going to make you do anything you don't want to."

"But you could if you wanted to," I say with a shudder. I didn't like the possibilities.

"Yes, I could, but I like your spirit. I wouldn't want to crush that."

"I don't believe you," I say quietly. "Not anymore." I wanted to believe him, I might even have a little bit, but I was scared, terrified of losing myself and becoming some sort of vampire marionette.

"You should believe me. Lesser vampires would have you locked in a dungeon somewhere until the new moon comes. Have I done that to you?" he growls, and I shudder again. *See!* There is a reason to be concerned.

"No, you haven't."

My new vampire best friend, Anton, who was the *biggest* gossip in the Vampire Guild, had told me as much. I really wish I hadn't heard some of his stories.

"But I haven't done that, have I?" Brigham grips my wrists tightly and pulls me towards him so that I have to look at him.

He is being much more aggressive tonight than he has ever been with me. As I wriggle on his body, the lines between anger and arousal start to blur. He is so much stronger than me, and this fierceness is so *hot!* Ugh…I need therapy.

"No, just bodyguards…" I say, staring him down, trying to ignore my lusty feelings. Was this the tip of the iceberg—having bodyguards? I'm unsure and it makes me feel uneasy to plunge in all the way.

"They are there to protect you—I have business to take care of during the night, and I can't watch you all the time. You're not as strong as you think you are, and your strength is hard to control. After the new moon, I won't need to worry as much. You'll be at full-strength and be more in control of your body, so you won't need any bodyguards."

"How do I know you won't parade me around like your puppet after the transformation is complete?"

Brigham face darkens and he looks *really* pissed off. "Have you ever heard of me doing that to anyone else?"

"No…" I say with hesitation. "But I don't think anyone would tell me if you had. You're pretty much the vampire bigwig around here."

I hadn't heard any rumblings about his mistreatment of his sired vampires. He didn't really have a bunch of vampires he sired hanging around—none, actually—and I hadn't heard anything from Anton either, but I didn't like the possibility of it.

"You think too much of this. Once the bond is completed, you will see that it is not that bad."

"Says the manipulative boyfriend," I mutter under my breath knowing he can still hear me with his vampire hearing. Brigham stiffens and releases my wrists. I turn from him and a breeze off the beach throws my wavy auburn hair in my face. The sea air had an edge to it that reminded me of myself, or at least who I used to be. "I do like this place, it's so vibrant and raw, not like your house. It can be so quiet there."

"Once the new moon arrives, we can move into something that is more us…or I'll get you your own place— wherever you like." I look at Brigham, trying to detect the lie in his words but cannot. I give him a small smile, and I see the tension leaves his body. He is always doing that, trying to make me happy as I broke his heart with my actions, thoughts, and feelings. Sometimes it is too much to manage, but at least I knew one way to make him happy.

I lean back into him, resting my back against his chest. Was I overreacting? Anton thinks I am being crazy, but I can't get this nagging fear about this whole thing out of my head. I wish I had more time to consider all of this. Had I known this was a part of it, I do not think I would have gone through with it. That is what was bothering me the most. I lost my ability to make my own choice—and now I was too far in.

"Is there some way around it? Can I go back to being human?" Brigham is silent for a long time. I already know the answer, but I want him to say it out loud. I wait, not backing down from this one.

After what feels like hours, he answers. "If we do not complete the sire connection you will die. You cannot go back to being human." *Damn!* It wasn't like I was longing to be a human again, but I liked the idea of having an out.

"Well, that's a horrible design. Who came up with this curse anyways?" I say, trying to make light of the situation even though my chest is tightening.

"It is told that the sire bond was gifted to the first vampire by the Goddess of Night called Nótt a very long time ago."

"So, we do not have a direct line to this Goddess of Night? I can't call her up and see if she'll amend the bond?" I joke. *That would probably be awkward—I might get smoted or smitted—either way I'd be dead due to pissing off a God.*

"No one has heard from Nótt in a long time. I do not know if she still graces Earth with her presence anymore," Brigham says gravely as he runs his hands through his hair.

I reach up behind me and run my hands against his jaw, feeling the faintest stubble against my skin. His hair does not grow as fast as a human, and he must not have shaved for a few days to have this much growth on his face. He must have been worried trying to find me if he had skipped shaving. We watch the ocean and I point out small, white, almost translucent crabs running across the shoreline in front of us hunting for food.

"Have you eaten recently?" he asks, skimming his hands along my throat.

The pain from the reopening of the sire connection had been painful enough that it had blocked out the pain I was feeling from not having drank blood in a day. I had only brought a few bottles with me, not wanting to look obvious that I was running away. I had tried not to leave a trail of victims that would lead him to me and I also didn't want to check into any vampire blood banks because he would also be able to track me through there.

"Not exactly," I admit now, becoming very aware of the burning in my throat. He pulls out a small golden metal flask from his back pocket and hands it to me. I untwist the top and the delicious scent of blood hit me. I gulp down greedily, feeling a satisfaction that is hard to explain. I never felt this good eating or drinking, even when I was hungry or thirsty. Drinking blood quenched an ache that was rooted deep inside me at my most primal level.

"Thank you," I say and hand him back the flask. Brigham gives me a smug look and I sink back into him. I wrap my arms around his torso and bury my head against his chest. This feels like how we were when I was still human and he was a vampire. It felt complicated enough back then, and I am reeling that it is even more complicated now. We did this to make things easier between us and now it feels messier than ever.

Brigham starts massaging my head and I moan at his luxurious strokes.

"I missed you," I murmur.

"I missed you too Butterfly, so much so."

"So, if you are going to get me an oceanside house, with a great view," I tease, remembering his earlier offer and wanting to lighten the mood. "What do I need to give you in return?"

"Please try not to leave me again," he says softly. I sigh heavily, I was thinking something more sexual, but that didn't look like that was happening. "Do not run away again so close to the new moon. If I can't touch you when the phase begins, you will die. I don't want to lose you that way—it'll hurt me so much." He wasn't taking the bait, sometimes he could be so serious. Not everything had to be dire this and end of the world that.

"This was the last time," I say, trying to sound convincing. I am almost fifty percent sure I mean it. "You always find me anyways." He'd been easily able to find me when I was out walking at night as a human, and I should have known it would be just as easy for him to find me as a vampire.

"I can sense you," he agrees, and gives me a sly smile. *Finally!* His grave mood is starting to lift.

"Is the sire connection always this strong between master's and newly sired vampires?"

"No, I can sense you better than most can," he says, and his face contorts for a moment and quickly disappears. "I could even when you were a human."

"Interesting…"

"Yes…"

"Do you think it means something?"

"Maybe," he hesitates and then bites his lip, "I—" Brigham's face goes stoney again. I shouldn't have started in on my questions, but everything about being a vampire was fascinating.

"What is it?"

"Nothing. We should return. It's going to be light out soon, and I for one do not want to see the sunrise."

He grabs my hand and stands up, pulling me to my feet. Wanting to stall on the beach awhile longer, I ask, "When I'm transformed, will I lose myself completely in your mind?"

"No. You will still be you, silly. I'll just be in your head with you." He gently taps my forehead.

"I'll still have my own thoughts and feelings?"

"Yes!" Brigham rolls his eyes. Another emotional response—I am doing well tonight. Usually, it takes me at least fifty questions before I get an eye roll out of him. "I'll be aware of them, that's all."

"And you are not worried I will drive you insane? This might be a bad deal for you, maybe you should be praying to Nótt for ways to break the connection," I tease, grabbing his arm and swinging it around myself.

He pulls me into him and whispers in my ear, "I am confident I made a good decision." I snort. Okay then, mister confidence.

I look up at him and see how unworried he is, and I cannot help the emotion that breaks across my face. "But you can stop me from doing things you don't want me to do, right?"

"What would I ever stop you from doing?" he asks and lets go of me, his arms falling stiffly to his sides.

"I don't know—" I lie, standing squarely to him. I had thought of a lot of things, actually, too many things. "That's what scares me."

"You have this idea that I'm a controlling monster. That's not who I am."

"That's what I thought as well, but I'm not sure anymore." I look at Brigham to see if my words had hurt him, but he stares blankly at me. If they stung, he wasn't going to show it. "I'm still angry because I feel like I was misinformed about this whole vampire business," I say honestly.

"I told you what I could about the connection between the sire and the newly made vampire before I turned you," he pleads and reaches out to me. "I was bound—I couldn't tell you more, or I would have."

"Yes, but I think you could have told *me* more! You could have given me hints, or, I don't know, left a book open for me to find that that spoke about it, something!" Brigham's brow creases ever so slightly.

"You're so very difficult."

"Yes, I am," I say proudly and cross my arms across my chest. "Get used to it." I bat my eyes at him and give him a seductive smile. I can't help myself—it is so fun pestering him. He takes a step towards me, and I back up a step. Something predatory flashes across his face, but only for a moment and then vanishes, making me wonder if I really saw it at all. He crosses his arms across his chest, and I glare back at him. It feels like we are two chess pieces positioned across a chess board.

"I should have tried harder to inform you of the sire bond," he says through gritted teeth.

"Thank you!" I say, "I appreciate you saying that." He stands rigidly in front of me, and I try not to let my eyes wander up his body. He is broad chested and much taller than me—he must be six feet, four inches tall at least. He looks like some sort of Viking God standing before me with his muscular shoulders and arms. I can see the upper part of his chest tattoo poking out from his shirt, the top buttons being undone. I want to unbutton the rest of them, revealing more of his skin, but I don't…because…*well, honestly, not doing that seems like a dumb idea, so I reach up and undo a button.* The corner of Brigham's mouth twitches upward.

"Come," he says and pulls on my arm gently. "I do not want to fight anymore. Let's go home—everyone is worried."

I snort. "No, they aren't."

They knew as well as I did that Brigham would find me before anything dire would happen. We walk hand and hand down the beach and I finally feel like I can relax. I had left my sandals somewhere on the beach—I honestly couldn't remember where—and the soft grainy texture of the sand massages my feet as we walk.

"Well, everyone was curious about how many days you'd be gone until I found you," Brigham says lightheartedly.

"How many vampires placed bets?" I ask, knowing what terrible gamblers they all were. Apparently, when you live a long ass time, you get really into gambling.

"The entire Vampire Guild, I'm sure."

"Really?" I ask, a little surprised. That was *a lot* of vampires.

"Yes," Brigham says, and I can hear a little irritation in his voice. He must not have liked this entertainment being at his expense.

"Interesting…"

Brigham stops and wraps his arm around my waist, pulling me into his body. I look at his steely blue eyes, trying to decipher what he is feeling. He strokes the side of my face and I close my eyes, feeling his fingertips ignite something under my skin. His touch sends tingles all over my body and I long for him to touch me in more places.

"I've missed you so much my Butterfly," he whispers softly and leans down, kissing my lips. I wrap my arms around his neck and let him pick me up into his arms.

"Have you really?"

He has said he loved me often enough, but sometimes I wasn't sure what that really meant to him. Was vampiric love as strong as human love? I didn't know. It was less complicated for me—I had fallen in love with him as a human and my feelings towards him hadn't changed when I was changed. Maybe vampire love and human love were the same. I bring my lips slowly to his neck and kiss his cool skin. He smells like sandalwood due to the body oil he rubbed onto his skin to give it a more human luster, and I breathe in his familiar scent. I had dealt with more than just physical pain being away from him. It had been lonely, and I missed our banter and lovemaking.

"Terribly." He hugs me closer to him and I nibble at his ear, letting my canines graze it gently. "I do understand, Butterfly, why you are doing this."

"Why am I doing this?" I ask innocently. I was very curious to hear his take on my excursions.

"To make a point," he says and looks at me squarely. I fist the back of his hair and tug on it, exposing his neck to me.

"And what point am I trying to make?" I graze my canines along his neck and he shudders.

"That I let you down and your heart is aching," he says softly. I pause and press my lips to his neck. *That was the point I was trying to make.*

"Yes, I suppose that is what I am doing," I murmur, barely taking my lips off his neck.

"I do understand, and I am sorry I disappointed you." I blink back tears and still in his arms. I feel so vulnerable right now, and I don't like that. I was always a love-them-and-drop-them sort of person before this. I would never have stayed in the relationship after a betrayal. It wasn't smart or safe, but with Brigham I felt such a pull that I didn't even know if I could leave him. It is scary. I didn't like having this sort of strong attachment to someone.

I try and relax my body back into him, but part of me feels too vulnerable right now to give myself completely to him.

"I've almost forgiven you…" I whisper and trace a finger along his jaw, keeping my face buried in his neck. Brigham tightens his grip on me and kisses my neck. "I like it when you do that," I moan, wanting not to think, but to feel right now.

"That's why I do it," he says and kisses my neck deeper, grazing his fangs against my skin.

The wind picks up around us, and the waves crash loudly against the beach. Brigham carries me closer to the ocean, and I see the hotel behind us glowing in the dark over his shoulder. None of the patrons inside know there are vampires on the very beach they sunbathed on and that fact thrills me. I kiss Brigham hard on the lips and he carefully lays me on the wet sand.

"I'm glad you went to the ocean," he says and runs his hand along my body. "I haven't seen it in years."

"Why not?"

"I had no reason to go, but now I have a reason to do a lot of new and fun things," he says, kneeling over me and stripping off his shirt. I reach up and run my hands over his chest muscles and down his torso, gliding over his abdominal muscles. I trace the large tattoo on the left side of his chest that swirls in knots around his shoulder and down his arm.

"Because of me?"

"Yes."

"Am I getting you out of a rut, Brigham?" He gives a soft growl and starts unbuttoning my shirt, exposing the black bra underneath.

"In the last month I've been to Seattle, Chicago, and now California, so yes, I think you have."

"We have had some interesting adventures, and it's only been a few weeks."

"But that's over now, right?" he asks and starts kissing the top of my breasts. He takes his canine and cuts through the front of my bra, and I let out a gasp. He nips at my nipples, and they grow rigid and aching at his touch. I want to agree to whatever demands he has as long as he keeps doing what he is doing.

"Yes."

He pauses and kisses by abdomen and starts making his way lower towards my core. "Good!" he says wickedly.

"But I would look into a credit card that earns you frequent flyer miles, just in case," I blurt out before I become undone by his kisses. Brigham laughs. I love the sound of his laughter. It is deep and thick like a redwood tree and surrounds me in a beautiful melody when he does it. It takes a lot of effort on my part to get him to laugh, so it is always an accomplishment when he does.

"I will look into that." I run my hand along his large muscular arms, marveling at his smooth and bulging muscles. I always felt so safe in them. Being here with him in this moment, I almost forgot why I had run away in the first place.

"I've really missed you too, you know. I missed us, missed this. The way it feels when we are together, and everything is right."

Brigham looks quickly at me and blinks. "I wasn't sure if I would get you back this time. I didn't know if we would... if things would be okay with us after you returned."

"Really?" I ask, pulling myself up to look at him better. "I thought you knew me better than that."

"Sometimes...I find you hard to read."

What is he talking about? He is the one with a stoney face. I am the one who is an emotionally reflective pool.

"Well, that will all change soon enough."

"Six days."

"Six days," I repeat trying to hide the sadness of my voice. It wasn't very long at all.

"Is there anything I can do to make this easier for you?"

"Well, it would be nice if I didn't have to worry about you snooping through my private thoughts when I become a full-strength vampire, but there really is no way around that, is there?"

"No," he hesitates, and something flickers across his face that I cannot discern. "Not a way that I know of right now."

"Then I'll settle for a little distraction. Maybe I won't worry about it so much if I'm busy with other things."

"What kind of distraction?"

"Oh…I don't know." I push my body up into his, grinding against him and pulling him down closer to me. "I have some ideas," I whisper into his ear. I tenderly bite his earlobe, breaking the skin slightly. He moans softly and I almost miss it with the sound of the waves.

"I always like your ideas," he says and holds my head in his hand. His eyes glisten in the dark and I feel his passion for me burning under the mask he always wears.

"All of them?" I ask sweetly, coiling a lock of his hair around my finger, tugging on it hard.

"Okay, maybe not all of your ideas, but will you settle for most?"

"I suppose. I'm not crazy about all of the ideas that come out of your head, either."

"I'm having one right now you might like."

"Ohhh—do tell!" I say playfully.

Brigham pushes his body deeply into mine, kissing me hard into the sand. I grip his arm with equal pressure as I crush my fingers into his skin, but I barely make an indent. His body had grown strong and hard over the years, and I would never be his equal physically. Although I did like being able to touch him fiercely as a vampire, sometimes it annoys me that I am still a fragile woman in his arms—some things never changed, even as a vampire.

Brigham pulls away from me and I can see in his eyes how hard it is for him to do. "As much as I want to stay with you out here my love, we need to go, it's a three-and-a-half-hour flight back to Minneapolis and we need to land before sunrise." Brigham says and eyes the horizon wearily.

I groan. "We don't even have time for make-up sex?" I ask, pulling his head back down hard into my breasts. Brigham kisses my skin and licks circles around my nipples, and I feel my core slicken for him. "You are making me so wet right now! We can spare a few minutes."

Brigham pulls my hips into him and for a moment I think he will concede to me, but instead he groans and lifts himself away from me. "Later my love, later—when we get home."

I groan loudly. "Oh, you're no fun!" I grind my hips against him harder, feeling his hard cock against my thigh.

He sucks in a breath. "Or maybe on the plane."

"Yay!"

"I'm sorry, if I would have known how enjoyable it would be finding you on the beach, I would have reserved a hotel room."

"We still could. We could stay another day here."

"Yes, we could, but…" his voice trails and again a strange look of concern flickers across his face.

"But what?"

"I'd feel better getting you home safe."

"Is this because I ran away? I'm not going to try to run…tonight."

"I worry about us being so far from the Vampire Guild's protection."

"Who would we need protection from out here? We're vampires. You worry too much."

"That's probably true." He pulls his shirt on quickly and dresses me. "Come, let us go." He lifts me up off the sand and begins to carry me towards the hotel quickly, using his vampire speed. I slump into his chest and breathe in his scent. "We'll be home soon, and I will make it up to you."

"I could get used to this," I say, and throw my arms around his neck and plant a tender kiss on his cheek." Brigham squeezes my body softly in acknowledgement and increases his speed. We are but a blur or gust of wind now, undetectable to the human eye. "So, can I fly your plane?"

"Absolutely not," Brigham says firmly.

"Why not?" Was it really that big of a deal? How complicated could it be?

"I've seen you drive, and you are the reason man painted lanes on the road."

"Rude," I huff in protest. "Are you saying I'm a bad driver?"

"No, I'm not that stupid," he quips, making me laugh.

"Can I fly one day?"

"Maybe."

"Your maybes are really no's."

"Maybe," Brigham says again and shoots me the tiniest of small smiles. *Clever vampire!*

"Fine, I guess I'll just have to amuse myself some other way," I say and cover his earlobe with my mouth and suck slowly.

"I'm sure you'll think of something."

CHAPTER TWO

"You cost me two hundred dollars!" Anton shouts as I walk into his room.

I roll my eyes at him and flop onto his king-sized bed. I love Anton dearly. No vampire could ask for more in a best friend, but he is such a drama queen! Everything is exaggerated and overemphasized. Sometimes when we talked it felt like we were acting out a play in a grand theatre. Maybe it was because our conversations usually occurred in Anton's bedroom, which did feel like a theatre—or at least a prop room.

I snuggle into Anton's bed like a dog. His bed stood on a raised, black-stained platform in the middle of the room with black silk sheets and duvet. The fabric feels heavenly against my skin. Being a newly made vampire, I am having fun experimenting with my new senses, and touch was one of my favorites. Everything I touch feels very different than it did as a human—it is more extreme, more real, and better.

I look over at Anton's walls, where he has hung brightly colored abstract artwork, against them he has numerous antique dressers that are much too ornate for my tastes. Everything in his room assaults your senses and elicits a response. There is an ungodly amount of metal and ceramic sculptures and lots of fabric draped everywhere, which I still don't understand—but if I point it out, Anton just huffs at me like I am an imbecile.

Anton and I had become friends right after my transformation. Our masters were old friends, and we spent many evenings hunting together. Anton had been turned a vampire two years earlier and was still living in his master's home. He had been very helpful teaching me the ropes of the vampire world. Anton and I both had been working as humanitarians in our human lives and those beliefs carried over for us into our vampire existence. I had been working in an animal shelter and Anton had been working in a women's shelter—so we hit it off right away.

"Two hundred? How did I do that?" I ask as I gaze at a newly acquired sculpture on one of Anton's dressers. It was a face of an old man made from a speckled stone—the details of his face were astonishing, and I couldn't fathom how the artist had created this masterpiece. Anton finishes buttoning his shirt, a shiny dark red number that glistens in the light when he moves and douses himself with a healthy dose of cologne. I knew nothing about fashion or designers, but knowing Anton, it was the latest and most expensive shirt available.

"I thought you would be caught on the second day," he groans and sits on the edge of the bed next to me. He looks down at me with his dark-black eyes and I marvel at his styled black wavy hair. He was a wizard with hair gel. I could never get mine to look as good as his.

"I was gone for two and a half days last time," I point out. "You should have figured I would be gone longer this time. It's not my fault you lost."

"Yes, but I thought Brigham would find you faster this time. I thought he'd have figured out your pattern or something," Anton says with a pout lying beside me. I reach up and touch his black hair, feeling the soft, feathery texture and he swats my hand away making it sting. I can't stop touching everything lately and Anton's hair really is a treat to touch. It is silky and feathery soft at the same time, and I wonder if it was as soft when he was a human or if it was some cool vampire side effect. Knowing Anton's meticulous grooming habits, I bet his hair was this fantastic as a human.

"Not likely," I snort. Brigham was good, but I was unpredictable which gave me a slight edge. I don't know what I am doing or where I am going half the time and never cared to plan it out. What fun was that? Everything usually worked out anyways.

"Yes, but he found you," Anton teases, waving his perfectly manicured finger at me. I bat it away in annoyance.

"Yes, he always does seem to," I sigh and rub my forehead. I still hadn't figured out how Brigham was able to find me and am getting very frustrated by it. I didn't like not knowing the answer to a question.

"Next time, I'm betting three days," Anton says confidently.

"Not four?" I ask, running my fingers along his duvet—it had a velvety smooth texture that was divine! Anton smacks my hand and I jump back at being struck and give him a dirty look.

"No one makes it four days," Anton says firmly. He sits up and smooths the invisible wrinkles from his shirt. He could be so wound up at times! I couldn't imagine being so fussy over my clothes. I look down at the black skirt I had thrown on and cringe. It is a little crumpled. I should have ironed it before I put it on, but I was so excited to see Anton and hadn't paid much attention. I try unsuccessfully to smooth a rather large crease out and catch Anton looking at me in disgust. I smile at him and shrug. Anton shakes his head, stands up from the bed, and begins walking towards his closet. What can I say, I am a disaster at times.

"Brigham told me one woman made it five days once."

"I've never heard of such a thing," Anton says dismissively and shakes his head in disbelief.

"It doesn't matter anyway," I say with a huff. "I'm not trying again."

I roll over on my belly and run my hand over Anton's silky sheets. The fabric slides under my skin causing small tingles to shoot up my arm. Being a newly made vampire is almost like being on ecstasy at times, with every sensation being exaggerated and pleasurable.

Anton gasps from the closet. "What? How will I make my money back?"

"There is always something to bet on here. I'm sure there are at least fifty things you could go bet on downstairs in Forseti's game room right now!" Forseti, who was one of the oldest vampires in the Vampire Guild, was also Anton's sire. His house served as the Vampire Guild's headquarters as well as the backdrop for any vampire function. If you were a new vampire in town, Forseti's game room was the place to be. "I never knew vampires were such terrible gamblers— it's sickening. There needs to be a Vampire Gamblers Anonymous set up stat!"

Anton stands in front of a long antique mirror and smooths out his shirt, turning in front of it and making various poses. He is tall, but not as tall as Brigham and had a lean muscular physique. His skin is not as pale as mine, which was due to the browner skin tone he had before he was changed. He is attractive like all the rest of the vampires here. It is like I lived on a movie set now.

"Hey, what else is there to do for fun?" he asks and adjusts one of his curly locks.

"I don't know," I shrug. "You could read or watch television, or something."

"Boring! Games of chance and luck are much more entertaining." Anton looks at himself critically in the mirror and turns to look at his ass and I see him clench and unclench his butt muscles.

"I suppose."

Anton examines his tight-fitting black pants, and I can tell he is trying to determine if they make his ass look good or not. He keeps clenching and unclenching his ass cheeks and it is disturbingly hypnotic.

"Your ass looks fine, stop doing that! I can't unsee you doing ass clenches now!" I yell covering my eyes, causing Anton to laugh.

"You would be very lucky indeed to have those images seared into your brain for eternity!" I laugh and shake my head.

I stand up from the bed and walk over to Anton's dresser, running my hand along the wood. I feel small divots and the wood's grainy texture against my skin. As a human, I doubted I would feel anything but a smooth surface. On the dresser, Anton has many glass bottles of cologne, and I trace my finger along some of the glass jars, feeling every ridge and design.

"You're touching everything," Anton says through gritted teeth. "I'll be so happy when you grow out of the touchy phase!" He turns the other way in the mirror and inspects his ass from the new angle. I roll my eyes at him. If I spent as much time getting ready as Anton did, I'd never get anything done.

"Sorry about the room groping," I say, stuffing my hands under my armpits. "I can't seem to help myself."

"How did I get hooked up with an OCD vampire for a best friend?"

"Like attracts like," I tease, and Anton laughs and then sticks his tongue out me. "I can't believe you only gave me two days! I'm a little offended, to be honest."

"Hey, that Brigham loves you. I thought after last time he'd be watching you like a hawk."

"He was," I grumble. "It was like being on suicide watch."

"I'm surprised you were able to manage it at all. How many more days until you're completely transformed?" Anton asks as he picks up a shiny red jacket that is neatly draped over an antique chair and slips it gently on.

"Five," I reply, trying to keep the anxiety out of my voice. It seemed like such a small number now and I didn't want to be reminded of it.

"Five, huh?" Anton adjusts himself in his jacket in the mirror and gives himself a small wink. I didn't know anyone who is more in love with themselves than him. I laugh softly to myself, and Anton shoots me a pouty look. "I'll be glad when you're at full-strength. Then you can come out with me and really light up the town! We won't have to drag around anymore babysitters."

"Do you really think Brigham will let me go out after the new moon?" I ask, trying not to sound too hopeful.

Anton shrugs. "Sure, why wouldn't he?" Anton looks at me as if I am crazy and shakes his head. He heads over to his bathroom where he has a barrage of cosmetics lined up on the counter and starts applying a bronze cream to his perfect face. I lean up against the doorframe and watch as he applies some eye liner and a light, shimmery eyeshadow.

"I don't know…part of me expects him to change when I change. Maybe he will become more possessive," I admit nervously. Okay, maybe I am a little commitment-phobic, but this was eternity we were talking about here!

"Hey, sure—some of the sires can be real control freaks, but not Brigham. You couldn't get a better sire than him." Anton applies a tinted lip balm and smacks his lips in the mirror, giving himself another wink. I roll my eyes again at his ridiculousness.

"What about your sire, Forseti? Does he make you do things you don't want to very often?"

"No, not really. He asks me to do things, and I usually agree to it, so he's never had to push the issue before."

"What is it like having your sire in your head all the time? Does it hurt? Can you feel when he is in there?"

"I never even notice it anymore," Anton says, waving my comment off.

"Really?" I balk. How could he not notice another mind butting up against his all the time? It seemed unlikely.

"Really, he's a quiet guy. Well, at least he is in my head. I doubt he listens much anyways—he's a busy guy."

"Hmmm…" I murmur as I rub my chin. I am not sure if I believe Anton completely. Maybe he is only saying this to not scare me more than I already was.

"It's nice having someone to talk to all the time. I do like that part. I don't get lonely anymore. It's not like it was when I was human. Sometimes we'll talk for hours in my head when we're miles away, it's kind of neat." He shrugs again and applies some black mascara. I didn't think it is possible to make himself more attractive, but somehow Anton is able to.

"I could see how that would be nice," I say slowly. It would be like texting, sort of—someone would be always available no matter what time of day it was.

"But?" Anton prods, raising an eyebrow at me.

"But I worry about what he'll find in my head. What if Brigham doesn't like one of my thoughts and has me marked!"

Anton laughs loudly and smacks me on the shoulder. "Brigham isn't some vampire mafia guy! You can be so stupid sometimes!"

"Thanks," I say sarcastically and try to smack him back on the shoulder. Anton dodges my smack, and I end up hitting the wall leaving a tiny divot. I had thought my aim would improve as a vampire, but it hadn't. Another disappointment. "Then why doesn't he have any other sired vampires around—where are they? Most of the vampires have numerous sired vampires, but Brigham doesn't."

"Brigham wouldn't have you marked! He loves you!" Anton exclaims as he eyes the small divot in the wall, and I smile guiltily at him. He throws his hands up and walks away from me sighing loudly.

"People fall out of love."

"People sure, but not vampires. Name one vampire that's fallen out of love." I couldn't think of one, but I hadn't met a ton of vampires yet. "See, you have nothing to worry about!"

"That's not fair, I don't know all the vampires like you do."

"You are losing it, my dear," Anton says and grabs my shoulder, looking me up and down while clicking his tongue. "What are we going to do with you? You *cannot* go out like this. I have a reputation to uphold!"

I move out of his grip. "I'm fine—no one will be looking at me anyways, not with you next to me."

Anton smiles and primps his hair. "Well, that is true."

"Does the transformation hurt?"

"Hurt? No—it doesn't hurt…it feels different. I'm not sure how to explain it. It's like you're having a person literally stuffed into your head. There's a pressure, but it goes away, or you get used to it or something." He laughs. "Since when are you worried about pain? I've heard the reopening of the sire connection is very painful, even after a few hours apart. I can't imagine what it is like after three days."

"It hurts," I gulp and rub my hands together, remembering the searing pain. "It hurts a lot." Anton smirks at me and shakes his head again at me. He's going to have terrible neck pain at this rate. "The pain is bearable, though."

"You confound me." Tell me about it, I confound myself half the time.

"I'm a complicated vampire," I say dryly.

"I guess. So do you want to go out vigilante style tonight?"

"Is there any other way?"

"Nope, not for us."

"I do feel like sucking a bad guy dry, tonight, really sucking him dry," I say excitedly. *Ew!* That sounded a little sexual. "You know what I mean."

"Can I pick tonight? You picked last time," Anton asks hopefully.

"Sure, I owe you since I made you lose *all* your money."

"Sweet! I want to get a baby killer tonight, or some jackass who beats his kids."

"Sounds good. Have anyone in particular in mind?"

"No, I thought we could hit a couple clubs and read people until we find the right one."

"I so enjoy being able to read humans minds now. People are fascinating!"

"Do you do it often? I mean, when you're not looking for someone to feed on?"

"Oh yes! Sometimes I'll go to a restaurant and pretend to eat, just so I can read everyone in the room."

"Why?" Anton asks curiously.

"It's interesting! Sometimes what people say and what they feel are completely contrary. Even close friends keep large parts of their lives secret from each other. I like trying to figure out why people project what they do."

"That just makes my head hurt. I don't understand people any more now than I did when I was a human," Anton shrugs.

"If I could go back to college now with my vampire powers, I would look into psychology or sociology, but I had a feeling that earning a degree as an undead member of society might be a little difficult. I don't know, maybe I'm weird."

"Maybe?" Anton teases.

"Oh, like you're normal. I haven't met anyone so obsessed with how they smelt before—seriously, is it necessary to own *hundreds* of bottles of cologne? It seems a bit over the top." Anton scoffs and claps his hands over his heart, feigning hurt and then turns to face the mirror again, flexing his arm this time and studying the way his bicep looks under his jacket.

"That's why we get along so well, we're both certifiable."

"Probably…" I step up beside him in the mirror and cringe at my reflection. I try smoothing a wrinkle out of my skirt to no avail. My hair looks good tonight—the long auburn tresses hang in waves down to my waist, and my jade green eyes pop out against my pale skin—but I am unsure about the clothes.

"Hey, am I dressed okay for tonight?" I ask Anton self-consciously. Maybe I should have paid more attention to the clothes I picked out. Anton looks at my clothes and brings his hand to his mouth and dry heaves. Now, I admit that I am not a fashion guru, but I don't think my outfit is that bad—just a bit crumpled.

"You should have dressed sultrier—the guys we're hunting are a sucker for a pretty girl in a short dress. I bought you something in case you came over here looking like a drowned rat."

The only other thing Anton enjoyed more than gambling was shopping, and now that he had an unlimited amount of money at his disposable thanks to Forseti's generous nature and limitless credit cards, there was always something new in his closet. Anton moves quickly to his walk-in closet using his vampire speed and flings open the doors dramatically. Vibrant colors leap out from tiered racks, and I eye the clothing suspiciously.

"Why would you assume I would look like a drowned rat?" I hiss, taking a step into Anton's closet. "And rats are very cute, by the way!" I finger a pair of corduroy pants that are hanging, and Anton slaps my hand away sharply before he moves down the line of clothes. He is right, and I am touching everything in sight. I couldn't wait until this needing-to-touch-everything phase wore off!

"I heard you were at the ocean," Anton yells over his shoulder, disappearing from sight beneath all the clothes. I follow his voice and find him unzipping a large blue garment bag. He shakes his head in disapproval and starts to unzip another one hanging next to it.

"You're such a gossip! Who did you hear that from?"

"I am not a gossip, and *I will not reveal my sources!*"

"Are too!" I challenge and make a face at him. I look at all the clothes around me and feel very overwhelmed. Anton's closet is five times the size of mine and stuffed full of clothes, shoes, and accessories. Where did he get all this stuff?

"Well, whatever, here! I found it!" Anton pulls a very short red dress out of a garment bag that is the same color as his jacket. "Try this on." He hands me the dress and a look of pure glee spreads across his face. Despite Anton's shortcomings, he is very good at picking out clothes. "Oh!" Anton claps excitedly and ducks beneath the clothes. "Wear these black pleather boots with the high heels." He pulls out a small box from his closet and hands it to me. "It'll make you look hot."

"Should I be concerned that you have a surplus of women's clothing in your closet?"

"Jeez, I bought this stuff for you—I just like to shop!"

"Whatever you say," I tease. Anton's face creases and he shoots me a dirty look.

"I have very eclectic tastes, and gender is fluid, anyways. It is not my fault if some women's clothes are more fabulous than the men's. Hurry up and try the dress on! I'm excited to see how good you'll look!"

"You better watch yourself. If Brigham hears you talking like that, he might get all territorial on you." I slip out of my skirt and put Anton's dress on. The dress hugs my curves and shows a lot more skin than the outfit I came in over. Anton scrutinizes me in the dress and walks around me in a circle with his hand rubbing his chin.

"Oh, he knows I have no interest in you. You're way too crazy for me," he says, smoothing out a crease in the dress. "Like *way* too crazy!"

"That's harsh! You're being so mean tonight!" I sit on his bed and grab the boots out of the box. The pleather is soft and pliable, and I rub them against my face before I even know what I am doing.

"Uh…I mean you're *too* much of a woman for me. *Too hot* to manage." Anton says sarcastically. He shoots me a sincere smile, and I laugh.

"Nice try."

"Sorry," he says guiltily. I laugh again.

"No worries, you're not my type either." I slip on one of the boots and zip them up almost to my knee. I rub the soft pleather emphatically.

"Why's that?" he asks and puts his hands on his hips, clearly offended. I shrug, enjoying tormenting him. "I'm very fetching for a vampire!"

"Yes, you're very handsome." I say in a sarcastic tone.

"Why did you say that so patronizing?" Anton barks. I laugh hard, enjoying taunting him.

"I didn't. You're paranoid."

"Well, I wasn't before, but now I am. What's wrong with me?" he challenges, putting his hands firmly on his hips. I roll my eyes at him.

"Nothing, drama queen. You're very sweet and sexy and if I wasn't worrying about the new moon transformation, I'd fuck you in a heartbeat—but, as it is, I've got other things on my mind." I slip on the other boot and try not to rub it. I didn't want to look like a complete crazy person in front of Anton.

"Alright…in a heartbeat, you say?" he asks, raising an eyebrow at me.

"Yes, a heartbeat. No pun intended. Now, how do I look?" I stand up from Anton's bed and do a little spin for him.

"Perfect!" Anton exclaims and claps his hands together.

Looking down at myself, I am impressed by my transformation.

"You have such good taste in clothes, Anton!" I would never have bought this dress. I wouldn't have thought I could have pulled off the look.

"Why, thank you madam," Anton says dramatically, giving me his best butler impression and bows slightly.

"Your talents were wasted at the women's shelter."

"No, they weren't. I had lots of fun shopping with the gals for clothes for job interviews, and collecting donations for our free store. It was a lot of fun," Anton says and looks sad for a moment.

"Well, they were very lucky to have you while they did."

"I feel bad I decided to become a vampire some days," he admits quietly. "I think I did a lot of good there."

"You could always find a way to help again, maybe even donate clothes. Plus, we do good now."

"I know, but it's not the same." Anton's face drops and he looks even sadder, and I reach out and touch his arm, trying to console him. I've never seen him like this before. But I understand what he is feeling—it is hard leaving parts of your human life behind.

"I know what you mean," I say sadly, "All the dogs I meet try to bite me now."

I used to work with animals, but now animals were afraid of me. They sensed I wasn't right. It hurt my feelings quite a bit when I tried to approach a dog the first time as a vampire and have it snarl and bristle up at me. It was so unexpected and unlike any experience I had ever had with an animal, but it really was for the best. It is safer for the animals to be cautious and afraid. I am something much more dangerous now.

"I know you do, and that's why I love you," he says and gives me a crushing hug as I hear my bones creak. "Now, let's go kill one for the good guys!"

"That sounds so wrong."

"Did you go on a Buddhist retreat when you were away or something?"

"No, but you just reminded me of something I've been wanting to ask you."

"What is it?"

"Do you think vampires are under the same karmic rules as humans?"

"I don't know . . .I assumed we were, but I guess that might not be true, since we don't exactly have to deal with the whole reincarnation thing."

"See, that's been bothering me! What if vampires are completely separate from the ebb and flow of the universe? What if what we do doesn't contribute to anything, and doesn't affect the balance at all because of who we are? What if all this good we think we are doing doesn't even chart?"

"I don't think it works like that," Anton says, shaking his head.

"No?" I didn't want to believe it either, but I wasn't very knowledgeable about vampire spirituality.

"Worst case scenario, everything I'm doing now only has a karmic effect on my human life," Anton says with a shrug.

"It doesn't bother you that the universe could be blind to your efforts?"

"Hell no, I see the difference I make in the lives of the people we help, taking out their tormentors. That's enough for me. I don't need a spiritual bonus prize. I'm not doing this for a reward. I'm doing it because it's the right thing to do, right now."

"What if we're just making room for another tormentor to enter their lives?" I ask and find myself rubbing the fabric of my dress as my anxiety gets away from me. "What if we were delaying the inevitable? What if the universe has a plan for the people we've helped and no matter what we do, bad things are meant to happen to them?"

Anton grabs my hand away from my dress and gives me an annoyed look. "That's fine, I'll take the next one out too, I've got lots of time," he says confidently.

I laugh. "I suppose we do."

"No worries, Butterfly, just because the rules have changed for us in this life doesn't mean our position in the universe has. I think there are a lot of different types of beings out there and they all have their part to play."

"You mean like aliens?"

"Yeah, and leprechauns, trolls, werewolves, gods, goblins, all those things. I mean, we exist, they might too."

Now that is a theory I hadn't thought of! It is entirely possible that other beings exist. I had always believed it, but now it seems much more probable. I wonder if Brigham has ever met any otherworldly beings before. I'll have to remember to ask him when I get home. It would be so cool to meet a leprechaun or a werewolf!

"You haven't met any though, right?" I ask, trying to hide my hopefulness.

"Not yet, but I've only been a vampire for a few years—who knows what might happen. Now c'mon, I'm getting hungry! Let's go give a bad guy a good dose of karma," Anton says, shaking my shoulder.

I laugh at his enthusiasm. "You're always so excited to hunt," I say watching him glow. "You look like a kid at Christmas."

"I love it! Don't you?" Anton exclaims, his eyes burning brightly.

"It's more appealing than I thought it would be," I admit reluctantly. I had never hunted as a human being—I had been an animal rights activist, but being a vampire vigilante was very appealing, and I was good at it. *Damn good at it!*

"You know what they say: Once you go red, you never go back."

I roll my eyes. "They don't say that."

"I know—I made it up, but I'm hoping it will catch on. What do you think?" Anton smiles hopefully at me.

"I think it needs work," I say gently, letting him lead me out of his room. We enter a large hallway with rich wood flooring and deep burgundy walls. We pass numerous paintings on the wall that are in golden frames—I assume they are worth fortunes.

"Oh, you're no fun," Anton huffs. "Forseti thought it was good."

I look at Anton doubtfully. "You're kidding."

Anton rolls his eyes at me. "Okay fine, he hated it too! *DAMN!*" Anton stomps his foot on his hardwood floors, making a loud thudding noise that resonates down the hallway. "I thought I had something there for a minute."

"How about: Once you go vamp, you never go back," I suggest.

"That's good! *DAMN IT!* It took you two seconds to come up with that! I've been working on mine for days."

I shrug. "Sorry, you can use it if you want."

"No, that's okay. *SHIT!*" Anton stomps his foot again and I feel the vibration go through the floor. The building had to have been well made to withstand vampires. I wonder if there is steel underneath the flooring. "Once you go vamp, you never go back! Why didn't I think of that?"

"Sorry."

"It's so good!"

"Jesus, use it, what do I care?"

"Are you sure?"

"Yes! For God sakes. Use it!"

"Great!" Anton says joyously.

We reach a large elevator. Anton pushes a button, the doors slide open, and we step inside.

"Alright milady, are we ready?" Anton motions to me.

"I think so," I say, inspecting Anton's ensemble. "You look good."

"Yes, I do, and now you do as well!"

"Well, I'm glad I meet your approval," I say dramatically.

Anton hooks his arm with mine. "You should be! Now, let's take you out for a night on the town!"

CHAPTER THREE

Anton and I scan the club, searching for our next victim. Scantily clad women and men wearing too much jewelry for my taste dance around us to the techno beats the DJ dishes out. We are in a very exclusive club and had to glamour the bouncer to get in—which annoyed Anton. He blamed me for that.

Anton and I both wanted to continue our humanitarian and animal welfare work as vampires. We knew that in order for us to survive as vampires, we needed to drink human blood, but how we obtained that blood was completely up to us.

It was Anton's idea to form an allegiance against *The Bad Guys,* or at least that's how we referred to them. Each night we hunted, we sought out a person who brought pain and suffering to their fellow man, animal, or environment. It was fun, and we both enjoyed feeling like we were making a difference somehow, even if it involved killing.

"Do you ever feel bad drinking someone's blood?" I whisper as I scan a group of men at a table in the back.

"It tastes too damn good!" Anton says, laughing darkly. "Do you?"

"No, I really don't," I admit. "But part of me feels like I should more. I mean, we *are* taking lives. These people have families."

"The people we go after deserve what they get," Anton says harshly.

"That's true, but I wonder if I killed a random person if I wouldn't feel the same way. Am I justifying it because it's what I want, or is it real?"

"You think way too much," Anton says dismissively. "If I thought as much as you do, I would go insane." He takes a fake sip out of the beer bottle in his hand as he watches a group of girls dancing across the room. These were good people who had no hatred or malevolence in their hearts...*unfortunately.*

"That's probably true, but do you ever wonder if we are deluding ourselves?" I ask and pretend to take a sip of my drink. I could drink it. It wouldn't kill me, but if I ingest something besides blood, my stomach starts cramping, and nothing tastes like it used to—it all tastes like ash.

"I am starting to worry about you now."

"Just now?" I tease and batt my eyes at him sweetly.

Anton rolls his eyes at me. "You are becoming a very esoteric person right before my eyes. You should be embracing this new life. Grabbing it by the horns and all that."

I scan the room, watching all the people flirt and rub up against each other. "Maybe." Was he right? Was I wasting this opportunity I'd been given?

"You know the images that flash through the victim's minds before they die?" Anton prods as he leans towards me and puts his hand gently on my shoulder. His eyes grow large and sad, and I wonder what he is thinking about.

"Yes," I say quietly. This is something else I hadn't been quite prepared for as a vampire. I assumed you drank the blood and all you felt was the ecstasy of drinking the blood. I hadn't been prepared for the connection between the victim and myself. When drinking their blood, their entire life would flash in my mind—the first time I drank, it was very disorientating and assaulting. It was like getting a giant download into your brain.

"If you drank from someone who was innocent, you'd feel different. There is no way you could see their life and not feel bad about taking it."

"But even our victims are not all bad. They've had times in their lives when they were sweet, loving, and kind. When they were children…mostly."

"Yes, but *overall*, they were not like that. We do a good job screening them. I think humans are humans and they have faults and imperfections, but we are going after the outliers."

Anton had a point. The people we chose were not average people. When all the images of a person's life came flooding back at you, you had to quantify them. Despite the images of their childhood when they were the most innocent, there was a lot of darkness in them overall.

I sigh in defeat. "That's true."

"What's got you thinking like this?" Anton asks, turning his gaze back towards the dancing women and men. I think he was more interested in chasing lusty feelings at the moment rather than bad guys.

"I don't know…" Why am I thinking about such things? "I'm feeling very reflective since I've gotten back." Reflective, unstable, lost—you name it, I'm feeling it.

"Where did you go, when you ran away?" Anton asks. He turns his gaze reluctantly from the dancing men and women and begins scanning the dance floor. I feel bad for Anton. He would never admit to it, but I did think he wanted to have a romantic relationship with someone. He never mentioned dating or being interested in anyone, so I wasn't sure what the issue was with him. I sensed loneliness in him, a loneliness that I was very familiar with because it was the same loneliness and need that I felt in me before I met Brigham.

"I went to California this time—I'd never been there before."

"Nice." Anton jerks his head to the left and stares at a short dark-haired man with a shiny green shirt and black pants ogling a woman in a blue dress near the dance floor. He is standing with a man wearing a black-and-blue striped shirt with dark pants. Anton nods towards the men. "I think I've found our guys."

I scan the men Anton is looking at. The one in the green shirt has a wicked mind. In his head, I see the wife he has at home who he berates daily and had left this evening crying on the floor with a black eye. In the background, I hear the baby crying with a lump forming on his forehead from a blow with the bottle. Reaching back further into this man's mind, I see previous girlfriends he had abused and a mother he had slapped around. This man is revolting, and everything about him makes my skin crawl.

"Ick!" I say in disgust. I shake my head, hoping to break up the images in my mind. "Reading that green shirt guy is like having bugs crawl under your skin."

"Yes, he's a bad one," Anton says excitedly, leaning towards the man in anticipation. Anton is practically drooling, and I have to admit I am right there with him. The man is an easy target. Not much grey in him.

"I wonder what made him like that," I say in disgust and close my eyes trying to escape the images. The images seem to be stuck in my head and I if I really wanted to know the answer to my question, I would have to go back into the man's head again, but drudging through the darkness there to find my answer is very unappealing. There is too much horror to go through to get there. Too many dark deeds to sift through.

"I don't know, but we'll find out in a minute when we suck his blood. Go up to him and his friend and try to get them to come outside with you. I'll be waiting in the alley."

"What about the other guy, did you read him?"

"Yep! He's just as disgusting, trust me. Meet me outside."

"I'm on it," I say and stand up from my barstool. Anton gives me a quick peck on the cheek and rushes excitedly out of the club.

I watch for a moment as the man in the green shirt mentally undresses the woman in front of him dancing. He wants her. He wants her on his knees in front of him with his cock in her mouth and then he wants to see her on the ground begging for him to stop while he bashes her face in. This is one sick fuck, and I am going to enjoy sucking him dry.

I say his name in my head and his eyes flash up to me. He didn't hear me say his name exactly. What he felt was a nudge in my direction. I like doing this to get human's attention. It is subtle and effective. I flash him with a seductive smile and slowly make my way over to him. I could see my reflection in his mind, and I know he thinks I am beautiful...too beautiful for him. And not to be too cocky, but I *am* too good for him. I feel a wave of anxiety flood over him, and I know I need to reel him in quick.

I smile at him again and bite my bottom lip, trying to look alluring. It feels weird to be approaching men like this. I had never flirted with men like this as a human, it had not been my thing—but as a vampire, it is starting to grow on me. There is a thrill of the hunt and using my body as a weapon to lure men in. I feel like some sort of praying mantis or spider.

"Hey," I say as I gently touch the man in the green shirt's arm. Physical contact with humans makes it easier to connect with them and lure them in—ironically, it is the same way with vampires. I turn to the man with the striped shirt and run my fingers along his shoulder. He grins wildly at me, and I smile at him as I swing my ass into his leg.

"Hey baby," the man with the green shirt says, trying to sound smooth. His eyes land on my exposed cleavage and I thank Anton mentally for my dress—it is making it easier to hunt tonight. I pretend I don't notice the obvious ogling and give him a sweet smile, twirling a strand of my hair. "What's a pretty girl like you doing alone tonight?" he flirts as he reaches a hand around my back and rests it just above my ass as I resist ripping his throat out. He's bold, and he wastes no time getting his sleaze on and my disgust for him rises a notch. I hate men like him that come on strong with the fondling, acting confident, especially since it is all an act. What they are really doing is trying to push your boundaries and see how far they can get with you before they get pushed off.

"I'm lonely," I say with a pout. "My girlfriend is making out with some guy over there." I gesture behind me. "I haven't found anyone to be with tonight."

"That's terrible," he croons and pulls me up tight against him. He grinds against my hip, and I have to fight the urge to rip his head clear off his shoulders.

I could do it too, and it would be *really fun*. But it probably would scare the other humans in the club, and then there would be a lot of screaming. Plus, people are always glued to their phones now and there would be lots of pictures. And I guess there would be blood everywhere, which would be bad, so I reluctantly resist for now.

I look deep into his eyes and start glamouring him—I send him images of what it would be like to sleep with me to entice him. I send him dirty images of me kneeling before him with my mouth around his cock, of him putting a collar on me and pulling on it as he takes me from behind, and of him tying me up and hitting me as he rapes me. I know what he would like, and he is *so* easy to manipulate.

You always have to be careful when you did this with humans. It is very easy to break their mind by sending them too much information. The trick is going slow and giving them a chance to focus on each image. Everyone's mind is different and could manage different amounts of data at a time—this particular man's mind was very slow, and I had to be extra careful, or I might pop his brain right here in the club. Then there would be brain goo, screaming, and pictures.

"Would you guys like to be with me tonight?" I ask seductively, already knowing the answer. I turn towards the man with the striped shirt and glamour him with images of me being held down and fucked by both. His eyes light up in lust, and he adjusts his pants. I look down at his growing bulge and smile wickedly at him. *This is too easy.*

"Absolutely, honey," the man with the green shirt says thickly, grabbing my chin and turning my head toward him. *I want to bite him so badly! God, what a grabby bastard!* He presses himself harder into me and I feel his hard cock through his pants. Seducing men like them is so easy it is almost criminal—well, I suppose it is criminal by human standards anyway, but this wasn't against any vampire code.

"Good, good," I purr and brush my lips against his cheek. I trail my fingertips across his chest, hoping he doesn't notice my cold touch. Out of the corner of my eye, I see a man sitting at the bar studying me. He has dark brown hair in a textured long crop cut and has a pint of beer sitting in front of him, half empty. He looks at me and smiles, cocking his head to the side. I can't tell if he is a vampire or human in the club lighting, but something about how he is looking at me makes me nervous. Something is off about him. He smiles wider at me, and my skin prickles. Who is this dude? I try and read his mind but can't sense anything from him. That is weird. His eyes flick to the man I am glamouring and back to me, almost like he is acknowledging my hunt. I turn my attention back to my victim, remembering that I am in the middle of a hunt.

"Follow me," I whisper in his ear and gesture for him to follow me with my finger. I lock eyes with him again and glamour him with an image of him pinning me up against a wall for good measure and he follows me out obediently. I move to the man in the striped shirt and palm his obvious bulge in his pants and glamour him images of me sucking cock and gesture for him to follow me.

Outside, the air is cooler than inside the club and it feels good to be away from all the human minds. It is much quieter out there. I grab both men's hands as I lead them into the alley behind the club. Touching their hands, I get the information that their names are Don and Jim, and they are in their forties. They follow me in a trance as I flood them with more dirty images, and once we were in a deserted spot away from any club traffic, I push them with one hand up against the brick of the building. They are almost drooling now with their eyes glazed over. It is daunting how much more powerful I am as a vampire. Humans were really at my mercy. Anton creeps out from the shadows smiling widely, and I gesture to the men in triumph.

"Any trouble?" he asks, focusing his eyes intensely on Don.

"No, it was easy." I say confidently, "I almost feel bad for this dope, he doesn't stand a chance. But—" I hesitate, thinking about the strange man at the bar.

"But?" Anton asks raising an eyebrow at me.

"I don't know—maybe it's nothing, I had a weird interaction in there."

"What is it, Butterfly?" Anton asks and his body tenses. I look at Anton and furrow my brows at him.

"It's nothing, it's just that there was a guy in there who smiled at me."

Anton laughs. "So what? Guys always smile at you all the time. Do you have low self-esteem now, all of a sudden?"

"This was different—it was almost like he knew what I was doing with Don and Jim here. There was some sort of understanding in his smile. I'm not sure if he was a vampire or human, and I couldn't read his mind."

"Does it matter?"

"I guess not." I say slowly, but something in me is really concerned that it did matter. There was something off about the whole situation. This wasn't a normal human guy checking me out, this was different.

"Do you want to do the honor, or do you want me to?" Anton asks excitedly as he looks at Don. Don was still plastered against the brick but was now being held by Anton's gaze. His face was getting pale, and his mouth had turned into a wince as if he was in pain. I had a feeling Anton was feeding him horrific images of his death. This was something new Anton was experimenting with, and if it gave him a little more pleasure with his kill, it was fine by me.

"I'll take sloppy seconds to make up for the bet."

"It was only two hundred dollars, and I am rich, Butterfly. I was only giving you shit—I really don't care about the money."

"I know, but I still feel bad—you go first, and I'll go first on the next set of victims."

"Alright, I'm not going to argue." Anton smiles wickedly at our victim, and I lift the glamour I have on him but still keep Jim glamoured and pinned against the wall.

"This is going to hurt, dear boy—and unfortunately not enough," Anton sneers, showing his canines to Don.

"What? Who are you?" asks Don as he comes out of his daze.

"Your worst nightmare," Anton growls, letting his fangs elongate further out. I snap my mouth open as well and give him a view of my canines while making a scary hissing sound. It is very horror-movie vampiresque, but it is actually pretty fun to be so theatrical. Don's eyes fly open wide in panic, and he tries to scream out, but Anton is on him in a flash. I watch the man wither under Anton and slowly go limp, his eyes dulling. Anton moans with pleasure and I hear him tear deeper into Don's neck.

The smell of blood hits me and my throat starts to burn with need. It is a shame how much suffering this man had caused—hopefully his wife would be able to get on with her life. Anton releases Don, his eyes blazing, and shoves him over to me as he snatches up Jim. I grab Don hard, making him groan. I look at his neck, see his pulse, and bite down hard, tearing into his flesh. Don tries to shove me away, but it is useless. He is much too weak, and now that the bloodlust has taken over, there is no way I am releasing him.

I greedily drink every last drop of him, savoring the sweet metallic fluid. Blood tastes different as a vampire. It still has a metallic taste, but there is also a sweet honey-like bouquet to it now. Images of the man's misdeeds flood my mind. I see him kicking a dog, road raging, committing a hit-and-run, and littering—which is just unnecessary and rude. *Have some respect for the planet, dude!* I make sure to get his home address before the last of his life force is drained from him— his wife deserves to find a bundle of money on her doorstep for a fresh start.

I unceremoniously drop him to the ground. His body makes a sickening thump on the pavement when his head hits the ground and somehow it seems cathartic. I stare at his body for a while, feeling the blood course through my body, invigorating me. He was so weak compared to me, but he had caused so much damage in his life. It is better that he is gone.

Anton breaks from Jim with blood dripping from his mouth and makes a disgusted snarling noise. "This guy was a complete fuck! You'll enjoy killing him—he tortured a litter of kittens in high school."

"*Asshole!*" I shout and grab Jim so hard that my hands tear into his shoulder ripping into his flesh. It made me insane when people hurt animals. I viciously bite into his neck hard, piercing his jugular. Blood fills my mouth, and I drink quickly, making the man draw faster into death. His heart becomes erratic as the last beats of his life begin and I take the final mouthful, stopping his heart completely. I let the man fall unceremoniously with his head whacking the cement loudly. *The fucker deserved what he got!*

"I love it when you let them fall like that," Anton says passionately. I wipe droplets of blood into my mouth as I stare at the man's dead body—not feeling any remorse.

"I'm still hungry," I say in annoyance. Killing these men didn't seem like enough to undo all the pain they had caused, but it was all we could do.

"Want to find another set?" Anton asks excitedly as he pulls his phone from his pocket and checks his reflection in his camera. He runs his hands through his hair, tames his locks, and checks his eye makeup, removing the smudges.

"Yes!" I need to do more good tonight and only killing Don and Jim would not satisfy my itch. "But first, I want to go see if the man at the bar is still there."

Anton and I lift the men into a garbage bin and check each other for blood splatter. It was all too easy to get carried away with the first kill and have to run back home for a change of clothes before continuing on into the night. When

Anton and I first started, we had to bring extra clothes with us, because it was hard to control our exuberance. Satisfied that we weren't going to scare anyone, we walk back inside the club.

Anton scans for our next victim as I search for the dark-haired stranger at the bar. His stool is vacant now and I try to find him among the other clubgoers. The club is more crowded now, and the dance floor is full of people grinding up on each other. I smell the sweat of the human bodies—which is still weird. I try to focus on the man's face while searching the minds of the people around me. I find a woman who had seen him leave a few moments ago and am disappointed. Anton puts a hand on my shoulder, and I turn to him, dropping the woman's mind.

"Find him?" he asks while scanning the crowd.

"No," I say, and continue to search. "A woman saw him leave a few minutes ago."

"That's too bad."

I shrug. "No big deal. Did you find anyone else?"

"No one good enough to kill, which is a good thing, really, if you think about it. Want to try another club?"

"Absolutely. I can't seem to quench my thirst after being gone."

"Didn't you kill when you were away?"

"No, I didn't want to leave a trail for Brigham to follow."

"How does he find you?" Anton contemplates as he rubs his jaw.

"I never know. I thought I had covered my tracks really well this time, too," I say dejectedly.

"Interesting," Anton murmurs softly to himself.

"I think I might be microchipped," I say seriously and rub my neck trying to feel for it. They do it to animals. It was entirely possible that Brigham injected me with something when I was sleeping.

Anton mouth drops open, and he inspects my neck. "Really? You think so?"

I slump against the bar. "No, not really, but there is something odd about it."

"Some connections between the vampires they sire are stronger than others," Anton offers. "Vampires vary in their strength and gifts, too. Maybe Brigham has some weird ability to track people."

"Did you ever try to get away?"

Anton looks at me in shock, his mouth hanging open. "Me? No, no way. Are you crazy?" He shakes his head rapidly.

"Why not?" *Was it really that weird running away?*

He looks at me, his eyes bugging out of his head. "The thought never entered my mind. I've never wanted to run away, Butterfly. Pain is not my cup of tea, I mean—inflicting it on assholes, sure—but pain in my body, no thanks. I love being a vampire. I love being here."

"You never felt the urge to run, even a little bit?" I ask in disbelief. I find that so improbable. *Wasn't he even a little curious about what happened when you separated from your sire?*

"Where would I go? I like living here—I have everything that I've ever wanted, and I like my sire. Don't you enjoy being with Brigham?"

"Yes. I wouldn't have accepted being turned if I didn't."

"It's going to be fine after the new moon, you'll see—you're worrying over nothing."

"I hope you're right."

"I am." Anton puts his arm around my shoulder. "Let's go to Tropix. There is always a grandma-beater there."

"Aw, Anton the Great Woman Avenger."

He smirks and stands taller, straightening his shirt. "I do good work."

"That you do."

Tropix was a large complex on the south side of the river. It attracted young thirty-somethings and college students who were out on the prowl for mutually beneficial hook ups. The men wanted pretty women that they could parade around with and be seen with in their expensive cars, and the women were looking for rich men who could fulfill their consumeristic needs. It was actually a very disturbing and twisted place filled with shallow and manipulative people. It wasn't the kind of place that I hung out at as a human, but it was the perfect breeding ground for hunting as a vampire.

Inside the club, there were three floors, each with a huge bar and dance floor. The upper lounge had more comfy chairs and private hide-abouts where hookups could be made. Large televisions flashed music videos and colorful lights danced across the dance floor, lighting up the clubbers. It was very chic and expensive inside, which made it all the more glamorous to its occupants. If it cost a lot of money to be there, then it had to be the in place to be. Image was everything in this place, and there was no substance to be found anywhere.

Scanning the minds of the clubbers is depressing. Everyone is so hollow and self-absorbed. I would have never hung out or associated with these people in my human life and being around them now makes my skin crawl. But I am here to hunt, I remind myself as I continue to scan the occupants. Ten people later, I have to give myself a break. If I hear one more woman criticize her girlfriend's figure in her mind, I am going to crack and go on a bloody rampage—women can be such bitches. Anton is feverishly scanning the people around us. Their inner banter doesn't seem to bother him as much as it does me, so I let him take the lead on the scanning. I am done with this crowd—give me a biker bar any day. They are much more civil than this bunch.

I take a fake sip of my mixed drink. I wasn't sure what it was, but Anton assured me it was in and trendy and that it made us look normal, so that was all that mattered.

"So, Anton, did Forseti tell you about the sire connection before you became a vampire?" I ask.

Anton snorts and shakes his head. "No, no one knows about it before they're turned," he says earnestly.

"Brigham mentioned it briefly to me when I was a human," I say, remembering. Very briefly, as in—*we'll be more connected once you change*. I had disregarded it as some romantic lofty love talk. I had no idea of the gravity of his statement.

"He couldn't have said much. It's impossible for him to talk about it. I think they ignite or combust or something if they say too much."

"Bullshit," I disagree. Vampires don't ignite…I didn't think.

"No, really, I've heard stories."

I roll my eyes. "More gossip? You can't believe everything that you hear, Anton."

"Some of it has to be based on fact."

"I don't think Brigham would have ignited if he told me about the sire connection." I wasn't sure what would happen, but I doubted it would be anything so dramatic.

"Ignite, implode, melt—something would have happened that would have ended in his death, one way or another."

"I don't believe that," I say firmly. That was complete fantasy. Yes, we were vampires, and we were real, but we were still governed by some of the same laws of physics. Weren't we? I thought about Brigham's ability to find me, my newfound strength and glamouring power, and suddenly I'm not so sure. A lot had changed when I was turned.

"What's not to believe?" Anton asks and smiles wickedly at me. He stands up from the table we are at and starts to gyrate to the heavy, beating music that is blaring around us. "I really like the music here—you can really dance to it!"

Ignoring Anton's dance moves, I shout to him over the music. "I think it's all vampire superstition or myths to help vampires gain control of their newly-sired vampires. Who would be willing to get turned if they knew how strong the connection was?"

"I probably still would have," Anton shouts back to me over the overpowering music.

"No way," I say, shaking my head as I stand up to join in his dance. I am tired of sitting and need some physical distraction.

"Yeah, it doesn't bother me in the slightest." Anton says as he grabs my hand and spins me fast around in a circle. It was much too fast for a human, but underneath the lights and crowded dance floor, no one noticed us.

"You're a weirdo then," I jab, but Anton ignores me and spins me faster. It really didn't seem to bother Anton very much, or any other vampires I had met, but it did bother me.

I focus on a young woman in the back of the club. She is pretty with her hair cut short in a bob and is wearing a black leather coat and boots. If I didn't find someone else tonight, I might go after her. There was no reason not to wear faux leather these days. I roll my eyes at myself, *lord I was desperate.*

"When you were first turned, did you find it hard to feed on humans?" I ask Anton.

"At first?" Anton makes a face at me, doing a perfect imitation of David Rose from *Schitt's Creek*. "No, I was ravenous. If Forseti wasn't there, I would have drained the city."

I try to imagine Anton with bloodlust that intense, but can only picture the happy-go-lucky Anton I know now.

"I can't picture you like that," I admit.

"It was nuts. I've never been so insatiable in my life," he laughs darkly. "Not *even* as a teenager."

Images of a young virginal Anton trying to pick up girls and guys in high school flash in my mind and I try to contain my laughter.

"I couldn't get enough blood in me that first week. I was draining five to six people a day!" he says and cringes a little.

"Jesus!" I exclaim, thinking about all the carnage. "That's a lot!"

"Well, I'm a guy, and I think we have a larger appetite to start with—faster metabolism or something." Anton shrugs.

I bit my lip, pondering this new notion. "Makes sense—human men have a higher calorie requirement than women," I say softly. I had never thought about that aspect before. What other differences were there between male and female vampires?

"Exactly. Plus, I think vampire bodies go through a lot of changes that first month and a lot of blood is needed to make us so powerful. Forseti and I were hunting like crazy when I was first turned."

"What's it like hunting with Forseti? I have a hard time picturing him doing it. He seems so refined." Any time I had ever seen Forseti, he was dressed immaculately—as prim and proper as a king. He was also very calm and laid back for a vampire. I had never seen him emit anything but pleasantness when in the presence of others.

"He's very smooth. He'll strike up a conversation with a random person and before I know it, they're willingly exposing their neck to him."

"Willingly?" I ask doubtfully. There was no way a vampire, even Forseti, could get a human to willingly give them their blood. There had to be some level of glamouring involved. "He must glamour them!"

"He does glamour them a little, but not much—everyone likes him, so it's not hard for him to get what he wants out of people. I don't know if he has some other power or what."

"He's a great guy, I admit, but I can't imagine people willingly giving up their lives for him. He must have some other ability—I wonder what it is. Brigham hasn't told me if he has any special abilities, although his eyes are always changing a different color of blue—I think based on his mood."

"Not every vampire manifests one. I like mine, though. It's fun turning stuff into metal."

"That is pretty cool—I hope I manifest with something when I am fully turned. Do you think maybe Forseti glamours everyone else to make it look like his victims are willing before he kills them?"

Anton rolls his eyes at me and says a little huffy, "He doesn't kill all his victims."

"Really? How does he manage that? I thought all vampires killed their victims."

"As I said, people give their blood willingly to him. He takes a little and moves on." Anton spins me around hard again, causing me to almost bump into a large man with a shaved head with many piercings and gauges in his ears who is trying to dance with a young blonde next to us.

"Hey!" I seethe at Anton. "Be careful where you're spinning me. I could hurt someone." The last thing I wanted to do when we were trying to be covert vampire vigilantes was accidentally break a guy's ribs. It might raise a few questions how a five-foot five-inch hundred-thirty-pound woman can cause that amount of damage to a six-foot four-inch two-hundred-sixty-pound beefcake.

Anton pulls me closer to him. "Sorry," he whispers into my ear. "I get a little carried away on the dance floor."

"No harm done." We dance closer together for a while, keeping up our cover as each of us scans the room. The lights are dancing around us faster now as the music's tempo picks up speed. The people dancing around us are generating a lot of heat and it feels good to be warmed by them. I scan the dancers around us and am disappointed. They are all innocent enough, which is actually a good thing. "Isn't that risky for Forseti to drink blood that way? Having all those people walking around with holes in their necks?"

"He heals them before they go. There aren't any bruises or marks on them."

"Oh right, I keep forgetting about our healing abilities," I snort. "We never use that—maybe we should start doing that to our victims, in case they are found by the police, so it is not so obvious that they were attacked by vampires."

"I think if they find a body drained of blood, the police will think vampire even if it doesn't have bites in it."

"Do you think we should do something different with the bodies? Like burn them or put them in a lake, so they are harder to find?"

"Nah, you know the guild owns the police. It's not an issue."

"Still, it's a lot to cover up, if you figure each vampire in the area kills an average of two people a day, which might be too low. Let's say it's three a day on average times how many guild members there are, which is like what, a couple hundred?"

Anton nods. "At least."

My eyebrows raise as I do the math in my head. "That's a lot of deaths per day! That's almost three hundred thousand a year! Is that even sustainable?"

"I think there are like over thirty thousand babies born each day, so it is probably fine."

"Wait what? Really? Well, that is disturbing."

"See, we are helping with the human overpopulation problem. We are definitely getting some karma points for that!" Anton says triumphantly and smiles at me like he truly believed that.

I scan a woman at the bar with short cropped purple hair—her skin is silky smooth and has a sheen to it. She turns towards me and flashes me with a smile, showing me her canines. I smile back at her, barely exposing my canines. We are not the only ones hunting tonight. It's a bit weird coming upon vampires out in public. There is a weird comradery with the guild members—we were all a part of this secret society. I had never been involved in a group like this before, and, at times, it is still a bit odd to be included.

"There's another vampire hunting here," I say to Anton and give a slight nod towards the purple haired vampire.

Anton looks over to her and raises his drink to her. "That's Rayna, she's cool."

I keep scanning the crowd but am having difficulty finding anyone up to my standards. My mind wanders back to Forseti and his unique hunting style. How does that work exactly? How can vampires, beings made for death and destruction, heal their victims?

"Do you know how we are able to heal our bites on our victims?" I ask.

"It's crazy. Forseti told me that our saliva has trillions upon trillions of antibodies—white blood cells, antivirals, antiradicals—all kinds of good stuff in it!"

"Sort of like chicken soup?" I joke. "How is that even possible? Those are living cells and proteins, and I don't know how to even classify them, but they are alive in a way. Aren't we kind of dead or are we reanimated?"

"You never take me seriously," Anton pouts. I laugh. It wasn't that I didn't take Anton seriously, I did. He is a wealth of vampire knowledge, but I'm not going to believe everything that comes out of his mouth—some of the stuff is really messed up.

"Could our saliva cure cancer?" I tease.

"Yes," says Anton seriously.

"Liar."

"I've heard we could from a buddy of mine." Here we go again with Anton's unmentionable sources.

"Who?" I ask. Maybe this time, he would actually give me a name.

"You don't know him." I look at Anton doubtfully. "If you don't believe me, ask Brigham about it."

"I will," I say sassily and raise my chin at him defiantly.

"Good, you do that," Anton pouts and crosses his arms over his chest. I smile sweetly at Anton and he tries not to smile back. "You think I'm stupid, don't you?"

"Not at all," I say seriously and then shoot him an evil smile. He is so easy to mess with, and I just can't help myself sometimes.

"Then why is it so hard for you to believe me?"

"I believe you eighty percent of the time," I say with a wink. "But I do find it hard to believe that vampires—bloodsuckers, nightwalkers, the damned, demons of the night—can sure cancer. It seems illogical, or unfair really. If it is true, we need to get our asses to a children's cancer ward."

"What part about vampires existing *is* logical?" Anton asks and throws his arms up in the air. I think for a moment on that—he is right. Being born a human with cells that grew, divided, and died and then being turned into a being that never aged, drank blood to survive, and had the potential for immortality didn't make a hell of a lot of sense.

"You've got a point. It isn't very logical."

"Exactly! We're in a whole new ball game. Old human logic doesn't apply anymore. Embrace the now already!"

"Sorry, I suppose I'm still thinking like a human. It's a hard habit to break," I admit. I wasn't really sure how a vampire should think but I was sure it had to be different than a human.

"I'm being too tough on you. You haven't been a vampire for very long—sometimes I forget. It seems like we've been friends forever. After a few decades, you'll feel differently."

"I guess…so why do you think Forseti hunts like he does?"

"He's a grazer," Anton answers, as if I am supposed to understand what that means. I laugh and hold my hands up. *What does that mean?* When I think of grazers, I think of deer or cows. He smiles at me and continues. "He likes sampling and enjoys experiencing the different tastes of people."

"You make it sound like he's at a perpetual wine tasting."

"That's exactly what it is. Hell, think about it. We live in a perpetually growing vineyard. Every human is unique and has a unique flavor. Why not try them all?"

"Did he ever try to convince you to hunt like he does?" I ask.

"I did at first. I did enjoy not having to kill people to quench my thirst, which was a plus. It only makes them a little dizzy and anemic."

"Why did you stop?"

"Having so many people's thoughts in my head was exhausting—plus I had to sample a lot of people in a night to get satisfied."

I nod, understanding that. "Information overload."

"Yep," Anton says and runs his hands through his hair and then quickly pulls out his phone to check his locks.

"Is that the only reason?"

"No, you know it's not. I like feeling like I have influence in this world—like I have a positive impact, even if I don't function within the same realm as I used to. I loved my old job, and I think I miss seeing myself as one of the good guys. Don't you feel the same way? Isn't that why you decided to hunt the people you do?" Anton asks.

"Yes. I feel just like you do, but I'm worried." I pause and scan the man standing next to me. He had short black curly hair with a goatee and large tattoos on his arms. He was a chef, liked working on his motorcycle, and had a wife and a little girl at home whom he adored. He is a nice guy and not on the menu for Anton or me tonight. I turn towards Anton and whisper, "What if when I'm changed completely, Brigham's take on killing will seep into me and I'll change my mind? Do you think your personality changes after the new moon?"

"Yes."

"Oh great!" I was hoping I was being paranoid.

"I'm more stable now after the change—more self-assured. The first month was rough, there was so much change. I felt more myself after the transformation, like the real me was more clear-crystalized," Anton explains.

"You don't think Forseti's mind left a fingerprint on you?" I wonder.

"If it did, I haven't noticed. I still feels like me," Anton answers.

I nod and sigh heavily. I couldn't shake the worry that I was about to change, and I wouldn't notice. I'd lose a part of myself and never know it was missing. *That possibility is terrifying!*

"Butterfly, becoming a vampire isn't like having your body snatched."

"I guess…I haven't met a vampire who is unhappy with the change, but people who have been brainwashed are usually very content. Look how happy children are when they've sat in front of a television for three hours. I want to be happy, but not at the expense of losing myself."

"God, you make everything so complicated and see it so negatively. What are you so afraid of?" Anton prods.

"I'm not afraid," I say defiantly.

Anton rolls his eyes at me and pretends to take a sip from his drink. "Uh huh…sure."

"I'm not!"

"You're terrified you're going to become Brigham's plaything."

"I already have," I say, smiling suggestively at Anton.

"*Ew!* Bad visual!" Anton waves his hands frantically in front of his face and I laugh and take a pretend sip of my drink. "Maybe it will be a good thing having Brigham having a little mind control over you—you might be nicer. I think you would do well with a little imposed-upon self-control, hopefully Brigham will be able to rein you in a bit."

"Okay, now I'm going to bite you!"

Anton flashes me with a wicked smile, exposing his bleached white fangs. Vampire fangs were already starkly white, but that wasn't enough for Anton. He had his bleached to perfection.

"I'd like to see you try," Anton challenges and I laugh. Yeah, that would be an interesting situation—Anton and I in a fight! He had me on strength, but I had no qualms about fighting dirty, and the dirtiest thing I could do to him would be to mess up his immaculately-coifed hair! It might be fun! I laugh again, thinking about how fun that might be.

"So, you think I'm being ridiculous?"

"Extremely, but I understand, I really do. I see how hard this all would be for you. You're much more independent than I am."

"I'll be glad when it's all over," I sigh and scan the room some more. "I'm tired of thinking about it and obsessing over it."

"You and me both, sister," Anton mutters under his breath. I lean over and punch Anton in the arm hard, causing him to spill his drink on his pants.

"Hey! These clothes were expensive! Don't make me bleed you in public!" Anton hisses at me, his fangs elongating.

"Oh! I like it when you talk dirty to me!" I tease and hand him a napkin from the counter. I try to dab at the spilled liquor, but Anton slaps my hand away hard.

"Get off me, you're making it stain! Are you even looking for victims anymore?"

"Oh right." I look up and scan around the room. "I forgot why we were here."

Anton blots himself frantically, his face contorting in strange ways as he looks at his clothes. "Attention span of an ant, you have."

"Like you are any better. When we go shopping at the mall, you are all over the place."

"That's different. I'm extremely focused when it counts, like now," he says, giving me an annoyed look and focuses on cleaning himself up.

I scan the room some more and see a man with dark black hair and a purple shirt in the back of the club. His back is turned to me, and I'm not sure if he is the mysterious stranger I had seen earlier or not. I focus on the man, trying to glamour him. Glamouring is hard for me to do still when I wasn't looking directly in their eyes. The man turns towards me, and I see it is not the same man as before, and I drop the glamour and sigh deeply.

"Damn," I mutter under my breath.

"What is it?" Anton asks as he looks at the man I was staring at.

"I thought I saw the guy from earlier, but it wasn't him."

"Why the obsession? Isn't one large handsome man enough for you?" I smile evilly at Anton, and his face contorts in disgust. "Forget I asked," he says.

"You're *not* into vampire orgies?" I ask innocently.

"What?" Anton gasps, almost spilling his drink again.

"I told Brigham you might be into it." Anton mouth drops open in horror.

"You did not!" Anton hisses and looks wildly around the club.

I laugh hard at Anton and ask, "Who are you looking for?"

"Brigham to burst through here and stab me in my heart! You didn't really tell him that, did you?"

"You're right, I didn't. The look on your face was classic though—pure terror."

"I hate you," Anton pouts.

"You love me," I say, winking at him and give him a side hug. He pushes me off of him hard, causing me to laugh harder.

"I think you lost a nut or bolt or something out on this last adventure of yours."

"Am I being that strange?"

"You're spiraling," Anton says seriously as he shakes his head slowly.

"Hmmm…I do feel a bit more reckless than normal." I just couldn't seem to center or be still.

"Contemplating vampire orgies is *not* a good sign."

I roll my eyes. "I wasn't serious."

Anton takes a fake sip of his drink and shoots me a smirk. "Sure, you weren't."

"I wasn't!" I growl, setting my drink down sharply. Rubbing my neck, I scan the crowd. "I think I'm stressed." Anton nods and gently squeezes my shoulder. "That and I'm curious about the guy I saw. I wonder who he is." There was something about the man that felt off that I couldn't put my finger on.

"Still not sure if he was human or vampire?"

"My mind didn't do the automatic scan thing it does when I see a human, so I think he was a vampire, but I'm not certain. I haven't met many vampires out and about to know for sure. Most of the vampires I've met have been at Forseti's parties or were business colleagues of Brigham's that have stopped by his house."

"Interesting…" Anton's hand went to his chin, and he began to rub it slowly as he looks at a couple coming through the door. They are all over each other and had been partying for a while. Both of them are benign and I dismiss them quickly, but Anton keeps staring at them.

"What is it?" I ask. Had I missed something in their minds?

"You said *Brigham's house*."

I shrug. "So? That's what it is." What point was Anton trying to make here?

"You didn't say our house."

"Huh…I didn't realize I did that. That *is* interesting."

"Can I ask you something…personal?"

"Sure," I say hesitantly. *That sounded ominous.*

"Do you feel intimidated in your relationship with Brigham because he's this big bad head honcho vampire guy?" Anton asks and looks at me closely.

"It's funny that you asked that. I didn't feel that way when I was human, but I suppose I didn't know the extent of his head honcho-ness, as you say. I knew he was handsome, rich, and immortal and that didn't intimidate me. I suppose a more intelligent person would have been," I admit and rub my temple. That was probably all very naïve of me, come to think about it—getting involved with him as a human. "I felt very special when Brigham decided to date me—I mean, getting attention and affection from a vampire is very romantic. But our relationship has changed since I've become a vampire. I knew my footing as a human—now that I'm in Brigham's world and have learned about his place in it, I feel like the bottom's dropped out. I don't know where my place is in it and where it is with him. He hasn't done or said anything to make me feel that anything between us has changed, mind you, but I do feel so much less certain."

"Why do you think that is?"

"I feel like a guest in his life—a fling, a passing fantasy—not a permanent fixture. Our relationship was *so* significant to me, and now that I've seen what the vampire world is like, I see how silly that was. We've only been together for a few months—how could any vampire out there see us and not think it's a laughable situation. How could they take our relationship seriously? Hell, I barely take myself seriously."

"Since when do you care about what anyone thinks, human or vampire?" Anton says, giving me hard look.

"I suppose since Brigham told me about the sire connection . . .he didn't tell me right away after he changed me."

"When did he tell you?"

"Remember when I ran away the first time?"

"Yeah, that was like ten days after you were changed."

"I found out that night."

"Freaked out a bit, did we?" Anton teases. I cringe and he gently puts his hand on my arm.

"That's putting it mildly. It made me realize how little I knew about being a vampire, and about being in a relationship with Brigham. I mean, if he didn't see the importance of telling me something *that* significant, what did that mean? Was I so unimportant to him that he didn't think he had to tell me that? Did he not think I'd care? Did he know me at all? I had a lot of doubts, and I didn't like the answers I was coming up with, so I left. And yes, I know how cowardly that was—no need to point that out."

"You seem to be doing okay with everything now. I mean, after this last episode."

"I'm nothing if not curious and I want to see what will happen next. It's hard to do that if I'm running away." That and I am running out of time. I may be unstable, but I didn't have a death wish.

"So, you ran away to get back at Brigham for not telling you about the sire connection?" Anton muses.

I grin sheepishly. The good and bad thing about having a best friend is they are your constant mirror. Nothing gets past them. I explain, "Aw…yeah…there has been some of that, but I wanted to evaluate the connections as well. I was not about to believe Brigham so readily again. I wanted to find out the truth for myself."

"That was kind of a juvenile response."

"I'm a young vampire," I say with a shrug. "It's my right to be juvenile. If Brigham doesn't like it, too bad for him. He made me, and now he was to deal with me."

Anton laughs and pats me on the shoulder. "You're terrible—you know that, right?"

"I know," I moan. "And I'm so full of shit. I'm lucky Brigham has been so understanding and has not kicked me out yet. Seriously, I wouldn't put up with this kind of shit from my boyfriend. I'm pathetic." I scan the club again and irritation fills me—there is no one here worth biting. *What the hell!*

Anton snorts. "Like he would, he loves you so much. It's all over his face, that's all there is when he looks at you."

"Really?"

"Yeah, even now after you're last adventure. I'd say there's more love there than there was before you left."

"When did you see him?"

"He stopped by Forseti's house after dropping you off at your house yesterday," Anton says as he scans the crowd and grimaces.

"My house?"

"That's what it is, silly. It stopped being only Brigham's house a long time ago."

"He has gone out of his way to make me feel comfortable there. He redecorated his bedroom since we've been going out—asked for my input and all that. It was actually a little awkward for me to give him any opinions—no one has ever asked me questions like that before."

"I think he wants you to stay there with him for a while."

"He calls me his immortal beloved."

"That's beautiful."

"It is, but. . ." I loved Brigham more than I ever knew was possible. No one I had ever met has even come close to being as connected as I was to him and so fast, but it scares me. There is a lot to gain and a lot to lose in a relationship like this. I'd always been able to walk away, and now that was an impossibility beyond my control and I am scared. I am going to finally have to deal with everything that comes up now—every fight, every emotion, every moment. I'd never done that before! Never wanted to.

Suddenly, I am the one who is vulnerable. I had never been in that position before and being it in now I found it hard to breathe. What if he didn't want me? What if I became attached to him and he changed his mind? What was I going to do then? There is a lot of responsibility in carrying such a deep love through time, and time was something that was now unending for us. Any mistake I made, every time I lashed out had an effect on the man I loved, and that was frightening. The power of myself is larger than it had ever been and I didn't like my careless tendencies or lack of foresight wounding him or us. There is so much more to consider now. Before, I would only be hurting myself, and that had all changed.

My momentary pause stretches into eternity as I contemplate my situation. Anton shakes me fiercely and I stumble out of my chair. "It's beautiful—but?" Anton prods, the annoyance thick in his voice. He hates it when I trail off into a thought and never finish it.

"Oh, ignore me. I'm certifiable," I say, waving him off. I don't want to get into my craziness with Anton tonight any more than I have already. I am tired of feeling like a lunatic in front of people. "I'm getting hangry. Can you see if you can find someone? I've given up on this place. I think we need to start hitting fewer trendy bars—the people we hunt aren't this classy."

"You're right, we do get an occasional wife/girlfriend beater, but if we want our type, we'll have to start slumming it." Anton sighs. "But then I have to dress down and I hate that, especially since I can afford nice clothes now!"

I put my hand on his shoulder and pat him sympathetically. I know he likes these kinds of bars because they fit his personality better and he enjoys people watching all the new fashions coming onto the dance floor. "Maybe you shouldn't have thrown out all my old clothes," I tease.

"Nonsense! *They were HORRIBLE!* We can still slum it and look good."

"Not without getting noticed. We'll need to tone it down."

Anton moans and rubs his face. "Figures, I become a vampire and can finally afford to dress nice but can't because it interferes with my hunting."

"It's hard being you," I say sarcastically and poke him in the arm.

"It *so* is!" Anton shouts and stamps his feet. "Oh well, I'm going to be positive. It just gives me another reason to go shopping for more clothes."

"That's the vampire I know and love."

"Of course it will have to be at thrift stores, but hey, maybe I'll get a good laugh or two," he says.

"Hey! I used to love thrift stores! That's the only way I could afford to get new clothes!" I scold him.

"I know, and darling, trust me—*everyone knew!*"

"My god, you're such a bitch! I didn't dress that badly!"

Anton laughs. "You're just so much fun to tease. Usually not much bothers you, but if I tease you even a little about your human life, you go batty!"

"Well, I am glad I can amuse you!' I say sarcastically.

"Oh, stop that! You tease me all the time!"

"Yeah, and you don't like it either."

"Sure, you can dish it out, but you just can't take it," Anton says playfully and bites my shoulder.

"Elitest!" I snub.

"Doormat!" Anton challenges.

"*I am not!*" I yell loudly. The bartender looks up at us and gives Anton a dirty look. I smile at him and glamour 'everything is fine' to him to keep him from thinking I am fighting with Anton. That is all we need, to look like a couple about to brawl and get kicked out of here. We'd be glamouring all night trying to fix that mess! "Look what you made me do!" I hiss, gesturing towards the bartender. "Let's get out of here before your juvenile behavior gets us into more trouble!" I jump off my stool and start heading towards the door.

Anton giggles as he follows behind me as we weave in between groups of people. "Ah, Butterfly—I have such fun with you! I'm sorry I called you a doormat—you aren't one, you just have self-esteem issues," Anton teases. I growl and Anton starts to laugh hysterically "So touchy!"

"You better find us someone quick here—you know how testy I get if I get hungry!" I snip. I had self-esteem, *damn it!* I wasn't some wishy-washy doormat, right? Suddenly, I'm not so sure. Maybe that's why I always feel so unsure about Brigham and my relationship, was it me??? *CRAP!!* I thought it was him!!! I laugh softly at myself. That is so me! Getting it backwards!

"What's so funny?" asks Anton. I turn to him as we walk outside and the look on his face is classic. His face is completely open and eyes bright with his head cocked slightly to the right. He always gives me this look like he is trying to figure out something I did or said.

"Oh, nothing—I was just laughing about myself," I answer as we start walking back towards Anton's car, passing numerous excited people about to enter the club.

"That's a very healthy thing to do, Miss Butterfly! I do it to myself at least five times a day!"

"I bet," I laugh.

"Come on," Anton says, looping his arm into mine, "let's go find my car and hit another place. Maybe we can even find someone as we drive around."

"Yay!"

We head out to the street, and the cold air hits me. It doesn't bother me, which actually wasn't that much of a change since I had grown up in Minnesota, but what had changed is the weird feeling of the loss of human presence that I seem to always be attuned to. It is like my body now sought them out. It sought out their blood, the heat of their bodies, their smell. It is very strange to feel predatory towards something.

We scan the people as we pass them, but they are as benign and boring as ever, which I keep reminding myself is a good thing. What if Anton and I ended up cleaning up all of the Twin Cities in a few years? What would we do then?

Anton steers me to the parking garage that is badly lit. I would never have parked here before becoming a vampire—it wasn't safe for women to walk alone in this area, armed or not, but now it wasn't an issue to walk around wherever I wanted. This must be what men feel like all the time. *How strange!*

As we near Anton's bright red Ferrari 812 Superfast sports car, he starts cooing to it, "Hello, my baby! Daddy's back! Did you miss me? I missed you! I love you so much! Yes, I do, my sweet red thing!"

"*Argh!* I think I am going to vomit," I mutter and look away from him as he gropes his car and notice a man standing back between some cars in the shadows. I scan him and touch Anton's arm. "Got one," I whisper, and Anton stands up straight and turns looking in the direction I am staring. He looks at me and grins and before I can barely blink, he runs over to the man and immobilizes him with a glamour.

I walk over to the man slowly and look into his blue eyes. He's shorter and wider than Anton and has acne-scarred skin and short brown hair. He looks at me wide-eyed, and I see that Anton's glamour has paralyzed him, and has drool running down his chin.

"You've been such a naughty boy," I purr at him and smile, making my fangs grow slowly all the way out. He makes a pathetic raspy sound, and a foul odor comes from him—I look down and see urine dripping to the ground and a large wet stain spreading over the front of his pants.

"Butterfly, looks like you made this poor boy piss himself," Anton says, clicking his tongue.

I run my hands over the man's face and he trembles. "Naughty, naughty boy. What will we do with you?" I slap him hard and the sound echoes around us.

I didn't always play with my food this much, but this guy had beat his grandmother half to death because she wouldn't give him her social security check. I grab a hold of the man hard and Anton steps back and looks at me gleefully. He takes out a small metal box from his jacket pocket and opens it, revealing a bunch of pointed plastic straws. He grabs one out and holds it in front of him and turns it into metal. He then takes the straw and jabs it hard into the man's heart, causing blood to start gushing out of him like a hose. Anton leans down, drinks, and then gestures for me to do the same.

The blood hits me and I feel myself ignite inside as it courses through my body, rejuvenating me. I smile at Anton. This was not the worst part about being a vampire. I love this euphoric empowering surge that happens every time I drink from a human. I wondered if, in Greek mythology, when it talked about the Gods drinking and eating ambrosia to get immortality and eternal youth, if they were really talking about vampires. Humans were ambrosia to me, and I loved it!

The man slumps against a pillar as we take turns drinking him from the straw. When he passes, Anton plucks the straw out and picks him up unceremoniously, throwing him over the side of the parking garage ledge into a dumpster down below.

"That was fun!" Anton says with satisfaction.

"Your metal-turning ability sure comes in handy."

"If only I could turn stuff to gold!" Anton says defeatedly. "I can do almost every straight metal, and I'm working on some fun alloys, but gold is eluding me. Forseti thinks if I keep trying, I will get it."

"Practicing is really the only way to get good at something. Maybe one day your nickname could be King Midas!"

"I like that King part! You can start calling me King Anton now!"

"That's not happening." I grab his arm, and we walk back to his car.

"Damn it!" Anton pouts. "I'd make a great King! If only the Vampire Guild let us rule over the humans!"

I punch him in the arm hard. "You are so full of shit!"

"I am. That would be really horrible, wouldn't it?" Anton grimaces. "The Vampire Guild isn't perfect, but I do like the rules for the most part that are in place. I feel like they try to keep a good balance of our power. We don't have any crazy vampires trying to murder or breed humans for food or anything."

"*Ugh!* I hadn't even thought of that as being a possibility," I admit. My stomach drops, I really didn't think this whole vampire thing through. I could have gotten in with some really bad people and not even known it because I was so mesmerized and in love with Brigham!

Anton looks at his watch. "I better get you home, sunrise if going to be soon and you will turn into sleeping beauty."

I groan and give him a hug. "Okay, but I want to go out with you hunting soon. I missed you!"

Anton hugs me back. "I missed you too, Butterfly. I'm glad you didn't die!"

CHAPTER FOUR

Home

Sunrise approaches. I can feel the force of the sun rising on the horizon. It is like the opposite of an undertow. It rises and I fall. It's continuous, at opposite ends of the spectrum. Brigham's house stands on a hill overlooking the Mississippi River below. The outside of the building reminded me so much of him. It is a large, four-story house painted a mellow slate blue with few windows from the front. In the back, there are many windows overlooking the river, and most of the rooms had a door leading out onto a balcony. The house looks cold and distant as I approach—much like Brigham did most of the time—but inside it is warmer. Inside, the house is decorated in warmer tones and had cozy lighting and plush furniture, completely in contrast to the outside.

Before I moved in with Brigham, he lived here alone—for how long, I wasn't sure—it was a topic that had never come up in conversation. Occasionally, he had business associates that would come and have meetings in his office, but now that I was here, Brigham bought a small building near Forseti's house closer to the guild where he could conduct business. He said he wanted the house to feel like a home and that was hard to do when business partners were constantly stopping by. I honestly didn't mind the added company since the house seemed so big and empty with just the two of us here, but it seemed like an important step for Brigham to take, so I didn't argue.

The sunrise is getting closer, and my legs ache from walking, my eyes growing heavy as I unlock the front door. I kick off my shoes and try unsuccessfully to shuffle them out of the way in the entry as I limp into the dark living room. I can't see Brigham in the darkness, but I sense he is here— the sire connection pulling me towards him. I fumble with the light switch and find him sitting in a dark brown leather chair reading a book. He looks up at me and smiles as he gently closes his book.

"I still find it disturbing when you do that," I say, shaking my head at him as I make my way to the couch and sink into the deep padding. It feels so good to lay down, and I didn't know if I will ever be able to make it to the bedroom.

"Read in the dark?" Brigham asks, setting his book on the table next to him. I couldn't tell by the cover what he is reading, but the binding is old. He loved to read musty old history books, and I assumed this was another from his collection.

"Yes," I yawn as I turn on to my back. My entire body feels heavy as if I am turning into stone.

"I don't need the light anymore—my eyesight has improved greatly over the years."

"It's creepy," I say crabbily. I always became fussy when I was tired, and now was no exception.

"That's your human prejudice shining through," Brigham says evenly. He was so good at deflecting my moodiness, and I don't think I would ever be able to deal with people like he did—not in a million years—but sometimes, he could be so condescending. I didn't even think he knew he was doing it. I mean, I know he was old and had experienced a lot of life, but did he always have to seem like such a know-it-all?

"Probably . . .but it's still creepy."

Brigham stands up and moves to the chair standing next to the couch. He gently reaches for my hand. I try to move it towards him, but it barely budges from the couch. He strokes my palm, and I feel a tingling sensation move between us. I begin to feel less heavy and some of the exhaustion lifts. Being apart from him for a few hours had had an effect on me, which is annoying. I was used to being independent in my human life, but now it feels like I am tethered to him.

"You had a good night," Brigham whispers as he strokes my cheek.

I close my eyes completely, enjoying the tenderness of his touch. "Yes," I murmur. Brigham moves closer and carefully lifts me off the couch, cradling me to his body. He sits back down and positions me so that my head is lying in his lap. He begins stroking the hair from my face back behind my ear, and I moan as tiny bursts of energy hit my skin. I didn't know if it was my attraction to Brigham that made his touch feel this way or if it was the sire connection, but I loved it and didn't want him to stop.

"What did you and Anton find?" Brigham asks as he leans down and kisses the top of my forehead, with another electric jolt moving from his body through mine.

"A man who beat his wife, baby, and tortured numerous animals—we also found a man who beat his invalid grandmother in a parking ramp." The last individual we found was particularly revolting, and both Anton and I felt like we had made a huge contribution to humanity by taking that asshole out. Even though at times it feels like we were only putting a drop in a bucket, I am sure that what we were doing added up—at least I hoped. Every little bit counts, right?

"That must have been exciting."

"It was a good night." If all of my hunting nights went as well as tonight, I would be a very happy vampire.

"You have a lot of fun with Anton," Brigham states evenly.

"Yes." I pause for a moment, contemplating Brigham's comment. I hadn't really thought about how my relationship with Anton might affect Brigham. There was no reason for him to be threatened by Anton, but Brigham was still a guy, and it wouldn't surprise me if he had a small amount of trepidation with our relationship.

"I'm glad," I look up at him, and he smiles sincerely at me. "You aren't worried?" I ask, trying to keep the surprise and doubt out of my face.

"I don't worry when you're with Anton," Brigham says confidently, and something about how he says that doesn't add up. He was fine with me and Anton being friends, but was he worried about me being out for other reasons?

"You weren't worried I would run?"

"No."

"Why?"

"You said you wouldn't."

I had said that, but I tended to change my mind a lot. What was true one day was not always the case the next. I wasn't the most trustworthy person out there—it's not that I was purposefully dishonest, but when you changed your mind a lot, the answer you gave one day might be completely different the next. Brigham's confidence in me creates a large lump in my chest. I wasn't sure I deserved it, and I didn't like the pressure. Now I had to worry about not disappointing him. My thoughts turned back to Anton, and I wonder why Brigham never seems to doubt our intentions for each other.

Was it because he knew how much I loved him? Was it my history of having men as best friends? *What?*

As I touch Brigham's hand, rubbing along his palm, I ignite tiny pulses of energy between us. "Why aren't you jealous of Anton?" I ask, really wanting to know the answer.

Brigham's watches my hand on his and says softly, "Do I need to be?"

I laugh and shake my head. "No."

"I didn't think so."

He wasn't really answering my question—sometimes it was so hard to get the answer I wanted out of him. It was like it existed so far deep inside of him that it couldn't be reached with one question. I remark, "I find it so odd how you can be so even-keeled about so many things."

"Would you rather I fly off the handle all the time?"

"No, absolutely not," I say tersely, holding my jaw hard. I was not the kind of person who would put up with an abusive relationship, no matter how much I loved the person. Anton had told me enough stories and I knew it wasn't that black and white, more like those types of relationships were a slow boiling—they got worse and worse over time, entrapping you in them, but I didn't need that kind of bullshit in my life or want it. Brigham looks at me, searching my expression, trying to uncover my thoughts behind my face. I soften my expression and look away from him. "If I were *you,* I think I would be more unstable in my emotions."

"You're much younger than me—when you're my age, everything is much easier to take in stride."

"I don't know if I'll make it to be as old as you," I say honestly. I didn't know how old he actually was, but I knew it was pretty old.

"You don't think so?" Brigham cocks his head slightly at me. He only did that when he found what I was saying to be very interesting—apparently my mortality in immortality was an interesting topic.

"I am much more reckless than you ever were," I quip. I hadn't known Brigham for long, but I could tell he had always been the slow and steady type. Slow to anger, slow to show emotion, and dependable. All things very different than myself. Maybe that was why we worked. I was the yin to his yang.

"That is true," he says, and a small smile grows on his face, with his canines poking out.

I smile at him ruefully. Brigham was being so much more expressional since my last escape—maybe our separation had loosened something inside of him. Maybe I broke him.

"Where you waiting up for me tonight?" I ask, looking at him suspiciously. He looks at me and cocks me a smile—I could tell he was stalling to answer my question. What could he possibly not feel comfortable saying to me?

"Yes."

I knew he had been, but I wasn't sure if it was something he would admit to doing. "But you weren't worried I'd come back," I tease and sit up from the couch. He blinks at me and shakes his head and a small smile creeps across his face, and his fangs break through beneath his lips. Brigham's fangs were beautiful. Which—yes, I admit—is a very strange thing to say, but they were. They were as elegant as ivory tusks, but hundreds of times more effervescent.

"I suppose I had a small amount of doubt," he says slowly, his eyes flashing playfully at me. *Now we were getting somewhere!*

"How small?" I ask, touching his arm. "What are we talking, ten percent? Fifteen? Twenty? What?" The thought that I had stirred some anxiety in him was amazing and a thrill ran through my body. *I had no idea I could do that to him!*

Brigham reaches for my face and holds it lovingly in his hands. "Always so many questions from you."

I crawl into his lap and brush my lips against him, gently slipping my tongue in his mouth, touching it to a fang. It elongates slightly and I pull back from him and look into his eyes. They were more vivid than normal tonight and I wonder why the color has changed so much. Had it been like that when he was a human? Was this a side effect of vampirism? Was it just him? At times, his eyes gave me more insight into his emotions than his facial features or words did, but I was still trying to figure all the colors out. Despite the little energy surge I had gotten off of Brigham's touch, climbing into his lap had taken a lot of energy and I feel my body slumping against his.

"I think my curiosity will have to wait—I'm exhausted." I lean hard against his chest, and he wraps his arms around me tightly. It was too bad I was still such a weak vampire. I would have loved to continue the interesting conversation.

"That you are my dear, that you are."

I yawn again, struggling to keep my eyes open. I hated being this weak.

"Come," he says as he picks me up effortlessly and carries me towards the bedroom. This was one of the reasons I wanted Brigham to turn me into a vampire. He was always very loving to me, and I felt safe in his arms. Maybe I had some weird 'daddy complex' thing going on, but I couldn't help how I felt.

"My poor Butterfly, I think your last excursion weakened you," he whispers gently into my ear and kisses my neck, sending shivers down my spine.

"I didn't really sleep well when I was gone," I admit, hoping he will not ask more about it.

"Where did you sleep?" Brigham asks, kissing my neck again.

"I couldn't sleep in hotels, because I thought it would be easy to find me," I say nervously. "So, I slept in the sewers, which is really gross, and I had to cling to stuff so I wouldn't float away." It was a pretty stupid move on my part and probably a little dangerous considering that when I was asleep, I was pretty much dormant and vulnerable.

"Why did you do that?" he asks, the anger rising in his voice. He shifts me in his arms so that I am looking at him and I groan and lower my eyes, not wanting to meet his gaze.

"I thought if I didn't do that, you would find me quicker," I say, unable to hide the embarrassment and shame in my voice. I had been pretty pissed off still and maybe had overreacted, but I was embarrassed that I had gotten into that situation with him, and I felt that was my only choice.

"That wouldn't have mattered, I still would have found you. You should have found somewhere safe to sleep. Just because you're a vampire doesn't mean you can stop taking care of yourself," Brigham says sternly and his eyes blaze at me when I sneak a peek up at him. *Oh, crap, I do have some weird daddy complex!* He sounded just like my father when he yelled at me for sneaking out at night! *How embarrassing!* I wonder if there are vampire therapists or psychologists. The thought of explaining why I thought I was attracted to Brigham to a vampire therapist makes me begin to laugh hysterically. Brigham looks at me curiously, which makes me laugh harder.

"What are you laughing about?"

"Nothing…nothing. So, after the new moon, will you tell me how you always find me?" I ask, trying to change the subject.

He gives a small smile. "Maybe."

"I hate maybes," I pout and jut my lip out at him for emphasis. This never worked on him, but I was hoping it might if I did it enough. At times, Brigham reminds me of a solid steel beam—unbendable and rigid. I am more like a feather—flimsy and prone to floating.

"I know, dear, I know. Come, we need to sleep."

As Brigham carries me down the hall, my eyes wander to all the old photographs hanging in wood frames on the walls. Brigham is an avid photographer and had photographs hanging all over the house of buildings and cityscapes.

"Why do you take so many pictures of buildings?" I ask, barely above a whisper. *I was so tired!*

"It's soothing," he replies vaguely. *Soothing?* I could see how a hobby was soothing, but what was soothing about taking pictures of buildings? Wouldn't taking pictures of landscapes, animals, and people be just as soothing?

"I don't understand," I huff in frustration. Maybe I wouldn't have to ask so many questions if he answered me the first time I asked! "You never answer my questions."

"I like buildings."

"Obviously." Sometimes it was like I was talking to an alien. "What is it about buildings that you find soothing?" I prod, trying to get him to understand what I was asking him. Brigham's face scrunches slightly. "As opposed to other things you could take pictures of—people, for example."

We reach the end of the hall and Brigham opens the door as he holds me with one arm. He is so strong—even for a vampire.

Brigham explains, "They are a little more constant than people—they don't change as quickly. I find their state of being soothing because that is an aspect I see in myself. When I see humans, I see how different I am compared to them—they change, grow, age, and die. I don't do anything of those things." *Huh… I didn't think Brigham concerned himself with such thoughts…interesting.* He continues, "I used to take pictures of trees—they can live to be very old, but they still change with the seasons, some species less so. I suppose I didn't like the reminder that I was different, so I stopped and began to focus on buildings. They still change, but at a less frequent rate."

As we enter the room, I smell vanilla. I had bought numerous vanilla scented candles before I ran off to California, and they made the air smell sweet. My eyelids are very heavy now and I can no longer open them. Brigham still doesn't seem tired as he lays me down in his mahogany bed—our bed. It still felt odd thinking that way. Brigham wraps the blankets around me and lays down beside me, wrapping his arms and legs around me tightly as if he feared I was going to disappear.

"Will you come out with me next time to feed?" I murmur as I nuzzle into him.

"If you want me to, my dear," he whispers and moves the hair from my face gently as I yawn again. It was taking all my energy now to fight back the sleep.

"I like watching you glamour them before you feed," I mumble, my voice barely audible.

"Why is that?" he asks as he kisses my neck softly.

"It reminds me of when we first met and you glamoured me."

"I didn't glamour you," Brigham says and kisses my neck deeper. The tingling was back, and I felt the sensation move slowly through my body. I try to open my eyelids and am only able to get a small flutter.

"Yes, you did," I protest, and lean into him more. He nips at my neck, and I feel the edge of his fangs against my skin. This causes a stronger jolt to pulse through me, and I feel my core throb with need.

"It was you who glamoured me," he says with his voice thick with need. I strain and open my eyes slightly, catching a glimpse of his eyes. They are the color of aster flowers now. A wave of exhaustion hits me again and my eyes close heavily. Brigham runs his hand through my hair, down my neck, over my breast, behind my back, and pulls me up to him. I reach for his face and find his lips tracing the curve. He opens his mouth slightly and I press my finger against his canine—it pierces my skin, and a drop of blood falls and lands on my breast.

"I like it when you bite me," I murmur, still unable to open my eyes.

"I like biting you," he growls and kisses me hard on the mouth and moves to the drop of blood on my breast, gently lapping it up. I moan and arch towards him. "You taste like crystallized honey," he adds.

"I thought I might taste like French fries," I joke. I could feel the energy from his touch, but it was not as strong as before. It was almost like my body was closing off and going dormant already. I didn't want to sleep. I wanted to make love to him.

"French fries?" he asks, curiously resting his head on my stomach.

"Ever hear of the phrase 'you are what you eat'? I ate a lot of French fries as a human."

He laughs. "You're so ridiculous. You make me feel young again." *That's good, I didn't like the thought of him feeling like my father—gross!*

"Don't feel too young, because I kind of get off dating older guys," I tease. I had received a bit of a reputation for dating two professors at once, but that wasn't something I wanted to share with Brigham—well, at least, not until I had to.

"Guys?" he asks with a tinge of concern. *Crap! I should have kept my mouth shut—I was always sticking my foot in my mouth.*

"Guy," I lie. Those player days were long gone. He kisses me ravenously and I try to kiss him back with as much enthusiasm. Why didn't I come home sooner?

"I missed you," he moans and presses his body into me.

"I wasn't gone long." Was he talking about tonight or my excursion? I couldn't tell.

"It feels like you were."

I kiss him harder. Since we met, three days was the longest we had ever gone without having sex and he was right that it did feel like I had been gone longer than that—it felt like it had been weeks.

"I like it when you're like this," I whisper into his ear. I could feel him rise above me and his hair fell on my face. I bet my comment had made him cock his head again, but I am too weak to open my eyes to me sure.

"Like how?"

"Playful—it reminds me when I first met you. Sometimes you can be very serious," I tell him.

He doesn't respond right away, and I strain against my closed eyelids, but they won't open. Not having full use of all my senses is getting annoying. Hopefully after the new moon I will be stronger when it is close to sunrise.

"It's hard for me to remain that way when I'm with you. I find myself laughing more than I have in years."

"I like trying to make you laugh," I admit. It took an insane amount of work and planning on my part to elicit a laugh from Brigham, but it was always worth it.

"Why's that?"

"It's challenging."

"And you always like a challenge," he states as if he was cataloging aspects about me somewhere in his head. He traces his fingers along my lips, and I bite it as hard as I can. His skin was so tough that I wasn't able to make him bleed. I had gotten close one time, but that had been right after I had fed.

"I do."

"Is that why you decided to date me? Because of the challenge of dating a vampire?" he asks seriously, with a layer of vulnerability hidden underneath.

I wish I could see his face now!

His change of tone gives his concern away, but I can get more clarity out of him by seeing the color of his eyes— if only I could! Was he really worried about my affections towards him? It seems so incredible that he would have any doubts about me. I mean, leaving your human life behind for a guy was a big commitment. I hadn't ever even lived with a guy before this! How could he not see how over the mountain I was for him? Had my little runaway stunt hurt him that much that he now doubted my affections? I would have thought that with all his years, he would have a better understanding of women than that, but maybe my reaction really was as unique and crazy as Anton thought.

"No, I would have dated you if you were a goblin, troll, or human. It wouldn't have mattered to me," I say, while trying to sound as convincing as possible.

Brigham touches my eyelids, and they begin to tingle intensely. I strain against my exhaustion and am able to open them a little.

"Really?" Brigham's eyes sparkle a deep blue color but his expression is as stoney as ever.

"Hey, as long as you looked as sexy as you do now, I'd give you a roll without hesitation no matter what type of beasty or non-beasty you were—I was pretty easy as a human," I joke.

That was actually pretty true, but everyone had their issues. What I wasn't saying was that I stayed with him because I felt much more for Brigham than I ever had with anyone else. Not many men could hold my interest for very long, but there was something about Brigham that made me burn, I didn't think it had anything to do with him being a vampire. That was just an added bonus. Brigham's face cracks and a small smile escapes his lips, showing the tip of his enlarged fangs. I wish I had more energy to suck on them—he really liked it when I did that.

"You're teasing me," Brigham says knowingly. He leans down and kisses the area between my breasts and I moan.

"Yes," I admit, I rarely wasn't teasing him, actually.

Brigham snuggles closer to me. "That's a very dangerous thing to do, to tease a vampire."

"I can hold my own," I say confidently, but there is a little flutter inside me where my heart used to beat. What I should have said if I was being completely honest was, *I hope I can hold my own.*

My eyes start to close again, and Brigham touches them softly, helping to keep them open. "That is true," he says. *It really wasn't true*—this moment disproved his declaration. I couldn't even keep my eyes open without his touch, but I did appreciate the lie.

"But I would rather hold you," I whisper softly. I did, too. Being alone was fun at times, but I liked having someone to love more.

"That is acceptable," he whispers and leans down and kisses my lips and gently lifts my arms around him because now I cannot even do that.

"Do you promise me that we will be like this after the new moon?" I whisper and I try and move my fingers against his back but am hardly able to get them to twitch.

"I promise, Butterfly," he says and kisses my forehead. "Sleep now."

CHAPTER FIVE

A Memory

The one thing I missed most about being a human is dreaming. Vampires don't dream—they remember. Last night, or morning, rather, I remembered when I first met Brigham.

He found me for the first time in a coffee shop. I was daydreaming while sipping my mocha and watching college students run from the rain pouring down on them. I was supposed to decide on my major. The registration paper sat in front of me, blank. My career counselor was frustrated with my lack of professional ambition. He didn't understand my appetite for new experiences and found my class choices contradictory and anticlimactic. He didn't understand why I took statistics, watercolor painting, world religions, and mammalogy all in one semester. He thought I was unfocused, but he was wrong. I was extremely focused on my goal of experiencing as much as I could in college. Experience was my goal, not choosing a career. I wanted a colorful, experience filled life, and cared little for being wedged into a one-word job title such as lawyer, doctor, or teacher. I wanted to be a skydiver-painter-psychic or a songwriter-accountant-seamstress.

Outside, the rain was coming down harder and I saw a tall man walking slowly on the sidewalk with a large black umbrella. As he drew closer, I was able to see his face. He was gorgeous! I mean, drop-dead-and-beg gorgeous. As I eye humped him and he neared me, something about him stirred a deep ache in me and before I knew what I was doing, I found my hand on the glass window. When he was a foot from me, I stood up from my table and pressed my hand against the glass and tapped it lightly. He looked up at me in surprise, and I shot him a Cheshire grin and raised my eyebrow at him suggestively. He laughed loudly on the other side of the glass and stopped to study me. His gaze intensified and I blushed and sat back down at my table. I gave him a small shrug and picked up my coffee. I didn't know what the hell I was thinking, but I couldn't let him pass by without doing something. I was so embarrassed now that I turned my gaze down to the table and pretended to be studying the paper in front of me. After a moment, I snuck a quick glance at the window and saw that the man had moved on. My heart sank a little. *Damn!* He looked interesting and I couldn't really understand the pull I had felt towards him.

The doorbell chimed and I almost fainted when I looked up and saw the man walk through the door. He closed his umbrella and ran his hands through his thick blond hair, shaking a few droplets onto the floor. Part of me wanted to hide, and the other part was extremely excited. He searched the tables and when he saw me, smiled widely.

I hadn't expected him to come into the coffee shop, or I might not have been so flirtatious through the window…maybe. He was the most handsome man I had ever seen in my life, and I smiled back at him. He ordered a coffee from the barista and turned and watched me as he waited for his drink. I set my coffee down on the table and crossed my arms across my chest and stared back at him. He seemed so sure of himself, and I found that *very* intriguing. Who was this man? The barista handed him his drink, and she batted her eyes at him flirtatiously, but he didn't seem to notice and turned and slowly strolled up to my table. I watched him, taking all of him in. He was older than me, but it was hard to gauge how old he was exactly. He had an air of confidence and knowing that was intriguing—he wasn't like anyone I had ever dated, that was for sure. He wore a medium grey sports jacket with a black button-down shirt under it with grey pants and looked sexy as hell!

"Hello," he said as he approached my table, giving me a sly smile. His voice had a nice timbre to it, and I got a sudden urge to hear him speak more to me. Maybe whisper something dirty in my ear while he was at it.

"Hello," I said with a smile and looked up at him expectantly. He was so handsome! His skin had a strange light translucence about it that I had never seen before. He must be rich and get some special facials or something.

"Do you mind if I sit with you?" he asked with his eyes sparkling a deep blue color. He was mesmerizing, and I found myself unable to breathe for a moment.

"Not at all," I replied, thickly trying to clear my head. A conversation with a handsome stranger would be the perfect distraction from my assignment.

"It's starting to rain hard out there," he said, sitting his coffee down in front of him.

"Is it?" I looked out the window, and the restaurant sign across the street was barely visible through the glass. "Hmmmm…"

"So, what are you doing flirting with men through coffee shop windows?"

"Flirting?" I look back at him and smirked. "That was hardly flirting—you'd know if I was flirting."

"What would you call it then?" he asked, taking a sip of his coffee.

"Experimenting!" I said excitedly and gave him a mischievous grin.

"Experimenting?" he said slowly and leaned on the table, studying me.

His eyes roamed over my face and down to my neck, lingering there for a moment. I swallowed hard, my heart racing. Something inside me, some instinct was telling me to run right now, but as I looked at him, I wanted to run *at* him and not away from him. His eyes moved from my neck down to my chest and I cleared my throat, drawing his eyes back up to my face. I gave him a knowing look, and he smiled at me with no guilt whatsoever even after having been caught eye humping me. *Who was this man?* And—fuck—please be as good in bed as he looks! The thought of that made my body heat and I rolled my shoulders, trying to focus on something else.

I took another sip of my coffee before answering. "I like to study cause and effect. What happens when I do *blank* is my favorite experiment."

"Was this your expected hypothesis?"

"No! This is much more interesting than anything I could have come up with," I said and took another sip of my coffee.

His eyes crinkled as if he is holding back a smile and asked, "What's your name?"

"Butterfly."

"It's nice to meet you, Butterfly. Am I interrupting your studying?" he asked and gestured to the paper in front of me.

"God no. I'm not studying! I'm stalling, if anything."

"What are you stalling about?"

"My career counselor wants me to decide on a major."

"Do you not know what you want to be?" he asked, looking at me intensely. With the way he watched me and waited for my answer, I didn't know if I've ever had a man this engaged with me before. It was startling and oddly grounding to talk with him like this.

"I already am what I want to be," I said confidently and waved the paper at him. "This is just frosting and garnish."

"What are you?" He looked at me, cocking his head slightly.

"A transient fairy," I said with a snort.

"A transient fairy?"

"Yes."

"Did you have to go to a special school to become that?"

"You have to go to numerous colleges to be able to claim that title."

"How many have you attended?"

"Six."

"Six colleges?" he repeated and I could not help but notice his raised eyebrow.

"Yes."

"That's impressive."

"As I said, I'm a transient fairy."

"I would have to agree."

"I know it's impractical, but I don't give a shit about having a degree or having a diploma on my wall. That's not why I am taking the classes," I said and frowned to myself. This might not be the right person to have this conversation with, because by the looks of him, he had his shit figured out. This conversation might seriously scare him away—*which oddly I didn't want.*

"Do you not like college? Is that the reason behind attending so many?" He leaned back and studied me again. My eyes lingered on his lip and his jaw for a moment, and I couldn't help but wonder what it would feel like to have his lips pressed against my skin. *Good lord, I was horny!*

"Oh no, I love college! I love taking all the classes, meeting different people, and attending all the different student groups. It's very exciting. I think I could attend college for years." I laughed. "I might be doing that anyway if I don't choose a major soon."

"What's your favorite subject?"

"At the moment? Hmmm, that's a tough one." I bit my lip thinking about that. "I don't think I can pick."

"I've always enjoyed philosophy."

"Oh yes, I've taken loads of those. I especially liked my philosophy of ethics class. Got an A in that one."

"What about math?" he asked as his face brightened and he leaned in closer towards me.

"I like statistics, it's fun making the graphs."

"Art classes?" he asked, his smile growing wider.

"I've taken watercolor, ceramics, art history, and drawing."

"Political science?"

"I've only taken one class on local politics—I had a roommate when I was in the dorms that was a political science major, so I've learned a lot helping her study."

"What are you going to write on that piece of paper?"

"Oh…I was thinking I might just write English and then change next semester, or maybe I'll try a different college next year and take a few more classes," I said and shrugged. "I haven't decided though."

"Eventually, you'll have taken so many classes you will fulfill a major requirement somewhere," he said with a smirk, and I laughed.

"Probably." I sighed, and my heart sank a little at that thought. Then what would I do? I studied him across the table at how relaxed he seemed talking with me. My curiosity about him and his life nagged at me and I asked, "So, where were you going when I so rudely interrupted your walk?"

"Nowhere in particular."

I snorted. "Nowhere?"

"No, I was walking for walking's sake."

"Do you like walking in the rain?"

"Yes," he said without a trace of self-consciousness and continued to stare at me. He held my gaze for a long time, and I noticed that he rarely blinked. *How strange!* As if reading my thoughts, he blinked slowly.

"I like walking in the rain too."

"What else do you like to do?"

"I volunteer at an animal shelter."

"Really?" His eyebrows raised in surprise.

"Yep, I've been doing that since high school."

"But you don't want to be a veterinarian."

"Nope."

"Why?"

"I don't think I could deal with people on a daily basis that are cruel to their animals."

"Don't people who bring their animals into the vet care for them?"

"Not always."

"Do you not think you could stomach it?"

"Oh, I could stomach it. I've helped clean dogs that were hit by cars with eyeballs hanging out, restrained cats with lacerations, you name it. Blood, abscesses, maggots, and guts I can manage, no problem. What I don't think I could manage is my anger. I'm not an idle person and I don't think I could sit idly by if I knew of an animal being abused or not taken care of. I'd probably lose my license within my first year as a veterinarian."

"Interesting…" he said slowly.

I shrugged. "But I suppose that can change, maybe one day I will be better emotionally equipped and will want to be a veterinarian. I'm leaving that window open."

"You like having options," he stated factually.

"I like possibilities. There are so many possibilities in every moment, thoughts, and actions. It's very exciting."

He smiled slowly at me, watching me intently. I wondered what I must seem like to him. Did I seem naïve? Flighty? I had never really wondered what type of impression I was giving off and now it seemed very important to know what he saw. Why was that? What was he stirring within me that was different? His eyes shifted and I found myself being drawn back into him. It was like he had reached out and touched me with his mind. *How interesting!* I settled in and reflected on his gaze. I liked the intensity we were sharing at this moment—the connection, the challenge.

His eyes shifted again, and I felt myself moving even closer to him. I grasped the side of the table trying to steady myself because the movement I felt, although not physical, was so intense that I needed more grounding. His mouth curved slightly more, and I felt the intensity relax as he let me regain my balance. *What was going on here?* This wasn't the normal flirty eye groping I was accustomed to. This was different...

"What are the possibilities of this moment?" he asked quietly, the challenge of our gazing coming out verbally. He wanted to know how much fire was really inside me, how brave I was—how bold.

Taking the challenge, I leaned in towards him slowly, never taking my eyes off him. Turning my head slightly, I gave a sly flirtatious smile and said, "Oh let's see...I could lean over and kiss you now."

His eyes widened. I wasn't sure if this was surprise or anticipation, but I liked the reaction, so I continued. "Or, I could slap you completely out of the blue and have a schizophrenic episode, an ex-lover of yours could walk through the door and see you with me and freak out, this place could burn down, you could spill your coffee, it could stop raining, or we could keep talking. There's so much that could happen, and I enjoy the ride."

"That's a lot of possibilities."

"There are so many more that I didn't name. There's an infinite number of possibilities in each moment."

"I like that," he said softly. He reached across the table and with the tip of his pointer finger gently touched the side of my hand. "An infinity of possibility."

It seemed like mere moments later, but after a while, I looked around the coffee shop and noticed that there was no one else in the store. The lights behind the counter were dimmed and the sign on the door had been flipped. I had been so immersed in our conversation that I had forgotten where I was. I looked down at my coffee cup and noticed it was empty. I hadn't even realized I had finished it.

"Where is everyone?" I asked, looking around the coffee shop. Did they leave? Did we get locked in? That was strange, why didn't they tell us they were closing?

"I told them they could leave," he said, not taking his eyes off of me.

The hair on the back of my neck stood on end. *When did he do this?* How did I not notice? I swallow hard. "You told them to leave?"

"Yes," he said steadily, still keeping his gaze on me, not blinking. *Why does he so rarely blink?* Did he do some weird eye exercises to be able to hold out from blinking for so long?

"Do you own this place?" I asked, as I looked around again. Why would they let us stay here if they closed down the shop? That did not make any sense.

"No."

"Do you work here?" I asked, knowing that it is not possible based on how he was dressed, but wanted desperately to make sense of what was happening.

"No," he said softly and shook his head, his hair falling a little in front of his face. My hand reached up to push his hair back from his face, but I stopped myself, and he glanced at my hand for a moment raised in midair and something crossed his face that I could not discern.

I moved my hand back quickly to the table and looked at him and around the empty coffee shop. "I don't get it," I admitted and looked at him, expecting an answer.

He laughed. "You will, you are pretty smart. You will figure it out."

"Are you some kind of celebrity?" I guessed and crossed my arms over my chest, trying to figure him out. He was good looking enough, but I didn't recognize him from the movies or television.

"I wouldn't say that."

"But you're famous?" I frowned, raking my mind for what kind of celebrity he could be.

"I'm known," he said, settling on that answer.

My brows furrow and I bit my lip. "Hmmm…" He watched me biting my lip and a lustful predatory look crossed his face briefly and just as quickly disappeared. *Interesting!* Did he find me attractive?

"Figured it out yet?" he asked, looking up from my lips.

I grimaced at him. "Not yet, but as you said—I'm smart, so I will."

"Think so?" he teased.

"I hope so," I said honestly. This was a fun little game and I did like to win.

"Me too," he said quietly, and we stared at each other across the table, the air becoming thick with a weird, charged tension. I bit my lip again and studied him. *Who was he?*

I glanced at the clock and tried to shake myself out of my daze. "Well, I better get going. I'm afraid my career counselor will be very cross with me since I haven't done my assigned homework."

"I hope I won't get you in trouble," he said, standing. He grabbed my empty coffee cup with his and tossed it in a nearby garbage. His movements were so fluid and quick, it was disorienting watching him move. I took a quick peek at his ass when he turned his back to me. It was perfectly round and muscular and I sighed—he was a little too physically attractive. He glanced back at me over his shoulder and my eyes shot back up at his face a little too fast. I knew he just caught me staring at his ass. *Damn it!*

"It was worth it," I said quickly, not really sure if I meant talking to him or him catching me looking at his ass. "I've enjoyed talking to you tonight. I don't have that many interesting conversations with men...uh, I mean, people, like this." Uh, awkward much, Butterfly? *Good grief!*

"I've enjoyed our time together as well," he paused and looked down at me, and I noticed how much taller he was than me as he stood beside me. He was like some Nordic God with his blond hair and muscular frame. "Do you have any plans tomorrow? I'd like to take you out for dinner."

"Dinner?" I asked, slightly surprised that he wanted to get together so soon.

"Yes."

"Alright, I'm game." He nodded and I hesitated for a moment, wondering how this would work. The guys that I have dated recently usually met me at a taco stand. That probably should have been my first red flag now that I think about it. "Do you want to meet somewhere?"

His face contorted. "We can if that makes you more comfortable, but I'd like to pick you up at your apartment."

"Why's that?" I asked, feeling a little suspicious. Should I be alarmed right now? Is this what a stalker does? What does a nice, normal guy do?

"It's the gentlemanly thing to do," he said, looking at me oddly.

"Gentlemanly thing…huh…okay." *Was he serious?*

"Yes," he said and cocked his head at me and gave me a teasing grin like I was the one being weird. *Gentlemanly thing?* What the actual fuck?

"I'll give you my address then," I said, pretending that I do this all the time for my dates.

"Or I could walk you home tonight…if you would like. That way, I'll know you made it home safe and I won't have to worry all day until we meet tomorrow."

I blinked at him, stunned by his words for a moment and then I looked outside at the dark and vacant street, my face twisted as I weighed my options. I didn't usually walk by myself in this part of town after dark. *Damn it!* I usually paid better attention than this.

"Alright…you could do that," I said slowly, waiting for the catch in this whole situation. I bent to pick up my jacket, but Brigham already has it open for me. I never even saw him grab it. *Was I tired or something?* Why was I missing so many details? I stepped into my jacket awkwardly, never having had anyone hold it like this for me before. I really needed to start dating a higher caliber of guy!

He squeezed my shoulder gently as he slipped my jacket over my shoulders and I felt such a shock by his touch. His hands are strong, like really, *really* strong! *Like not normal man strong!*

"You're not a firefighter or something, are you?" I asked, my voice feeling thick as I thought about his touch again.

"No, why?" he asked as he leaned over my shoulder and I felt the coolness of his body, which was strange because I would think he would generate more body heat than me, being so much bigger.

"Never mind, no reason," I muttered and zipped up my jacket and turned towards him.

"Did you bring an umbrella?" he asked, looking down at me, his eyes having now turned a steely blue grey. *Why were his eyes changing color?*

"No, I forgot mine. It wasn't raining when I left this morning."

"We shall share mine then," he said with a satisfied grin.

"Alright."

We exited the coffee shop, and he turned off the lights. I didn't see him with any keys, but I heard the door lock behind us. I found him very interesting and the mystery surrounding him was getting more and more intriguing. It was starting to really bother me that I didn't know who he was. I had never seen him around campus, and I was beginning to doubt he had any connections to the school at all.

"I don't live very far, just past Caufman Hall," I revealed as I pointed to a large brown square brick building in the distance.

He opened up his umbrella and I stepped under it, being very aware of how close I was to him. He smelled delicious. It was a spicy musky smell, and I wondered what brand of cologne he was wearing. I might have to find a bottle for a future boyfriend to wear. As we walked down the street, I felt his hand gently pull me closer to him, pulling me in from the edges of the umbrella."

"I don't want you to get wet," he said quietly, and I let him hold my hand.

"Thanks," I said awkwardly. It was like I had lost all my game.

"My pleasure," he said, his voice thick. His nostrils flared a little, like he was smelling me. *Weird!* I looked away from him quickly. I was losing it and letting my mind run wild. This was all fine—he was being nice and walking me home, nothing to worry about.

I snuck another glance up at him and noticed how light his skin tone was under the light of the streetlights we passed. It was unnaturally light. My heart started to beat a little faster. Maybe having him walk me home was a bad idea. I hardly knew him. *He could be a rapist!* I looked around and there were few people on the street, which was a bad sign. If he tried something, I was going to have to scream really loudly. Maybe I could nonchalantly pull out my rape whistle as we walked… I took a deep breath, trying to get my emotions under control. I was sure I was overreacting.

"So, are you a student here?" I asked, hoping to get some clarity about him so I can feel better.

He laughed. "No."

"Professor?"

"No."

"Hmmm…tricky." He laughed louder and I looked at him in irritation. "Am I close at all?

"No."

"Fuck," I said under my breath, and he chuckled softly as I rolled my eyes. At least I was entertaining him.

"Politician?"

"No."

I groaned and bumped up against his arm and stiffen at how hard his body is. He looked down at me, and I knew he caught my reaction. "Professional athlete?" I asked, trying to fit the puzzle pieces together.

"No," he said quietly and squeezed my hand slightly. His touch was so cold and his fingers felt like metal bars grasping me. My heart raced a little as thoughts that didn't seem possible started to form in my mind. *His skin…his coldness…his strength…fuck!*

"Damn, I thought I had it that time," I said a little shakily. "But that's okay, I hate sports or at least watching them…might not mind watching you though." I cleared my throat and rubbed my neck. *I sounded like a lunatic!*

He didn't seem to notice and squeezed my hand again. "Why did you think I was a professional athlete?"

"Because of your build. You're tall, muscular, and handsome—uh, not that I've been paying attention to those things," I said awkwardly. He chuckled and I blushed and turned my face away from him. I couldn't believe what a dork I had just sounded like. That was the problem with being a transient fairy—I didn't always think things through, especially the things that came out of my mouth.

I felt a gentle tug at my hand, and I turned and saw him smiling at me kindly. He reached for my face and lifted my chin up to him. My heart skipped a beat as I looked into his eyes. They were on fire as he looked at me, and I saw something in them that I didn't understand. *No man had ever looked at me like this before!*

"Do you want me to tell you what I am, or do you want to keep guessing?" he asked. *What I am?* He said *what* I am not *who* I am! *Double fuck buckets!*

This was the closest I had ever been to him. Mere inches separated us from a kiss. I studied his face and I began to notice things that had not been as clear in the dimly lit coffee shop. His face was smooth. There were no wrinkles, scars, acne, or enlarged pores—no flaws or imperfections at all. His skin was very pale, milky white with a hint of grey, and even though it was late in the evening, he didn't have an after shadow—there was no stubble or even a hint of hair growth on his face. All of these things were not normal, they were unnatural, really, and I felt a hint of fear start to grow inside me. There was something not right about this man.

His eyes darted back and forth as he studied my face and asked, "What are you thinking?"

"I'm trying to decide if I want to know the answer."

He smiled slowly at me, and I saw it. When his lip curled up, I saw the gleaning white sharp point of his upper canine. It was too pronounced, not grotesquely so, but enough to stand out.

"Oh…" I said knowingly, trying to keep my voice even. He was a vampire. *Fucking figures!* The most interesting man I had ever met was a bloodsucker—that was extremely disappointing.

"Have you guessed it?" he asked while searching my face, his eyes moving over me rapidly, too fast, much too fast.

"Yes…but I don't want you to tell me," I said slowly and took a small step from him as he released my chin. A flicker of sadness moved across his face.

"Are you going to tell me what you've guessed?" he asked, moving closer and tilting the umbrella so I didn't get wet. What a strange thing to do if he was about to drain me.

"No, not tonight," I said, my mind doing a million rotations a minute as I tried to understand what was happening. "I'll save that for a future date." *If I don't die tonight—logistics, and all that.*

"Fair enough," he said.

We started walking and my heart raced faster in my chest. Which, if he was a vampire, he could probably hear. Which will make him think of blood. *I was so fucked!* Even though it was only a theory, I knew I had figured it out and I was suddenly very nervous walking beside him. I felt the edge of danger in him that had been hiding under all the sexual tension, and I was feeling incredibly vulnerable. *Not a fan of this feeling!*

I had read that vampires were very strong and good at mind control. Looking at his physique, I would be in danger if he had only been a mere human, but if he was a vampire, I was seriously toast. If he had any mind controlling abilities, I was also utterly screwed. In the meditation classes I had taken, I had never been able to center my mind, and I doubted I could block out an onslaught on my mind.

"Your heart is racing," he said, interrupting my thoughts. Yep, I was right about that one.

"Yes," I said quietly. "I suppose I can't really deny that with you, huh?"

"Are you scared?" he asked. I heard the strain in his voice which made me glance up at him as he looked ahead down the street and I noticed his jaw clenching.

"Yes," I answered honestly. He looked at me out of the corner of his eye and I quickly looked away.

"Because of your theory?" he asked quietly. I shot him a quick glance and swallowed hard before answering.

"Yes."

"Is it that bad of a theory?" he asked, and there was a vulnerability there that made me hesitate. Why was he asking me that? Why did he care? This whole situation was so bizarre, and honestly, I didn't know how to feel about it all right now.

"I'm not sure."

We reached a crosswalk, and the light said: DON'T WALK.

"You're very interesting," he said tensely, and I saw his jaw clenching again, his face tensing like he was conflicted. His words were surprising. I thought he was much more interesting than me.

The sign changed to WALK, but we stood together under the umbrella contemplating each other.

"Why do you say that?" I asked and glanced down the street. The streets were still empty, which I didn't know if that was a good thing or not. If I needed help, bad. If I'm talking with a nice vampire, good.

"Most people who have guessed what I am run the other way," he said looking down at me as I tried not to shudder.

"I feel like doing that a little," I said, scrunching up my nose at him and trying to not look afraid.

"Why don't you?" he asked with a demanding tone, and I looked away from him as I tried to find an answer that would explain why I wasn't freaking out more. There were a lot of reasons why…some of them…were surprising…even to me, which was saying something.

I sighed and decided to go with humor. "I don't think I'd get very far."

He laughed and I saw his canines even more clearly and a pang of fear hit me again. "You wouldn't," he responded.

I looked at him and my heart pounded faster. Was he saying this because he wasn't planning on letting me escape from him tonight? Had the innocent walk home become my death march? He saw the fear in my face, and he rubbed the top of my hand gently. His skin was cool and soft like silk sheets.

"I'm sorry, that came out wrong," he said.

"What did you mean to say?" I asked.

He looked at me for a moment, and a flicker of sadness crossed his face. If I had blinked, I would have missed it. "I wanted to say something that made you feel better, but I didn't know what to say."

I inhaled deeply and let my breath out slowly. What did I want to hear? I'd like to know if he was planning on killing me, but I wasn't sure I could believe what he would say. Don't killers always say they were going to let you go so you would cooperate with them? I took another breath and thought about what I wanted most at that moment.

"Can you kiss me?"

"What?" His eyes opened wide. *Cool! I can take a vampire off his guard!*

"Can you kiss me?" I said now with more determination in my voice. Yes, a kiss would give me a lot of information.

"You want me to kiss you?" he asked suspiciously, having gained more control of his facial expressions. "Why?"

"Because you want me to feel better, and a kiss will make me feel better."

"How would it make you feel better?"

"Are you a bad kisser or something?"

He blinked slowly at me and shook his head.

"Yeah, I didn't think so, hence the feeling better." I bit my lip and looked down the empty street again. "Okay look, I have no control over what you're going to do to me." He flinched at that, and his mouth opened to protest, but I continued. "I want to have one more beautiful experience. A kiss from a vampire would be a nice notch on my life rope and it was the best I could ask for in this situation."

His jaw clenched and his gaze got steely as he looked at me and I started to rethink having said all of that. "Okay," he said and his gaze softened, and he started to look at me curiously.

He closed the umbrella and awkwardly wrapped an arm around my waist, drawing me close to him. His arms were like steel beams grabbing me and I gasped as he lifted me off my feet effortlessly.

I looked in amazement at the distance between my dangling feet and the ground. Raindrops hit my face, and I gently wiped them away. He stared at me as if he was unsure how to continue and I closed my eyes for a moment. Thunder rumbled above us, and I felt my excitement and fear brewing under my skin. His hand gently brushed against my cheek and I opened my eyes, meeting his gaze—which was so soft right now as he looked at me.

"Hey stranger," I said shyly. He laughed and caressed my cheek. I brought my hand to his face and hesitated a moment before touching him as I searched his expression, looking for approval. He gave a slight nod, and I touched his face. His face was as soft as his hands and only slightly warmer, but still much colder than a human. I ran my finger across his cheek to his lips, and they were even softer than his face. "I must feel like sandpaper compared to you," I said quietly.

"I haven't done this for a while," he admitted, his voice thick. I cocked my head at him.

"How long has it been?"

He raised an eyebrow at me and smiled.

"Never mind," I shook my head. I didn't want him to give away too much about himself. "It's like riding a bicycle, you never forget how to do it. Besides, I've done this recently—well, not with someone like you…"

He opened his mouth to say something, but I wrapped my legs around his body, distracting him. He moved his arms to my ass and held me there, staring at me intensely and I felt the stiffness and reluctance in his touch.

"You're very unpredictable," he said, sounding very unnerved.

I looked at him challengingly. "Are you trying to turn me on?" I joked.

"What? No, I—"

I pressed my lips hard against his, stopping his words. If this was my last kiss, I wanted it to be a good one. I squeezed him between my legs and ran my hands through his hair, drawing his face closer to mine. At first, he didn't respond to my touch, but when I flicked my tongue against his lips trying to coax my way inside, he began to kiss me back with equal intensity. I kissed him even harder and he held me with one arm, pulling my ass into him as his other arm ran up my back to the back of my head as he pressed me into him.

We exploded into each other and I tore at his shirt, wanting to feel more of his skin and his buttons flew off in my exuberance. He reached up and cupped my breast, pinching my nipple hard, making me moan and I ground my core against him. I suddenly realized what I was doing and broke from him, gasping for air with my heart racing. *Holy hell—I just grinded on a vampire!* That was extreme, even for me! I laughed and hugged him against me. His body was like a rock—it was hard and unmovable and so strangely cool to the touch.

I cleared my throat. "Thank you for that," I said quietly, very much aware that he is still cupping my ass. He let me slide gently off of him and I blushed and looked up at him slightly embarrassed, but absolutely not regretful. He stood there looking at me with a stunned expression on his face, his hair dripping from the rain and a bit disheveled. I wiped the raindrops from my eyes so I could see better.

He cleared his throat. "I don't remember bike riding being like that."

"No, that was a good ride…a good last ride," I slipped and looked at him apprehensively. Was he going to bite me now? His eyes narrowed and I shrugged. I grabbed his hand in mine and yelled, "Let's go!" I pulled him and ran across the street.

We walked in silence for a moment, holding hands. The rain started to come down harder and he began to open his umbrella out, but I put my hand over his, stopping him. "It's okay, I want to feel the rain."

He opened his mouth to say something then stopped abruptly.

"When I was a little girl, I thought I could call the rain." I looked straight up into the sky and closed my eyes, feeling the raindrops hit my eyelids. "When I was sad, I would call for the rain. There was a whole summer in my teens where I think I caused a lot of flooding. I'd sit in my room and concentrate on the rain, and it would come.... every time…it would come. There were so many rainy days…"

"Why were you sad?" he asked, and I could hear the concern in his voice.

"Regular teenage depression and rejection," I said dismissively. I could feel his eyes lingering on my face, but I stared down the street looking away from him. I didn't want him to really know why I had been calling the rain. "The rain always made it better, though," I whispered.

"How did the rain make it better?" he asked with a slightly stronger tone. There was something to his voice now that was more commanding, and I found myself letting out an unguarded answer.

"It made me feel connected to something bigger— the universe, if you will. I liked that, and even if it was only a connection in my mind, it helped." My voice stopped and I realized all that I had let slip. I looked at him a little startled. *Why did I just say all that?* What was it about him that let that secret come out?

"Did you make it rain today?" he asked as he looked up into the sky and many raindrops landed on his ivory skin. He was beautiful, even wet, and I tried to keep images of his naked body covered in raindrops out of my head. Unable to keep the images at bay, I shook my head and laughed at myself. He looked inquisitively at me.

"No, sometimes it just needs to rain," I said with a smile. "Yep, sometimes the world just needs a good dowsing of water."

"I'm glad you weren't sad today," he said.

I nodded shyly. What he said was very sweet and I didn't know exactly how to take it.

I saw my apartment in the distance, and I slowed to a stop.

He paused and looked at me questioning. "What is it?" he asked.

"That's my apartment," I pointed to the large lit up brick building.

"Why are we stopping here? Don't you want me to walk you to your door?"

"I'm giving you your chance," I said seriously, trying to sound confident. This was the moment when my life would change. I could feel it, the gravity of our present crossroads. I didn't know what was going to happen in the next few moments, but I was sure it would be life altering…and hopefully not life ending.

"Chance for what?" He stepped back from me and scanned my entire body, trying to find answers to his question. I squirmed under his scrutiny and sighed deeply. *Was he really going to make me spell it out?* I gave him an annoyed look, and his face swam with emotions.

"Look, I know what you are…or at least I think I do. Obviously, I don't know all the details, but I know enough. I know you're not letting me get away, you said it yourself—"

"Do you think I'm going to kill you?" he interrupted with a scowl and then quickly returned to his original stoney gaze.

"Yes." *What else would I expect?* He's a fucking vampire—they suck people's blood—read any vampire book, that part is pretty standard. He made a low and guttural noise that I don't understand. "Did you just growl at me?" I asked, my voice raising slightly. *Killing me was one thing, but growling at me was rude!*

"No," he muttered unconvincingly as he gave the slightest of embarrassed grins. My eyes widened, knowing that I had been right and I couldn't help but smile at him.

"Yes, you did!" I said loudly and poked him hard in the rib. His torso was solid stone, and I couldn't even make an indent into his skin. "Wow…" I said in awe. He must be really strong, which should scare me, but it was a little bit of a turn on.

He grabbed my hand gingerly, and I was amazed at the strength in his fingertips. I bet he could crush my entire hand in an instant. He raised our hands up and gently kissed the top of my hand. "I didn't mean to growl. It was an accident, and I apologize."

I stared at him for a moment and wondered what the hell was going on. *Was he real?* Was this happening? Was I already dead? I didn't know, but all this confusion and mystery was starting to wear on me. I just wanted to get on with it already. I took my hand back from him, or rather, he let me go when he felt me pull away from him.

"Look, I don't want to make a scene at the apartment. I don't want to scare anyone by having him or her find my dead body in there. I live alone and I don't have any family, so I might not be found for a while, and I'll stink up the place—it'll be a whole embarrassing thing. So, if you're going to kill me, I'd like you to do it here," I said roughly, not feeling courageous enough to look at him. I knew that was a little harsh, but I was getting tired.

"I'm not going to kill you! I asked you out on a date tomorrow, God damn it!"

He took a step towards me, and I recoiled unintentionally. He noticed, took a step back, and clenched his fists. His eyes filled with rage—which again, I should find terrifying, but found it more curious than anything. *I really had like no survival instincts, apparently.*

Did I really just hear him say he wasn't going to kill me and that he wanted to date me? *Was I dreaming?* I blinked hard and looked around in a daze. No, this still seemed like Earth.

I looked back at him and asked, "What did you just say? I think I may have lost my mind somewhere along here."

"You heard me!" he gritted out between clenched teeth. *Wow!* He was really upset that I thought he was going to kill me…interesting.

"Oh…sorry…I thought—" I stammered.

"Yes, we covered what you thought was going to happen," he interrupted. He looked away from me towards my apartment. There was a softening around his eyes, and I could see a mound of sadness underneath his impenetrable exterior. My heart ached at the thought that I may have caused that to be there and I found myself walking towards him and putting my hand on his shoulder.

"You're still planning on taking me out for dinner tomorrow?" I asked softly. I squeezed the rock that was his body and wondered if my touch even registered to him.

He looked down at me softly and whispered, "I would like to."

"And you're not going to kill me then?" I asked, searching his face for the truth. He looked back at me and his face softened further. I could see no malice or ill-intent inside of him, only yearning—I got lost in his eyes for a moment, feeling the strong pull to him.

"I wasn't planning on it, but now I'm beginning to rethink it," he replied, his tone lighter. I laughed loudly and moved my hand off his shoulder.

"Interesting…" I whispered to myself softly and looked up at my apartment.

Well, I was glad there wasn't going to be a blood bath there tonight. I'd hate to be in the newspapers that way. I giggled slightly at myself. I always ended up in strange situations without even trying. Remembering our kiss, I unconsciously brought my fingers to my lips and laughed again. I looked at him guiltily and his eyes grew slightly wider.

"Wait a minute. Did you kiss me like that earlier because you thought it was the last kiss you were going to have?"

I smiled mischievously at him and raised an eyebrow. "Maybe."

He growled and this time I liked it.

"That's a little sexy," I joked.

He grinned and I saw his white fangs fully. They were very large now, almost like they could elongate. He caught me looking at his teeth and grabbed my hand, rubbing my palm with his palm, and I looked at our hands, not understanding what he was trying to do.

"I really wasn't planning on killing you." He held my hand in his and gently traced a line across the palm as if he was trying to read it.

"Really?" I asked, watching the pattern that he traced.

"Really," he said seriously. He let out a large sigh and squeezed my hand. He traced a small circle in my palm and looked down at me.

"I wasn't really planning anything. When you knocked on the glass, I couldn't help myself. I wanted to meet the girl who was so brash she flirted with a vam— stranger." He bit his lip and grinned at me.

"That's all you wanted?" I flirted, giving him the sexiest expression I had. His smile widened at me, but he didn't answer. "Can you read my mind?

"A little," he said in a low voice.

Not being able to hold my curiosity any longer, I began to rapidly fire out questions at him. "Can you fly?"

"No," he answered, giving me an incredulous look. "Do you really think that is a possibility?"

I shrugged. "They do all kinds of stuff in books and in the movies. Sometimes they have special abilities. Can you turn into a bat?"

"No."

"Do you drink blood?"

He hesitated and gripped my hand a little tighter. "Yes," he whispered so softly that I barely hear his answer. I could feel the air around him stiffen. Admitting that he drank blood to a human made him uncomfortable—or maybe it was uncomfortable because he was admitting it to me.

"Do you like it?" I inquired without thinking.

His eyes jumped as my question hit him, and I winced, realizing how rude and awkward my question might seem to him. He was a person, after all—or at least something very close to it, and having one's lifestyle choices questioned was breaking a pretty big boundary. I hoped he understood I was only trying to get to know him and not being judgmental. I looked awkwardly up at him regretting asking him that as he contemplates my question. If I could have taken my question back, I would have.

After what seemed like an eternity, he formed his answer for me. "Yes, I do enjoy the taste of blood," he said evenly, holding me in his eyes. His eyes searched rapidly across my face, searching for the slightest reaction or facial twitch that would give away my thoughts or emotions about his answer. I tried as hard as I could to not give anything away as I thought about it.

"Huh…" I responded, trying to sound nonjudgmental. It was probably good that he enjoyed drinking blood—it would be such a horrible existence to not enjoy eating your food. Although, for humankind's sake, it would be better if we didn't taste so good.

"Are you disgusted by me now?"

"No, I'm not." I really wasn't, what that good or bad? *Should I be morally disgusted?*

He turned from me and looked out into the night and whispered, "Why do you think that is?" I knew he was contemplating a deeper idea than he was letting on.

"I try to be open-minded, and I don't think…" I hesitated. Maybe it would be prudent to keep some thoughts to myself, self-preservation, and all that.

"You don't think what?" he prodded and stepped a little closer to me, his eyes moving over me rapidly.

I was going to have to watch what I said to him. I doubted he was going to let much slip by him. "I have a good feeling about you," I said honestly and ran my hands through my now soaking hair, wringing out some water out.

He watched the water drip from my hair to the pavement, and I gave a little shudder as the wet and coldness seeped into my body. I glanced at him—he was equally soaked but didn't seem to be bothered by the wetness or the cold. I bet that was nice.

"You thought I was going to kill you," he said quietly, and he looked at my neck. His eyes shifted away for a moment, and a look of guilt stayed on his face as he looked back at me. I really did think he was going to kill me for a minute there.

"Yes, but I didn't think you were a bad person to kill me. I figured I was at the wrong place at the wrong time." I looked at my apartment and wondered how many college students inside knew that vampires existed. I guessed very few, if any, and I felt a little special knowing the truth. "I have a lot of questions."

"Good, then we'll have lots to talk about on our second date."

"Yes, I suppose we will." I squeezed his hand and turned away from him, walking towards my door. "Goodnight," I called over my shoulder.

"Don't you want me to walk you to your door?" he called after me.

"No, I'm fine from here." I glanced over at him over my shoulder. He had his hands in his pockets now as he watched me walk away, I felt a pull to go towards back to him, but I should go in and change and take a hot shower before I get hypothermia.

"What about another kiss?" he taunted, and I considered running back at him.

"Next time—maybe, if you are good," I teased, flashed him a big smile, and walked away. *I really hope he is good!*

"Promise?" I laughed and kept walking. "I'll pick you up at six." I turned and waved at him. "You never asked me my name," he yelled.

I laughed. "I didn't?"

"No—it's Brigham."

I winked at him. "Nice to meet you Brigham—see you tomorrow at six!"

CHAPTER SIX

Awake

I wake with a smile. Brigham holds me, stroking my hair behind my ear and I snuggle into him, breathing in his scent deeply. He is wearing a different cologne today and the blend smells like a mixture of vanilla, lavender, amberwood, anise and elemi. I had no idea what brand it is, but it smells heavenly, and I want him to wrap me up in himself so I will smell like him all day. I bet Anton knows what the fragrance is, and I make a mental note to ask him about it later.

"Morning—uh, evening," I yawn and stretch. "I can't get used to the change of saying 'good evening' in the morning and 'good morning' in the evening."

"You don't have to say it that way if you don't want to," he whispers and presses a kiss to my neck, sending little shivers through my body. *God, it felt good when he did that!* It is like my body is lying dormant for him and his touch makes my cells come alive.

"Won't everyone think I'm silly if I say it the old way?" I ask, peeking at him. He is already dressed for the day and is wearing light-colored pants, a light-colored button-down shirt, and a medium-blue sports jacket.

"No, I like the old way better." He lays another kiss on my neck, and I arch up into him.

"Oh good, because I can't say it the new way," I say breathlessly. *Why the hell did he get dressed already?*

"What were you remembering in your sleep?"

"Why, what was I doing?" I ask, wondering what gave my memory away.

"Smiling and laughing."

"Oh good, nothing too embarrassing then," I say and reach for him, pulling him closer to me.

"I like it when you talk in your sleep," he whispers and pulls me closer to him. I can feel his hardness against my skin and my body starts to ache for him.

"I've always done it—for some reason I thought I would stop when I became a vampire."

"A lot of aspects of our human life come over into this life," Brigham says softly as he grabs my hip and pulls me hard into him, making me gasp. *Good lord, he is hard!*

"Hmmm…" I say, completely distracted by his touch.

"What were you remembering?" he presses and nips at my nipple through my dress, making me moan in pleasure.

"The night we met," I say, trying to focus on the conversation but finding it hard to do so with his constant touch.

"Aw…a good dream," he says and pulls my dress up over my head, kissing my breasts poking up over my bra.

"Yes." I reach up and run my hands through his hair, enjoying the silky texture of it. It would never be this soft if he was still human, not with all the beauty products in the world. "I like when I remember that day in my sleep."

"Do you ever regret meeting me?" he asks, raising his head up to look at me.

"God, no! Why would you ask that?" I ask, feeling like a bucket of cold water has just been dumped on me.

His eyes change to a deep sky-blue color, and he hesitates, looking down at me. "Your life is very different now than it was before."

"Yes, but in a good way," I say and cup his cheek. Why was he asking me this right now?

"A bit more complicated," Brigham says, his face going stoney as he tries to hide his emotions.

"Maybe."

"Do you regret me turning you so far from the new moon?"

My brows furrow, not understanding why he is asking these questions right now. I thought we were okay. Did he not think so? *Damn it, I thought we were about to have sex!*

"No, I couldn't have waited a day longer. I think I might have really hurt myself if I tried to stay apart from you."

"I would have changed you closer to the new moon if you had been ready," Brigham says, his face tensing.

"I didn't want you to—I didn't have all my questions answered yet." I run my fingers across his chest and unbutton a few buttons so I can feel him better. His skin felt very different than a human's and it feels like touching a polished marble statue. "Why didn't you tell me about the transformation before you changed me?"

Brigham looks at me guiltily. "You know we're not supposed to discuss it with non-vampires. I've been clear on that."

"Yes, but why didn't you tell *me*?"

"I can't break the rules, even if I had wanted to.

"Seriously?"

"I didn't think it would matter as much to you as it does."

"You were wrong."

"Yes, I was wrong. Do you regret the change?" he asks, and a tension hangs in the air.

I pause, contemplating the question. Did I regret it? I think about my human life. I did have a full life as a human. I was busy with school and volunteering. My sex life was active enough to be satisfying, but I didn't feel any sort of great connection with anyone, friend, or partner. I did enjoy that part of my life now. It was like my life had reversed. Now it was all about finding ways to fulfill myself outside of Brigham and my relationship, which was weird, but being friends with Anton helped. It will just take some time.

"No, I don't regret you changing me. I'm disappointed, I suppose—maybe a little disillusioned. It reminds me of being human again. Honestly, men can be very disappointing, and I suppose you are still a man even if you are a vampire, too," I say and Brigham winces.

"Butterfly—"

"It's my own fault for believing that this would be a different kind of relationship," I say quietly and bite my lip, taking in all that I had just revealed to him.

"Is there anything I can do to ease your mind about all this?"

"I don't know. I think I've almost come to terms with the whole thing, and my alternative is not very attractive."

"It's not very attractive to me either. I don't want you to die."

"If I wanted to die—would you let me?"

He hesitates and something flashes across his face so fast that it almost doesn't register as regret. "Is this another one of your theoretical questions?" he asks quietly.

"Yes."

"Then the answer is yes."

"Interesting answer."

"Interesting question."

The tension builds between us. *I hate this!* I hate feeling so fragmented from him!

"I'd rather be a vampire and hunt with Anton and be a little…hindered…than be dead, but I suppose my answer to that question may change after the new moon comes."

"Why do you keep punishing me with your words? I'm not—"

"Guilty conscience?"

He sighs loudly and hangs his head a little. "I suppose there is a little truth to that. I don't like feeling like I let you down. That was the opposite of what I intended."

"As I said, I'm almost over it. I need to deal with it or off myself, so—"

He bares his teeth at me and his canines flash. "I don't want to talk anymore about this. I don't want to think about you dead."

I flash him a smile and kiss his forehead. "As you wish, *master.*" He raises his eyebrows at me. I know I am being a brat, but I can't seem to help it. "Just trying it out. After the new moon I might be saying that a lot."

He grabs me and throws me on top of him so that I am straddling his waist. I laugh loudly in surprise as he positions my core above his hard cock. I knew that my comment would get a reaction from him, but I didn't know what kind of reaction I would get.

"If I had any idea how naughty you were, I might not have picked you up at that coffee shop."

"I thought I picked *you* up."

His eyes blaze and turn light blue. "You had no chance with my vampire powers."

"I don't know, my measly human woman powers had you wobbling by the crosswalk pretty good."

He smiles and his canines pop out. I reach down and lightly rub my finger across one and he shudders.

"True…I was a bit unsteady for a moment. I did enjoy that kiss," he admits.

I think about how human I was back then and how simple and innocent our relationship had started, and my chest clenches.

"I'm worried it's going to be different after the change," I blurt suddenly and quickly cover my mouth. I am no good at holding in my emotions and they always seem to come out at the oddest times.

"You like change," Brigham reminds me gently, but there is a glint of worry in his eyes.

"I don't want us to change," I whisper. Was that even a possibility? How could our relationship and love not evolve over the years? What if we had already hit the high points and after the new moon it took a nosedive? Nothing was guaranteed, and I had been naïve in believing that by changing myself into this unchanging creature, somehow that would transfer over into our relationship.

Brigham reaches up and grabs the back of my neck, pulling me down to him. He presses his forehead to mine, looking at me deeply. I stare back at him, feeling him and feeling how close we are in this moment.

"Everyone changes, even vampires, Butterfly." My stomach drops. *FUCK!* This is not what I wanted to hear from him right now. "I'm not the same man I was when I first turned. I have a lot of new interests, ideas, and opinions that I didn't have as a young vampire."

"You're not helping me feel better," I say, scrunching my face at him. He gives me a weak smile and nods.

"Hmm…" He puts his hand over the place where my heart used to be. "Do I mean that much to you that you would worry about us changing? Do you worry that my love for you will change?"

"Yes."

"I didn't expect to fall in love again," he whispers softly.

"You were in love before?" I ask, my eyes going wide, unable to hide the surprise in my expression. This was huge! *Like huge HUGE!* I couldn't wait to tell Anton!

"Yes," he answers simply.

I had never appreciated this idea before. *Of course,* Brigham had been in love before! It was impossible to think he hadn't, but the idea was still surprising to me. I had never entertained this possibility of him being in love and the questions flooded me.

"What happened?" I burst out, practically falling off of him in my amazement. I wince at how abrupt the question was and did a quick glance at Brigham to see if I had offended him, but he is staring off into nothing, lost in his memories.

"She died," he answers, his voice thick.

"Was she a vampire?"

"Yes." A vampire who died? *That was so rare!* There were only but a few tales of this happening and I had chalked them up to cautionary fables for young vampires—in the same realm as bedtime stories for young children.

"When did she die?" I ask. Brigham had told me when he first kissed me that it had been a long time since he had done that, but how long were we talking?

"Before you were born…" Brigham says and rubs my arm. He looks up at me and studies my face, his face returning to his unreadable stoney look. He didn't like talking about her, but I had too many unanswered questions, and I couldn't stop asking them quite yet.

"What happened? How did she die?" He places a finger gently to my lips.

"Shh…I'll answer your questions. I promise I will, but not tonight." He removes his finger from my mouth, and

I considered biting the tip of it clear off. I wasn't a child, and I didn't like being shushed.

"Can I ask one more question?" I ask, trying to keep my irritation out of my voice.

He sighs deeply and gives me a small smile. "One more question."

"Why won't you tell me tonight?"

"You have the most incorrigible spirit!"

He grabs my wrists and folds my hands across my chest, tucking me into myself and flips me onto the bed on my back. He holds me down, adjusting himself on top of me, pinning me down. I try to squirm away, but he holds me down tightly. Unhappy about this situation, I stick out my lower lip at him in a pout, which makes him grin wickedly.

"Tonight, I have other plans for us, and it is too sad of a tale to tell right now. First, I'm going to make love to you." He leans down and bites my lower lip gently. "Then, we're going to Forseti's house for dinner. He's having some guests over and there are a few people I want you to meet."

"Dinner!" I moan, throwing my head back dramatically. "It's not dinner if no one eats anything."

"What would you call it then?"

"A bunch of old fogies hanging around talking about their glory days. Maybe call it a Bore-A-Thon," I suggest as I struggle underneath him, trying to get leverage.

"Old fogies?" he quips as he presses down harder on me. I struggle harder but am unable to budge him. Feeling defeated and helpless, I decided to try a new tactic and completely relax my body, hoping Brigham's grip would also relax.

"Yes, you and Forseti are old fogies. You all need to hang out with people from this generation."

"Do you see me that way?" *What's this? Paranoia? Self-consciousness? Very interesting!*

"When you talk to Forseti about living in New York, yes—yes, I really do."

Brigham's grip finally relaxes, and I push hard against him trying to break free—but as soon as he feels me pushing against him, his grip clamps down even harder against me and he pins my arms up over my head! I snap at him with my teeth and he pulls away—it is no use. I am trapped.

"Well, Anton will be there, so you won't have to be bored all night."

"*Thank God!*" I say in relief.

"You really like Anton, don't you," Brigham asks softly as he moves my wrists into one hand. He reaches down and strokes my cheek, looking at me closely.

"Yes," I say, scrunching up my face at him. He is acting really weird tonight.

"And you're not attracted to him at all?" Brigham asks, his face expressionless as he peers down at my pinned body.

I snort. "He's not my type."

"What's your type?"

"Old fogeyish," I tease. His brows knit together and I giggle. He leans down and kisses me hard. His tongue moves into my mouth, claiming me as I moan into him, feeling him grind against me. *Fuck, that felt good!*

"You're so evil," I moan as I feel my body burn for him.

"Well, I am a vampire after all," he says hoarsely and uses his fangs to tear through the fabric in the front of my bra. My breasts spring out, and he gives a growl and sucks in one of my nipples, tugging on it slightly and then moving to the other side. I feel my core throb with need and slicken, which is weird that it does that since I am now a vampire, but apparently some things didn't change.

"It was so hard staying away from you," I say and try to pull my wrists free. He releases me and I grab a hold of his head, digging my fingers deep into his scalp as he kisses a line down my stomach. He reaches the area just below my belly button and uses his fangs again and snaps the fabric of my panties off one side and moves to the other side and tears through it. "That's such a handy little trick," I moan as he removes my panties with his teeth and throws them off of the bed.

He looks up at me and grins wickedly.

"You're the most expressive when we make love. Did you know that?"

"I think it is just being around you, Butterfly. I haven't felt this alive in a long time," he says as he puts his head down and licks up my core making me call out, "Brigham!"

He laughs, and the sensation of his laughter through my core as he licks at me causes me to orgasm right there. "Fucking hell!" I say breathlessly. "I really needed that!"

"We're not even close to being done."

I look down at him, and he grabs one of my legs and lifts it over his shoulder, kissing my inner thigh. Tiny little pulses of lightning shoot through my muscles with each kiss, making me quiver.

"How do you do that?"

His eyes darken with lust, and he kisses up to my core, licking at my clit and flicking it with his tongue. I grind into him, grabbing the bedsheets while trying to get some leverage. He moves his hand up and pushes two fingers in me he starts pumping into me as he sucks my clit, and the pressure and tingling sensation from his tongue on my clit sends me over the edge again as I cry out his name again.

He gently lays my leg back down and looks down at me as he throws off his sports jacket and slowly unbuttons his shirt.

"You are taking way too long," I moan, trying to get my wits about me while still recovering from my colossal orgasm.

"Did you like that?" he asks, his eyes sparkling as he throws off his shirt.

I bare my teeth at him and sit up and grab at his belt, undoing it and throwing it on the floor. "It was okay."

He growls and pushes me down to the bed and I laugh. He unbuttons his pants, his eyes blazing at me and gives me a deadly look, and I cannot help but shudder. He looks like the classic vampire demon, and he is all mine! He steps out of his pants but leaves his boxers on and I whine. *That just wouldn't do!*

He raises his eyes at me and I lunge at him and grab his head, kissing him hard and pressing my naked body up against him. I grind over him, wanting him so deep inside of me, and reach down and rip his boxers off. I'm done playing hard to get.

"I need you!" I growl at him, feeling my more vampiric personality traits surging through me. I felt much more possessive about him now that I had changed into a vampire.

"Say it again," he commands, fisting the back of my hair.

"I NEED YOU NOW!" I growl louder and bite at his lip, drawing blood as I grab his cock in my hand and pump it, needing to feel more of him. He is so hard right now and his skin on his cock is so smooth it is like running my hand over polished stone. I grip him harder and he moans, his eyes snapping to me, blazing with a blue fire like lit propane.

He pulls my head back hard and I release his lip. He kisses me, and I taste his blood.

If I had a heartbeat anymore, it would be racing. *He tasted so good*—better than any human I have ever tasted. He bites down hard on my lip, and I feel him break through my skin. The pain ricochets through me and he tastes me and moans. He smears my blood across my neck as he moves to it with his lips and bites down hard on my neck and breaks the skin again. He sucks deeply and the pain slowly turns to pleasure as he pulls me into him.

I line his cock up with my entrance and jump at him, wrapping my legs around him as he sucks and slowly begin thrusting my hips as he holds me, drinking from me. Between the feel of him inside me and the sucking on my neck, I orgasm again, and he roars and releases my neck and carrying me to the wall where he pins me to it, my back pressing against the wall. He licks the wound at my neck, and I feel it slowly close and heal, my head woozy from the blood loss and the ecstatic release.

He grips my head and kisses me and then turns and slits his wrist open and presses it to my mouth. I grip his wrist and drink it greedily and he slowly rolls his hips into me, watching me as I drink him. I'd never really gotten into blood play, but as a vampire, this is sheer ecstasy. I could not get enough of him physically. I wanted every ounce of him touching me and inside me.

He pulls his wrist back and licks it, closing the wound. I kiss him tenderly as he pushes harder and harder into me, filling me completely. I roll my hips to him as he thrusts and presses my forehead to his as I cling to his neck and shoulders, needing to touch more of him. I dig my fingers deep into his skin, but still only make the slightest of impressions. Brigham's body is so strong, and I wonder if I will ever be as strong as he is.

He looks at me and his eyes turn almost violet. I kiss him, pulling him harder into me and he growls. I adjust my hips to have him get deeper and I shudder as another orgasm hits me and he shudders in my arms, moaning my name as he finds his release. He holds me against the wall, and I rest my head on his shoulder.

"I love you, Butterfly," he whispers and presses a kiss to my neck.

"I love you too," I whisper back to him and kiss his shoulder. It might not be perfect, right now, but I love how safe and loved I feel with Brigham. I just had to get through to the new moon—after that, things would get even better than between us…hopefully.

CHAPTER SEVEN

Brigham pulls up in front of a huge cream-colored stone mansion, and a burgundy tuxedoed human valet opens my door for me. I step out of Brigham's blue sports car and try to look like I do this all the time and not step on my dress. Forseti's house is the largest house I have ever seen, and it still feels weird that I come here regularly.

Brigham leads me inside and we make our way to a large game room ornately decorated with lush, burgundy carpets and plush chairs and couches. There are many vampires milling around various gaming tables, and, as we enter, Anton and Forseti spot us and make their way over to us.

"Ah, Butterfly! How good to see you, my dear!" Forseti pulls me into his arms and hugs me tenderly.

I smile at the large man, slightly embarrassed. I hadn't known him that long and he always greets me the same way, like I am some long lost relative or something.

He pulls back at me and looks me over, his golden eyes shining at me. "My goodness, darling—you look amazing tonight!"

I look down at myself awkwardly. Anton had helped me pick out my outfit and I am wearing a jade-colored, crinkled, metallic fabric evening gown that is sleeveless and has one shoulder strap with a slit in the bodice which shows a little cleavage, but not an indecent amount—I hoped. It has a high slit at the hem, which shows off my muscular leg. The fabric is soft and has a cool texture due to whatever is woven into it to make it shine and I love it!

"Hello Forseti, thank you—Anton picked this out for me," I say with a half-smile. Forseti pulls me into another hug.

I never know exactly what to do when he shows me this kind of affection. Forseti's auburn hair falls forward, and he brushes it back over his shoulder. His hair is longer than Brigham's and he keeps his beard cut short, which had to have taken him hundreds of years to grow, I guess, because not many of the vampires I had seen had much facial hair. Maybe he was turned with a beard—I didn't know how it really worked. I didn't think our hair grew the same anymore. When I brush mine, I never seemed to lose strands, which is weird, and Brigham never woke up with any stubble on his face. I had to start doing some experiments and measure my hair to see if I could figure out if it still grew or not.

Forseti looks at Anton, who looks dazzling in a blue and gold jacquard fabric blazer with a paisley pattern and blue shirt, vest, and pants. I really had no idea how he could pull something like that off and not look ostentatious, but he always seemed able to.

"Yes, Anton has a particular talent for picking out clothes. He picked this out for me tonight and I think he did quite well, don't you?" Forseti looks down at himself and smiles. He is wearing a cream-colored three-piece tuxedo with a grey shiny tie that had swirls of cream making little circular patterns on it. It is tailored to fit his muscular form perfectly and looks quite nice on him.

"You do look marvelous," I agree and sneak a glance at Brigham. His face is neutral, but I can tell from his eyes that he is finding this very amusing by the slight twinkle there. My eyes roam over him for a moment and I bite my lip, looking at how handsome he looks in his tuxedo. He is wearing a deep taupe-colored three-piece tuxedo, and the vest is shiny with taupe, metallic-colored paisleys against a black background. It was really hard getting out of the house with him in it. I kept wanting to jump his bones.

"I heard you went to the beach, how was it?" Forseti's eyes dance with delight and my eyes turn back to him.

"It was beautiful!" I gush.

"Did you find it different looking at the sea with vampire eyes?" he asks, and I notice a longing in his voice.

"Yes, there were more…dimensions to it. It's hard to explain. It was like I could see every angle of everything all at once."

"Yes, exactly! It's been years since I've seen the ocean. Maybe we should go see it sometime soon," he says with longing, turning towards Anton.

Anton shrugs as if that was the last thing on the planet he wanted to do. He probably didn't like the idea of the wind or sand messing his hair or clothes up.

Foresti makes a disgusted sound. "Your friend here is such a homebody. I can barely get him to go anywhere with me. That's why I have to have these parties—if I didn't, he wouldn't meet anyone at all!"

"I go out all the time. I'm just not interested in traveling. Why should I go anywhere, anyways? There's always something exciting going around here," Anton huffs and gives Forseti a dirty look.

Forseti looks at him ruefully. "That is true, there is always a lot going on here—I can barely keep up, but still, the ocean! I forgot how much of the world is still out there! How I would love to go see it again soon!" Forseti smiles as me. "Well—maybe, my dear, you and I should go one day—with Brigham's approval, of course." Forseti nods at Brigham.

"That would be lovely."

Forseti loops his arm with mine and pulls me closer. He smells like one of Anton's fancy colognes and pleasant hints of bergamot, citrus and musk hit me. "Now dear, how are you doing with the change?" he asks in a low tone.

"Good, I do like being a vampire. Anton and I have been having a lot of fun," I say, trying to deflect, not wanting to talk about how I really feel about all this.

"Oh, yes! I hear about all your exploits!" He laughs loudly. "It's all very amusing! It's so…freeing…to hear about some of the things that you and Anton do. It's been so long for me, but I do suppose it is nice not having to worry about silly human concerns any longer. That must be quite a change for you!"

"I am very excited to no longer get my period."

Forseti laughs loudly, wiping a bloody tear from his eye. He turns and looks back over his shoulder at Brigham. "Oh Brigham, I am so glad you found this girl. She makes me laugh, and that's so good for an old man like me to do!"

"She is a character," Anton says, rolling his eyes. He shoots a smile at Brigham, who looks only the slightest bit amused.

"Come my dear, there are a lot of people I want you to meet." Forseti puts a hand around my shoulder and leads me away. I look over my shoulder at Brigham who is turning to Anton, talking softly. I can barely see his lips moving but I can tell from Anton's eyes that he is listening to something.

Forseti steers me into a small group of vampires. "Hello, everyone. There is someone I'd like you to meet." He smiles at them coyly. "This is Butterfly, she is Brigham's partner."

I stiffen slightly, I hadn't really ever been introduced this way before and it is a little odd. Girlfriend yes, but partner? That seems very committed and stable. Was that what Brigham and I are? I glance back towards Brigham and catch him watching us. He is probably trying to gauge my reaction to the introduction, so I pretend it doesn't faze me and smile at the vampires.

The eyes of the vampire nearest to me with red hair fly wide open as he looks at me and I notice the stunned expressions on the other vampire's faces. I smile awkwardly, not understanding their reaction to me. The man with red hair seems to recover and he smiles kindly at me, his blue eyes shining brightly. He straightens his light blue tuxedo with black lapels and gives me a small bow.

"Well, hello dear, it is so nice to meet you, Butterfly. My name is Leroy, and this is Anastasia." He gestures to a short woman with almond colored skin and beautiful hazel eyes with long straight dark-brown hair that goes to her waist. She gives me a small smile, and I marvel at her long, black-sleeved gown with three-dimensional flowers embroidered into the fabric and the sheer waist cutaways of her dress. I am going to have Anton dress me for every event from here on out. I am way out of my league here!

"Hello," I say, trying not to seem awkward and like I belong here. *Which I of course do…*

"This bloke over here is Dermot." Leroy gestures to a man with dark skin and warm-dark almond shaped eyes who gives me a smile. He's wearing a dark blue, shiny tuxedo, and I again thank God I let Anton dress me. "And this beautiful woman here is my love, Lillian," he says as he plants a kiss on woman with tan skin and beautiful, dark, curly black shoulder-length hair wearing a dark blue-and-white tulle embroidered long-sleeved evening gown.

"It's nice to meet you," I say, trying to keep my anxiety down. This was so formal and weird.

"How long have you been a vampire?" asks Lillian as she takes a sip of her wine glass that has a red liquid in it. I forgot that Forseti catered in blood for these events, and suddenly I am very thirsty.

"Twenty-two days," I say quickly and then realize this may be an odd answer being so precise. I glance over at Brigham, but he has his back to me and is still talking to Anton. *I was going to kill him later for making me come to this!*

"Oh my, you are brand new!" she exclaims, and I don't really understand what is so fascinating about this. Maybe they don't sire vampires that often.

"Yes." I nod and look around for a waiter who might bring me a drink.

"Are you enjoying it?" asks Leroy as he puts his arm around Lillian.

"Oh yes, I'm having a great time." I wince at how disingenuous and sarcastic my tone sounds, but no one seems to notice.

"I would expect the transition to be easy for you. Brigham is such a good teacher, he was always so patient with..." Anastasia's voice trails off, and a sad expression crosses her face. She quickly snaps her eyes back up to me and shoots a guilty smile at Forseti.

"Oh yes, Butterfly is doing wonderfully. My Anton is helping her as well," Forseti says quickly. *That was fucking strange!* Brigham was patient with who?

"Anton has been fabulous!" I agree with Forseti and see a waiter holding a large tray of drinks.

I wave him over, probably looking like I am trying to direct a plane, but it is what it is. He hands me a glass with sparkling red fluid. I take a sip, letting the blood-infused concoction invigorate me. Drinking from a human was the best, but this drink was divine! I would have to find out from Anton later who the caterer is and how they came up with this magical drink! There are hints of berries in it and they had somehow made it carbonated, which is completely fun!

"He is very entertaining, isn't he?" Dermot laughs. "He is always getting me to place bets around here! I think he is working for Forseti to get me to go broke!"

"Oh please, no one needs to encourage your gambling habit!" Lilith teases. "But I agree, Anton is a riot! It has been much more fun around here since he has arrived."

"I feel very lucky to have him as a friend," I say and look for Anton, but cannot find him anywhere. I take another sip of my drink and suppress a moan. *It was so good!*

"Well, good, I'm glad Brigham has someone in his life. It's been so long since Jacqueline," Leroy says with a sad expression, and I try as hard as I can to keep my expression neutral and not let on that I have no idea who the hell this Jacqueline is. *God, I hate these parties!*

"Yes, much too long," Forseti nods sadly and pats my shoulder.

Forseti introduces me to more members of the Vampire Guild, and I try my best to remembers everyone's names, but after a while, they all blur into the same immaculate-skinned, fanged beautiful anonymous person. Forseti releases me from the introductions, and I quickly find another glass of the delicious blood wine and search for Anton. Everyone has been nice enough to me, very nice actually, but these parties are just weird to me—this isn't how I used to spend my time as a human. I was usually studying or trying to go on some crazy adventure exploring ruins somewhere.

I spot Anton looking bored while talking to a vampire wearing a dark blue suit who has sandy brown hair cut in a messy quaff. He is, of course, gorgeous, like everyone else at the party and I wonder if there is some sort of code or regulation on who you are allowed to turn. Is being beautiful a requirement? He nods, smiling as the vampire talks to him, but his eyes keep drifting away to other people in the room. I catch his eye and gesture for him to come over to me. He makes a face, gesturing to the vampire he was talking to, and I laugh at his displeasure. Apparently, he is stuck in the conversation with the vampire. I walk up to them and grab Anton's sleeve frantically.

"So sorry to interrupt, Anton, but Forseti asked me to get you. Apparently, there's a problem at one of the tables," I lie.

"Oh dear," says Anton dramatically. "I better see what is going on." Turning towards the old vampire, he says, "Terribly sorry, Demetrius, we'll have to continue this conversation later."

"Yes, I am terribly sorry," I say to Demetrius. The vampire nods and I lead Anton away to the far side of the room.

"I love you," he whispers into my ear. I laugh softly. "We're so even for that bet now."

"Hey, we were already square for that, remember? You owe me now, buddy!"

"Alright, fine! Since when are we keeping score?" Anton hisses.

"It doesn't matter anyway, because I'm going to ask you for a favor in a second, so we'll be even again," I whisper.

"Oh, a favor! How exciting! Hey, wait a minute, you're not escaping again, are you?" he groans and looks around the room frantically, his face pales and tenses. "Because I don't want to get on Brigham's bad side—there's something about him that scares the bejesus out of me, and I am *too pretty* to die!"

I laugh and look at him in disbelief. "Really? He wouldn't hurt a flea. I've only seen him get barely angry before."

"I've heard stories," Anton says in a low tone and glances around the room. "I couldn't get many details—my sources were afraid to talk!"

"Bullshit! About Brigham?"

"Yep," Anton nods vigorously.

I take a sip of my blood wine and finish the glass. "Have you had any of these? They are delicious!" I exclaim.

Anton waves a waiter over to us, grabs two glasses from him, and hands one to me. I take another sip greedily and ask, "Have you heard anything about Brigham having a former lover?"

Anton chokes on his wine as he asks, "He had a mate?" He quickly recovers and takes another sip of his drink and lets out a low moan. "This is so good, you can thank me for this, by the way. I made Forseti do a blood wine taste tasting with me and then convinced him to buy a million bottles of this stuff. We may have enough for the next party if I don't drink it all first."

"Call me over to your place if you start drinking— I'm in!"

"I can't believe he had a former lover. I thought you were the first one," Anton whispers to me.

"Why would you think that?" I spot Brigham at the other end of the room, but his back is turned to us and damn, the suit makes him so hot that my core starts to throb again. He is way too hot to have been single long—he probably has had a slew of women.

"He acts like you are the only person in his universe, the way he looks at you…" Anton shrugs. "It's hard to imagine him being like that with anyone else."

"Apparently he has, and she was a vampire and died!" I whisper to Anton, leaning closer to him so no one hears. It was really tricky telling secrets in a room full of vampires!

"No way!" Anton gasps.

"Yep," I say and take another sip of my drink.

"Where'd you hear that?" Anton asks. "Vampires rarely die, it's almost unheard of!"

"From Brigham directly," I say, causing Anton's eyebrows to rise. "He wouldn't give me many details about it, as he distracted me with sex."

Anton snorts. "You are so easy!"

"It's not about me being easy! It's about how good Brigham is at sex."

"Well, now we know why," Anton teases and I cringe at that thought.

"I hate you," I hiss.

Anton gives me a side hug. "No, you don't." He glances around the room and smiles at a tall blonde woman immaculately dressed in a sleeveless red gown and raises his glass to her. "Wow! I still can't believe that Brigham has another lover. I mean he is old—like really old—but still."

"Yeah, I know right. Didn't see that coming. I mean, I didn't ask him directly about his past relationships, because honestly, I've had some I'm not exactly proud of and didn't really want to discuss them."

"You were a slut? What?" Anton teases and puts his hand over his chest, pretending to look shocked.

"One, that is *NOT* what I just said," I say sternly and hit him in his shoulder. "And two, easy for you to say, you're a man. It's not fair—you can date a slew of woman, and no one gives a crap or judges you."

"Okay, one, I can date a slew of women and men, and no one cares, and two, yes, having a magical penis is a great life choice."

I groan. "Anyways, I didn't get a lot of details before the mind-blowing sex."

"Mind-blowing, really?" Anton narrows his eyes at me and then looks across the room at Brigham and seems to study him.

"That's what I said, and I stand by it."

Anton's lips twitch as he watches Brigham. "What did he say exactly?" Anton presses.

"That's all the information I have. He said it was too sad of a tale to tell right then or some bullshit. I was hoping you could find out more for me," I say, batting my eyes at him.

"Why don't you just ask Brigham about it?" Anton asks suspiciously.

"Because…I want to know the whole story, not just Brigham's version," I say and run my hands over the fabric of my dress. *It is so fun and feels so good!* Anton taps my hand, and I look at him gratefully. I didn't want to look like a crazy person touching myself here tonight.

"Isn't it good enough that he said he'd tell you later? I mean, what does it matter? If she's dead and long gone, there's not much you need to worry about there."

"I guess you're right," I say dejectedly.

Anton groans and then looks quickly up at Brigham. "Well, I can try to see what I can get out of Forseti—he's always good for a yarn, especially if I can get him drinking some of this blood wine—but it will cost you."

"You owe me, remember? Oh, forget it, you're too expensive! I'll just go ask someone else for help—they might have better sources than you, anyways."

Anton scoffs. "No one has better sources than me! And I haven't even told you what I want."

I roll my eyes. "Okay, what is it that you want?"

"I want you to go shopping with me," Anton says triumphantly, and I groan and stomp my feet…but only a little…in a cute way.

"I hate shopping!"

"I know, but I need a woman's opinion, and I always accidentally glamour the saleswomen so I can never get a good assessment of what they actually think and what looks good."

"How do you manage that?"

"I get nervous, it just happens, and they get glamoured," Anton says and rubs his neck.

I laugh. "You are telling me you are a premature glamourer," I cry, and Anton slaps his hand over my mouth.

"Shut up! It's very embarrassing!" Anton hisses at me and I stifle a laugh, trying to make my face serious. He releases his hand from my mouth slowly.

"Sorry, I made fun of you. I had no idea how hard it is for you," I snicker and try again to look serious, but fail and Anton glowers at me.

"It's much harder than you think. You'll see when you're up to full-strength—you'll have trouble controlling it," Anton says seriously and crosses his arms over his chest. "You might even get some weird ability that's even harder to control. I was accidently turning stuff to metal for weeks." I look at him doubtfully. "Okay, maybe not, you were meant to be a vampire—it's freaking annoying how good you are at taking down assholes."

"Jealous?" I smirk and Anton rolls his eyes at me. "I hope I get some cool ability like laser eyes or something! That'll make it so fun hunting with you!"

"That is the stupidest thing I have ever heard. Have you not read any Marvel comics or seen the movies? Cyclops had a hell of a time!"

"You are such a nerd!"

"Says the woman who has how many hundreds of college credits?"

"Man, you are so spicy tonight!"

"I need to get laid," he says and runs his hands through his hair. "But that's beside the point, I'll get over it.

Come on, please go shopping with me! I don't have anyone else to ask, and I'll bring you some of this blood wine!"

"Why can't Forseti go with you?" I whine.

"Do you see how that man dresses?"

"He always looks nice."

"That's because I dress him. Trust me, it's scary—he is stuck in some weird century where everything was fastened with bone buttons and strange clasps. The man is fascinated by elastic!"

"Alright fine, but I think I'm getting a bum deal, and you better bring me lots of wine!"

He kisses my cheek. "Thank you!"

"Yeah, yeah, but you owe me, even with the wine and looking up information on Brigham's former lover. I think her name was Jacqueline—or, at least, that's what Forseti said."

"Jacqueline, huh?" Anton pauses and bites his lip.

"What is it?"

"Nothing, I mean, I don't know for sure yet. I heard a story about a woman named Jacqueline once when I was a newly made vampire, but I can't remember all of it now. I was so disoriented when I was first turned, and some of the things I learned are a bit foggy now."

"Interesting, I didn't realize you had a hard transitioning phase."

"Yeah, I know it was easy for you, but it's not like that for everyone. I had bloodlust for a while and barely remember how I got to be the dynamic vampire you see before you today. Most newly-sired vampires are not seen for months—they are too out of control."

"I wonder why that is. Is there something wrong with me?"

"I mean, knowing you, I would say yes," Anton quips. I glare at him, and he laughs. "I wouldn't worry about it, Butterfly, everyone is different. Everyone goes through the change differently."

I sigh and contort my face. "Are you gambling tonight?" I ask, wanting to change the subject.

"No, these old guys can always tell when I'm bluffing. I've lost enough money this week. How about you?"

"I'm not much of a poker player. I like throwing dice, though—maybe the craps table?"

"How good are you at it?"

I shrug. "Fair, I guess. Never really thought about it."

"Alright, you roll, and I'll place the chips. How much money do you have on you?"

"Umm, I don't know—let me check," I rummage in the bodice of my dress and pull out a wad of cash and count it.

"Five-thousand dollars!" I say triumphantly.

Anton looks at me in awe. "You're carrying five-thousand dollars in your bra?"

"What bra? Now that I'm a vampire, these puppies stay up all by themselves," I say and gently cup my breasts.

"Seriously?"

"Yep, it's another perk I was not expecting. I have a list going."

"But I've seen you wear a bra," Anton points out, not believing me.

"Well, Brigham likes—"

"Never mind, never mind, I get it," Anton says, making a face and I smirk at him.

"Since when are you a prude?"

"I'm not a prude, but I don't really want to picture Brigham naked."

"Why, it's fun—I do it all the time."

"Sorry, not really into guys that look like him," Anton says and scans the room.

"That's too bad because I would highly recommend Brigham. *Highly recommend*," I tease.

"Okay, now you're grossing me out and annoying me. God, I need to get laid."

"Okay, I'll stop. Here." I hand Anton my money. "You get the chips, and I'll meet you at the table."

I look around the room and see Brigham having a conversation with Demetrius and he is drinking from his wine glass. He nods his head and listens to what Demtrius is saying, but his eyes slide to me, and I give him a wink, heading to the craps table. At the table, there are three vampires, and one of them is the man from the bar who smiled at me. I stare at the man for a minute, not really believing it is him, but he has the same dark brown hair and textured, long crop cut but now is wearing a deep grey tuxedo.

"Hey, I saw you at the club the other night, didn't I?" I ask, taking a chance.

The man looks up at me, and his eyes are dark, and he gives me a sly smile. "Yes, that's right! Small world."

I stare at him for a moment, waiting for that uneasy feeling to come again, but it doesn't, and I look at him curiously. He has a strong jaw and sharp nose and looks like he is in his late twenties from when he was turned, but it is so hard to tell.

"I'm Butterfly, and this is my friend, Anton," I say, gesturing to Anton who has joined us, carrying the chips in his hands.

"I'm Darren," he says, extending his hand to me. I shake it and he holds it a little too firmly before he releases it and the uneasy feeling tingles through me. I move a little closer to Anton but try not to look like I am moving closer to Anton.

"How do you know Forseti?" I ask, wanting to figure out more about this person.

Darren looks down at the table and places a few chips on the table. He answers me while not looking at me, "My sire and him go way back."

"When I saw you at the bar, I wasn't sure if you were human or vampire," I admit, and then wish I could kick myself for admitting something like that to him.

"Really?" he asks, looking up at me in a predatory way as I repress a shudder.

"Yeah, I'm new to this whole vampire thing and I'm not good at recognizing our own kind," I admit again, wishing I was better at keeping my mouth shut.

"How long have you been a vampire?" he asks and looks between Anton and me.

"About twenty days," I say, trying to make it sound more ambivalent this time and not as exact. That might give the wrong impression if I say the exact number again.

"Twenty days, wow—you haven't even been through the new moon phase," Darren says, giving me a knowing look. Odd that he is tracking the phases of the moon so closely.

"Nope, it's coming up," I say, trying to sound unconcerned.

"Are you nervous?" Anton laughs and Darren looks at him curiously.

"A little," I say through gritted teeth and shoot Anton a warning look.

"What's the joke?" he asks, looking at Anton. He gives him a smile which shows off his canines.

"Butterfly just got back from an excursion away from her sire," Anton says and puts some chips on the table.

"Really?"

"Uh…yeah," I say, grabbing the dice and throwing them.

"She's been testing with the connection," Anton says with a smirk, and I glare at him. *What the hell!*

"How long were you gone?"

"Three days," Anton says quickly and I elbow him in his gut. I mean yes, probably everyone knew already, but *FUCK!*

"No way!" Darren says in amazement and his eyes go wide as he releases an appreciative sigh. "That's amazing!"

"Yeah…" I say and take a sip of my blood wine. Anton places more bets down and I grab the dice and throw them, not really paying any attention to the table.

"I can't imagine. Did it hurt when you reconnected?" he asks. *I nod and look around for Brigham. I really wanted to stop talking about this.* "Why did you go? Sorry, that was forward of me. You don't have to tell me." *I laugh uneasily, trying to sound unconcerned.* "I'm just really impressed that you have that much self-control so soon after being turned," he adds.

"It's okay, there are no secrets around here anyway." I shoot Anton a deadly look and he laughs again. "I'm not crazy about the thought about losing my autonomy."

"I completely understand that," he says and smiles warmly at me. "You won't have anything to worry about if you have a good master," Darren says and then something dark flickers across his face. His expression contorts and it makes my hair on my arms stand on end.

"That's what I hear," I say in a low tone and hold his stare.

The darkness dissipates from his face, and he smiles at me. "You don't believe it?"

"Ever hear of the saying 'absolute power corrupts absolutely'?"

Darren snorts. "Yeah, I've heard that." He flinches as if he had gotten a sudden pain. *What is with this guy?* Anton elbows me and gestures to the table, and I throw the dice again.

"Well, my sire is great, he really is, but I still worry that things will change afterwards."

"If your sire cares about you, that won't be an issue." A look of sadness flashes across his face for a moment, but was quickly replaced by a smile. *This guy had some serious Dr. Jekyll and Mr. Hyde vibes!*

"I keep telling her that, but she doesn't believe me," Anton sulks and finishes his glass of blood wine. He places more bets and elbows me again towards the dice.

An arm reaches around me, and I stiffen until I look up and see Brigham and immediately relax.

"I see you and Anton are doing well tonight," Brigham remarks, looking at the pile of chips Anton and I have amassed. I look down at the chips and my mouth drops open—I hadn't been paying any attention.

"Your woman's making me tons of money!" Anton says excitedly, rubbing his hands together looking at his new amassed wealth. *"I'm taking her to Vegas!"*

"Making you money?" I question and put my hand on my hip. "Wasn't it *my* money to begin with?"

"Technicality," Anton says, waving me off.

Brigham gives the slightest of smirks and then looks across the table at Darren. That's when I notice Darren staring at Brigham silently with a grim expression on his face. His eyes stray to Brigham's arm around my waist and his face darkens, making me feel uncomfortable. *Why would he care if I was with Brigham?*

"Darren," Brigham says tensely.

"Brigham," Darren says with venom in his voice. I look at Anton, and he shrugs and looks between Brigham and Darren, his eyebrows raised.

"How are you?" Brigham asks, his voice strained. I stiffen hearing Brigham's tone. I've never heard him this tense before, and I study Darren trying to understand what is going on.

"Not as well as you," Darren says with an edge to his voice and his eyes flicker to me. There is an awkward silence as the tension builds in the air, and I look to Anton. He tenses and places a few more chips down on the table and slowly hands me the dice. I throw the dice as Darren and Brigham have their silent standoff and a few of the other vampire players at the table pick up their chips and leave, looking wearily between Brigham and Darren. I watch them go and look at Anton, wide-eyed. *What is happening right now?*

"I hadn't heard you were in town," Brigham says in a low tone that is almost a growl, and I feel him pull me into him slightly.

"Just arrived yesterday. You can't be on top of everything, Brigham," Darren says with a cockiness that makes me flinch. I can't believe anyone is talking to Brigham like this. I've only seen people be respectful to him.

"Is Shawn here as well?" Brigham asks and again he pulls me tighter to him.

"No," Darren says with irritation and rolls his shoulders. "He chose to stay in New York for this trip. He has too many bad memories of this city."

"I've been meaning to visit him, but…"

"I wouldn't advise it—he's still upset with you," Darren says curtly and picks up his chips from the table.

"I was hoping enough time has passed that he—"

"I don't think enough time will ever pass for that, do you?" Darren says insolently and glowers at Brigham.

Brigham doesn't answer and when I look up to him it looks like he is barely containing his rage. *It's scary.* I've never seen Brigham look like this before! I feel like I'm about to be in the middle of some sort of vampire brawl.

Darren studies me closely and his eyes narrow and get darker, his face contorting back and forth between a menacing demon and a friendly face. It was like the vampire I had met and been joking with earlier had vanished and a completely different person is looking at me now.

"If you're going to be in town for a while, I'd like to get together with you. Maybe you could give Shawn a message from me to try to explain," Brigham says, and I can hear how hard he is trying to sound diplomatic.

Darren laughs loudly and several vampires at the poker table next to us glance at our table as Brigham's face darkens again.

"I'm sorry Brigham, but if you think I can change Shawn's mind, you're insane," Darren says, and the darkness seems to lighten. He looks at me, and I see a shadow of sadness flicker there. Brigham sighs deeply and I am surprised by how much emotion he is showing in public—it's a bit unnerving.

"Maybe more time will—"

"Good luck with that." Darren cuts him off and then laughs again a little manically and I shudder. He looks at me, and a small smile crosses his face. I don't like the way he is looking at me—it seems predatory. Brigham must have sensed it as well and his hand tightens on my hip. "Butterfly, it was very nice meeting you. Brigham…have a good life." He turns and walks out of the game room.

"That was one weird dude," Anton says under his breath. I look up at Brigham, but he is focused on the retreating Darren, and his face looks deadly, his eyes on fire and his jaw clenching tightly. I squeeze his hand trying to get his attention, but he keeps watching Darren until he has left the room.

"What the hell was that about? And what is that guy's deal?" I ask.

"Sorry about that," Brigham says, turning back to me, his face now neutral as if nothing odd had just happened and he loosens his grip on my hip.

"Who was that man?" I ask in irritation.

"Darren Jennings is an old acquaintance of mine," Brigham says without emotion.

"Yeah, I gathered that," I say, my anger growing. "That doesn't answer my question."

"His sire and I had a difference of opinion years ago and I'm afraid he got caught in the middle of it," Brigham says dismissively.

"What was the difference of opinion about?"

Brigham ignores me and looks back in the direction that Darren had left, and I consider making a scene to get him to answer me. I glance at Anton and raise my hands, gesturing to him to see if he knew what was happening, but he is studying Brigham, trying to read him as well.

"Brigham, are you going to answer me?" I ask through gritted teeth. I feel like I am about to explode. I am tired of being out of the loop on important matters.

"Anton, I meant to ask you earlier, but can you accompany Butterfly tomorrow? I'm finding it difficult to fill her bodyguard position after what happened to Brandon," Brigham asks looking at Anton and I step on his foot hard, putting my full weight on it, which makes him finally look at me.

"I don't need a bodyguard, remember—I'm not going to try to *escape* again," I grit out and consider leaving this stupid party if he is going to be an ass.

"Oh, I know that dear, it's purely for my peace of mind," he says as he leans down and kisses my cheek, but I pull back from him.

"But—" I start.

"Anton?" asks Brigham.

Anton bites the inside of his cheek looking at us. "Sure, no problem. We were going to go shopping anyway."

"Great. What do you think about heading home?" Brigham asks, looking at me. His eyes have changed to the color of storm clouds, and I feel the slightest pressure on my back pushing me towards the exit.

"Sure, that's fine." I mutter. "Anton, I'll see you tomorrow." Anton nods and waves as Brigham puts more pressure with his hand to my back and we make our way to the door.

The drive home is tense, and Brigham drives without saying a word to me, focusing on the road. His face is stoney and deep in thought. I can't tell if he really isn't aware he is being an asshole or he doesn't know he is being an asshole, and I try to calm myself and wait for him to give me more information.

Finally, unable to handle the silence anymore, I turn to him with my fists balled and growl, "You have three seconds to tell me what the hell is going on, or I am leaving. I'm not putting up with this male-dominant-whatever it is!" I spit at him, and he takes his foot off the accelerator and looks at me out of the corner of his eyes. "I don't even know what the fuck alpha display you got going on. It's fucking rude not answering my question and dismissing me."

Brigham turns to look at me fully and I see the surprise on his face. He pulls his car over to the shoulder and parks, blinking at me as if he has no idea what I am talking about, and this makes me even madder.

"Where are you going to go?" he asks, keeping his voice even.

"I'm not telling you, and wherever the fuck I want," I say, sneering at him, having lost all control over my anger.

Brigham stares at me without expression, his hands gripping the steering wheel tightly and saying nothing.

He continues to stonewall me, and I snap. "Fine!" I say and reach for the door handle, but he pops the locks down and I turn and attack him with my fangs fully out and clawing at him like a madman. *"What the actual FUCK!"* I growl at him, and he restrains me by pulling me tight to his lap, which is extremely uncomfortable with the stupid steering wheel and this being a sportscar.

"I'm about to explain," he says calmly, and I lunge at him trying to bite his neck, but he pulls me back.

"LIAR! You are stonewalling me! Let me go, *NOW!"*

Brigham releases me and I pop the unlock button and start to open his door, but he pulls me back in the car. I growl at him, and he restrains me again.

"I wasn't stonewalling you—I was distracted. I'm sorry, please, can we talk?"

"Bring me home," I say and try to get to my seat—he resists but then releases me.

I'm so angry right now—I can feel the dawn coming and I can't think straight. *FUCK! What have I done?* I live with a vampire that is being an asshole and now I have nowhere to go! *FUCK, FUCK, FUCK!* This is terrible! I've gotten myself into a very bad situation and it's not like I can go back home, because I gave up my apartment. I'm not even human anymore! I couldn't even go back to school unless the classes were at night or online. And then what? What the hell would I do for money or for a job? I'd have to work at night or remote. *Damn it!* I am so stupid!

"What are you thinking right now?" Brigham asks and I ignore him, staring out my passenger window.

He waits for a few minutes, but I don't answer. I don't want him to know what I am thinking. He puts the car in gear and speeds home. I can feel dawn coming and I start to feel sluggish. He pulls into the underground garage, and I stumble out of the car, barely able to walk. He comes around to my side quickly and picks me up and I stiffen in his arms, not wanting him to touch me.

"Let me get you inside," he says softly and runs me up into the bedroom before I can tell him no.

He sits me on the side of the bed, and I struggle to get my balance due to his speed, sagging forward as my body drains of energy. I hate this part about being a vampire. He pulls my shoes off my feet quietly, not looking at me, and I feel my anger waning as he lifts the dress up over my head and quickly returns with some comfy pajamas. He helps me into them and lays me down on the bed.

Brigham's face is stonier than normal, and I watch him curiously as he undresses, staring out and not looking at anything in particular. I yawn loudly and this draws his attention back to me and his face softens.

"Dawn is coming soon," he says and tentatively sits on the bed next to me and reaches for me, letting his hand sit on my arm. As much as I don't want to forgive him right now, his touch against my skin feels so good and I moan as he rubs the muscles on my arm.

"How long will it affect me like this?" I ask. "As it nears, I lose my ability to function—it's horrible."

"We should have come home sooner, I wasn't thinking. I'm sorry," he says and he looks at me with such sadness, and I know he is apologizing for more than our arrival time at home.

"It's fine." I snuggle heavily onto the pillow, too tired to continue arguing with him right now. "I'm so glad we don't sleep in coffins. I would miss pillows." Brigham laughs and unbuttons his shirt.

"I never liked that part of the vampire fable."

"I'm also glad we can see our reflections in the mirrors—it would be very difficult applying makeup if I couldn't see myself." Brigham stands and removes his pants, throwing his clothes over a chair. I watch as he stands before me in his boxers and removes his watch. His body is so sculpted with muscles and it's hard not to marvel at his form. Did he have these before he was a vampire, and if so, why?

"You don't need to wear makeup—you're beautiful without it," he says and climbs into bed beside me, pulling me close to him.

"It's fun to wear it sometimes."

"I wouldn't know."

"Never had a glam vampire goth stage?"

He kisses my forehead. "No."

"That's too bad, I bet you would look hot covered in glitter and dark mascara."

"I doubt it, but we can try it if you like," he says and kisses my lips. I laugh at that thought. I might take him up on that later.

"I'll remember that." He kisses my cheek and I yawn again. "It's getting closer."

"Yes."

"So that Darren guy—" I feel Brigham's body stiffen against me, but I don't stop my line of questioning. "He didn't seem to like you very much."

"I don't suppose he does," Brigham says, his voice guarded.

"What did you disagree with his sire about?"

"It's a long story…"

"I have lifetimes." I yawn again and try to keep my eyes open.

"Yes, but not at the moment. Right now, you need to sleep."

"Will you tell me tomorrow?" I ask, unable to keep my eyes open any longer. Brigham kisses my lips, and I fade into a memory.

CHAPTER EIGHT

Rainclouds Memory

I could smell the rain in the air. I pulled my black army jacket that I had found at the thrift store around me tighter. I looked up at the large pine tree that was protecting me and turned the volume up on my headphones. Lightning flashed in the sky and the thunder followed quickly behind it and I watched the dark grey clouds move swiftly in the sky. I felt so empty inside—nothing made sense—*nothing*. How was I supposed to fit into this world? Why did I feel these feelings? Why did I always feel so out of place?

More thunder clouds rumbled overhead, and I closed my eyes and felt into them as rain began to sprinkle down upon me, making me smile. I looked up into the dark clouds and felt into them as more rain poured down on me, soaking me. Lightning flashed across the sky followed by another boom of thunder. I wrapped my jacket tighter around me and leaned against the pine tree, feeling the ground underneath me, and was safe within the limbs of the tree.

My ass was soaked, and I shivered from the cold rain, but I didn't want to go back inside. I wanted to stay out here feeling connected to something greater than myself. This was the only time I felt like it was okay to be me. I wiped the rain from my face—eventually I would have to go in and change and get ready for high school, and that thought made my stomach drop. I hated it there. Everyone was so fake and only had silly thoughts—there was no one of substance there and it felt like a huge waste of time. I felt like my life, my real life, was out there somewhere. *Somewhere, not here, but where?*

I sighed and another flash of lightning flickered across the sky. The rumbling of the thunder felt like it was rumbling through my body, and I tried to hold onto that feeling. The thunder felt real, the force and pressure of it. That's what I wanted—something real.

CHAPTER NINE

Shopping

When I woke, Brigham wasn't there. I lay back on my pillows thinking about the memory I had dreamt, the feelings of wanting and despair still haunting me. Things are different for me now and I no longer sought out the storms, but with all those feelings I am having with the new moon drawing closer, sitting out in a storm sounded fantastic!

After I dress, I search the house trying to find Brigham, but he is gone. Brigham always leaves a note for me if he has to leave before I get up, which happens on occasion, because, as a new vampire, I need more sleep than him—but I couldn't find a note anywhere. It is unsettling and not like him. I wasn't meeting Anton until later, so I had a few hours to kill. If I was going to shop with Anton, I would need all the energy I could get, which meant I needed to feed.

I grab a jean jacket and decide to head to the park. I might not be able to find an animal abuser there, but I likely would find someone who liked to beat up on the homeless. It is really depressing that I am getting to know where bad people hung out, but good for the vampire part of me that needed blood. It doesn't take me long to happen upon two college students harassing an elderly woman trying to sleep on a bench and I make quick work of them, practicing my glamouring. I hide their bodies behind some trees and head towards the mall.

"Sorry I'm late," I say as I enter through the mall's doors and try to straighten my hair from running. Anton is sitting on a bench fake sipping a smoothie, looking bored.

"Where were you?"

"Disposing of a very heavy college student."

"You fed without me?" Anton shrieks, making me flinch.

"Sorry, I didn't think you'd mind. You look really nice," I say, hoping a compliment will distract him. He is wearing black jeans, a black t-shirt and a short-sleeve button-down deep blue shirt that is partially unbuttoned.

"I thought we were going to feed together," he pouts, not even hearing my compliment.

"I'm sorry, but I needed energy for shopping. We can still feed after we're done here."

"I don't need your charity."

"Oh stop! You know I like going out with you! I didn't want to ruin your fun tonight by feeling weak and hangry. I was thinking of you, you big baby."

"Oh, so you still want to feed later?" Anton asks hopefully and gives me puppy dog eyes which makes me laugh.

"Yes, I'm sure I'll need to."

"Good."

We walk past stores filled with clothing. Anton seems to know exactly where he wants to go and I barely look at the stores, not exactly hiding my disinterest.

"Please tell me you found some information for me."

"About Jacqueline or that weirdo Darren?" Anton says, crinkling his nose in disgust upon saying Darren's name.

"Both—I still don't know what the hell is going on," I admit and feel my anger at Brigham stir again. I knew that Brigham, having lived so long and being a vampire meant he had a different view of time, but I am irritated that he keeps putting off answering my questions. Since he obviously is avoiding me this morning, I feel less bad about attacking him last night.

"What did Brigham say about that Darren guy?" Anton asks as he looks into a shop window.

"Nothing! He avoided answering me when we got home and was gone this morning when I woke up. I lost it on him and attacked him in the car on the way home."

"You attacked him?" Anton sucks in a breath and looks me up and down, nodding his head with approval.

"*I know right!* I snapped. He was being so dismissive, and I lunged at him. He had to restrain me!"

Anton claps my shoulder. "I would have paid good money to see that!"

"You may not have to pay if he doesn't answer me soon. There may be another opportunity yet."

"That's weird that he didn't' answer you, isn't it?" Anton pretends to sip his smoothie.

"Yeah, I don't know what's going on and I don't like it," I say in frustration. "He hasn't been the most loquacious person, but this is a new level for him."

"Well, *I* did find out a few things!" Anton purrs and gives me a mischievous look.

My mouth drops open wide, and I grab his shoulders shaking him. "You did? You're a God, Anton!"

Anton shoves me off of him. "Yes, I know," he says and straightens his shirt, walking into a store with lots and lots of mannequins wearing men's underwear. I look around at the store in dismay. Where was Anton taking me?

"What did you find out?" I ask as he mills around the store, picking up different pieces of underwear and holding them towards me. I give a thumbs up or down depending on what he holds up. He holds up a red thong, and I give an aggressive thumbs down and he looks disappointed.

"Well, you know how Forseti likes talking about Brigham's and his glory days in New York?"

I sag and roll my eyes. "Ugh, yes. It's so boring."

"Well, I was telling him about my, uh…premature glamouring problem, and asked him if in his young vampire days in New York if he ever had that problem. Which yes, he wasn't a young vampire then, but he totally took the bait." I move my hands in a circular motion for him to move his story along faster and he rolls his eyes at me. "And it turns out it's a very common thing to have."

"Uh huh."

Anton slides a hanger aggressively. "It is!"

I wave him off. "If you say so."

"Forseti was telling me about how you need to focus on—"

"I don't care about the glamouring!"

"You will when you find out that Forseti showed Brigham how to control his glamouring problem by helping him glamour a woman named Jacqueline," Anton says slyly and holds up a red fishnet shirt and I grimace.

"I don't think I am the right person for this shopping spree. What are you buying these for exactly?"

Anton huffs. "I am trying to be prepared for all possibilities."

"What kind of possibilities?" I ask and look around the store again. "Sexual possibilities?" I whisper, leaning closer to him.

Anton stomps his foot a little and turns towards me with a menacing glare. "Yes, as it happens."

"Oh," I say and look around the store again. "Then maybe, yes, to the red fishnet thingy, but I think maybe get them in different colors—you know, depending on if it is a playful or more…domineering mood."

Anton smiles at me. "I knew I had the right woman for the job!"

"Okay, so back to this Jacqueline person—and I don't believe you that Brigham had a premature glamouring problem."

Anton growls and pretends to strangle me with his hands. "Fine! I was lying about that—Brigham didn't have an issue—but this next part is true. Apparently, Brigham glamoured this woman and eventually turned her into a vampire," Anton says in a low voice.

"Wow," I say, my mouth dropping open. I'm completely stunned.

"Brigham and Jacqueline were together for *years* after that."

My stomach drops a little, and an unease settles in me. What is this emotion I am feeling? Is it jealousy? Apprehension? Inadequacy? "How many years?" I croak out, surprising myself that I am feeling thrown off that they had been together so long. Brigham's and my relationship was the longest I had been in, and suddenly that seems very pathetic.

"Forseti didn't say exactly, but it sounded like a long time," Anton huffs, looking through the rack and pulls out some shiny, tight—looking shirts and puts them on his arm.

"Did he say how she died?" I ask and move to the rack, looking for something for Anton. I find a section of open-front-bikini-and-boxer style underwear and gasp. I had no idea they even made these. I hand Anton a few of them and keep moving down the rack.

"He didn't mention that, but he did mention that mid-century Brigham and Jacqueline separated," Anton purrs, enjoying dishing out his story slowly to me.

I gasp and look at him while holding up a pair of G-string underwear with a cock ring built in it. "Separated?"

He grabs the garment from me and looks at it and smirks, adding it to his pile of clothes. "He said she went off to the country with another vampire."

My mouth drops open. "Brigham was dumped?" I can hardly believe it! Who would do that? I was absolutely floored.

"Sounds like he was," Anton says, smiling at me with satisfaction.

"I'm so shocked right now. This is blowing my mind. She had to be insane, right? Who would dump Brigham?" I move to a table with small velvety bags with ties and hold one up trying to figure out how someone would wear it, then look at the model who has the bag tied to their junk and realize what I am looking at. I shake my head—that doesn't even look comfortable or fun.

Anton looks at the mannequin and then looks at me hopefully, and I shake my head, and he slumps and looks dejected. "I'll keep digging for info."

"What about this Darren guy? Who is he?"

"I didn't get a chance to ask Forseti about that. Once I got him started on New York, he went on forever," Anton moans. "I barely made it out alive."

"Yikes, sorry about that."

"You so owe me, but I did asked Gregory about him, and he gave me some good info too." Anton holds up a black pleather half-shoulder tank, and I give him a thumbs up and blush.

"This is getting awkward."

"I have to do this before the new moon and before Brigham can see in your head. He may not approve of this kind of shopping with me after that," Anton says, as his head tilts down and he frowns.

"Yes, we can. He'll be able to see that I am not thinking about you that way—it will be fine."

Anton rolls his eyes and holds up a pair of black, mesh boxers with a pleather front-panel that can detach. "Do you think he will like me showing these to you?"

I laugh. "I don't even like you showing me those. Okay, point taken, and those go in the yes pile." Anton raises his eyebrows at me and looks at the garment again. "Just get it, trust me. Who's Gregory, again?"

Anton sighs. "He's the really tall red-haired vampire that runs the Crystal Club."

"Oh yeah, sorry, I've met a lot of vampires this month."

"Anyways, he said Darren used to live here maybe a hundred years ago with a vampire named Shawn."

"We knew that already," I groan and aggressively sort through some garments. I needed to feed again soon. Maybe it is because it is so close to the new moon, but I seem ravenous lately.

"Shawn, I guess, is not a favorite among the vampires."

"Why is that?"

"Gregory said he's not very discreet about his victims and would leave big, gory scenes and draw a lot of attention to the Vampire Guild—and that's a big no-no."

"My guess is he wasn't into vigilante vampirism like us."

"Butterfly, most of the vampires don't hunt like we do," Anton says, giving me a pointed look.

"I try not to think about that," I say, scrunching up my nose.

"Me too," Anton says with a sigh. He looks around the store and moves to the toys and gestures, and I give the thumbs up again.

"I say go wild—one of everything!"

Anton looks at the display and bites his thumb. "Really?"

I nod. "Some of the stuff that looks fun doesn't end up being fun and some of the stuff that you'd think isn't fun ends up being the most fun."

"Good to know, thanks. I guess this Shawn guy has a very borderline personality. He was into torturing his victims, real sick stuff. Everyone was really happy when he left."

"Good riddance."

"My thoughts exactly."

"Hmm…"

Anton stops his shopping and looks at me. "What is wrong?"

"Well, it's Darren," I say and rub my cheek. "Why would he live with a sicko like Shawn? He seemed like an okay guy until the whole Brigham conversation got weird."

"I don't understand vampires any better than I do humans." Anton shrugs and grabs some vibrators off the wall, and I point to a large purple one and he grabs it as well.

"Hmmm…very interesting." I give Anton a side hug. "Thanks for sleuthing for me, I appreciate it."

"I love a good gossip, it was fun!"

"Do you think there is a connection between Darren, Shawn, and Jacqueline?"

"It's possible."

"Brigham was weirded out after seeing Darren, and I thought he was avoiding me to get out of answering my questions now. Now I *know* he is." I push a garment on a rack a little aggressively and it makes a screeching sound, making me flinch and I continue, "Which is so freaking weird. It's cowardly, which is so unlike him."

"That's what I do when I don't want to tell you something," Anton mutters under his breath.

"Nice," I say sarcastically.

"You can be pretty relentless when you want something—sometimes it is easier to avoid you and get out of your way."

"I'm not that bad."

"Do I really need to mention Brandon's arm?" I flinch and rub my forehead.

"That reminds me, I should apologize to him," I sigh heavily. I had been avoiding it since I'd been back.

"Good luck with that," Anton says sarcastically.

"I feel really bad about it."

"He'll get over it."

"You think so?"

"No, not really, but I don't want you to freak out," Anton says, giving me a small smile and turns and heads to the checkout counter.

"Damn it!" I groan and run my hands through my hair. "So where are we going shopping next?"

"I think the question is where *aren't* we going shopping." I let out a small whimper and rub my face. Anton responds with, "Hey, none of that! If you complain at all during this outing, I'll stop asking about Darren and Jacqueline."

"Fine," I huff and jam my hands in my jacket pockets. *This is torture!*

Many, many shops later, I am Anton's packing mule, carrying more bags than I care to count. It is a good thing I was a vampire, or I wouldn't be able to carry all the bags, and I am beginning to think Anton wanted me for this purpose and not my fashion opinion after all.

"Hey, look!" I point across the food court to a tall man with dark hair in a textured, long crop-cut. "It's Darren!" I whisper to Anton.

Anton looks to where I am pointing and smirks. "I wonder if he's looking to glamour himself some dinner."

"Should I go talk to him?" I ask, setting Anton's bags down on a bench.

"Do you think that's a good idea?" Anton asks, looking at me like I am crazy.

"I don't know, that's why I asked you," I say honestly. "You are supposed to be the stable one."

"Well…" Anton looks towards Darren and hesitates. "You *could* talk to him. I mean, whatever beef he has with Brigham has nothing to do with you."

"Right—besides, maybe I can find out what the whole big issue is and fix it!"

"I say go for it—but if Brigham gets pissed, I officially tried to discourage you, for the record," Anton says and counts his bags, making sure I hadn't dropped any.

"Alright, wait here," I say excitedly and smooth out my shirt.

"Why can't I come?" Anton pouts, sticking his lower lip out.

"Because—well—I don't know why, just let me try to talk to him alone." Anton's face looks hurt. "I'm going to tell you everything he said as soon as I get back."

"You better!" and says as he sits down on the bench in a huff, glaring at me.

"I will. Wish me luck," I say and try to walk like a human at a decent, normal speed, which is really hard to do now.

"Good luck," Anton says with so much attitude in his voice that I look back at him and stick my tongue out at him.

I walk cautiously over to Darren. He is wearing stone-washed, ripped jeans, and has on a tight, white t-shirt that shows off his physique. I don't know why, but I feel like what I am about to do is wrong. Was it a strange loyalty to Brigham that made me feel that way? I'm not sure, but I am too curious about what the disagreement is about to head back to Anton.

I notice Darren is talking to a young teenage girl who is sipping a yogurt drink and staring wide-eyed at him with a huge grin on her face. He is obviously glamouring the young girl and as I approach, I hesitate. I didn't want to rudely interrupt him. I am about to turn back to Anton when Darren sees me. He stares at me for a moment with a look of uncertainty. I smile at him meekly and he grins back, dropping the glamouring spell on the girl. She looks confused at Darren and walks away from him in a daze.

"Sorry," I say as I approach. "I didn't realize what you were doing until I got closer—I'm still figuring this whole vampire etiquette thing," I whisper.

"No worries, there's lot of fish in the sea." He gestures around the mall. He is right about that. The food court is filled with teens and preteens. "I'm sorry I was so rude yesterday—it had to be unpleasant for you to be caught in between Brigham and me."

I blink at him in surprise. "It was interesting, that's for sure, but I didn't really understand what was going on to be honest."

"Really? Brigham has never mentioned Shawn to you?" Darren asks, tilting his head at me, his brows furrowing.

"Shawn?" I shake my head. "No."

Darren rubs his jaw for a moment, looking at me curiously. "Interesting."

"Shawn's your sire?"

"Yes," Darren says and there is an edge back in his voice again.

"You don't like talking about him," I blurt out and Darren's eyes go wide for a moment. He bites the inside of his cheek. "What is his problem with Brigham?"

He flinches. "I'm not sure if I should be the one to tell you."

"Why is that?"

Darren looks at me for a few moments, and I think he is not going to answer me but says softly, "It's not my story to tell." I sigh and look back at Anton who is watching us, trying not to look too obvious. "So do you love Brigham?"

I turn back to him., not sure he really just asked me that flat out. "Excuse me?"

"Sorry, I'm just curious," Darren says, and his eyes seem to darken.

"Yes, I do," I say, studying his face. *Why does his mood change so much?*

"And does he love you?" Darren asks, with the same edge in his voice again.

"Yes."

"Has he said it to you?" Darren asks, his voice seeming strained.

"All the time." Darren pauses and looks at me closely. I don't understand why Darren is so interested in Brigham and my love life—it is a little odd.

Darren shudders and rolls his shoulders. "Well, I'm glad for him." He looks away from me. "He deserves the best," he growls coldly. I take a step back from him, and he smiles weakly at me and bites his lip for a second. "Sorry, I know I'm being confusing."

"Emotions can be complicated," I say slowly, and I notice his eyes are lighter again. "Did Brigham do something to you?"

"Me?" Darren laughs. "No, to my sire."

"What did he do?"

"This isn't something that we should discuss here." Darren looks cautiously at the people eating around us.

"Why not?" Darren's eyes drifted to where Anton is anxiously standing now, and his eyes darkened again. "Because of Anton?"

"I've heard he's a bit of a gossip," Darren says and gives me a wicked smile.

"Not any more than the other vampires," I lie.

"Either way, I'd feel better discussing this in private," Darren says, giving me a big smile that shows his canines, as a shudder runs through me. My body is telling me to run right now from him. *Like, right fucking now!*

I smile at him, trying to hide what I am feeling, and feel so grateful that Anton is with me today. "I don't think that's possible."

"Why do you say that?"

"Brigham's being very protective of me as the new moon is drawing near."

"That's because he's a good sire," Darren says sincerely. I did not understand this guy. He ran so hot and cold. One moment he seemed to be bubbling with anger and the next he was very sweet.

"He is."

"He must trust Anton a lot to let you out with him," Darren says, gesturing to Anton.

"Anton's a good guy."

"Do you think Anton would let us have a discussion in private?" he asks and smiles at me again with his predatory smile.

"We're doing that now."

"I mean, alone, without him being around."

I hesitate. I don't really want to be alone with Darren, but I did want to know more about this grudge Brigham and

Darren's sire had with each other. "I don't see why not. Do you want to go somewhere now?"

"I have plans tonight, but tomorrow I am free. How about I meet you at a coffee shop? How about Café Enlightenment? I'd feel more comfortable discussing the situation if I knew Anton wasn't eavesdropping."

"Okay," I say slowly. "What time?"

"Let's say eight o'clock."

"Okay, I'll see you then." I say and turn from him feeling slightly nauseous. *This guy is freaking weird!*

"Until then," Darren says a little too darkly and I turn back to look at him, noticing his eyes oscillating from pitch black to a dark brown, and the hairs on my arm stand on end.

I walk back to Anton trying not to move too quickly, which is hard because I really want to run the hell out of this mall. There is something not right with Darren. I hadn't spent a lot of time hanging out with many vampires, so maybe I am overreacting, but the hairs standing on end on my neck told me I'm not.

"So, what did creepy guy say?" Anton asks, keeping his eyes on Darren.

I start grabbing Anton's bags. "Not much, he wants to meet me at a coffee shop tomorrow," I whisper.

"Why the hell would he want to do that?" Anton hisses, leaning towards me.

"To tell me more about Shawn and Brigham's disagreement, but there's a catch," I say while grabbing up the last of Anton's bags.

"What's the catch?" he asks, his eyes wide.

"You can't be there," I say and start walking away from the food court quickly.

Anton scoffs loudly and follows me. "Why the hell not?"

"He thinks you're a gossip," I say over my shoulder at him. I can tell he is really pissed because he has his fists balled at his sides and looks like he is about to strike out at something.

"What the hell would make him think that?"

"I don't know, but that was his excuse to meet me alone."

"*Bullshit!* I'm not a gossip!"

"Well, he won't talk to me if you're there, so you'll have to stay away. It's the only way I can find out what is going on."

"Brigham will be pissed if I let you go there alone," Anton groans and rubs his temple.

"Too bad for him."

"Easy for you to say—he's not going to tear your throat out when he finds out."

"Oh, he wouldn't do that," I say, shaking my head. "You can be so dramatic sometimes!"

"I've told you—I've heard stories about him!" Anton says, grabbing my shoulder and making me stop walking.

"Look, if I don't meet him, I might not find out what's going on, and I really need to know."

"Brigham will tell you eventually. Can't you be patient?"

"I don't know. I don't think he's going to tell me. Not before the new moon anyway. This all feels wrong, and I am freaking out!"

"Why do you have to know before then? What's the difference?"

"I..." I hesitate. "I want to make sure I have all the information about Brigham and this vampire thing before I turn completely."

"Why? You said you weren't going to escape again. You can't not go through with it—you will die!" Anton angry whispers and lips tremble slightly.

"I know, and I am going to go through with it, but I..." My eyes start to well with tears and I desperately try to keep them in. I don't want to look like a freak in the mall. Anton squeezes my shoulder.

"It's alright, you don't have to explain. I get it," Anton says softly, and I lean my head on his shoulder, trying not to squish his bags.

"So, you'll help me?" I mumble into his shirt.

"Yeah, of course I will, but if you sell me out to Brigham, we're through—and I mean that because I will be dead."

"I won't sell you out. I pinky promise."

"Good, because I like this whole vampire lifestyle and I want to be a vampire for a long time. This looks good on me," he quips as he gives me a vogue pose, and I can't help but laugh. *He does make a good vampire!*

CHAPTER TEN

Avoidance

It is minutes to sunrise and Brigham isn't home yet. I am starting to worry. He never cuts it this close, not even when I was still human and we were dating. I walk through the halls, checking the rooms making sure he hadn't come in and I had missed him. I find Brandon in the library putting a folder of papers on Brigham's desk. He is wearing all black and looks rather ominous standing in the room with his big muscular frame.

"Brandon?" I whisper as softly as I can, trying not to startle him. Brandon jumps a foot at the sound of my voice, dropping the papers he had in his hand on the floor. "Sorry." I rush over and pick up his papers from the ground. I try to hand them to him, and he reaches for them cautiously.

"Thanks," he mumbles, avoiding my gaze.

"I've been meaning to talk to you."

Brandon's posture stiffens and he begins to slowly make his way to the door. I follow, trying not to seem aggressive.

"I wanted to apologize for breaking your arm."

"I should have let you leave," he says tensely as his eyes shift to the door.

"You were only doing your job. It's my fault."

"Don't worry about it—Brigham fixed it."

"I know, but I still shouldn't have done that to you."

Brandon reaches the door, and his eyes dart down the hallway as if he is looking for help. The horror of that fact makes my chest hurt. I want to fix things between us so badly!

"It's fine," he says gruffly.

I reach for his hand, and he jerks away from me.

"Don't touch me!" he growls, and I flinch at his words.

"Sorry, I wasn't going to do anything."

"I'm so sick of you fucking vampires!" he yells and takes a step towards me, and I back up as he raises his clenched fists. I wasn't afraid of him physically hurting me, but if he did strike at me, I might really hurt him—and I didn't want to do that again.

"Sorry?"

"You think you can do whatever you want without any consequences!"

I blink at him. *I didn't think that!* I was trying to apologize. "Brandon, I know—"

"Butterfly, I don't care! I don't care if you feel bad, and I don't care if you're sorry!" He glowers down at me, and his face darkens. "I just don't care. Tell Brigham I can't do this anymore. Tell him I quit." He turns and walks quickly away from me, and I stare at him in disbelief.

"Fuck, that didn't go as well as I had hoped," I mumble to myself and slump down in Brigham's chair. Now I'll have to tell Brigham that Brandon quit! He's going to think I did something else to him! I get up slowly and head back to the bedroom, feeling utterly defeated.

I sit on the edge of the bed with my head between my hands. It is seconds from sunrise, and I am exhausted. I can feel the sun pulling me to sleep, Brigham still isn't here, and I am worried. We had never been separated the entire night since I had become a vampire. I worry something bad has happened to him. Would anyone from the Vampire Guild come tell me if it had? Was I his emergency contact? *I had no idea!* I couldn't call or text him because I'd be damned if I am going to come off like the clingy girlfriend.

Suddenly, the door opens and Brigham walks in.

"Where were you?" I cry.

Brigham freezes and then rushes towards me. "Sorry, Butterfly.

"I thought you were dead!" I scream and try to move towards him but stumble off the bed and fall to the floor.

He kneels down to me and holds me to his torso, and I slump against him. "Why would you think that?"

"I didn't know where you were, and you've never been this late before. You didn't leave a note! I had no idea where you were."

Brigham looks around the room at our nightstand and sighs. "I'm sorry, Butterfly, I wasn't thinking. I got caught up talking with the Vampire Guild about an urgent matter and I lost track of time. I knew you were going with Anton today and I must have forgotten to write you a note. I'm sorry."

I try to raise my head to look at him but cannot as my body seems to be turning to stone. "What were you talking to them about?"

"It's nothing you need to worry about, Butterfly," he says and presses a kiss to the top of my head.

"God damn it!" I yell—or try to yell—but it comes out more like a whimper. I had *had* it. I am exhausted and had been holding back hysteria for too long. "What are you keeping from me now?" Tears well in my eyes and I try to brush them away, but my arms are like lead weights at my side and the tears run down my cheeks, soaking his shirt in red.

"Why are you so upset?" he whispers as he carries me to the bed.

"Because you're being so *GOD DAMN SECRETIVE!*"

He brushes my tears away and starts rubbing my arms and they start to tingle, and I feel some relief as energy trickles back into them. "No, I'm not."

"Yes, you are!"

"Butterfly, you're exhausted. I'm sorry I'm late—I meant to be back here sooner. I'm sorry I didn't leave a note." He tries to hug me, but I push him away, having some use in my arms now.

"Don't touch me, I'm leaving." More tears run down my cheeks. I try to stand, but my legs give out and I fall forward, and he catches me and holds me up.

"You can't go out there, the sun is out now," he says and rubs the tears away from my face.

"I don't care." I try to pry his hands off my arms, but they grow heavier by the second, the little surge of energy that was just in them dissipating rapidly. I groan in frustration and sag in his arms and begin to sob harder. *This sucks!* I can't trust Brigham anymore and I am stuck in this form.

"Oh, Butterfly," he murmurs to me, gently picking me up and holding me in his arms.

"I hate you," I cry. Brigham gently carries me back to bed. He lays me down and encircles his body around mine. I try to turn away from him, but he holds his hand against my face, making me look at him. I close my eyes, trying to shut him out and he laughs softly.

"Don't laugh at me," I growl at him.

"I'm not laughing at you," Brigham says seriously—but I keep my eyes shut, trying to block him out.

"I was worried," I hiss.

"I realize that, and I'm very sorry I did that to you. I am not used to having someone depend on me like this. I'm sorry if I hurt you—that was not what I intended."

"I don't want to sleep—I need to know what's going on," I say and try to open my eyes, but they are heavy, and it takes all my effort to get them to flutter.

"Nothing is going on," he attempts to assure me as he touches my eyelids. They tingle a tiny bit, and I get them to open up the slightest amount. I can see his shirt but can't see his face.

"Yes, there is!" I insist. Why is he lying to me? What is he hiding from me?

Brigham kisses my forehead. "Shhhh…honey, you need to sleep."

"Brandon quit. I tried to apologize, but he hates me," I say quietly.

"Ah…"

"I didn't mean to hurt him."

"It was my fault, my dear," he says as he pulls me in closer to him and wraps his arms tightly around me.

"I don't want to sleep," I groan and feel myself sinking into darkness.

"I know," Brigham says and runs his hands through my hair, and I feel myself relax and grow heavier.

"You have to tell me about Jacqueline and Darren," I murmur, fighting as hard as I can to stave off sleep.

"I will, but first, you have to sleep."

"I—"

"Shhhh…everything is going to be okay, Butterfly," Brigham runs his hand across my cheek, and I feel myself slipping into a memory. "You'll feel better in the morning, but you need to sleep now."

CHAPTER ELEVEN

Brigham stood next to me on a small hill overlooking a lake. It was cool outside, and he was wearing a dark wool coat. Below us, a path was lit by streetlights. It was early into the evening, and the sun had set minutes ago. People walked, ran, and biked the path below, unaware that there were two vampires watching them.

"What do you feel?" Brigham asked, gently touching my back.

I closed my eyes and searched myself.

"Restless, hungry, but I don't want food…I want something else, but I don't know what that is."

"That's the bloodlust."

I scrunched up my nose at the sensation. "It's a weird sensation. It reminds me of the same ache I feel when I'm lonely."

Brigham cocked his head and his hair fell into his face. "When were you lonely?"

I shrugged. "Before I met you."

"But you have lots of friends," Brigham said, looking at me curiously.

"Yes, but I don't always connect with them—not on a significant enough level to ease the loneliness." I shrugged again. "Maybe loneliness is the wrong word—it's more of an emptiness, a missingness."

"I understand that," Brigham said slowly, and his eyes lingered on me for a moment before he looked out at the park.

"Do you?"

"Yes, I've felt that way for years," he said softly and I felt him rub my back.

"I would think that must have been very difficult, living as a vampire with that feeling."

"It was," he said and gave me a slight smile.

"Do you feel less lonely now, since you've made me?" I asked and studied his face. His eyes gleamed and he smiled at me.

"I've felt less lonely since I met you."

I smiled at him and then winced and grab my throat. "I'm getting very achy," I said and turned my head back to the people. "But I don't want to do something I will regret—I'm afraid I'm going to lose control and bite someone I don't mean to." I tried to keep the panic out of my voice, but the possibility of losing control was bubbling to the surface. I tied my jacket tighter around me as if it would restrain me and looked at the people with apprehension.

"That might happen—it's very difficult controlling your thirst when you're young," Brigham said solemnly. I cringed—that was not what I wanted to hear.

"But you'll help me, right?"

"Of course."

"Good," I sighed in relief. "So, how do I scan humans again?"

"First, focus on one person." Brigham looked down at the park. "Do you see the man by the light post tying his shoe?"

I followed his gaze and saw a man in his mid-forties kneeling on the ground. He was large and balding and had worked up a sweat with his jog. "It's easier if you look at him—eventually, you will be able to scan an entire room without looking up at anyone, but for now, look at him and feel his presence."

I bit my lip. "How do I do that?"

"Focus on his movements—his breathing, his heartbeat."

I stared at the man and watched as he inhaled and exhaled rapidly. I strained my ears and heard the faintest of heartbeats.

"Okay," I said, feeling relieved. *I had done it!* "Now what?"

"Now, let go of yourself. Let the barriers of your mind drop. Feel yourself moving into him."

I imagined myself merging with him, and suddenly my body moved towards him. Brigham's hand shot out and held me in place.

"That's okay, that happens to everyone. The first time I tried to scan someone I bumped right into them. Imagine your spiritual self, your soul, merging with his—not your body." I nodded and focused back on the man. *This was hard!*

I felt myself getting closer to the man. I was standing next to him, touching his skin, and then I was inside of him. I saw his nearest memories—walking to the park, getting ready at home, watching television, driving his car home, sitting at his cubicle.

"I see his memories, but what about his emotions? Right now, it's like watching television without the sound," I whispered, trying not to lose the connection.

"That'll come, it takes practice. Now, scan further—see if you can see his childhood."

Images of playgrounds and classrooms flashed in my mind.

"He went to grade school in Iowa," I said, smiling. *It was working! I was doing it!*

"Good," Brigham said with pride in his voice.

"He's never had any pets, and barely went to the zoo," I said, my voice filled with disappointment.

Brigham chuckled. "It might be challenging to find victims that meet your criteria. Are you sure you want to continue with that?"

"I'd like to try," I said and touched my forehead. The ache inside me was growing larger and my head was starting to hurt. "But I need to drink, and I don't feel right."

Brigham noticed the pain and panic in my voice, and his brows furrowed. "I found someone that will work a few days ago, he lives nearby," he said, looping his arm in mine.

My mouth gaped. "You found someone for me?"

"I knew it would be hard for you the first few days and thought it best to have a few people lined up. When you get your stamina built up, you'll be able to find your own victims."

I jumped at Brigham and threw my arms around him, hugging him. "That's the nicest thing anyone has ever done for me!"

"I knew it was important to you. Come." He grabbed my hand and began to lead me away from the park. "We'll knock on the door and I'll glamour him. Once we're inside, we can practice your scanning and glamouring techniques."

"I don't know if I can wait that long."

"If you can't wait, I'll glamour him and you can drain him, then we'll go to the next house and practice there."

"I can't believe you lined up victims for me," I said quietly, feeling so overwhelmed with emotion. *He really cared about me!*

"I love you, Butterfly. I would do anything for you," he said and his face softened. Brigham threw an arm around me and pulled me in close to him. I wrapped my arm around his waist, and we walked to my victim's house.

I woke up late into the night. I slept much longer than normal and am disoriented as I look around the room. Brigham is no longer lying next to me, and in his place, a note had been placed. It read:

Butterfly,

You were so exhausted that I didn't want to wake you when I left. I love you very much and am very sorry I got home so late. Unfortunately, I am going to be tied up with the Vampire Guild today and will be home late again. Please don't worry, I will be home before sunrise. I promise I will discuss Jacqueline and Darren with you as soon as I can.

Love,
Brigham

I crumple the note in my hand. Something is up and I know that Brigham is avoiding me now. If he isn't going to tell me what is going on, *I am going to find out for myself!*

CHAPTER TWELVE

Secret Meeting

"You're not wearing that, are you?" Anton asks, looking at me like I am wearing a clown suit.

I look at the red, sleeveless dress I had slipped on. "What's wrong with it? This is something you bought for me."

"It makes you look sexy."

"So?"

"You can't go on a secret date with a guy looking like a harlot," Anton says, running his hand through his hair that was perfectly coifed, per normal. He is wearing a grey vest and pants, with a white and grey shirt and looks very nice, again, per normal.

"Oh, please," I say shaking my head. "It's not a date."

"If Brigham sees you, that's what he'll think."

"No, he won't. Anyways, what do you think I should wear?"

"A lumpy sweater," Anton quips and crosses his arms over his chest.

"What?" I ask and shake my head. There is no way he was serious!

"Yes, something big and baggy."

"You're being insane—plus, you threw away all my sweaters for that same reason. I think you said to me, and I quote, 'you're a vampire now, and vampires do not wear lumpy sweaters' end quote."

Anton rolls his eyes. "Vampires don't usually go on secrets dates either," he mutters, and I stick my tongue out at him. "I'm finding you something else," he huffs and searches my closet, throwing clothes on the floor. "How about this?" He pulls out a black knit long-sleeved dress with a V-neck and holds it up to me. I slip on the dress.

"How do I look?" I ask, turning in a circle for him.

"It'll do, but you still look a little sultry," Anton says, twisting his face as he looks at me dissatisfied.

I look down and inspect myself. "It's covering everything up."

"I know, but that just gets guys more excited."

I huff and roll my eyes. "What doesn't get guys excited? Why are you being so weird?"

"I don't know," he groans and moves to the bed, flopping down on it. "I'm nervous, I think. I've got a bad feeling about all of this. What if Brigham thinks I let you go on a date, gets pissed and decapitates me before I can explain to him what you're up to?"

"Are you really that scared of him?" I ask and walk over to a vanity and start pulling out makeup.

"Yes," Anton says, his face scrunching up as he walks over to me, looking at the cosmetics I have pulled out. He grabs the powder out of my hand and selects something else, spinning me around to face him as he starts applying it to me.

"Are you going to tell me the stories you've heard about him?"

Anton hesitates and his jaw clenches. "You won't like them."

"Tell me already—I want to know why your undies are in a bunch. I've seen what kind of undies you have now, and they are probably bunched," I say with a snicker.

"I wasn't going to tell you this even though I said I would get you info on those Darren and Shawn guys," he says, shaking his head and using a makeup sponge to blend in my foundation.

"What did you find out?"

"Apparently, Shawn and Brigham had a huge blowout over a woman."

"A woman?"

"Yes."

I gasp. "Was it Jacqueline?"

"The vampire I talked to didn't know the woman's name, but I wouldn't be surprised if it was her. He said Brigham almost decapitated Shawn during a fight over this chick."

"Really?" My chest tightens. If Brigham almost decapitated Shawn, it must mean he really loved this woman. I suddenly feel very uncertain—I've never felt that passionate about anyone besides Brigham…

"Yeah, know, right? It's a lot!" Anton says and looks at the colors of eyeshadow I have laid out. He rubs his temple and then reluctantly selects one.

"Jesus, I can't picture Brigham angry enough to do that."

"Guys can get crazy when a woman is involved," Anton says with a shrug. "Close your eyes."

"I guess," I say and obediently close my eyes.

"Anyways, it was bad, and the Shawn guy barely got out alive."

I open my eyes and Anton hisses at me. "He's already dead—he's a vampire," I point out.

Anton makes a face at me in the mirror. "You know what I mean. Now *CLOSE* your eyes!"

I close my eyes and Anton starts applying more eyeshadow. "I don't believe it. How reliable is your source?"

"Reliable. I've gotten a lot of good information out of him in the past."

"But Brigham never gets mad. Last night, I had waited up for him—it was seconds before sunrise, and I was exhausted. He came in and I freaked out on him, crying and hitting him, and he barely reacted."

"Hmmm…"

"I even said I hated him and he didn't even flinch."

Anton pauses with a makeup brush held midair and I peek at him. "You said you hated him?"

"I was exhausted, out of my mind. I didn't mean it."

Anton's eyes narrow. "Can I ask you something personal?"

"Go ahead."

"When is Brigham the most emotionally expressive with you?" I smile at Anton and get embarrassed, and he makes a face. "When you're having sex, right?"

"Yeah."

"Would you say he's a very passionate person?" he asks while selecting a lipstick for me and handing it to me.

"Oh, God yes!" I say and apply the lipstick.

"Well, think about it. Brigham is capable of exhibiting strong emotions. I bet when he gets mad, *really mad*, he's explosive."

I pause, remembering our first night together after he had made me, and frown.

"What is it?" Anton asks.

"I think you might be right. I'd never thought of it that way." I grab a necklace off my dresser and clasped it around my neck.

"Maybe you shouldn't go out tonight. Be patient—Brigham will tell you what you want to know eventually."

"I don't think he is going to tell me before the new moon phase, and I need to know before then." I give Anton a pleading look and he groans.

"Okay, but you have to call me the second you're done meeting with him."

"You're still going to let me go by myself?"

"Sort of. I'm going to wait in my car around the block after I drop you off."

"He'll see you if you drop me off." I put an earring in my ear.

"I'll drop you off a block away—you can walk in."

"Great! So how do I look?"

"Still too good. Don't you own any frumpy clothing?"

"You threw them all out, remember?"

"Oh, right," Anton sighs and smiles to himself. "They *were* pretty horrible. I wasn't thinking I'd ever want you to look less attractive to someone."

"See, if Darren falls in love with me tonight, it'll be your fault. Or, at least, that's what I'll tell Brigham," I tease.

"That's not funny! We already know he got dumped once—if he gets dumped again, it might set him right over the edge!"

"Jesus, chill. You're really worried, huh?"

"I really like my head—it looks good with all my clothes. I kind of want to keep it!"

I pat Anton on the shoulder. "I promise I won't let Brigham decapitate you."

"Thanks," Anton says, unconvinced, flicking my hand away from him.

Anton drops me off a block away like we agreed, and I walk nervously up to the coffee shop. I didn't know exactly why I needed to know what the story was between Brigham, Darren, and Shawn, but I couldn't let it go. I had a feeling there was something big I still didn't know about yet. I wanted to know everything about what had happened between them before becoming a full-strength vampire.

As I enter the coffee shop, patrons joke and drink coffee on small tables. It is always a little disconcerting when I enter stores these days, because now, I am an apex predator. Whenever I come across a human, I scan their mind, searching for a hint of badness in them that would give me an excuse to feed on them. I used to enter a coffee shop scouting for hot guys—a lot had changed in a month.

"Butterfly, you made it!" Darren says excitedly from the back of the coffee shop. Standing up from the table, he pulls out the chair for me to sit next to him. He is wearing khakis and a checkered black-and-tan button-down shirt and had his hair gelled and styled. *Oh crap!* Did he think this *was* a date?

"Did you not think I was going to show?" I ask innocently. I sit down at the table and notice that Darren had bought a cup of coffee, and I wonder if I should do the same—it was important to look like a normal person these days.

"I had my doubts Anton would let you come," he says, shrugging and giving me a warm smile.

"I explained everything to him, and he was fine with letting me come," I say honestly.

"He knows you're here?" Darren's face contorts.

"Yes," I say, giving him a direct look. I wasn't a complete idiot—even though I was a vampire now, I was still a woman, and safety was always a concern.

"Huh…" Darren says and he stares down at his cup as his brows furrow.

"Is that a problem?"

"What? No, of course not. I'm just surprised, that's all. I assume Brigham has no idea you're here. He wouldn't like you talking to me."

"Why is that?" I ask, not answering his question. This guy *is* a little weird.

Darren smiles at me, his eyes doing that weird color fluctuating thing again. "Has Brigham ever told you about his disagreement with Shawn?"

"Bits and pieces—he's not the biggest talker," I lie.

"Interesting."

"What's their problem with each other, exactly?"

"I don't think we should discuss this here, do you? I mean, if a human overhears us telling vampire tales, they might get the wrong idea."

"That we're vampires?"

"Yes, exactly."

I look at him, and an uneasy feeling starts to grow in me. Why the hell did he suggest this place then? Wasn't it a rule to never go to a second location with a creeper?

"Where do you want to go?" I ask, trying to keep the suspicion out of my voice.

"My hotel," he says with a smile and my stomach drops. *Gross!*

"*Your hotel?*" I say, raising my eyebrow at him. *Was he serious right now?*

Darren laughs. "Don't worry, Butterfly, you're not my type. I'm gay."

"Oh," I say, but continue to stare at him, giving him what I hope is my stoniest face.

"Shall we go?"

I stare at him a moment more before answering. What is with this guy? This is starting to get annoying. Maybe

I should listen to Anton and wait for Brigham to tell me the whole story.

"How far is your hotel from here?"

"It's really close—I am staying at the Marriott." I nod, not really believing him. This is the part of the movie where the audience is screaming at the damsel to run. I should leave now—that would be the smartest thing to do.

"Okay…" I say slowly. "Let me touch up my makeup, I'll be right back." I stand and walk towards the bathroom.

"You look fine," he says quickly and tries to reach for me.

I dodge him, hoping no humans notice how fast I had just moved and say over my shoulder to him. "I'll just be a minute." I head to the bathroom and enter a stall to dial Anton's number.

"Hello?" Anton says, his voice strained. "Butterfly— what the hell is going on in there? *The suspense is killing me!*"

"Darren wants me to go to his hotel room. He says he's staying at the Marriott."

"I told you he's making the moves on you!" Anton hisses.

"He's not—he said he's gay, but something is not right."

"It's a line! I use it all the time, on women, and then they miraculously turn me straight. Or, I tell men I'm straight, and then they miraculously turn me gay. Being bisexual really *is* the best!"

"You don't really do that, do you? It's wrong on so many levels!" I hit my head with my hand. "Okay, after all this, we are getting you some therapy!"

"Yes, I do—it's fine! I'm fine! It makes—oh never mind—I'll tell you about it later. Look, you can't go with him to his hotel room. Brigham will hunt me down if he finds out about this!"

"I know it is a bad idea, but I haven't found out anything yet. That's why I am calling you—in case things go south."

"Come on, Butterfly! I don't like this! Things are already going south—we are in the Southern Hemisphere, already! You never go to a second location with someone! That is the number one rule on how *not* to get murdered!"

"Can you please follow us to the hotel?" I plead.

"I still don't like this. I'm picking you up," Anton says harshly.

"Please, Anton—just give me an hour, then you can call me, and I'll leave." Anton groans.

"Fine, but that's it. If you're not out of the hotel by then, I'm breaking down doors and calling Brigham."

"Thanks—see you in a bit."

"Bye, be careful!"

When I walk out of the bathroom, I find Darren rubbing his temple and standing by the door.

"Headache?" I ask.

"What?" Darren looks up at me distractedly.

"Do you have a headache?"

"Oh—yes I, suppose," Darren says and puts his hands in his pockets.

"I haven't had a real one since I was turned—if I get thirsty, it feels weird though," I say, looking at him suspiciously.

"You're lucky. I tend to get them often." Darren looks sad for a moment and then his face changes completely and a large smile spread across his face. "My car is around back—shall I drive us?"

"That's perfect, I walked here," I lie.

"You walked here?"

"Uh…yes."

"That's five miles," Darren says, narrowing his eyes at me and his eyes darken.

"I like walking at night." Darren looks at me in disbelief but then smiles and gestures at the door and we walk out of the coffee shop.

Darren is driving a black Mercedes. He opens the passenger door for me, and I climb into the plush seats.

"Nice car," I say, trying to sound impressed. *I really don't give a crap about cars.*

"Thanks, but it's not really my taste." Darren's face twists slightly in disgust. I stare at him curiously, trying to understand his reaction. Why drive a car you hated? I mean, it is obvious that Darren had money, and I hadn't met a vampire yet that is thrifty, so the question burned in me—why own this car that you hate? He can afford to buy a different one, so why make yourself miserable?

Hoping to understand the motivation behind the action, I ask, "What would you prefer?"

"Anything else," Darren replies in a low grumble. Darren's eyes reveal a sadness that I don't understand.

"Then why are you driving this?"

Darren smiles at me but doesn't answer.

I search his face for an explanation, but Darren's face has closed down and is unreadable. I sigh in annoyance—a vampire's silent smile is a force I am coming up against lately and I am beginning to think that this is the tactic they all used to get out of difficult questions.

"I'm so glad you decided to come out tonight," he says and hits the automatic lock button. A slow panic is starting to rise in me. Why would he lock the doors? We're immortal, and there isn't any safety risk for us driving. What is going on in Darren's head? My brain frantically searches for probable answers, and the loudest one in my head at the moment screams that he wants me to keep me in the car with him—by force, if necessary.

"Why is that?" I ask cautiously.

"It's going to make my life much easier," he says softly. If I had a pulse, it would be racing.

I swallow hard. "I don't understand."

"There's someone who wants to meet you very badly," he says, trying to sound lighthearted, but it comes out flat.

"Who?"

Again, Darren smiles and doesn't answer my question. The hairs on the back of my neck were now standing on end, and I know I need to get out of this car *now!*

"Darren, I think I need to go," I say tensely and he grabs my arm hard, and I wince as his grip cuts through me. Darren looks at me tensely as I feel fear rising in me. *Anton was right! This was a horrible idea!*

"Please don't make me hurt you," he pleads, and his face contorts as if he is battling something off. *What the fuck did I get myself into?*

"Why would you want to hurt me?"

Darren stares at me and I can see the conflict in his eyes. "I beg you, don't try to get away. You're not at your full-strength yet—it won't end well for you." I gulp, realizing the truth of his words. I am an idiot for meeting him tonight and an even bigger idiot for getting into his car. "Please hand me your phone."

I slowly hand him my phone, my panic rising. "I don't understand why you're doing this."

"I don't either," he whispers to himself and let's go of my arm. Suddenly, he shifts the car into drive, throws my phone out the window, and starts driving quickly down the street. He focuses his attention on driving as if it takes all his energy to drive the car.

"Are you taking me to see Shawn?" He gives a slight nod. "Is he going to kill me?"

Darren looks at me and his mouth tenses, then his face changes and an icy malicious grin forms on his lips. I turn away from him and shudder. I look around in the car for a weapon, trying not to look obvious, but find nothing useful.

"You have a very creepy Jekyll and Hyde thing going on," I say trying to keep my voice steady.

Darren laughs softly as if he is in pain. "You have no idea." Suddenly, his entire body goes rigid and his grip on the steering wheel tightens as he presses the gas pedal to the floor.

"I think I do," I say sadly. His sire is controlling him, and it looks like Shawn is a very cruel and powerful vampire. "It's okay," I whisper. "I know you're not in control." Darren's head slightly tilts towards me, and I see a flash of sadness in his eyes before the steely black gaze of Shawn creeps back over him.

We drive for hours in silence, and I consider breaking through the car door or windshield, but I'm not sure how much stronger or faster Darren is than me. I also don't know if Anton is following us, and I am afraid to look in the mirror to check in case Darren notices. Darren and Shawn struggle over control of Darren's body for the first hour, then Darren seems to give up and only Shawn remains. He drives fast out of the city, leaving the city lights behind. I know that Brigham will be worrying as I start to feel the strain being so far from him, and I know he would be feeling it as well. He probably thinks I am running away again, and it makes me sad that those will be his last thoughts of me. Hopefully, we will stop soon, and maybe Anton might be able to help me get away.

After we'd driven five hours north, Darren finally pulls into a large warehouse.

"Is this where Shawn is?" Darren doesn't answer and parks in front of the warehouse, turning the car's engine off.

"Don't run," he whispers, sounding exhausted as he rubs his head.

"Okay," I say quietly, knowing full well that if I get an opportunity, *I am running away as fast as I can!*

He exits the car and opens my door for me, offering me his hand and I stare at it. Was he really trying to help me out of the car right now? "I'm sorry," he says, not looking at me.

"I know." Darren's face twitches and he grabs my hand hard and leads me into the warehouse. Inside, there is a large black van with two vampires sitting near it. The smallest vampire jumps up upon seeing us and runs to the van and starts the engine. The other, taller vampire approaches us cautiously—he is very muscular and has short black hair cut short and tan skin. If I hadn't noticed his fangs showing as he sneers at us, I wouldn't think he is a vampire at first glance. With his black t-shirt and tan, tactical pants, he looks like he is in the military.

"She's not going to escape," Darren says to him and moves his hands to my shoulder, holding me tightly. I flinch at his touch, not liking how his icy hands cut into me.

"Good," said the taller vampire gruffly. "I don't want to piss Shawn off by losing her. He's already pissed because you were resisting him."

"I don't like him in my head using my body like he does," Darren says with disgust.

"Not much you can do about it," says the shorter vampire walking back over to us. He looks at me curiously and runs his hands through his curly, sandy-brown hair. He is wearing the same type of clothes as the other vampire, and I wonder why they are dressed like that. "Might as well accept it and not make him mad."

I look at Darren, and he gives me a weak smile. "At least you won't ever have to experience that." I gulp and look at the other vampires warily.

"Shawn wants us to keep moving," the shorter vampire says.

"I know," Darren sighs and he pulls me gently towards the van.

"We're driving again?" I ask, the fear in my voice becoming uncontrollable. I look back towards the road and see no other cars around and my bond with Brigham aches a little more, making me wince. *Is he trying to find me right now?*

"We need to keep moving—master's orders," Darren says with an angry tone.

"You call your sire 'master'? That's beyond gross. Why do we need to keep moving?" I ask, digging my heels into the ground, trying to stall.

"We need to keep as much distance between you and Brigham as possible."

My stomach drops and my throat goes dry. "Because of the new moon?"

Darren looks up at me, and I see the guilt in his eyes. "Yes."

"That's kind of a pussy way to kill someone," I say and plant my feet in the ground, but unfortunately this does nothing to stop Darren from moving me forward. The shorter vampire laughs at my comment and the taller one shoots him a warning look.

"What? She's funny," the shorter vampire shrugs.

"Let's go," says the taller vampire and the shorter vampire moves to the driver's door.

I try and brace against the van door, but Darren easily folds my arms and pushes me inside. He climbs into the back of the van behind me, and we start driving again. Darren sits me down along the side of the van and I notice that there are blankets and a few pillows on the floor. The windows are tinted in the front, and I see some rope and what looks like chains behind the driver's seat. I decide I really don't want those on me, so I don't resist sitting in the van. I look at Darren—he's slumped against the other side of the wall and is rubbing his temples hard.

"Darren, is Shawn in your head right now?" I ask quietly.

"No, not at the moment," Darren grumbles.

"Does it hurt when he is?"

"The way he does—it can," Darren says darkly.

"Why are you telling her these things?" asks the taller vampire, looking at us with panic in his voice.

"What does it matter? She's going to be dead either way," Darren mutters and puts his head back against the side of the van.

"Master wouldn't like you talking to her," the taller vampire says quietly.

"All the more reason to tell her," the shorter vampire whispers. Darren shoots him a smile. "I'm Embry, by the way," the shorter vampire says, turning back to look at me.

"I'd say it's nice to meet you, but—" I gesture to the van and Embry laughs. "Why isn't Shawn in your head anymore?" I ask Darren.

"I don't know."

"He's probably making plans for the grand finale," Embry snorts. "He's a bit of a drama queen." The taller vampire's lip curls and he makes a disgusted sound.

"Oh, lighten up Renard. You're not going to get in trouble—you're Shawn's favorite pet," Embry quips.

"*DO NOT CALL ME THAT!*" Renard growls.

"Why? That's what we are," Darren says sadly.

"It's not that bad," Renard urges and rubs his chin aggressively.

Embry snorts. "Says you."

"Have you guys been vampires long?" I ask. I still couldn't tell how you could age vampires, and these guys could be hundreds or decades old.

"I've been a vampire for ten years, Renard for sixtyish, and Darren—how long has it been for you?" Embry asks.

"One-hundred-and-fifty fucking years," Darren curses, and hits his head against the wall of the van.

"Jeez, I don't know how you have made it with Shawn for one-hundred-and-fifty years!" Embry exclaims.

"What choice do I have?"

"That's true. It's not like Shawn will let you kill yourself," Embry adds.

"Yeah, no sunbathing for me."

Embry lets out a low whistle. "Wouldn't that be something! Man, that's the way to go," Embry says quietly.

"I don't know. I think when you tried to pick a fight with that older vampire last year was much cooler," Renard says with a smirk.

"I almost got him to decapitate me before Shawn stopped him," Darren says proudly, and my mouth drops open. *Did he really try to get himself killed?*

"Shawn was so pissed at you," Renard says and a small smile creeps over his face.

"Yeah, it was pretty cool," Embry agrees and changes lanes, increasing his speed as he looks in his rearview mirror. *Did he see something? Was it Anton?* My bond with Brigham aches harder again and I fear I am getting even farther from him.

"Why isn't Shawn in all of your heads all the time?" I ask, hoping to keep them all distracted.

"It takes a lot of concentration to control a vampire and read their thoughts. He has a lot of vampires under his control." Darren grimaces. "He has to do a lot of spot checking—he can't be in our heads all the time."

"It's really not that bad," Renard says quietly as if he is trying to convince himself.

"But when he is in there, you're completely gone, and you have no control of your thoughts or actions. You become a vampire marionette," Embry says with a sigh.

"Yikes," I say, not really surprised. This is what I'd been fearing.

"It can be very unpleasant," Darren says and stares at his hands, flexing them as if he is remembering having Shawn in his body.

"You guys make it sound so much worse that it is. Shawn asks very little of us for all of the things he gives us," Renard says confidently and Darren rolls his eyes at him.

"Not all masters are like him," Darren points out.

"Some are worse," Renard points out and this makes me flinch. *Is he serious?*

"That's true," Embry says dully.

"Most of them are better, like Brigham," Darren gestures towards me. "Butterfly wouldn't have to deal with the crap we do."

"Yeah, but look what Brigham let Jacqueline do," Renard says quietly, glancing at me quickly and then looking back out the front window.

"I'd love to have Brigham as my master," Darren says honestly and looks at me with envy.

"Shut up!" Renard hisses. "He'll hear you!"

"How? He's not here." Darren points to his head.

"Be careful Darren, Shawn has a long reach," Embry says cautiously and makes a sharp right turn, and we all hold on to the van as the force shifts us. I have the same amount of ache through the sire bond, and I consider that a good sign for the moment.

Darren moves to the front of the van and looks in the mirrors, watching for a moment and then sits back down. "I don't care if he heard me, it's true."

The vampires are silent as they contemplate what Darren has said, and the air grows thick with tension. They seemed to all really hate Shawn—maybe I could use that fact to my advantage.

"Darren, can you tell me what happened with Brigham, Shawn, and Jacqueline? I still don't know what is going on. I'd like to know before I die," I say, my voice wavering more than I want it to. Darren looks at Embry and Embry nods yes. When he looks at Renard, Renard's eyes open wide and he shakes his head violently.

"Don't be stupid—Shawn will kill you," Renard whispers to Darren and Embry laughs.

"Well, now he's going to tell her for sure," Embry chuckles and gives Darren a knowing look. Renard sighs and crosses his arms over his chest.

"What do you know about the situation?" Darren asks.

"Very little. I know that Brigham had a lover named Jacqueline, he was her sire and that she died. I don't know how that happened."

"She killed herself."

The shock of that stuns me. Jacqueline killed herself, and Brigham let her. What the hell happened between them? I try and recover from the shock and ask, "How did she do that?"

"She walked into the sunlight."

"Why would she do that?" I gasp, thinking about how badly that would hurt.

"I think she felt guilty for the things she and Shawn had done over the years," Darren says and looks away from me and down at his hands.

"When was she with Shawn?"

"Let me start at the beginning. When Brigham initially made Jacqueline in New York, they weren't together like you and Brigham are, but they were close. You always have a strong connection to your master, even if you hate him. Brigham and Jacqueline hunted the streets of New York for years. Back then, Forseti and Shawn were very close. In the early 1940's, they all went on a hunt together in upstate New York. When Shawn saw Jacqueline, he wanted her right away—she was very beautiful."

"What did she look like?" I ask, unable to hide my intrigue.

"She was tall, and thin, with long straight-black hair and dark-brown eyes." Darren shrugs, seeming not interested. Maybe he really was gay.

My face contorts. "She doesn't sound a thing like me."

"You thought she would?"

"I thought maybe Brigham had a type," I say, slightly embarrassed, and Darren laughs. "What was she like?"

Darren pauses and rubs his chin. "She was very quiet—reserved—some might say cold, but after you got to know her, she could be very friendly," Darren says thoughtfully.

"Brigham definitely doesn't have a type," I snort and Darren smiles at me. "Did Shawn like her right away?"

"Oh yes, I think especially because she was with Brigham," Darren says, nodding his head.

"Gross, but they weren't together then, Brigham and Jacqueline?"

"No, that didn't happen until after she was with Shawn."

I contemplate this for a moment. "How did she end up with Shawn?"

"He was a very cunning vampire back then, and when he wanted something, nothing got in his way. He can be very charming, especially with women," Darren says with a shrug as if he didn't see the appeal.

"Gross," I say, grimacing. Embry snorts from the driver's seat.

"You have no idea," Darren says under his breath. "I think Jacqueline liked the attention Shawn lavished on her and got swept away. He was always giving her presents and taking her out to see the city. Who wouldn't want a rich and powerful vampire doting on them?" *FUCK!* I was so easy, wasn't I?

"Point taken."

"When Shawn asked her to come away with him, she was more than willing to go."

"Was Brigham mad?"

"I don't think so—if he was, he didn't show it."

"How long was she with Shawn?" I rub my palm as the sire connection starts to ache again, and Darren's eyes move to my hand. I stop rubbing it, but he catches me. I'd have to be more careful about that.

"Ten years."

"You said she killed herself because she felt guilty. What did she and Shawn do during that time?" I press, causing Darren to cringe and shift uncomfortably.

"Too many horrible things to mention. Jacqueline didn't know the real Shawn when she left Brigham. He only showed her one side of his personality. She didn't know the depth of his insanity and cruelty."

"So, after being with Shawn, she came back to Brigham?"

"Yes."

"And that's when they fell in love?"

"She stayed with Brigham for three years before she took her life." *Three years!* That was a long time to be in a relationship, or at least it was for me! I rub my forehead as a pit of anxiety forms in my stomach. I wanted to know more information, but God, it kept getting worse!

"Why is Shawn mad at Brigham for that? She had already left him," I ask.

"Because Brigham didn't stop her from killing herself."

"You can't stop a suicidal person from killing themselves—they'll find a way to do it," I argue, not understanding why Shawn was mad.

"You can if you're their sire," Darren points out and I gasp.

"Oh…right…"

I remembered teasing Brigham about killing myself and a wave of guilt hit me. I would never have joked about it if I knew what he had gone through with Jacqueline! *No wonder he had gotten so upset!*

Darren leans his head back against the wall of the van. "I don't know what all happened during that time. Shawn sent me a few times to bring Jacqueline back, but I couldn't force her—not with the Vampire Guild there."

"Did you see her with Brigham?"

"Yes."

I hesitate to ask any more questions. Did I really want to know more about Jacqueline and Brigham's relationship? Why am I doing this to myself—it isn't the most pleasant conversation. The palm of my hand starts to burn and I ask, "Were they happy?"

"Yes."

"I don't understand why she did it—killed herself—if she was with Brigham and they were happy," I say, shaking my head.

"Maybe the happiness made it worse," Embry says softly. I look at him and he quickly looks back to the road.

"She had a lot of guilt," Renard adds and looks at me sadly. "Guilt can destroy you if you let it."

"Yes, it can," Darren says quietly. "Maybe she felt she didn't deserve happiness because of the things she did.

Maybe the happiness she felt being with Brigham made it easier to see her demons. You can make amends for the things you've done, but if you're happy when you do that, you're rewarding yourself along the way. Maybe she didn't like adding to her deficit."

"That's silly," I say, but it actually did make some sense, and it was so sad. *Did the Vampire Guild not have therapists for their members?*

"Maybe, but I could see how she might feel that way," Darren says with a shrug.

"Is that how you feel?" I ask him and he looks at me for a moment and doesn't answer.

"It's different for me. I can't stop what Shawn makes me do or say."

"How much could Jacqueline stop what was going on?" I point out. Who knew how much control Shawn had over her. From what Anton has told me about his experience working with abused women, sometimes when you are in an abusive relationship you contort yourself into a pretzel to keep the peace, and maybe that's what Jacqueline found herself doing.

"Not very much, but Shawn couldn't take over her body or mind, so she had more free will. Much more compared to what Renard, Embry, and I have."

"Enough to feel guilty enough for self-destruction," Embry adds.

"I think so," Darren says with a nod.

"That's so sad," I say and look at the vampires. *Good God, this was a mess!*

"Yeah," Renard says quietly and then realizes what he had just said, and his face turns stoney.

"I'm glad Brigham was there for her in the end," I say while feeling bad for this woman I never knew.

"I am too," Darren says, his voice barely audible. No doubt he is hoping Shawn doesn't hear him.

We drive in silence for a while, and I try to contain a yawn. I try and look out the front window but am unable to see much from my position. I pray that Brigham is searching for me. *He had to be, right?* Even though we hadn't been together as long as Jacqueline and him—he wouldn't let me die…

I mean something to him…even if I am a little troublesome…right?

I swallow trying to keep my emotions contained. *He loves me. He would come.* Another bolt of pain shoots though my body from my palm and I try to fake breathe through it.

"Dawn's coming," I say quietly and rub my palm on my leg, feeling the ache getting harder to bear. Darren nods. "Are we sleeping in here tonight?" I ask.

Embry spasms and his hand flies to his ear. Darren watches him silently. "There's going to be another warehouse about ten miles up. We're supposed to turn in there. We'll switch vans and there's a human there that will take over the day driving duties."

"Shawn must be real worried Brigham will find you," Renard says, watching me rub my palm on my leg.

"He loves her quite a bit," Darren says and looks at me sadly. "I doubt the daylight will stop him from searching. He's had practice searching for her already."

"What do you mean?" Embry stutters and looks in the rear-view mirror.

"Butterfly was testing the connection between them and tried to see how far she could stretch it—she ran away a couple times after being turned. Brigham found her every time," Darren says with a smirk.

"Are you suicidal, too?" asks Renard, looking at me in disbelief.

"No, just curious," I say, realizing how stupid it probably sounds. The connection with Brigham stings and I close my eyes trying to rub the pain away, but it doesn't help.

I yawn and slump against the wall of the van—at least if I am sleeping, I won't be in pain.

"The sun is coming," I mutter, struggling to stay awake.

"Go to sleep—we'll carry you," Darren says kindly. I try to keep my eyes open, but the pull of the sun is too strong, and I feel my body become immobile.

CHAPTER THIRTEEN

I remembered the night Brigham made me a vampire…

We started the evening out at his house. I was standing out on the balcony, wearing a long grey silk dress, watching the wind blow through the trees along the river. I was trying to take everything in, like the feeling of my heartbeat in my chest, the pulse of blood through my veins, and the way a deep breath felt in my lungs.

Simple things, human things.

Brigham approached soundlessly behind me and surprised me by wrapping his hand around my waist. My heart quickened and my body warmed from his touch. I would miss the way this body responded to him the most.

"What are you thinking about?" he asked and I looked guiltily at him. He brushed a strand of hair from my face. "Tell me."

I looked away from him, out back at the river—he grabbed by chin softly and turned my head towards him. His eyes were the color of a calm sea, and they moved over me, trying to decipher my thoughts.

"I was thinking about what I would be losing no longer being human," I said, slightly embarrassed.

"You can still change your mind."

"I know." I did know that, but the thought of aging and having death separate us sounded terrible.

"What things were you thinking about that you would miss?" he asked as he caressed my cheek.

"I was thinking about no longer having a heartbeat and a need to breathe, but there are more things, too," I whispered.

"Such as?" he asked as he kissed my neck, and I leaned back into him, loving the way his body encircled me.

"I won't need to eat—normal food—so I will lose taste."

"You will taste blood," he said quietly, and I recoiled at that thought. I was *not* looking forward to drinking blood.

"It won't be the same."

"No, it won't be the same," he agreed and rubbed the skin on my arm, sending little tingles throughout me. "What else?"

"Babies."

I felt Brigham stiffen. "Babies?"

I nodded. "I can't have a baby as a vampire."

"Do you want to have children?" Brigham asked and he stopped rubbing my arm.

"I don't know…" I'd never really thought about it before, or at least I'd never been in a relationship where that was even a remote possibility. I would have liked to have children with Brigham, but that wasn't possible, and for some reason that made me a little sad.

"I don't think we should do this tonight. You're not ready," Brigham said firmly.

"Do you regret not having children?" I asked and looked up at him, and so many emotions moved over his face that I could barely catalog them all.

Brigham hesitated before answering. "It's different as a vampire. You don't have biological children, but the vampires you sire can feel as close as children."

"Maybe it won't be such a loss then. Will I be able to turn people into vampires?"

Brigham turned me in his arms and looked at me in alarm. "It's not something that can be done lightly," he said, trying to read my expression.

"I know that. I'm not saying I want to do that. I'm asking if it is something I will be capable of at some point."

Brigham sighed loudly and I turned away from him and looked out at the river. When I looked back up at him, his face hardened for a moment and then relaxed back to his neutral expression. He rubbed my back, and I arched into him, enjoying the sensation.

"Eventually, you will be able to do that," he answered quietly.

"How many vampires have you made?"

"Not many."

"How come?"

"I haven't wanted to."

"Is that normal?" Brigham's eyes crinkled and a small smile appeared on his face. The tips of his fangs showed, and I reached out and touched the tip lightly, breaking the skin of my thumb and letting a small drop of blood out which I offered to him. He gently sucked on my thumb, his eyes glazed over for a moment, then released me and kissed the tip of my finger as the wound healed.

"No, other vampires have sired many more," he replied and cleared his throat. I watched as he tried to get control of his bloodlust, and I gave him a wicked smile.

"What's average?"

"I don't know."

"What's your best guess?" I pressed.

"Maybe one every five to ten years. Some vampires sire a vampire yearly, but that's an extreme case. The Vampire Guild doesn't really approve of that."

"How old are you?"

"I'm still not telling."

"But if you were average, would you have a whole auditorium full of vampires made by now?"

"Maybe not that many…"

"But a lot."

"Yes."

"Why not very many?"

"I haven't liked how everything turned out in the end."

"What happened?"

Brigham stared out towards the river and I noticed he was biting the inside of his cheek, but he didn't answer me.

"Will I want to hurt people? I mean, will I be a danger to all the humans around me?" I asked.

"Not necessarily. You're not a danger to people now."

"Does my personality matter that much?"

"Yes."

"I won't become a different person as a vampire? A demon doesn't take over?"

"Not unless you let the demon already within you out."

"Huh…"

I turned back to the river and leaned into Brigham, and he encircled me in his arms again. They were heavy and solid against my body. He leaned down and kissed my neck gently and I felt his fangs gently touch my skin. "Is it hard not biting me?"

"Yes." The wind blew harder around us and I shivered.

"Do you get cold?" Brigham rubbed my bare arms, trying to warm me.

"Sometimes, if it's been a long time in between feedings."

"What type of people do you feed on?"

"I don't have a type."

"Huh…I've been thinking about it, and I will have a type."

"You've been thinking about feeding?" Brigham asked.

"It's all part of being a vampire, isn't it?"

"Yes. What have you decided?"

"It's always made me mad to see animals suffering at the hands of humans. As a little kid, I was always rescuing animals. I really feel like I make a difference at the shelter, and if I become a vampire, there will be one less person doing good out there. So, I've decided to feed on people who make animals' lives worse."

"So, animal abusers."

"Yep."

"Interesting."

"Does that seem silly to you?"

"Not at all. I envy your passion on the subject."

"Do most vampires kill without prejudice?"

"Not all of them."

"But you do."

He hesitated and I feel his arm stiffen. "It's not what you think."

"I'm not passing judgment—I'm trying to understand."

He looked at me closely, trying to judge my sincerity. "I don't feel I can't pass judgment on people. Everyone has a past, a background that they are dealing with, that affects the decisions they make today. I can't ignore that. I've found that, if you get to know a person long enough and well enough, they all have redeeming qualities. But everyone has a dark side and flaws as well, and I'm not comfortable separating out the bad people from the good. I can't see a clear line of separation between the two, so I don't discriminate—and, when an opportunity arises for me to feed, I feed."

"But you have to agree that there is a spectrum with people—there are people who in general are worse than others."

"Absolutely."

"But you still won't discriminate."

"I'm in no place to pass judgment—I've done things I'm not proud of just like everyone human I meet on the street."

"Do you think I'm being naïve choosing to go after people who have hurt animals?"

"No."

"Really?"

"I think that if that's what you want to do and it's important to you, then it's important to me."

"Will you show me how to hunt when I become a vampire?"

"Of course," Brigham whispered and kissed my forehead. "There are all kinds of things I want to show you."

"Like what?"

Brigham smiled suggestively at me.

"It's all about sex with men—even as a vampire, guys still are obsessed with it."

"If you weren't so good at it, I might not be." He leaned down and kissed my neck again, this time pressing his teeth against my skin a little harder.

"To become a vampire, is it a, you-suck-me-I-suck-you kind of deal?"

He laughed. "I've never heard it described quite like that, but, yes, pretty much."

"Has anyone ever died in the process?"

He turned me to face him, and his face broke with emotion. "I'm not going to let that happen."

"But you've only done it a few times—how do you know it won't happen?"

"Do you want me to find a vampire who's more experienced with changing vampires? If you do, I will."

"No, I want you to do it." I traced my finger against his jaw and looked up into his eyes. "I think I've finally run out of questions."

"You're ready?"

"Yes."

Brigham cocked his head and leaned in closely to me. "There isn't anything else you want to know?"

"I can't think of anything, unless there's something you can think of that I should know."

A flash of something crossed over Brigham's face that I can't discern but was gone in an instant. "We'll be more connected when you change," he said quietly and drew me closer into him. "I'm excited to show you the world."

"Haven't you already?"

"Not even close."

He leaned down and kissed me hard and gently picked me up in his arms. I kissed him harder and wrapped my legs around his body, squeezing him tightly like I had done on the night we met.

"I love when you do that," he growled into my ear.

"I've noticed," I whispered and grinded against him, feeling exactly how much he enjoyed it. He carried me inside to his bedroom and laid me down on his bed, straddling above me.

"Are you sure you want to do this?

"Yes," I said, trying not to let my voice shake. I was nervous, despite how much I wanted this. I ran my hands up his chest, marveling at how different he was than a human.

"I love you very much," he whispered, brushing his lips against my neck.

"I love you more."

"I don't think that's possible," he said, shaking his head as he kissed me tenderly on the lips, his hair fell around us as I kissed him harder.

I broke from him and gasped. "You better bite me before I start biting you."

He pressed hard into me, and I felt his hard cock at my entrance, while I moaned and arched my body into him.

"I like it when you bite me."

"It's going to hurt more when I do it from now on."

"I know—I'm terribly excited about it," he said flatly, and I laughed. His excitement was a far cry from anyone else's excitement.

"Masochist."

"Look who's talking—you're trying to get a vampire to bite you as we speak."

"Not just any vampire," I said quietly. He looked up from kissing my chest. "I want *you* to bite me."

"I'm so glad you tapped that window," he said, and his eyes glazed over for a moment.

I touched his check, feeling the smoothness of his skin. "Me too."

He moved up my body slowly and my heart raced. "It'll hurt for only a moment," he whispered and kissed my neck.

"Okay," I said swallowing hard, trying to keep the anxiety out of my voice. He arched up from me and put his hand over my breast and closed his eyes.

"What are you doing?" I asked.

"I'm feeling your rhythm—it's the last time I'll feel it." He opened his eyes and looked down at me as if he was memorizing what I looked like as a human. I leaned up to him and kissed him hard. He kissed me back hard and slowly and made his way to my neck. "My Butterfly," he whispered softly and kissed my neck.

I inhaled deeply and tried to relax my body as he kissed the spot he was going to bite. My heart pounded in my chest, and I knew the blood was pulsing in my jugular millimeters from his teeth, enticing him. He kissed deeper, and I felt his teeth again against the skin.

"I love you Butterfly, forever." He pressed himself deep into me and his fangs pierced my skin.

CHAPTER FOURTEEN

I wake up aching and crying. I curl myself into a small ball trying to escape the pain. Darren comes over to me and wraps his arms awkwardly around me as I sob, and I appreciate the gesture. My body aches for Brigham and the distance separating us is unbearable. *Why did I meet Darren in the coffee shop? Why am I so impulsive?* I will pay for it with my life now, and I regret so many of my actions over the last few weeks. I sob uncontrollably seeing so clearly now how much I have fucked up.

"Bad memory?" Darren asks as he gently touches my shoulder. I wipe the tears from my eyes, but they keep coming as I think about Brigham, and it takes me a few moments before I can speak.

"No, a good one," I say, trying to stifle my sobs. Darren nods in understanding. I look at all the blood covering me from my tears and groan. *I hate crying now!*

"How do you feel?" he asks, looking me over.

I sit back from him and lean against the van's wall weakly. I notice that we are not moving and wonder why we have stopped.

"Awful," I admit. My head throbs and my stomach is in knots. I am so tired, my entire body aches from the distance between Brigham and I, and my throat burns from not feeding. "We must be very far away from Brigham," I say, and my voice catches as I stifle a sob. *FUCK! This is really bad!* The mention of Brigham's name brings tears back to my eyes and I try to unsuccessfully wipe them away. I look at my hands and groan again—they are covered in blood. *Now I am sad and gross!*

"We drove all day." Darren says darkly and moves back across from me in the van, pulling his knees up and resting his hands on them. I try to move to look out the front window and see Embry is gone from the driver's seat, but I can't see anything of significance from where I am sitting— and we aren't moving.

"Do you know where we are?"

"No."

"Shawn hasn't told you?"

"No—he's pissed at me."

"Because you were resisting him?" I guess and try to move my legs into a more comfortable position, but nothing seems to help.

"Yes," Darren says gravely.

"Will he punish you?"

"Probably." Darren shrugs. "That is his favorite activity lately."

"Then why did you do it?" I ask.

Darren smiles weakly at me. "I had to try," he says barely above a whisper, looking at his hands.

"Thank you for trying," I say sincerely. It might not be enough to keep me from dying, but if I had to die, at least I had someone who cared about me here at the end.

"You're welcome, but I'm afraid it didn't help you much."

I shrug and try not to laugh bitterly. "Sometimes, it's the thought that counts." I look around the van and notice that Renard is not inside with us either. "Where is everybody?"

"Hunting."

"Oh." I adjust my position and wince at the pain. "I haven't been this far from Brigham, and it hurts more than I expect. He's never let me get this far before—or maybe it hurts so much because we are so close to the new moon." Again, the tears well in my eyes. I know I am going to die far away from Brigham, and it makes me so sad. I wish I hadn't gone on my excursions earlier in the month. Now I wanted every moment I wasted without him back.

"You'll feel better if we go feed," Darren says with determination in his voice, and I look at him and see how much he wants to help me.

"Will Shawn let us do that?"

"We could try and see how far we can get before he stops us," Darren says with a smirk, and I laugh a little.

"Such a rebel," I tease. "I don't want to get you in any more trouble."

Darren cocks his head and smiles. "I don't mind."

"I'm fine," I lie, and the mere thought of blood makes my fangs and throat ignite with an intense burning sensation. I might start attacking Darren soon if I didn't feed. *Good to know there is still a rock bottom to this nightmare.*

"Please let us try—think of it as a favor to me. I don't like seeing you in so much pain," Darren says seriously. "Besides, Shawn didn't say specifically that I couldn't let you hunt, just Embry—and if he is not listening, we might be able to get around that."

"No, I only kill people who hurt animals or women. I don't think we'll be able to find someone like that without some effort, and I don't want to kill someone who's an innocent if I'm going to die anyway. I don't need the bad karma."

"You're a very strange vampire," Darren says, tilting his head to look at me closer.

"I suppose I am. Anton tells me that daily." I think of Anton and cover my mouth as a sob escapes me. I am going to miss Anton so much when I am dead—*for real dead!*

Darren looks away from me and rubs his neck. "It's no wonder Brigham is so fond of you."

"I don't want to talk about him," I say sadly, and feel a surge of pain through my palm, causing me to wince and rub it on my leg. It feel like I am being branded, and I start to laugh at that thought, feeling the pain that animals feel right before I die. That is cathartic in a twisted way.

"Sorry."

"It hurts too much," I groan and close my eyes.

"What do you want to talk about?"

"Tell me about Shawn," I say with distain, hoping that focusing on something that pisses me off will distract me.

"What do you want to know?"

"Why did you let him turn you into a vampire?" I ask, trying to keep the judgment out of my voice unsuccessfully.

"I didn't let him do anything," Darren says calmly, and I open my eyes.

I swallow rapidly. *"He changed you against your will?"*

"Yes," Darren says, his tone low and holds my gaze. I can tell he's telling the truth, and the horror of that is overwhelming.

"That's awful!" I reach out and put my hand on his leg, wanting to comfort him. "I'm so sorry that happened to you, Darren!"

"It happens all the time," Darren says, slowly and I realize all he is saying to me. How could this be? How could the Vampire Guild sanction this?

"How can that be?"

Darren laughs. "Shawn plays by the old rules."

I pull back from him. "Old rules?"

"Before the Vampire Guild was formed, vampires did whatever they wanted. It was utter chaos. A century ago, the guild was formed to try to rein in some of the more audacious vampires. The humans were on to our existence with all the rash killing sprees that vampires would go on. The guild was formed to create a code of conduct, if you will."

"I didn't know this. I thought the guild was some sort of country club where all the old vampires hung out."

"Oh, it is that too—but initially, it was created to bring order to the vampire nation."

"What kind of rules did the guild set up?"

"There aren't many. Number one is you must be discreet about your hunting. They don't want the humans to be onto our presence."

"No leaving bodies with holes in the necks lying around everywhere."

"Right."

"What else?"

"You can't change a human unless they want to be changed."

"But Shawn changed you against his will," I say, not understanding how this could have happened.

"He's not a part of the Vampire Guild," Darren says, his face dark.

"Is membership optional?"

"Yes. There are a few older masters like Shawn who refuse to join, but they don't get the privileges of the Vampire Guild."

"What privileges?"

"They can't live or hunt in the cities."

"Where does Shawn live?" I ask. Darren hesitates and his mouth opens and shuts a few times as his face strains. I can tell he is trying to tell me but is unable to. "Never mind, it doesn't matter. What other kind of privileges?"

"There are some definite financial perks of being a member of the guild. They have many financial wizards under their employment who invest the vampires' money. If you're a member of the guild, you don't have to worry about money."

"That makes sense—all of the vampires I know are all very well off."

"Compounding interest is an amazing thing—plus, they have a lot of investments."

"What other privileges?"

"I don't know about all of them, but I know there are voting rights and protection offerings."

"Protection?"

"The guild looks after its own. Every now and then a vampire might slip up, and the guild will help them out."

"They are kind of like a secret government?"

"Yes, I suppose."

"Cool," I grab at my throat as the burning and pain grow more intense. "Maybe they could help you."

"There's nothing they can do."

"Have you tried to talk to them?"

"Shawn would stop me."

"There needs to be a Vampire Amnesty International Group to help vampires like you." I affirm, and Darren laughs. "Especially if there are rogue sires out there doing this sort of thing. If I get out of this alive, I'll see what I can do. This is bullshit in my opinion that they are not doing that already, or better yet, monitoring these crazy old vampires."

"That would be nice if there was something set up like that."

"My friend Anton would love that—he worked in a woman's shelter before he was a vampire," I say through a sob. I wipe the flood of tears away. *Poor Anton!* He is probably freaking out right now!

"Really?"

"Yep."

"How does he like being a vampire?"

I laugh and wipe more tears away. "He loves it—we go hunting together all the time. He likes to go after men who abuse their wives."

"Vampire Avengers?"

I nod and let out a long breath. "We like to think so."

"How fun!" Darren says, his eyes sparkling.

"We enjoy it. He's going to be very upset with himself when I'm dead. I hope Brigham doesn't hurt him."

"Do you think he would?"

"No, I don't—Brigham is very mellow. But Anton heard a story about Brigham almost decapitating Shawn. Is that true?"

"Oh yes!" Darren says excitedly and his eyes sparkle again.

"Where you there?"

"Yes, it was great!" Darren leans forward excitedly, showing his canines as his smile widens.

"What happened?"

"Brigham came out to talk to Shawn after Jacqueline took her life to explain and Shawn was hysterical. He called Brigham a coward and said that he should have handed her over to him when he asked him to."

"Shawn wanted to take Jacqueline prisoner?"

"Yes—we came to the cities to get her back, but Brigham wouldn't let Shawn see her."

"Shawn must have really loved her."

"He didn't love her—he wanted to control her," Darren says in disgust. "He couldn't stand the thought that she left him. I'm sure he wished every day that he had been her maker."

"I'm glad Jacqueline was able to get away from him. I'm sorry she couldn't escape all the demons, but at least she got away from one of them."

"I helped her get away," Darren says barely above a whisper, and I lean towards him, not thinking I heard him correctly.

"You did?"

"Yes," Darren whispers and his eyes go wide, realizing what he just admitted. "Shawn doesn't know."

"That was very brave—or suicidal."

"She had a chance to get out. I don't. I had to do what I could." Darren looks sadly at his hands again and sighs, running his hands through his hair, tugging it slightly as his expression turns pained.

"Can you tell me about the fight?" I ask, hoping to change his mood.

Darren stops tugging his hair and looks up to me. "As I was saying, Brigham tried to explain why he let Jacqueline kill herself and Shawn was irate. He launched himself at Brigham and they struggled for a long time. There was broken furniture everywhere and blood."

"They were bleeding?"

"Very briefly—we heal very quickly."

"I've never seen a fight before."

"It's like watching dogs fight—it's intense."

"There's so much I didn't get to experience as a vampire," I groan, thinking about my impending doom. "It's all very disappointing. Anyways—go on, they were fighting."

"Shawn broke off a wood leg off a table and tried to run Brigham through."

I gasped moving my hand to my chest. "Would that have killed him?"

"No, but it would have hurt."

"Oh…so it really is only decapitation, sunshine, and…the new moon separation," I say glumly. *Just my freaking luck.*

"Yes…" Darren looks away from me with a guilty expression. *Poor guy! I feel bad that he has to kill me!*

"Did Brigham get some good punches in?" I ask hopefully.

Darren's face lights up. "Oh yes!"

"Good!"

"Brigham is spectacular in a fight. He's so fast and fluid."

"It's hard for me to imagine it."

"Have you ever danced with him?"

"No," I whisper sadly, adding another item I will miss out on because of the whole being murdered thing.

"Oh," Darren says and cringes. "Never mind."

"What were you going to say?"

"When he fights, he's as graceful as watching a dancer."

"Oh." It didn't look like I would ever see Brigham dance, so I was going to have to take his word for it.

"At the end of the fight, Shawn tried to bite Brigham's jugular, but Brigham got him in a head lock. They struggled like that for a while and Shawn said to Brigham, 'You should have kept her locked in a dungeon until she rotted' and something in Brigham's expression snapped. His eyes grew the darkest blue I had ever seen, almost black, and I could see him struggling with the hate inside him. It was so quick when it happened. He grabbed Shawn's head with one hand and jerked it, almost tearing it off. He dropped Shawn's body on the floor and blood squirted out of Shawn's neck, covering everything in the room. Shawn laid there gasping, trying to stop the bleeding."

"He did it one handed?" I gasp and then wince as I feel a stab of pain through the sire connection. *Is that a good or a bad sign?* The pain is getting so intense that I can't tell if it is lessening or increasing anymore.

"Yes, his neck was almost completely severed. Only a little skin and the right jugular were connecting the two parts together," Darren says with the biggest grin on his face.

"Gross."

"It was awesome! I could feel Shawn dying and his power over me slowly slipping away." Darrens face dulls and his smile disappears.

"What did Brigham do then?"

"He just looked sad. He turned to me and said, 'I'm sorry' and walked out of the house."

"Why do you think he said that to you?"

"I like to think it's because he couldn't kill Shawn."

"Why didn't you kill him at that point? It wouldn't have taken very much," I ask, leaning heavy against the van walls.

"It's impossible to kill your master," Darren says with disgust.

"Really? I assumed it would be hard since they were older and more powerful, but we really can't kill our sires?"

"Nope."

"Huh," I say and suck in a breath as a stabbing pain starts to move from my head down my body. What is that? I didn't think I am going to last until the new moon at this rate! "Why were you at Forseti's house that night?" I gasp, and Darren moves closer to me, and starts rubbing my arm. "Did Shawn send you to check on Brigham?"

"No, Shawn gave me a few days off from the compound, and I wanted to visit the Vampire Guild. It's my fault he found out about you," he says, barely able to look at me.

"It's not your fault," I choke out. *This hurts so bad!* "What is the compound?"

"That's what we call Shawn's house," Darren says and rubs my back. The pressure from his hand gives me something other than the pain to focus on and I appreciate the distraction. "It's a creepy old house with all of Shawn's…toys…that he uses for his demented hobbies."

I groan. "Oh F! I bet we're heading there. That sounds bad. "

"It is," Darren says and squeezes my shoulder and goes back to sitting across from me. "I've been trying to be more obedient to Shawn—it makes life easier. I like to visit members of the guild when I can. I never get to see them and Forseti was a vampire who I'd come to respect. He used to be very close with Shawn."

"Back in New York?" I ask, and Darren nods. "I have a hard time picturing Forseti with Shawn."

"As I said, Shawn can be very manipulative. I don't think Forseti knew how bad Shawn could be—he hid a lot of it and then left before more of it could be proven. I spent time with Forseti in Massachusetts before New York. Forseti is very kind and understanding…" Darren voice trails off, and I hear a hint of longing in his words.

"Anton likes him."

"Are they mates?" Darren asks and his lips tremble and then press together.

"What do you mean by mates? Like partners?"

"Vampire mates are different. Sometimes vampires form a bond stronger than the sire connection—they don't have to be lovers, but usually they are. It is very rare."

I make an annoyed sound. "Brigham has this huge library that usually I would have devoured going through. I probably should have done some digging on all this vampire lore—I might have saved myself from some trouble. This is *so* not my norm to get sidetracked by mind-blowing sex and not do my research," I add, and Darren's face cracks as he laughs loudly. "Anton and Forseti are friends, nothing more than that," I clarify.

Darren looks at me pleased. "I thought maybe they were together."

"No, I don't think Forseti is seeing anyone. Not seriously, anyways."

"Hmmmm…" He shakes his head, dispelling his thought. "Shawn didn't know that Brigham had made a new vampire. When I saw Brigham put his arm around you, Shawn caught the image and tried to jump into me. I'm sorry—all of this is all my fault."

"It's not your fault a psychopath can hijack your mind and body."

Darren's face breaks and he rests his head on his hand as he looks at me with tears welling in his eyes. The red fluid made him look like sort of heartbroken demon. "Yes, it is. If I was stronger, Shawn wouldn't have pushed through. I tried to keep him away but he's much stronger than me with this stupid sire connection."

The back of the van opens up, and Embry pokes his head inside and balks when he sees Darren crying. Darren quickly wipes his tears away and clears his throat.

"Everything alright?" he asks, looking at Darren shifting uncomfortably.

Darren clears his throat. "Yes, fine."

"I brought someone back for you," he says, and Embry looks at me apologetically, pushing his curly hair out of his eyes. "I'm sorry, but Shawn won't let me feed you."

"It's alright, Embry—she wouldn't feed anyway." Darren climbs out of the van and Embry climbs in.

"How are you feeling?" Embry asks, his face paling as he looks at me hunched over now. *I must look really bad to make a vampire pale!*

"Fine," I lie and wince as another bolt of pain shoots through me. "Did you have a good hunt?"

Embry laughs.

"What?"

"Nothing, I just can't believe how nice you're being about all this."

"Well, I know you don't have a lot of free will in this situation, so I'm not going to hold it against you," I groan and press my head to the floor. *FUCKING HELL! THIS HURT!*

"Thanks for that," Embry whispers.

"Did you have a good hunt?"

"Yes, there is a small town a mile south where I found a drunk passed out outside a bar."

"I fed on a drunk man once—I felt weird afterwards," I say while raising my head up from the ground. *No matter what I do, I can't dispel this pain!*

"It's fun getting a drunk or high person—you feel the effects of the substance they ingested for a little while. It's a nice little bonus."

"I wasn't expecting the inebriation when it happened to me. Someone really needs to write a guidebook for the newly turned vampire—the whole experience threw me at first."

"My favorite is getting a person who's taken cocaine. You don't feel the drug as intensely as they do, but it's a nice little rush," Embry chuckles.

"I'll have to take your word on that one."

"So where did you meet Brigham?"

I look at Embry, trying to understand why he would want to know that. He smiles and then looks at his hands, and I see he is wearing a wedding ring that he starts twisting around his finger. I didn't know vampires got married.

"A coffee shop." Brigham's face flashes in my mind and I try to keep the tears at bay. I could get through this if I didn't think about losing him, but it was getting harder to do. "Where'd you meet Shawn?"

"He found me walking home from work. It was my wife's birthday," Embry's answers in a low tone. He was married before he became a vampire! *That's so tragic!*

"Did he force you to be a vampire against your will, too?" He nods sadly.

"I'm sorry."

Embry twists his ring again slowly. "It was a long time ago."

"Have you seen your wife since then?" I ask, thinking about how hard it must have been for Embry.

"Once, but I didn't approach her. I didn't want to scare her." I nod in understanding. "And I didn't want to endanger her or let Shawn know about her."

"What does she think happened to you?"

"I don't know—they searched for me, but I worry she thinks I ditched her and hooked up with another woman," he says darkly and folds him arms in front of him.

"Has she remarried?"

He looks up at me, and I see the pain in his expression. "No."

Darren enters the van followed by Renard. "Renard says Shawn wants us to get moving again," Darren says, his tone gruff.

"What's the rush? We drove all morning," Embry asks in an annoyed tone. Darren smiles at me and I see a twinkle of something in his eye that I don't understand.

Darren shrugs at Embry. "Don't know, but Shawn was adamant."

"He practically split my head in two with all his shouting," Renard says, rubbing his head making his short black hair go in every direction. Embry moves up to the driver's seat, starts the van, and starts driving.

I lose track of time sitting in the dimly lit van after a while, trying to focus on my fake breathing as the pain overtakes me. After a few hours, the throbbing in my head starts to lessen and I wonder why that is. Am I getting used to the pain, or is Brigham closer? I am afraid to hope. I know that Anton would have followed the van as long as he could, but he would have had to sleep when the sun rose and would have lost the trail at that point. I hope he is okay and didn't walk into the sunlight from his guilt.

I close my eyes and focus on the sensations I am feeling in my body, trying to decide if I can tell where Brigham is. Sometimes, it feels that there is a pull backwards and to the right of me, but other times to the left, and it did seem to be consistently getting easier to bear. I want to believe he is getting closer so badly that maybe it is all in my head. Maybe none of it is real…maybe he is not coming. Maybe he realized I'm too much trouble…

That thought leaves me feeling hollow inside.

After a few more hours of driving, I open my eyes and see that Darren and Renard are busy playing a game of cards and Renard keeps glancing at his cards with a huge smile on his face.

"You have the worst poker face," Embry jokes, glancing back at him from the driver's seat.

"Why do you say that?" Renard asks and rubs his chin, trying to look disappointed as he looks at his cards.

"Because—when you have a good hand, you can barely contain yourself," Embry teases.

"Maybe I'm good at bluffing," Renard huffs.

"Doubt it—I'm calling." Darren smirks and puts a pile of chips in the pile forming between him. "Okay, let's see them."

They show their hands, with Darren revealing a pair of sevens as Renard boasts a flush.

"See, I knew you had good cards," Embry says cockily to Renard. Renard ignores him and begins stacking his newly won chips.

"How are you feeling?" Daren asks, looking at me closely as he reshuffles the cards. Embry's eyes narrow at him and then looks at me, and I pretend to wince, moving my shoulders around as if I am in pain. Darren's eyes dance in delight and he keeps his mouth closed tightly and nods.

"I'm fine," I answer cautiously. The pain is markedly less now, but I don't want to alert Shawn to that fact, even though I have a feeling Darren's already knew. Embry looks at me closely and I put my hand to my stomach and wince again, pretending I'm in pain. Satisfied, he returns his eyes to the road.

"Do you need anything?" Darren asks as he looks at me from his cards.

"Besides a great escape plan?"

Renard snorts.

"Besides that," Darren says with a light chuckle.

"No, that's okay—I'm going to rest." Darren nods and turns back to their game.

I close my eyes and focus on the sire connection with Brigham and rub my palm where it burns the most. I wish I could communicate with him somehow, but I can't—or at least, I didn't know how to through the sire connection. I massage the inside of my palm deeper, hoping maybe he will feel something. *He had to get to me before the new moon!*

With no windows in the back of the van, I have no idea where I am, and it is too hard to see out the front window from my position in the van without making it obvious. I didn't want them to have to tie me up if Shawn thinks I am getting too bold—*that would suck!* I close my eyes and continue to press into my palm—*please work! Please feel me!*

CHAPTER FIFTEEN

I remembered the first night Brigham and I made love together.

"You're trembling," Brigham whispered in my ear as we laid in his bed. His chest was so solid and cool against the skin of my back. My nipples peeked through my bra as he ran his cool hands over my breasts, and I kept my eyes closed, savoring the feel of his touch. He pressed his hand flat over my stomach and then my hip as he gently turned me towards him and leaned over me, propping up his forearms.

"I'm nervous, I suppose," I said, surprising myself. *Since when was I nervous about sex?* "Which is not really normal for me."

"Why are you nervous?" he asked and kissed my neck as he pulled me in tighter to him. His body pressed up against mine so hard, his erection even harder, which didn't seem possible. Would it even feel good inside of me? *Okay, that was crazy—of course it would!*

"I've never slept with a vampire before, remember?" I said quietly as I traced my fingers down his bare chest. I pressed my palm over where his heart would be beating and felt his utter stillness. It was so strange not to feel a heartbeat—I didn't think I would ever get used to it.

"There's no need to be nervous. I'm not going to hurt you," Brigham whispered, and I lost myself in his cobalt-colored eyes. I had never seen them change to this color before, and I wondered if other vampires' eyes color changed like his.

"Have you ever slept with a human—I mean, as a vampire?" I asked, hoping he would say no.

Brigham furrowed his eyebrows. "No."

"Really? Never?" I asked, with a little too much hope in my voice to be sounding neutral.

Brigham turned his head and looked at me, his eyes shifting to a slate color. "No, never. Did you think I have before? Did you think that I go around enticing human women?"

"No," I said unconvincingly. "Okay, maybe, but not in a judgmental way." Brigham nose wrinkled in distaste at my words. "It is interesting that you haven't. Do I have to worry about getting vampire cooties or anything?" Brigham's eyes turned azure.

"No."

"Getting pregnant?"

"No."

"Well, that's a load off my mind," I said and sighed in relief, snuggling into him. "Having some mutant demon baby was not on my to-do list."

"Were you worried about those things?" Brigham asked quietly and ran his hand down my back and up over my hip, pulling my ass into him.

"I guess—I don't know how all this works. Plus, I've seen a lot of vampire movies, and there usually is some sort of demon spawn twist," I rattled, moving my hips and grinded against him. It was such a turn on to know how ready he was for me.

He stilled and his eyes narrowed. "You're a virgin?" I laughed so loudly, I'm sure the neighbors heard me.

"Uh...no…"

"I don't understand why you're worried then," Brigham said quietly, and I looked up at him and noticed his eyes are now an admiral blue. He leaned down and kissed my lips tenderly. "It's just me."

"You're not nervous?"

Brigham blinked at me but held my gaze, his eyes turning azure again. "I wouldn't say that—I want to give you pleasure. I have a goal in mind that involves you screaming my name," he said factually. I chuckled at that—*that sounds fabulous!* He goes on, "I meant, I don't understand why'd you would be worried about being with me."

"As I said, I've never slept with a vampire before. Maybe you won't like or respond the same way a human man does." Suddenly, the truth of my words hit me, and I realized I was a little more than a little nervous.

"I think you get me to respond to you pretty well so far," he pointed out and pressed into me, making me gasp.

"That's true," I said softly and wrapped my arm up around his neck. He leaned in and kissed me hard, my lips almost bruising as I kissed him back, my tongue exploring him. The inside of his mouth was cooler than a human and I licked at his fangs, being careful not to impale myself on them.

He broke from me. "There's no need to be nervous. I'm not going to hurt you—it would break me to do so, Butterfly."

He cupped my cheek, and I looked deep into his eyes and felt into the depth of his affection for me. *Was this real?* Was I deluding myself by having a relationship with him?

Was there any way to be with him where I didn't get hurt? I didn't know, but I wanted to try and find out what it was like to be Butterfly and Brigham.

"Could you hurt me, physically?"

"If I wasn't paying close enough attention, I could."

"Because of your vampire strength?"

"Yes."

I considered that for a moment. "Well, I suppose being fucked to death isn't the *worst* way to go."

Brigham let out a low laugh. "I could think of worse fates."

"Such as?" I asked and he rolled me to my back, kissing the skin at my clavicle, and then he used his canines to pull my bra strap down off my shoulder. He kept pulling it down so that my breasts popped out and he leaned back, looking down at me and smiled. "You are so beautiful."

I touched his abdominal muscles. "Do the muscles come with the change, or were you this ripped when you were human?"

He unclasped my bra from the front and pulled it off me, kissing me between my breasts and I grabbed his head, pulling him harder into me. He moved down, layering my skin with kisses and pulled my panties off. As he moved to my hips, I gasped as he bit gingerly along my pelvic bones, sending shockwaves of energy into my core. My clit throbbed and I felt myself get wet as he bit into my skin, moving towards it.

"Have you thought anymore about my proposal?"

"About becoming a vampire?" I gasped as he bit tenderly at my folds. *Holy fuck—I didn't think that would feel good, but here we are!*

"Yes," he said and ran his tongue up my core, and I arched into him, grabbing the bedsheets.

"A little," I lied, as he pressed his hand to my hip, holding me down and licking me deeper and harder, making me shudder. Becoming a vampire was all I had been thinking about these days. I'd barely been getting my homework done.

"And?" he asked as he stopped licking and I made an embarrassing whimpering sound, not wanting him to stop.

"I don't have an answer for you yet."

"Why not?" he asked and flicked his tongue at my clit, making me jump.

"I want to see how tonight goes first."

"Is sex that important to you?"

"Are you sure you want to be hanging around with me for an eternity if I'm bad in bed?" I asked, looking down at him, he gave me a small, wicked smile.

"I'm not worried. I'm a good teacher," he retorted, causing me to snort.

"We'll, I'm worried. You might not be an attentive lover," I challenged, knowing fully well that he was *very* attentive.

"I am," he said with a confidence that sent a tingle down my spine and buried his head between my legs as he began to suck hard on my clit.

"FUCK!" I said breathlessly as a million tiny bolts of electricity shatter through me from my core. *What the fuck kind of orgasm was this?*

"Still no answer?" he asked as he released me for a moment and I tried to catch my breath and stop convulsing.

"I want this experience," I said in a daze and reached for him, pulling him up to me. My hip touched his hip, and I felt his smooth skin and noticed he was naked—somehow, he had removed his boxers without me noticing. I looked down at his hard cock and stared at it for a moment, surprised by the sheer size of it. *How was I going to fit that inside me?*

"Of sleeping with a vampire?" he asked seriously, and I looked up at him and noticed his eyes are now the color of lapis. I flinched, trying to get the image of his cock out of my head and focused on his question.

"I want to sleep with *you*, because of who *you* are, not because you are a vampire. Am I giving off a vampire groupie vibe? Because that is *not* why I want to do this." I sat up off the bed and pressed my forehead against him. "You know that, right?" Something flickered so fast across his face that it made my head hurt for a second as I tried to register his emotion but was unable to. "I do want to feel you in this form," I gestured to myself. "Maybe that makes me shallow."

"I understand."

"Do you?" I asked, looking deep into his eyes which were changing back to cobalt.

"Yes."

"If you were still human, I would want to do you in that form too," I said with a smirk, trying to lighten the mood. He let out a low laugh as I question, "You're not disappointed in me because I'm not ready to be a vampire yet, are you?"

"No, I know you'll come around eventually," he said, giving me sly smile.

"How can you be so sure?"

He smiled at me and didn't answer my question right away as he rubbed the skin on my arms. "You are a curious being—that's one of my favorite things about you." He paused for a moment before continuing, rubbing his hands over my body. "I've been looking forward to tonight." He pressed me back down to the bed. His cock pressed against the inside of my thigh and I gasped at the pressure.

"Have you? I would think sex with a human may seem dull to you," I said as he kissed my neck and I moved my hands along the muscles of his back. My breasts pressed against his cool skin, making them hard. I rubbed them against him, and he made a low growling sound that made my body goosebump and my heart started racing. *Fuck, I love when he does that!*

"I do not think making love to you will be dull," he answered, his voice thick and gritty, making my heart race even more. I reached down and found the tip of his shaft and touched it finding moisture there. I looked at my fingers and saw blood—*interesting!* I reached down again and rubbed up along his shaft and he growled again. Okay, so that part was the same in vampires as it was in humans. *Good to know!*

"I wasn't sure if sex was still important to vampires," I said, my voice heavy. He kissed down my chest again and this time sucked in one of my nipples hard—I felt his teeth tenderly nip at it and it made me suck in a breath and lose my grip on him.

He released me and moved to the other breast and asked with his mouth pressed against my skin. "Still?"

"Maybe after a few hundred years it gets old. I don't know," I gasped as he took in my other nipple. *Fuck, it was getting hard to think!*

"No sex never gets old, not even to vampires. I'm very excited to be with you tonight," he growled, and I felt myself start to drip. *Why the hell was that growling sound so sexy?* He moved his body, and I felt his hard cock pressing up against my core. I let out a low moan as the size of him became more real.

"I can feel that."

"How about you? Are you excited to be with me?"

"Uh…yeah." *Was he kidding?* I had to restrain myself from grave digging to find him today. Which after seeing this big bed would have been a waste of time. "I think my body is making that pretty clear. Don't you think?"

"You feel pretty wet for me," he said, his voice gravely, and I looked up at him as he bit down on his lip.

"Are you alright there? You look like you are about to lose control," I teased and slid my opening over the tip of his cock, making him groan.

"Tell me you want me," he demanded and pressed ever so slightly into me, making me gasp.

"I want you," I said, and pulled him down closer to me, making him inch into me. His eyes blazed, changing to indigo, and he bared his teeth, showing me his canines as he slid a little deeper into me and my pussy clenched tightly around him. He was so wide that I felt like I was about to split open as my body adjusted and he gently pressed forward slowly as I felt every inch of him fill me. I shuddered slightly and he paused as all of him was inside me and held me in his arms.

"I love you, Butterfly," he whispered and kissed my lips tenderly as I grabbed the back of his neck, pulling him closer and rocked my hips back and forth as I felt the full length of him ease in and out of my body. The friction of our bodies against each other and the fullness of him inside me sent me over the edge again and I shuddered against him as pleasure rolled through my body.

"I didn't know it could be like this with someone," I whispered, holding him tightly. I didn't mean the sex. It was so intimate with Brigham, and my emotions were overloading me.

Brigham kissed me again and his tongue found mine—he sucked and claimed me, leaving me breathless. He moved to my neck, and I felt his canines prick my skin as he kissed me rougher and began to thrust in and out of me at a quickened pace. I felt the limitless strength and stamina of his vampire form as my body becomes overwhelmed with sensation.

I wrapped my legs around him tightly and pulled him closer to me, needing to feel every part of him and he growled ferally as I dug my fingers into his back using all my strength. I wanted more of him—all of him. He started to move faster, grabbing my ass and pulling me up into him off of the bed as he continued to thrust into me at an inhuman pace and I shattered around him, my pussy clenching him tightly. He roared his release, and I felt him pulsing inside me as I slumped down against his chest as he held me in the air.

"Are you okay?" he asked, his voice strained and I looked up at him and saw his eyes were rapidly over my body as if he thought he had hurt me.

"I'm fine. Are you?" I said breathlessly and reached up and touched his cheek, still feeling him very hard inside of me. He leaned into it for a moment and closed his eyes as I kissed his forehead. *What was he thinking? What was he feeling? Was he as discombobulated as I was right now?*

"I didn't know it could be like this with someone either," he said, and gently laid me down on the bed. I reluctantly released him, and he pulled me tight against him.

It was weird snuggling with someone after making love and not feeling them breathe or have a heartbeat. Brigham also didn't sweat, so I had no real indicators of how successfully I was executing some things as we went along— I had to pay attention to a whole new set of cues, like how his eyes changed color, how much I could tell he was restraining from biting me, or how loud he growled or moaned. Given how many times I saw him biting his lower lip, I think it had gone well. My body was heated still from all the effort, and I pressed myself into him further, loving how cool his body felt—he was like my own personal air conditioner. It was also weird to have gone through a love making escapade and still be next to a fully awake male—so much was different, but oddly, it felt good and right.

"Does it hurt when you become a vampire?" I asked and Brigham tucked me closer to him and ran his hand over the back of my head as if he was protecting me from something.

"A little."

"Does it take very long?"

"No...seconds, maybe minutes, but there is a small amount of time after you're turned where you are vulnerable. You're not a full-strength vampire right away," he whispered.

"Why is that?"

"I think it's part of vampire evolution. For about a month or less after the change, it's important to remain close to your sire. I think it's so young vampires have a chance to learn about their new abilities."

"Kind of like vampire adolescence?"

"Something like that."

"Interesting..." I bit my thumb, thinking about that. "How close do you have to stay to your sire after you're changed?"

"Very close, within a few miles—otherwise, you start feeling some effects of the distance."

"What kind of effects?" I asked as a wave of nausea hit. *This sounds like a major drawback!* I didn't like the idea of being tethered to someone—Brigham or not.

"It can be very painful."

"What happens if you stay apart?"

"If you stay apart long enough, the newly made vampire will die."

I pulled back from him unable to hide my shock, "Really?"

"Yes," Brigham said, and his eyes changed to a steely grey.

"That's disturbing," I muttered as I snuggled back into him.

"It's a very critical time, that first month," he said and gripped me tighter. I loved how his arms were heavy and strong around me. This was the best feeling I had felt in a long time, it felt so safe in Brigham's arms.

"Has anyone ever died in the first month?" I whispered.

"It's very rare."

"Oh," I paused, considering that. *He was saying that it had happened though, right?* "That's interesting," I commented, trying to make my voice sound neutral, when in reality I was freaking out inside.

"What are you thinking?"

"Nothing," I lied. I was wondering if I became a vampire if I would die that first month. Maybe I'd have a weird accident or get on different planes and get accidently separated or something—but I wasn't going to say that. *That would be crazy and unlikely to happen, right?* Maybe like a 0.000001% chance. I cleared my throat. "I'm surprised a little. I didn't realize becoming a vampire was so complicated."

"It's not, really."

"After that month, you're a full-strength vampire?"

"Yes."

"And you're super strong, read humans' thoughts, glamour them, and do whatever you want?"

"More or less…"

"What's less?"

Brigham hesitated. "The Vampire Guild has rules— we are hindered by sunlight, and we need to feed to survive…you also have a very strong connection with your sire."

"How strong?"

"I suppose that depends on the vampires."

"What kind of connection?"

"I can't say," he said quietly and looked away from me as he rubbed my upper arm.

I made a face at him. "Why not?"

"Vampire rules," Brigham said and still avoided my gaze, and I noticed his jaw clenching.

"Oh…" We laid in each other's arms in silence for a while as I thought all of this over. *What wasn't he telling me or able to tell me?* "Are you glad you became a vampire?" I asked finally as I pressed my head against his chest. Still no heartbeat. *Still weird.*

"Yes—I would not have met you otherwise."

"Do you like it better than being a human?"

"Better? I'm not sure. It's an entirely different type of existence. It feels like I had two separate lives and I remember them both." He stroked my hair softly and frowned. "It is a bit strange, I suppose."

"One life is much longer."

"Yes."

"How old are you?"

Brigham's eyes twinkled. "I'm not telling."

"Why not?"

Brigham tensed and I looked up at him expectantly. He looked at me and sighed. "It makes me feel dirty."

I smirked at him. "Because I'm so young?"

"Yes," he said, his tone irritated.

"It kind of turns me on," I admitted.

His lips twisted ever so slightly making me laugh. "Really?"

"I've always liked older men," I said airily and ran my hand along his jaw, feeling his jaw tense under my touch.

"Men?" he gritted out between clenched teeth, and I laughed. Was he really being jealous now? Sleep with a guy one time, *I tell ya!* "How many men have you been with?"

"I'll tell you when you tell me how old you are, maybe. Hmmm…yep, I definitely have a thing for zaddies." I teased.

"I'm much older than most zaddies," he pointed out and I cringed a little at that inwardly. Maybe I would not keep that in the forefront of my mind.

"Oh yeah, say that again," I teased, and he flipped me on my back so fast I lost my breath and kissed me hard.

"You're so very different than anyone I've ever met," he said, pulling back from me.

"Is that a good thing?" I asked breathlessly. *Damn, he was a good kisser!*

"Yes."

"Good. I'm feeling less nervous and I have a few ideas for round two."

"I'm glad, I feel less nervous as well, and I have a lot of ideas as well."

"I thought you weren't nervous."

"I lied."

"*Bad* grandpa vampire," I teased and kissed his neck. I looked up at him hovering above me. He was so handsome, and I wondered why this was unfolding the way it was. "I wasn't planning on falling in love with a vampire in college."

Brigham face broke into a smile. "After college?"

"Nope…wasn't in the playbook for this life."

"I'm glad you did."

"Me too."

CHAPTER SIXTEEN

I wake up feeling awful. My body is completely limp, and I can barely lift my head. The relief I had gained during the night yesterday is gone, and I feared Brigham had lost track of me during the day. I try to sit up, but pain seizes me, and I groan loudly.

"Fuck," I say under my breath. Darren sits beside me and rubs my back.

"We're getting closer to the new moon," he says in a worried tone.

"One more day and this will be over, one way or another," I grit out. I was starting to look forward to my end—this was unbearable.

"You were feeling less affected yesterday," Darren says in a low tone.

"We must have driven far last night," I whisper, tears welling in my eyes.

"We did," Darren says with a defeated sigh.

"Too far, I think, for him now—it hurts really bad," I say and gasp as another wave of pain hits me and my throat feels like it's on fire. *I need to feed.*

"Tomorrow, we're meeting Shawn."

"Why? Wouldn't it be better to keep me moving? So that Brigham never catches up to me?"

"He wants to meet you…watch you die," Darren says, and I look up at him.

"That's a really stupid plan—hopefully, Brigham can still find me. God, he's one sick fuck," I say and Embry laughs. I had forgotten there were other vampires in the van with all my pain.

"Yes, he is," Darren, says darkly.

"Jesus, Darren, can't we feed her? I can't watch this," Embry says, pushing his hands through his hair.

"No…" I groan and press my head to the floor of the van. I didn't trust myself around any humans—I would kill a child with how thirsty I was, and I didn't want that on my conscience, no matter how much longer I had left.

"It has to be someone who's abusive—to animals, preferably," Darren says to Embry.

"That shouldn't be too hard, we're in farm country, after all. I'm on it. Shawn's not in my head right now." Embry leaves the van in a hurry.

I look around the van to see if Renard is still inside, but I can't see him anywhere. "Where's Renard?" I choke and gasp as my throat spasms sending shockwaves of pain into my torso and head. *Fucking hell, I wasn't going to make it to tomorrow!*

"Hunting."

"He won't like it that you're trying to feed me," I growl, trying to get a hold of myself.

"He'll just have to deal with it. He doesn't want to see anyone get in trouble. As tough as he looks, he's a big softy."

"You'll get into trouble."

"Shawn's too busy to stop me right now."

My palm surges with a stab of pain and I cry out, "I think Brigham lost me for good this time." I make a terrible hiccup sound, tears form in my eyes, and I start to sob uncontrollably.

"It's because of the sun—it just went down. The pain will lessen as the night progresses—he'll get closer, you'll see. Don't worry, Butterfly, it's going to be okay," Darren says desperately and puts his hand on my back, patting me rapidly. I think I am scaring him, which makes me feel bad and also terrified. I had to be in bad shape to scare Darren— he was an older vampire and had seen a lot in his lifetime. *I must really be fucked!*

"No, it isn't, but thanks for saying it anyway." I respond as he strokes my face. I close my eyes trying to rest, slipping in and out of consciousness.

I didn't know how long Embry is gone, but when I come to, Darren is carrying me out of the van.

"What's going on?" I ask, putting my hands to my head trying to try to stop the throbbing—it feels like I am about to explode. "Please tell me you are going to kill me— I can't take much more of this."

"Embry's back," Darren says softly, walking me off the road into the edge of the woods. He gently stands me up and my legs wobble underneath me.

"I can't stand," I say frantically, clinging to him. I am so much weaker than I had thought.

"I've got you," Darren says and holds me up. "Embry, can you bring him here?"

Embry emerges from the edge of the woods and that's when I smell the human and a feral growl rips from my throat—I whip around, almost losing my footing. Darren grips me harder, keeping me upright. Embry leads a short, fat man dressed in overalls over to me. He stinks like cow manure and is extremely ugly, with a bulbous nose and pock- marked skin.

"Sorry that he's so foul smelling, but he was the first guy that I found who fit the bill. This sicko gets a kick out of torturing the cows as they go to slaughter. He gets a little too slaphappy with his electric prod," Embry says, cringing and pushing the man hard towards me.

"Perfect," I growl, and my canines snap out. Embry positions the man in front of me, and I bite hard into his neck. The warm blood flows into me and I feel a surge of energy from the first drop as it hits my tongue. He is delicious and I bit harder into him, ripping the wound open more. I suck in deeply as the man's memories flooded me. Not only did this cretin like to torture cows, but he had a dog at home he liked to kick around as well. I bite at his neck harder and felt my strength increase with every drop of blood that I ingest. When the last drop is drained, I let the man hit the ground hard. I gave his head a swift kick and spit on him. "You got what you deserve, asshole." Darren looks at me in amazement.

"Thank you, Embry," I say softly, wiping the blood from my mouth. "I know you might get in a lot of trouble for it."

"It was worth seeing you drain that ass," Embry smirks and grabs the man's legs and drags him back deeper into the woods.

"I'm glad I got to kill one more asshole," I say, feeling a little defeated despite the surge of energy the blood is giving me. I close my eyes and feel the blood move through my body, energizing every cell. I still feel weak, but at least I can stand on my own now.

"How do you feel?" asks Darren.

"Better," I say, taking an unsteady step. I still feel the pain of the sire connection, but my throat wasn't doing the horrible burning thing.

"Good, but don't let on how good you feel when Renard comes back—he has a harder time keeping his thoughts out of Shawn's reach," Darren says quietly.

"That's why Shawn likes him so much," Embry adds, walking back towards us.

"Poor Renard," I say, looking around for him, but I don't see him anywhere in the shadows. I look up at the sky, and the moon is barely a sliver in the sky. Usually, when I look up at the moon, I feel peaceful, but looking up at it now fills me with dread. I am running out of time.

We climb back into the van and wait for Renard to return. I lay back against the van's wall and take stock of the pain I feel. I want to try to figure out if Brigham is getting closer. After feeding, it is difficult to tell if I am feeling better because of the blood meal or if he is closer. I'd have to wait and see what would happen throughout the night.

"Are you going to hunt?" Embry asks Darren.

"No, I'm still fine from yesterday. I'll be good for a few more days."

"Is that because you're older? Vampire-wise, I mean," I ask. Darren's human age couldn't have been more than twenty-six.

"Yes."

"Brigham barely needs to feed," I say, and feel a pulse through my palm upon saying his name. *Did he feel me think about him?*

"He's quite old," Darren says seriously.

"He won't tell me how old he is. Do you know?" I ask hopefully and feel another pulse. I rub my palm, hoping he can feel me through it.

"No, but he's older than Shawn."

"How old is Shawn?"

"He's three-hundred and eighty-six."

I gasp. *BRIGHAM IS OLDER THAN THREE-HUNDRED AND EIGHTY-SIX!* Oh, my God, I needed to talk to Anton, *right now!* "Jesus!" I exclaim as I gape at Darren.

"How old did you think he was? Forseti turned him when he was a newer vampire, and he's over a thousand years old," Darren says with a laugh and my jaw drops open. *HOLY FUCKING GRANDPA VAMPIRE! I'm such a dirty girl!*

"Forseti is Brigham's master?" I sputter. *What else didn't I know?*

"You didn't know that?"

"No, I had no idea. *Damn it!* I don't know anything apparently!" Darren laughs and shakes his head. "Christ— I've been sleeping with a *very* old, dirty vampire—no wonder he didn't want to tell me!" Embry and Darren laugh loudly, and I shake my head again in shock. *How old is he?*

Renard enters the van, rubs his lead and looks at us curiously. "What's so funny?"

"Nothing, Renard, nothing," Darren says, wiping tears from his eyes, still chuckling.

"We need to get going—Shawn made me stop half-way through draining a young woman outside of town.

"That sucks," Embry jokes and I can't help but roll my eyes. Renard shrugs and gets in the van gloomily and Embry goes to the driver's seat.

I look at Renard closely and he avoids my gaze, looking down at his hands awkwardly and slumps his massive form against the side of the van.

"Renard, what's wrong?" I ask. Renard looks at me and bites his lip and then looks at Darren and Embry with a pained expression.

"Shawn's been talking to me a lot," Renard whispers, his voice catching as he puts his heads in his hands. Darren and Embry exchange a tense look.

"Has he told you about his plans for me?" I guess. Renard's eyes shoot to me quickly and then to Darren and Embry again, going wide.

"Yes," he whispers and rubs his temple.

"Is it bad?" I press, not really wanting to know what Shawn had in store for me, but at the same time wanting to be prepared. Maybe it would be easier to take? I didn't know, not having been tortured to death before, thankfully.

"Yes," Renard groans and gives Darren an agonized look. Darren sighs deeply and crosses his arms over his chest.

"Fuck, all the guy has to do is keep her out of Brigham's reach. What else does he have planned?" Embry asks, his voice rising as he hits the steering wheel with his hand. Renard looks at him gravely and shakes his head, his lip trembling. *He really is a gentle giant!*

"It's okay, Renard," I say soothingly, trying to keep my voice calm. Inside, my anxiety feels like I have thousands of bugs crawling under my skin, but it won't help Renard if he knows that. "No matter what happens, or what Shawn makes you do, it isn't your fault."

"It doesn't feel that way," Renard says hollowly. "It would help if you were more of a bitch or had at least *tried* to attack us or something."

I give a halfhearted laugh. "Sorry, I'll keep that in mind next time you abduct me."

"What is he planning?" Darren asks Renard.

"Remember Maggie?" says Renard weakly. Embry lets his breath out in a gasp of horror and hits his head back against the seat.

"No way!" Embry growls in disbelief. Renard nods his head. Darren sighs deeply again and looks out the front window and rubs his face.

"What he's planning for Butterfly is ten times worse than what he did to Maggie," Renard says darkly and cracks his neck.

"What did he do to Maggie?" I ask, not really wanting to know the answer, but unable to help myself.

"He tortured Maggie for years in his dungeon. He did every horrible thing imaginable to her—cut off limbs, starved her, bled her—" Embry says darkly, staring out into space.

"Embry—" Darren tries to interrupt him.

"Maggie was a mother before she was turned—she loved children, especially babies. Every couple of days Shawn would bring in a baby and set it in front of her out of her reach and leave it to die in front of her…crying and struggling to be picked up," Embry says, shuddering and shakes his head.

"Embry!" Darren shouts.

Embry opens his eyes and looks at me with such sadness that I reach for his hand, trying to comfort him. "Then he would take children to her and change them in front of her, let her mother them, and then kill them while she watched."

"It was horrible the way she screamed," Renard said, as he rubs his ears and I notice the slightest of tremors run through his body.

"Embry, please stop," Darren says quietly, looking at me with a dejected expression.

"What did Maggie do to him?" I ask, noticing how scared and far away my voice sounded. It felt like I was having an out-of-body experience, my subconscious kicking in, trying to protect me.

"Nothing," Darren says softly. "He was bored and needed entertainment." My stomach drops. *She did nothing to him? Holy fuck, what a psycho!*

"Jesus! That is the most messed up thing I have ever heard," I say and start to rub at my palm frantically. If Brigham could feel anything through this, *I needed him to come now!*

"He's a sick fuck, that's for sure," Embry says through gritted teeth and even Renard nods this time.

"It won't be that bad for me," I hear myself say, but I am starting to feel disconnected from my body as my fear takes control. I press hard into my palm, drawing blood. *Come on Brigham! Please feel this!* "He won't have that much time to toy with me."

Renard looks at me sadly and I see that my words had not convinced him. Darren looks at the expression on Renard's face and looks back at me hopelessly. He didn't believe my words either. *FUCK!*

I slump back against the van and press into my palm hard with my fingernails piercing more of my skin. "I'll try not to scream, Renard," I say quietly and close my eyes—I could at least do that for him. A pulse of pain through my palm makes me flinch. *Come on Brigham! You have to find me!* I push my nails further into my skin until I cannot take it anymore and another pulse flares through my palm.

"Thank you," Renard whispers and turns away from me.

We sit in silence for a moment, and I turn my back on the vampires as I curl into a ball on the floor. I hear Embry start the engine and start driving. There is nothing I can do but wait. I have no more questions. My curiosity is finally extinguished. I didn't need to know any more about Shawn. As I wipe the tears away, I hope that Anton and Brigham won't take my death too hard.

CHAPTER SEVENTEEN

The ache inside me isn't as bad when I wake up in the morning—or evening, rather. That is never going to get easier to say—good thing I didn't have much longer to worry about it. My head isn't throbbing, and my stomach is only mildly uncomfortable. I had expected to be in much more pain and wonder what had happened in the day that was different than the last few nights. The vampires in the van look grim and stare stonily at each other. They weren't looking forward to this day any more than I was.

Thunder rumbles overhead and I can hear the rain hitting the metal roof. That familiar sound and pull of nature soothes me. I remember being a teenager and calling in the rain—I focus on that feeling, and the thunder overhead rumbles harder. I am happy that it would be raining when I died. It seems cathartic in some odd way, like coming home.

"Is Shawn close?" I ask Darren, while moving into a sitting position. He nods. "I can tell—you guys look much grumpier than normal."

A small smile crosses Embry's lips. "The closer we are to him the easier it is for him to jump in," Embry says, pointing to his head in a warning tone.

I nod in understanding. "Makes sense."

"If I do anything…cruel, to you, Butterfly, I'm sorry," Embry says, looking at me sadly. "Feel free to kick me in the balls."

I smile at his attempt at humor. "Don't worry, I can take a hit. Maybe I should apologize to *you* all now. If I hurt you while trying to escape, it's not personal. I can become *quite* feral."

Darren and Renard laugh. "Thank you, Butterfly," Darren says, giving me a weak smile.

"For what?" I ask.

"For making this easier," Darren says simply and Renard and Embry nod.

"I have a good feeling about today," I lie. The vampires look at me in disbelief. "Maybe I'll get to take a shot at Shawn—that could be *fun*, right?"

"Hit him once for me," Embry mutters under his breath. Renard shoots him a panicked look and Embry shrugs back at him.

"Twice for me," Darren echoes, tilting his chin up in the air defiantly.

Renard's eyes go wide, and he looks between Darren and Embry. "Ditto," he whispers, and a conspirator grin grows on his face as he looks at us.

"Any other requests?" I ask.

"Call him a spineless coward," Embry suggests and taps the steering wheel. "He *hates* that!"

"Will do." I say, adding that bit of information to my memory. "Darren, can I ask you something?"

"Anything."

"When you resist Shawn, how do you do it?"

"It depends on what he's trying to get me to do. If he wants me to move right, I focus on moving left. He wants me to speak, I picture myself with my mouth closed."

"So, opposites?"

"Yeah, that usually works for a little while, but it's exhausting to do for very long."

"What if he wants to search your mind?"

"That's even harder to stop—sometimes, if I have a thought I don't want him to know, I picture a wall around it, or a locked box—something like that."

I bit my lip. "Sounds tricky." It sounds like it takes a lot of concentration.

"It is," Darren says and rubs his head. "It's hard to think of something indestructible, strong enough to protect whatever you want to hide, especially being a vampire."

"It's too bad Shawn can't read my mind."

"Why do you say that?" Renard asks in disbelief.

"I'd like to stun him with some of Brigham and my love-making memories—I bet he wouldn't like that." I answer, causing Embry to snicker.

"No, I bet not," Darren chuckles and leans forward and looks out the front window apprehensively.

Embry pulls the van off the main road, and we drive down a long gravel driveway as my chest tightens. He soon pulls through a large garage door, drives through a dark tunnel, and parks the van. They all look at each other and then at me gravely.

"We're here?" I ask, trying not to sound panicked. I want to sound brave, but my voice catches and I dig my nails into my palm harder. Darren glances at my hands but quickly looks away, not wanting to give me away to the others.

"Yes," Renard replies, his voice low and body tensing.

"Good—I'm getting tired of this game." I look out the front window nervously. "I feel like the song 'The Final

Countdown' should be playing in the background. If this was a movie, it totally would be."

"I didn't ask you this morning, but how are you feeling?" Darren asks, looking at me briefly and then rises and looking anxiously out the front window.

I look at the other vampires in the van and hesitate to answer. *Would it matter if I told them the truth now? Would that information backfire on me somehow?* I press into my palm again and feel a pulse back right away and start to feel hopeful.

"I feel better than I have in days," I say, deciding to go with honesty. Embry smiles at Darren and he looks at me with a twinkle in his eyes.

"We better get moving—Shawn wants to start the show," Renard grumbles and looks at me apologetically.

"I have a feeling it's going to be a bigger production than Shawn is anticipating," Darren smirks as he gently helps me out of the van.

I step out into a huge underground garage that is lit by large overhanging fluorescent lights. It smells musty and wet, and I cringe at the smells.

"Is this the compound?"

"One of them," Daren says grimly.

"Pretty stupid of Shawn to take her here," Embry says.

"Well, Shawn's cruel—not intelligent," Renard mutters under his breath and I look at him in surprise at his bravery insulting Shawn when we are so near to him.

"That might work out for Butterfly," Embry says hopefully and rubs the back of his neck.

"Let's hope so," Darren says and leads me to a large metal elevator. He presses the small round glowing button, and the doors open wide. We walk inside and the doors close with a large metallic thump, making me jump a little. We start to descend, and the vampires become tense and silent around me.

"Well, this is quite ominous—doesn't Shawn believe in elevator music?" I joke, trying to lighten the mood.

"Butterfly, try to keep Shawn talking as long as you can," Darren whispers under his breath.

"That shouldn't be hard for her—she's had us jabbering this entire trip," Embry quips, giving me a smirk.

"It'll be better for you if you do," Renard whispers softly next to me. "He wants to brag about his scheme anyways—let him, give Brig—"

"Shh, Renard—not here," Darren hisses and his grip on my shoulder tenses slightly. Renard nods. The elevator comes to a stop, and I brace myself as the doors open, not sure what I am about to find.

Darren presses me gently in the middle of my back and we walk out into a large open room that is dimly lit. The room has very high ceilings and antique tables and chairs strewn haphazardly throughout it. Against the back wall I see a large ornate throne, the kind that kings use, next to a fireplace that has a fire blazing.

"Where are we?" I ask, "And why in the world is there some creepy-ass throne? *That's the most disturbing thing I have ever seen!* Does Shawn really sit on that thing? Talk about red flags!"

None of the vampires answer me and I assume Shawn wants it this way. He is trying to build my fear, which he is succeeding at. Suddenly, Embry grabs my arm roughly, making me flinch and leads me towards the back of the room. I don't need to look into Embry's face to see that he has no control of his body—his rough touch says it all. Darren and Renard follow behind us as we pass the throne and enter a dark hallway. I can hear voices in front of us growing louder. If I had a heart, it would be beating through my chest. I don't see how Brigham would ever be able to find this place. We had to be hundreds of feet underground.

Light floods over us as we stepped out into a large, well-lit room with numerous medieval torture devices. I notice a guillotine, an iron maiden, a strange metal pyramid on three legs that has blood stains on it with a dried pool of blood underneath it, and a large chair covered with large metal spikes before I look away, gulping down my panic and pressing my fingers into my palm, keeping them there. There are so many horrific looking contraptions that I have never seen before and assume I will find out what they are meant for soon. I shudder, making the mistake of looking up to some shelves, seeing various metal masks with sharp objects boring into them.

A young-looking vampire with short, black hair is animatedly talking to a tall, thin blond vampire against the far wall near a contraption with numerous straps and pulleys. The small vampire screams and violently strikes at the tall vampire, making a horrific bone-crunching sound. The tall vampire stands there motionlessly taking the blows, looking dead inside. The small vampire had to be Shawn. Darren clears his throat, alerting them to our presence and the smaller vampire shoves the tall vampire away and then turns to us.

"Ah, Darren, you've arrived! I'm afraid I've been so busy with my preparations here that I hadn't noticed," he says, giving us a wicked grin as he straightens his dark clothes. "Is this Miss Butterfly?" Shawn asks, eyeing me greedily, making my skin crawl. Darren gives only the slightest of nods. "Marvelous!"

Shawn walks around me, and I try to hold in my trembling. He looks innocent enough, boyish almost due to his small size and angelic face, but there is something distinctly dark and sinister lurking under the surface—his eyes give him away. They burn a deep red ochre color I have never seen before on a vampire. All the vampires I knew had normal-colored irises, but Shawn's eyes made him look demonic.

"What is it, my dear? You look frightened," Shawn says and laughs evilly.

Unable to contain my curiosity, I ask, "Why are your eyes that color?"

Shawn's eyes grow wide, and he shoots Darren an angry look. I feel Darren stiffen beside me and I began to worry if this is a question no one has ever dared to ask before. Figures—within a minute of meeting a psycho, I would stumble on his trigger. Shawn turns back to me and a wide smile slithers across his face, making his large canines stand out. I try to not look scared as he opens his mouth to speak. "Why are they red, you mean?" Shawn's eyes dart over me and I feel like he is trying to dissect me with his mind. *Why had I blurted that question out?* Shawn's gaze makes me increasingly uncomfortable, and I can feel my throat tightening.

I clear my throat trying to ignore my thirst and stare directly back at Shawn, trying to look confident. "Yes, they are very pretty…uh, scary…sorry, I don't know what you want to hear right now."

Shawn blinks and cocks his head at me and I feel Embry brace himself. *SHIT!*

"I don't know—they were a golden-brown when I was human—when I was turned, so did the color." Shawn takes a step closer to me and I brace myself, forcing myself to hold my ground and not back away.

Jutting my chin out slightly I say, "It's creepy."

"I know, isn't it fabulous!" Shawn shrieks, his voice raising a few octaves. His voice is so shrill—I couldn't see how anyone could stand around him without wincing. Shawn steps closer to me and my body involuntarily shies from him, and he claps his hands together joyously, seeing my repulsion. *This guy has serious issues!*

Trying to avoid his gaze I, say softly, "I suppose that depends on your perspective."

Shawn smiles at Darren and gives an approving nod. "Oh, I like her! *She's fun!*" Shawn shrieks as he turns his gaze from me to Darren, and I feel Darren's body jerk slightly. "I bet you all had a lot of great conversations in the van." Embry and Renard shift nervously as Shawn paces predatorily in front of us. *This guy really has some serious issues!*

Shawn stops in front of Darren and gives him a hateful glare and Darren looks away from him. "Oh, don't even try to deny it, Darren—I know what you've told her." Darren doesn't respond. "Not going to answer me, Darren? That's so rude." Shawn sighs deeply. "I've never had so much resistance with a vampire before."

"I'll take that as a compliment," Darren mutters softly and I look at him like he is insane.

"You would, wouldn't you." Shawn walks up to Darren and plants himself squarely in front of him, staring at him coldly. Suddenly, Darren is on the floor squirming and flailing his arms while screaming in pain. I try to move to Darren, but Embry's grip on my arm stops me.

"Stop it!" I scream. Renard flinches and I remember my promise to him. "Please—he didn't tell me anything," I say quietly, trying to sound convincing. *He only told me that you were a mad psycho!*

Shawn turns to me and stares at me with a curious expression on his face. *Oh fuck!* Darren flops against the floor like a fish out of water, hitting his head hard on the cement floor and I cringe. The sound is sickening, and I turn away from him, unable to stand the spectacle.

"Fine," Shawn says with a bored shrug and Darren's body stops moving. I look to see if he is alright and he blinks up at me, completely dazed. "We don't have much time anyway since the new moon is almost upon us. I'll deal with Darren's insolence when I have more time to enjoy it."

Renard bends down to help Darren up, grabbing his arm gently.

"Leave him, Renard!" Shawn shouts. Renard jumps and drops Darren's arm. Darren pulls himself off the ground and gives me a weak smile. "I wish I had known sooner that Brigham had a woman in his life. I would have *loved* to have gotten hold of you when you were still human. Vampire bodies are so boring to torture—now—*human* bodies, on the other hand, have lots of body fluids and parts that you can decorate with!"

"You want Brigham to find my mutilated body?" I ask, my voice sounding hollow.

"Oh, yes—dear, yes! I think that would be much more fun!" Shawn's eyes sparkle and his face darkens.

"But I'll turn to ash. He won't know it's me."

"You don't understand, Miss Butterfly—Brigham is going to watch you die," Shawn explains as Darren looks at him as if he has lost his mind, *which he obviously has.* "I've been working on this plan for days—Brigham knows where to find you tonight, and he's making his way here as we speak. He'll arrive just moments before the new moon starts, but he won't get to you—he'll have to watch helplessly as you turn to dust!"

"That's risky," Darren warns, giving me the slightest of hopeful looks.

"No, it's not! I have an army of vampires here—he's not going to arrive until I want him to. The hardest part was keeping him from you the last few days. He was relentless in tracking you, even during the day—him and that vampire named Anton," Shawn says in disgust.

"Anton?"

"Yes, I was very disappointed to learn that he followed you and Darren from the coffee house." He gives Darren a disgusted look. "A better vampire might have figured out you were being followed, but not Darren.

Luckily, the daylight gave us the time we needed to put some distance between us and him."

"Why all the games, Shawn? Why let Brigham come at all?" Darren asks.

"I want to *see* his face when she dies! I want to see all the pain and loss when his heart breaks," Shawn spits.

"He'll decapitate you completely this time," Darren says assuredly and Shawn slaps his face, hard. The sound of the slap echoes across the room and I shudder.

"That's not going to happen—as I said, I've got an army of vampires here—he's not getting through until I want him to. Now, put her on the Judas Cradle—I want to try this one out." I look at the devices around the room, trying to figure out which one he is talking about, but they all look equally horrible.

"No," says Darren softly. Shawn turns quickly to him and grabs his shirt and spits in his face. Darren wipes away the bloody glob, avoiding Shawn's gaze.

"Do you need me to make you do it?" Shawn hisses, his red eyes blazing, making him look crazier.

Darren turns and looks at him and gives him a cold stare, his jaw clenching as he seethes, "Yes."

Shawn huffs and turns from him, releasing him. "Unbelievable!" he screams. "Renard, can you believe this man? I swear to you, Darren, as soon as this business with Brigham and Butterfly is done, I'm dealing with *you* next. You won't live to see the next new moon!"

"Good!" Darren says defiantly, his eyes burning into Shawn.

Shawn sneers and creeps up to Darren. "You'd like that, wouldn't you, to be free of me? Well. That's not happening. No, there are far worse things that I can think of for you to experience." Shawn pulls at his hair and scowls at him. "*Argh!* Darren, you're ruining all my *fun!* We don't have much time, and I have a lot of plans for this girl!" He starts pacing back and forth across the room, muttering to himself.

"Well, you do whatever you're planning yourself, you spineless coward," Darren says coldly. *Oh, crap—he just called him a spineless coward!* Why is Darren egging him on? Shawn turns from his pacing and lets out a loud hiss, and I stiffen at the sound. *He sounds like an actual snake!* His face contorts and he snarls at Darren. I could see why Embry wanted me to call him that—it really did make him mad.

"How dare you!" Shawn yells and Darren is suddenly on the ground, clutching his head in pain.

Renard grabs my arm gently and moves me away from Darren as he begins screaming in pain and I watch helplessly. Shawn laughs and watches Darren as he thrashes and begins to dance around him, kicking and spitting at him. It is too horrible to watch, and I turn my head and bury it into Renard's chest. I want to stop Shawn, but there is nothing I can do—*I can't take on four vampires!* I'm not a full-strength vampire and am no match against the vampires in this room. I hate feeling this vulnerable and I vow that if I get out of here, I will never get myself in a situation like this again.

The tall, blond vampire that Shawn had been screaming at enters the room and looks anxiously at us.

"Master," he says quietly. Shawn ignores him and kicks Darren's head, making a horrible thudding sound. "Master!" the man says louder.

Shawn is wildly laughing now as Darren sobs on the floor curling into a ball, his hands tearing at his face as he tries to escape whatever torment Shawn is unleashing on him. Bloody claw marks appear just as soon as they heal, and I find myself getting nauseous watching him suffer.

The tall vampire looks imploringly at Embry and Embry rolls his eyes and clears his throat loudly, but Shawn ignores him.

"MASTER!" Embry shouts. Shawn looks up from Darren distractedly and Embry gestures toward the tall vampire.

"Yes, Cedric—what is it now?" Cedric looks uncomfortable and fidgets in place. "What is it, Cedric? God, you try my patience."

"There is some trouble upstairs," Cedric whispers and Shawn stares at him, trying to decipher what he means.

"Is Brigham here already? Hmmm, that's unexpected," Shawn murmurs and rubs his chin looking worried and starts to pace. "He got here sooner than I expected—this girl must be very important to him."

My eyes fly wide open. *Brigham is here?* I realize that it has to be true, as I feel no pain anywhere in my body except for the thirst for blood. *He is close, very close!* I hadn't paid attention because I had been so busy watching Darren get tortured—or rather, trying to *not* watch Darren get tortured.

"Embry, put Miss Butterfly in my bedroom. I'll send for you when it's time. Renard, come with me."

Shawn walks off with Cedric and Renard trailing behind him down the dark hallway we had entered from. Renard looks at me over his shoulder and gives a hopeful smile. My chest tightens and I hope Renard will be safe with Shawn—and that Brigham doesn't accidently kill him. It wouldn't be fair if he got killed working for a psycho. I look down at Darren who is lying in a pile on the floor, blood seeping out of him as his wounds slowly heal. Embry stands with me, grasping my arms hard—when the elevator door shuts, he lets go of my arms and we rush to Darren's side.

I grab his head and set it in my lap and try to wipe the blood off of his face. Blood has leaked out of his eyes, ears, mouth, and nose—plus, with him tearing at his face, he is a complete mess. He looks up at me, blinking at me rapidly.

"Butterfly?" he gasps.

"Why did you make him so mad?" I scold. I use the end of my dress to dab at the blood on his face, which didn't really help, but it smears away a little.

"That was pretty stupid calling him a spineless coward," Embry says grimly, kneeling next to us.

"Better me than her," Darren mutters, rubbing his head and letting out a small groan as he touches his nose.

"That's true," Embry says and turns to listen to something. There's what almost sounds like thunder rumbling above us and I feel a strangely familiar sensation in my body and close my eyes, sensing the storm. *I must be losing it.* "Brigham's here," Embry says, his face darkening. "Earlier than expected."

"Good, then it worked. I was trying to stall him to keep him from going after Butterfly. I figured Brigham would get here before Shawn expected. Brigham is much smarter than Shawn—Shawn's an idiot. How do you feel?" Darren asks, looking up at me.

"Jesus, I'm fine—you're the one covered in blood and was just beat almost to death by a psychopath. How do *you* feel?"

"Like I was hit by a truck a couple hundred times." Darren grimaces and tries to sit up.

"You're an idiot. Do you know that?" I say, my voice shaking.

Embry laughs. "I've been telling him that for years. He has a serious death wish," Embry says, grabbing Darren's arm and helping him to his feet. "We're supposed to take her to Shawn's bedroom."

"Good, I need to lie down," Daren says, swaying on his feet. Embry puts an arm around him and helps him move toward a door in the back of the room. I move to Darren's other side and try to help him walk but am too short to help much.

"Butterfly, can you open that door?" Embry gestures to a large wood door.

"That I can do!" I say, happy to find a way to help.

Behind the door is a large bedroom. There are large tapestries and pictures covering almost every wall surface inside. The carpet is a deep, red color and what little you could see of the wallpaper seems to be the same red color with gold vines running vertically. There are a couple sawhorse looking apparatuses with various metal attachments and protrusions on them decorated with dried blood in the room that I try to ignore.

"Jesus, his bedroom is right next to the torture chamber!" I say as a shudder ripples through me.

"He likes to hear the screams," Darren groans and clutches at his stomach for a moment.

"Poor Renard has had torture duty one too many times, and he can't take the screaming anymore," Embry adds.

"That's awful!" I say, covering my mouth.

"The vampire that does most of it now really enjoys his work, he—" Embry starts.

"Okay, I don't need to know any more," I interrupt.

"Sorry," Embry says, looking guilty and gently sets Darren on the bed.

"Can I get you anything?" I ask, looking frantically around the room. I notice more torture devices and shudder.

"No, I'm fine—in a few minutes, I'll be good as new," Darren smirks at me.

"I was prepared for the torturing. You didn't have to antagonize Shawn. I would have been fine."

"Yes, I did," Daren says softly and I see the tears welling in his eyes. I move to him and hug him gently.

"Don't worry about it, Butterfly—Darren's always looking for a chance to antagonize Shawn," Embry says, looking anxiously towards the way we had just come.

"You were resisting him too. I saw how hard Shawn was pushing you to hold onto Butterfly," Darren challenges and Embry runs his hands through his hair and shrugs.

"I don't know what you're talking about," Embry says, giving us a sly smile.

"Liar," Darren challenges and Embry smiles wider at Darren, showing his canines.

"Well, I thought maybe I could resist him just enough that he wouldn't be able to have his full focus on you, idiot," Embry says and turns, rubbing his chin and looking back at the door again. "Poor Renard, I'm worried about him."

"He's tougher than he looks," Darren says confidently.

Embry looks at Darren, and his face goes cold. "No, he's not."

Darren grimaces. "No, he's not…" Darren agrees and lays down on the bed and closes his eyes.

Darren's wounds are healing fast, and I wipe the remaining blood from his face.

"I'm fine, Butterfly, really," Darren says, grabbing my hand. I look at Embry for reassurance and he nods.

"He's a tuff old goat," Embry says assuredly as he claps Darren's shoulder.

"You guys are close, aren't you?"

"Yeah—me, Darren, and Renard are like the three musketeers around here," Embry says grimly.

"Brothers in arms," Darren adds, keeping his eyes closed and rubs his arms.

"It's kind of like being in a P.O.W. camp," Embry says and chuckles, rubbing his chin again.

"Not every vampire feels that way," Darren says, struggling to sit up.

"Most of them do," Embry says as he looks at him.

"Yes, most of them do," Darren sighs and loud boom of thunder makes me jump as my palms start tingling. I rub them together and then a huge crash overhead makes me jump again.

"What do you think is happening up there?" I ask as I watch dust fall from the ceiling.

"I think Brigham is kicking ass and taking names," Darren says and rolls his neck around. I rub my palm, looking up at the ceiling. "I'm serious—I think Shawn bit off more than he could chew with his plan."

"I hope so."

"Me too," Darren says, looking at me intensely.

I stand up from the bed and pace nervously around the room. "I feel like we are in a bomb shelter as a nuclear war is waging above us," I mutter as another loud crash booms above us. I can't tell if it is thunder or the fighting. I try to feel the storm, and I can almost feel the air outside. Why is this happening now, I wonder? Another loud crash above us makes us all jump.

"That's exactly what this is," Embry says and looks at me wearily.

I move around the room, frowning at what I find. I gape in horror at some of the pictures on the wall. They are all very grotesque. There are pictures of vampires ripping heads off humans, babies being eaten, vampires fornicating with blood dripping off their bodies, and *entrails, entrails, entrails.*

"Shawn has horrible taste," I say in disgust. "How the hell can he sleep in here?"

Embry laughs. "I dare you to tell him that," Embry crosses his arms and looks at the ceiling as another loud crash sounds above us.

"I don't think so. I was feeling braver before Darren ended up covered in blood," I say honestly. As I pace, I suddenly felt dizzy and clutch the bed for a moment, trying to steady myself. A large rumble of thunder overhead makes Darren and Embry jump, and I swear I can feel the storm as if it is inside of me.

"Butterfly, what is it?" Darren asks, moving towards me.

"I don't know—I don't feel right," I say with panic in my voice. Darren looks at Embry and Embry pales.

"What time is it?" Darren asks Embry.

Embry looks at his watch and his expression looks grim. "She has twenty minutes," he says quietly and another loud boom overhead crashes and more dust falls from the ceiling. Darren kneels next to me, holding up my chin, trying to get me to look at him.

"Listen to me, Butterfly—this is very important." I wince from the pain that is starting to fill my entire body. "Are you still with me?"

"Yes, but hurry—something is wrong." My body spasms and I sink to the floor, clutching at Darren. Painful jolts of electricity pulse inside of me cause me to convulse, *it feels like I am being electrocuted! What is happening? Am I dying?*

"Embry and I will do everything we can to get you close enough to Brigham, but you *have* to be touching him when the new moon phase starts," Darren says, his eyes wide with panic.

"I don't know if I'll be able to," I gasp and let out a loud moan as the pain grows more intense. "This hurts so much—I don't know if I'll be able to get to him." The panic in my voice is unmistakable I try to fight back the tears.

"You have to try," he says determinedly, gripping my shoulder roughly.

I nod and try to keep the tears from falling. "I will," I say and nod vigorously. *I've made it this far, and I am not going to die now! I can't do that to Anton and Brigham!*

"Shawn is going to be preoccupied with everything else going on and I think we'll have a good chance to stand against him. He has a hard time controlling numerous vampires at the same time."

"It takes a lot of energy for him to control Darren, Renard, and me at the same time and that's even when we're not fighting against him," Embry says, stuffing his hands in his pockets and looking down at me as his face hardens.

"Right, and if we fight against him, it'll be worse for him," Darren says excitedly.

"Do you think it will work?" Embry asks Darren, taking his hands out of the pockets and flexing his hands in and out.

"It's worth a try—hopefully Renard will catch on," Darren adds.

"He will, Renard will come through," Embry says, nodding.

My body spasms again and pain shoots through my palms, almost making me pass out as another boom of thunder sounds. The walls shake from the sound echoing around us.

"What the fuck is happening with the storm?" Embry mutters and then loud shouts above us make Darren and Embry turn towards the door in a readying stance.

"It's alright, Butterfly—they'll come for us soon," Daren whispers and adjusts me in his arms. As the words escaped his lips, Cedric enters the room, wiping fresh blood from his face.

"It's time," Cedric says grimly.

"How many vampires did Brigham bring?" Embry asks.

"The *entire* Vampire Guild of Minneapolis," Cedric says, his voice shaking.

"Really?" Darren gasps and a huge smile creeps over his face.

"We've lost a lot of people so far. It doesn't look good for us," Cedric says and wrings his hands.

Darren gently picks me up and holds me in his arms. "That's one perspective."

Darren carries me into the torture hall, and I lean my head against his shoulder. The pain inside me is immobilizing and I wonder if Brigham feels it too—I hope it's not as bad for him—*otherwise I am fucked!* Thunder rumbles louder overhead and it doesn't make sense that it is so loud when we are so far underground. *Were we not as far down as I thought?*

I fight hard to remain conscious as the new moon phase draws near, more thunder booms overhead and weirdly it seems to help stabilize me. Inside the hall, there are at least a hundred vampires lined up looking apprehensively at a hidden elevator door I had missed earlier. Many of them are healing from fresh wounds and there is a distinct smell of blood in the air. In front of the vampire mob, Shawn stands talking to a muscular vampire with long brown hair. Shawn sees us approaching and a wide grin appears on his face, making me want to run from him.

"Good, Darren, you've recovered just in time. God, she looks awful!" Shawn says, looking down at me. "That's also good!" Darren doesn't say anything and adjusts me in his arms, holding me farther away from Shawn. Shawn notices the gesture and laughs. "So chivalrous, Darren—it's pathetic." Darren doesn't take Shawn's baiting and remains quiet. "We're going to open the doors and let them in. Brigham will be in front, and once he's inside, we'll close the doors. I don't want the entire guild down here. Once he witnesses Butterfly's death, we can kill everyone in the room. The guild will stop once Brigham is dead."

Anger flares in me and I glare at Shawn. Another loud boom of thunder and the lights flickered around us, and I swear I have just called it. *What is going on? Am I in some weird state of delirium?* I feel into the storm and a thunderous boom makes the lights flicker again—*no, that was real!*

Darren tenses and looks at me and I give him a weak wink and he looks back at Shawn. "You think so?" Darren asks, his tone sarcastic as he grips me tighter.

Shawn waves him off. "Yes, I do, it's like cutting the head off a snake. There's no need for them to continue fighting."

"You don't think they want to take you out as much as Brigham?" Darren asks innocently as Shawn's eyes flash and he snarls.

"I'm not a threat to them," he growls.

"Whatever you say, *master*," Darren says while feigning obedience.

"I might just let Brigham take you out, after all," Shawn says in disgust. Darren doesn't respond. Shawn's eyes turn back to the elevator and he looks at his watch.

"Open it!" he shouts. Darren grips me tighter and I can't tell if it's Shawn or him behind it. Embry moves in between Darren and Shawn, and I wonder if Shawn is drawing him closer for protection.

The elevator opens and Anton and Brigham leap out with their fangs bared as they begin ripping the heads off of the vampires standing nearest the doors. I look at Anton and Brigham in awe—both of their clothes are tattered and covered in blood strains. They looked like a pair of feral demons, their faces filled with a darkness that would make your blood run cold—but their faces set me on fire, filling me with hope. *They had come for me! They both loved me so much that they were willing to risk their lives for me!* And the guilt and shame hit me like a brick.

The other vampires pull back in fear from Anton and Brigham as snarls and growls fill the room. Brigham searches the room for me and spots me in Darren's arms. His eyes move across my body, when he sees the blood-covered dress I am wearing, his face distorts into something truly demonic. He snarls loudly and I realize he thinks the blood on me is my own. Anton looks to where Brigham is staring and his fangs flash. In one fluid motion they are leaping in the air towards me. Behind them, I see a rush of movement as dozens of vampires charge out of the elevator. Shawn's men try to close the elevator doors and soon there is a large fight going on in front of the open elevator doors as more Vampire Guild members stream in. They had to be coming down the shaft!

As Brigham and Anton near, two vampires standing in front of us launch themselves at them. With one hand, Brigham throws the first vampire hard against the wall. The sound his body makes when it hits the wall is incredible. It sounds like an avalanche, and the vampire's body leaves a huge impression on the wall. The second vampire swings at Brigham, but he gracefully outsteps him and twists his arm off. The vampire falls to the floor screaming as blood gushes out of him.

The screaming reminds me of Renard, and I search the room for him. He is watching me from across the room, gripping on to a large beam in the room looking like he is trying to hold himself there. He isn't fighting yet, and he gives me a grim smile. I can't believe he is resisting Shawn! My chest tightens and I turn my attention back to the scuffle happening in front of me between Brigham and a group of vampires.

Brigham is *magnificent!* He moves quickly, taking out his enemies, his muscles pulsing and his hair flying around him like he is some sort of Vampire God. Darren sets me down roughly next to Embry, and I look at him questioningly. He doesn't look at me, and I know that Shawn is in control of him now. I look at Brigham, and he is watching me. I try to move towards him, but Embry's arm clamps down on my shoulder hard, causing me to wince and let out a cry of pain. *To say this makes Brigham mad is an understatement.*

Brigham's fangs flash at Embry as he lets out a hideous snarl that makes the vampires around him shudder and back away from him. Brigham turns and picks up Anton, launching him at Embry. Anton flies gracefully through the air and hits Embry square in the chest, knocking him to ground. Anton's blow sends me falling to the ground as well and I hit my arm hard on the floor and hear a distinct *crack*. My arm is broken and the pain burns, but I know it will heal if I can set it back in place. Quickly, before I can overthink it, I pull my arm so that the bones are closer in alignment and feel them start to knit together. *What's a little more pain at this point!*

All around me, vampires fight with each other, their movements so fast that it is hard to identify anyone. I try to find Anton and Embry amongst the fighters and see Anton punching Embry as they struggle with their fangs baring at each other. Anton lands a superb punch, knocking Embry off his feet and pins him down as he tries to rip his arm off.

"Anton, please don't!" I cry, but it is useless. Anton can't hear me in all the chaos.

I turn towards Brigham and see he is busy fighting off two vampires as well as Darren now. Shawn is nowhere to be seen as I search for him in the crowd. *Coward!* I try to drag myself towards Brigham. The pain from my arm is nothing compared to the pain in my body now.

My skin burns as if I am on fire, and more thunder booms overhead. I feel a surge of power in me and the lights flicker followed by a loud boom of thunder. *What is happening right now?* I close my eyes and call the storm. I feel the energy of the storm build as if it is inside me and I let it build and build as I inch my way towards Brigham. As I get closer to him, I release it, and large flashes of lightning hit the vampires in the room, turning them instantly to dust followed by a deafening boom of thunder, causing everyone to pause—*everyone but Brigham.*

He sees me and moves towards me, swiftly decapitating the vampire that he is fighting. The red-haired head falls to the floor and turns to ash mere feet from me. Darren is on Brigham with full force now and I watch in horror as Brigham tears at Darren's face. Blood pours from Darren's wounds, and he lashes at Brigham wildly. Brigham grabs one of Darren's arms and snaps it backwards, breaking the bone. My stomach lurches and nausea hits me as I look at the odd angle of Darren's limb. *Brigham is going to kill Darren, and I am going to watch it happen!*

Suddenly, I feel my body rising and I find that Renard is next to me, lifting me up off the ground.

"He's going to kill Darren!" I sob, pointing at Brigham and Darren.

Renard looks where I am pointing, and his face turns gray. "Hold on," he whispers. He grabs me roughly by the waist and for a moment I think Shawn has taken over Renard's body. He leaps over the vampires standing between Brigham and us and lands inches from Darren and Brigham. I fall from Renard when we land and hit the floor again. Renard tackles Darren and pins him to the floor. Brigham looks at Renard and snarls and moves to finish off Darren.

"NO!" I cry. Brigham head jerks towards me, and he sees me on the ground. I reach towards him, and he quickly falls to the floor next to me, grasping my hand.

"Butterfly!" he yells and pulls me into his lap, hugging me so tightly to him that I feel my bones creak.

"I knew you'd find me," I sob, grasping him as tightly as I can.

"I always do," he whispers into my ear, and I cling to him harder. *He is here! He came for me!*

"Is it too late?" I ask, unable to keep the fear out of my voice. "Am I going to die?"

Brigham shakes his head, still holding me tightly. "No, we're just in time." Suddenly, the burning inside me intensifies and I pitch against Brigham. He holds onto me tightly, digging his fingertips into my flesh like he is afraid to let me go.

My entire body burns, and I feel myself separate inside, melting under the heat. I am a volcano…I am a meteor…I am a full-strength vampire, and I scream as every cell in me hardens and sharpens. The lights flicker and bolts of lightning erupt around us followed by a boom of thunder that causes the entire building to shake violently.

My body begins to cool just as quickly as the fire has started within me, and I feel the new hardness of my body. It is like I had been dipped in liquid metal and am now cooling into something harder and stronger. *I've been forged!* I open my eyes and stare at Brigham and then I feel another surge, and I look up to the ceiling and feel into the storm. It feels like it is a part of me and I close my eyes and call another bolt of lightning that causes the lights to flicker followed by a boom of thunder. *The storm obeyed me! I can call and control it! I have an ability!* It is just like when I was a teenager, but more powerful!

"Are you okay?" Brigham asks, pulling back from me slightly but keeping me tight in his grip.

"Yes," I say in surprise.

"I thought I was going to lose you," he admits and I notice how pale and gray his face is. He looks completely haggard! "Did Shawn hurt you?" he asks, his tone dripping with venom.

"No, but can we kill him now? I really don't like him," I say, and Brigham gives me a feral smile.

"As you wish, my love." Brigham pulls me to my feet, and I notice Darren and Renard are still struggling on the floor. Brigham sees them and snarls, reaching for Darren again.

"No, don't!" I yell, grabbing his arm and am amazed by my strength as I am able to stop Brigham.

"But this is the man who took you!" he says, his face twisting demonically.

"It wasn't him, it was Shawn," I explain. "That's Shawn in there now—Darren would never hurt me."

"You're covered in blood," Brigham points out and turns towards Darren again, seething.

"It's not my blood. It's Darren's—he antagonized Shawn so he would torture him instead of me."

Brigham tries to reach for Renard, but Renard moves out of his reach.

"Don't," Renard says, shaking his head. "He's trying to jump into me as we speak. I think the only reason he can't is because he's busy trying not to get Embry killed." Renard gestures to the back wall where Anton and Embry are still fighting.

"Shawn's been controlling Renard, Embry, and Darren's will this entire time, but they've been fighting him trying to help me."

Brigham looks at me and hesitates and then looks back to Darren and Renard. "You saw the amount of power a master has over the vampires he sires, and you still reached for me before the new moon?" Brigham says quietly.

"You're not like Shawn."

"No, but you saw what I would be capable of," Brigham says grimly.

"You wouldn't ever do that to me." Brigham stares at me and then looks down at Renard and Darren struggling on the floor. Darren is snarling and trying to bite Renard, and it pains me to see him like that.

"Do you know where Shawn is now?" he asks Renard.

"No idea," Renard says and narrowly avoids another bite from Darren. Brigham scans the room, searching for Shawn—his jaw pulsing.

"I need to tell Anton not to hurt Embry any more than he needs to," I yell and step away from Brigham. His arm shoots out and grips me hard. I look at his hand, and he looks down at it in surprise as well.

"Sorry," he says while easing his grip. "I can't let you go off by yourself yet."

"Because of the new moon?"

"No," he says, shaking his head. "Because I can't do that yet." Brigham looks at me sadly, his face breaking with emotion, and I realize how hard the last few days must have been for him.

"Okay, let's go together," I say softly and wrap my fingers around his. Brigham steps in front of me and shoves the vampires out of our way as they fight amongst us and we make our way to Anton. He rubs his fingers over mine gently and I follow him towards Anton, feeling so relieved that we are back together.

Anton pins Embry to the ground and Embry's fangs snap and lash out at him. "Oh, Brigham, thank God you're here! This guy is annoyingly strong—he will not give it up!" Anton growls.

"That's because you're fighting Shawn," I inform him.

"I am? Cool!" he exclaims and hits Embry hard across the face.

"Don't," I say and put my hand to Embry's face. Embry tries to bite at me, and I quickly withdraw my hand.

"Are you insane?" asks Anton.

"Don't hurt him," I plead.

"Brigham, can you tell me what's going on? Butterfly has Stokholm Syndrome and isn't making any sense."

"This vampire is a friend of hers. He's been sired by Shawn—you've been fighting Shawn through this man's body."

"Embry," I correct.

"Embry," Brigham says as he rolls his eyes. *Oh! He is so crabby!*

"Aw, no fair, that's cheating!" Anton seethes.

"Embry is a sweetheart—he doesn't like Shawn controlling him. He didn't even want to become a vampire—he was turned against his will!"

"Really?" Anton gasps, as his jaw drops open. He loosens his grip on Embry for a second and Embry charges up at him—Brigham quickly helps hold him down, his face grim. "You *would* find a way to pick up strays while you were abducted, Butterfly."

"Most of these vampires here were changed against their will—they're Shawn's prisoners. Brigham looks around the room and sees the situation now in a new light, his face tenses.

"That changes a lot of things. I knew Shawn was a bad guy—Jacqueline told me stories—but I had no idea what he was doing here. I doubt the Vampire Guild does either," Brigham says through gritted teeth as Embry thrashes harder at him and Anton.

"We have to kill Shawn—it's the only way to set these people free!" I say, looking around the room in a panic as I see more and more of the Vampire Guild turning Shawn's vampires to ash.

"You're right, but I don't know where he is. He is not here," Brigham says tensely as Embry bucks at him.

"Are you sure we can't kill this guy?" Anton asks as he puts all his weight into Embry.

"*DO NOT KILL HIM!* Shawn has to be close, it's easier for him to control the vampire if he's close," I say and search the room again.

"Do you know where Shawn's bedroom is?" Brigham asks me.

I shudder. "Unfortunately, yes. Why?"

"It's something Jacqueline once told me—there's supposed to be a secret room there, behind a painting."

"Which painting?"

"Something gory. I don't remember the specifics."

"Well, that's not going to help, because all the pictures in there are disturbing," I mutter. Next to us, a guild member decapitates one of Shawn's vampires and he disintegrates into dust. "We need to hurry, or more vampires are going to die unnecessarily. I can't tell which ones are fighting because they want to and which ones are under Shawn's control. The room is this way." I grab Brigham's hand as Anton struggles to keep Embry pinned, leading him towards the bedroom.

"Hey, I want to see the dirty pictures!" yells Anton.

"You have to keep Embry safe," I yell back and Embry snarls at me with feral eyes.

"I always miss out," Anton pouts and punches Embry hard in the face.

A vampire with numerous tattoos jumps in front of me, blocking the entrance to the hallway. I launch myself at him and send him sailing across the room. He hits a large metal chest with several large spikes sticking out of it and is impaled.

"That was so cool!" I say, looking at my hands in astonishment. *I am so strong now!* Brigham looks at me in amazement. "Can I kill Shawn?"

"No way—he's mine," Brigham says firmly and grabs my hand.

"Party pooper," I say, frowning as I lead him down the hall. "How about we both do it, like a double tap?"

Brigham lips purse together and he scowls. "Maybe."

"You and your God damn maybes! If I get a shot at Shawn, I'm taking it. I think I can control storms now, too. I'm pretty sure I fried a couple vampires back there with lightning. Which, I do feel a little bad about because Shawn was probably controlling them, and I might have hit Vampire Guild members by mistake. Will I get in trouble for that?" I ramble, fueled by adrenaline.

Brigham pulls short and his face pales. "Wait, what? That was you?"

"Vampires can die from lightning, right? Asking for a friend. But, yeah, pretty sure I fried some vamps back there."

"Are you sure you're, okay?" he asks, and touches my face gently.

"I'm fine—as I said, the boys were very nice to me. As nice as they could be," I say, and another vampire jumps out at me. I grab him by the neck roughly, sending him sailing over my shoulder back into the fight. Brigham looks at me with raised eyebrows. "Too bad I can't hurt anyone—this fighting could be fun."

"What about the pain from the separation?" Brigham asks.

"There was one day when it was pretty bad. I thought you'd lost me," I say quietly.

"I did too, for a while," he says softly as he rubs my hand slowly.

"Are you going to tell me how you always find me now?" I ask.

"You can find out for yourself now. You only need to search my mind," Brigham says with a smile.

"How do I do that?"

"It's all about concentration," Brigham says and punches a large male vampire dressed in red that charges us, sending him back hard against the wall, caving it in. The vampire is knocked out from the impact, and I look at Brigham, impressed. He had made that look effortless and my eyes linger on his torn shirt and visible muscles for a second. He catches my gaze and smiles ferally at me, and I shake my head and turn back towards Shawn's bedroom. *I need to focus!*

We reach Shawn's room and Brigham walks around the room looking at all the pictures, unable to hide his disgust.

"You were in here? This place is obscene," he says under his breath.

"I told you," I say, sidestepping some odd-looking metal gadgets on Shawn's nightstand. *I really don't want to know what Shawn does with those!*

Brigham starts pulling down pictures and I go to the opposite end of the room and start doing the same. After three pictures, I find one I can't budge. It is a large picture of a woman being feasted on by three vampires.

"I can't move this one," I yell to Brigham.

He runs over to me and pulls at the picture and can't get it to budge either.

"Did Jacqueline say how to get into the room?" I ask, pulling at it with my full-strength.

"No."

"Damn!"

A loud scream from the torture hall makes me shudder.

"We need to hurry," I say quickly while pulling at the picture frantically. I couldn't bear the thought of my friends getting hurt.

Brigham moves his hands around the picture frame, searching for anything out of the ordinary. "There's something here," he says, pushing against the picture frame. There is a loud snap and the picture swings out at us. Cold, stale air rushes out at us from a small dark hole. I look at Brigham and cannot control the tremble that moves through my body.

"*Oh crap!* We have to go down the creepy hole of death now, don't we?" I say grimly.

"I'll go first," he says and crawls inside the hole. I follow behind him, trying to keep his feet within my reach. If Shawn grabs him from the front, there isn't much I could do but hold on to his legs—and that thought terrifies me. We crawl for what seems like ten minutes, but it could only have been a few moments—the hole is so tight that it makes me feel claustrophobic. There isn't even enough room to turn around inside of it. If I had to go back out, I would be doing it backwards. Brigham's feet suddenly disappear out of my reach.

"Brig—" I cry, but a large hand wraps around my mouth and pulls me out of the tunnel. I struggle against my captor until I realize it is Brigham who has hold of me. I try to speak, but he holds his hand over my mouth and gestures to the right.

We are in a large cave with dark passages. Leaning against a large stalagmite, I see Shawn with his hand on his head. His lips are moving rapidly, and he is unaware we have entered the tunnel.

Brigham motions for me to stay put as he starts to sneak up behind Shawn, but I follow close behind him. *If he thinks I'm not going to get a punch in, he is crazy!* All of Shawn's attention is focused on controlling his vampire army and he doesn't see Brigham's approach. Brigham grabs Shawn's shoulder and spins him around to face him, crushing him in his hands so tightly that I hear Shawn's bones snap and crackle. Shawn screams and the sound echoes around us.

"I didn't touch her!" Shawn cries, looking back at me.

"You've done enough," Brigham growls as his face goes feral and with one quick movement, Shawn's head is falling off his shoulders. It explodes in dust before ever touching the ground and Brigham drops Shawn's body as it turns to ash just as quickly. Brigham looks at the ash in the air and I see his body relax. He looks down at me noticing how close I am to him and frowns.

I look at Brigham in amazement and stare at the ash flying in the air in shock. Brigham looks back at me, his stare penetrating and brutal and I inch closer to him.

"That was quick," I say, putting my hands on his chest. "I didn't even get to double tap."

"I didn't really want to hear anything that man had to say, did you?" Brigham asks, brushing some ash off my dress.

"No," I say and lean my head on his chest. Brigham encircles me in his arms and the weight of him on me feels so good. *He feels like home.*

"Next time there is an evil villain, you can take the first shot as long as you are not in danger. We can try out your new storm powers. I'm not sure if lightning blasts will kill a vampire or not, but if you think you killed some vampires up there, I believe you."

"Are there going to be more evil villains popping up from your past?" I ask as Brigham shrugs and gives me a sly smile, pulling me tighter to him.

"I've missed you," he whispers into my ear.

"I've missed you too."

Brigham kisses me and lifts me up into his arms. I wrap my arms around his neck and kiss him back harder. *I can't believe he killed Shawn!* I can't believe I am not dead! I had survived and I am a full-strength vampire now! *It has been a good day!*

"I want to go home," I whisper. "I'm tired of adventures and traveling."

Brigham laughs. "That's something I'd never thought I'd hear you say," he says, kissing my neck.

"I mean it. I want to go home and hibernate for years—no shopping, no parties, no nothing but you, me, and our very large bed," I moan and wrap my legs tighter around him.

"We'll need to feed."

"There's not a vampire take-out?" I ask hopefully.

"No."

"*Damn!* I thought I had the perfect plan."

"We should go upstairs and make sure everything is being sorted out," Brigham says and starts to put me down, but I cling to him harder.

"Not yet," I say and my voice breaks.

"What is it, Butterfly?" Brigham asks and cups my cheek.

"I'm emotionally exhausted. If I were human, I'd take a stiff drink right about now," I joke.

"When was the last time you fed?" Brigham asks, looking at me closely.

"Darren and Embry found me a farmer the other day, which was the only time. Shawn wouldn't let them feed me."

Brigham's face darkens and he looks at the ash in the air. "You haven't fed tonight?"

"No."

"You'll feel better after you do."

I nod and rest my head on his shoulder. "Can you hold me for a few more minutes first," I whisper and press my body harder into him.

"I'll hold you for as long as you want," he whispers and runs his hand along my spine.

"That's a dangerous offer," I joke, my voice cracking again.

"I'm not worried," Brigham says with such love in his voice, and I choke down a sob pressing as much of my body as I can into him. I want to feel him and feel safe. I thought I would never feel him again like this and I shatter in his arms, as the last few days finally catch up to me.

CHAPTER EIGHTEEN

Two hours later, Brigham and I emerge out of the tunnel into Shawn's bedroom. Brigham swings open the picture and steps out quickly, pulling me out with one arm. Anton is pacing, biting his fingernails and looking fashionable as ever with a fresh outfit—when he sees us, he runs over.

"What the *hell* took you so long?" Anton yells. "Is Shawn really dead? Embry, Renard, and Darren say they cannot feel the sire connection anymore, but I'm not sure if I trust those guys quite yet."

"Brigham decapitated him—tore his head off with like one flick of his arm," I say, grimacing.

"*I FUCKING TOLD YOU!!!* Your Nordic Vampire God boyfriend is a vicious killer!" Anton hisses and grabs me by the arm. Brigham gives him a deadly look, and he quickly drops my arm.

"How is everybody?" I ask, looking for Embry, Renard, and Darren.

"Your *friends* are fine," he huffs, rolling his eyes. "*Me,* on the other hand, was near hysterics trying to locate you."

"You knew where we were." I brush the dust from the tunnel off my arms.

"Yes, but I couldn't get the damn picture to open," Anton says, wincing as he gestures to the picture.

"Why didn't you punch through it?" Brigham asks.

"Oh…I didn't think of that. *DAMN IT!* Sorry, but my go-to is not to destroy art, even if it is hideous."

I laugh at him and try to hug him. Anton jumps away from me and pokes me in my chest with his finger. "Don't even, missy—I'm still mad at you!"

"What did I do?"

"You got abducted!" Anton says and crosses his arms over his chest, glaring at me.

"That's not my fault! That's victim-blaming mentality! *You* of all people should know how messed up that is to blame me!" I say stomping my foot.

"I had to tell Brigham about what happened, and he almost *murdered me!*" Anton seethes and glares at Brigham.

"He did not," I say and look at Brigham who nods and gives me a semi-guilty look. "What did you do to Anton?"

"Strangled me," Anton whispers in my ear while using me as a shield between him and Brigham.

"What?" I turn and look at Brigham with my mouth open. "No, you didn't!"

"Yep, he did—it took Forseti and three other vampires to get him off me," Anton scoffs.

"Why did you do that??"

"I was upset," Brigham says with a shrug, not looking even remotely remorseful.

"I felt my flesh starting to tear," Anton's says his voice raises an octave, sounding disturbingly screechy as he rubs his neck. "I think he was trying to decapitate me!"

"BRIGHAM!" I shout, hitting him in the shoulder hard making him stumble back a step. I look at my hand in shock. *My new full-strength vampire body is cool!*

"So, you owe me big time now—you can't ever complain when we go shopping," Anton says, holding up a finger. "I get to pick every victim from now on when we hunt." Anton holds up another finger. *"And* you have to pay off all my gambling debts," he says, holding up three fingers to me.

"Gambling debts?"

"It's been very stressful with you being gone! When I'm stressed, I gamble, and lose—badly, I might add," Anton says. He pulls out his phone to look at his reflection and scowls.

"How did you even have time to gamble?"

"You can gamble online from your phone in the Vampire Guild," he says, shaking his phone in his hand.

"You can?"

Anton sighs in frustration. "Yes, it was one of the first things I got set up when I became a vampire. These guys were not running their operation full cylinder here—I had to get them with the times! I've racked up a lot of debt these last few days stress gambling!"

"Fine, fine, I'll do whatever you want—I'm glad you're okay." I hug Anton and he hugs me back lightly and I feel his head turn towards Brigham. Apparently, he wasn't comfortable having Brigham seeing us touching, and I squeeze him tighter.

"Don't you dare cry! I just changed my shirt!" Anton says, his voice faltering and sounding like he is about to cry, the big softy!

"Tell me what happened after Darren and I left the coffee shop," I say with tears welling in my eyes. "If you hadn't have followed me, I'd probably be dead right now. Thank you, Anton."

"Well, I *never* liked that Darren guy," Anton says with full sass in his voice and squeezes me back.

I sigh and release him, wiping away my tears. "Yes, I know—you were right, *sort of.*"

"Well, when you left the coffee shop, he tore out of the city and I knew something was up, so I called Forseti right away. He told me to keep following you and that he would get to Brigham and try to catch up with me. When the second van left the warehouse just before sunrise, I knew I was in trouble. I couldn't follow you in the sunlight, so as soon as they left, I parked in the warehouse and waited for Forseti and Brigham to arrive. I was woken up by Brigham pulling me out of the car by my neck!"

"Really??" I ask, turning towards Brigham and he nods cockily and glares at Anton.

"Scared the shit out of me!" Anton says, rubbing his neck. "I was trying to explain, and he kept squeezing me harder and harder! It was horrible!"

"I hope you apologized to Anton," I say sternly to Brigham. "It wasn't his fault I was abducted. He was trying to be a good friend."

"I did apologize to him," Brigham says, crossing his arms over his chest and scowling at Anton.

"No, you didn't!" Anton says and crosses his arms over his chest while staying behind me.

"Didn't I?" Brigham asks, feigning innocence and brushing some dust off his arm.

"No!"

"Anton, I am *very sorry* you got Butterfly abducted," Brigham says, turning his face up to look at Anton with a dark violence on his face that stuns me. Anton's mouth drops open and then he bares his teeth at Brigham and snarls.

"Brigham!" I shout.

"I mean, I know it wasn't your fault she was taken. Even though *you're* an older vampire and *you* knew there was something off about Darren," Brigham says with a harsh tone.

"Brigham!" I yell and pinch his arm—I can put more of a dent in his skin now. *Cool!*

"What? He knows I'm kidding," Brigham says and shoots daggers at Anton. Anton throws his hands up in the air dramatically.

"Do you see what I've had to deal with since you've been gone? I knew those stories about Brigham were true!"

"Okay, so what happened after the strangling?" I ask, trying to position myself between them to keep the peace.

"There was more than one strangling," Anton says sulkily.

I glare at Brigham. "How many?"

Brigham finally looks guilty and rubs his neck. "I'm not sure."

"Five," Anton says hotly and puts his chin in the air.

"Five?! Brigham, you can't strangle Anton ever again! No matter what happens! No matter how mad you get, and even if I sleep with him."

"Ew!" Anton cringes and I pinch him hard, and he cries out. "Damn, Butterfly—you're strong now!" he yells as Brigham laughs.

"Thanks Anton," I say, rolling my eyes.

"Butterfly, you don't understand how upset I was, you mean a lot to me, and—"

I hold up my hand to him. "I don't care! Promise you won't strangle Anton again."

"Fine, I promise not to strangle Anton again."

"And that you're sorry for the five strangling's."

Brigham hesitates. "But I'm only sorry for three of them," Brigham replies and gives me a feral grin.

"FORGET IT, Butterfly!" Anton spits in annoyance.

"I'm very sorry Brigham was such a jerk—thank you for rescuing me." I hug Anton again. "If you hadn't followed me, I would be dead now."

"You're welcome," Anton says quietly and looks me over. "You're okay right? Nothing too damaged?"

"I'm fabulous!" I say with a fake light heartedness. I really am not sure how I am at the moment. I think I am still in shock—but I don't want to worry him. "I got a cool ability when I changed!"

"What is it?"

"I can call storms!"

"That's so freaking cool! Did you do that lightning thing when all the fighting was happening?"

"I think so!"

"Great! Maybe next time we hunt I can impale our victim with metal, and you can try and electrocute them!"

"That would be so cool!"

"Are you sure you are okay, though? This place is scary as hell," Anton says, looking around Shawn's bedroom.

"Yes, yes, I am fine," I say quickly—I don't want to deal with how I feel right now. "I was barely here and was mostly in the van."

"Good, because we have a lot of shopping to do when we get back home." I groan. "After an appropriate recovery time, of course."

Out of the corner of my eye I see Darren, Embry, and Renard talking to Forseti. I break away from Anton and Brigham and run to greet them.

"Butterfly!" Forseti shouts and wraps his arms around me, giving me a big hug. "There you are—we were so worried. How are you?"

"Fine, fine, thanks to these three," I say, gesturing towards Darren, Embry, and Renard.

"Your friends were telling me about what's happened over the last few days—it's horrific," Forseti says, his face grim. I notice his shirt is torn and there are blood stains on his clothing. *He had fought for me, too!* Tears well in my eyes. I didn't know how much my new vampire family cared for me.

"They've been through much worse that I have, and for much longer," I point out and quickly wipe the tears away.

"That is true..." Forseti says and rubs his beard, looking at Darren sadly. "If I had any idea what was going on, I would have stepped in, I truly would have," Forseti says softly.

"I know you would have, Forseti," Darren says. Forseti smiles at Darren kindly, and I think I see a hint of affection pass between the two of them. Brigham comes up behind me and rubs my shoulder affectionately.

"Are you guys coming back to the city with us?" I ask hopefully. Darren, Renard, and Embry look at each other awkwardly. "You're more than welcome there."

"I'm not sure..." Darren hesitates and I notice his eyes shifting quickly to Forseti.

"I have a house there that you could stay in near the river. You could have it, for what you've done for Butterfly," Forseti insists.

"I'll set up some accounts for you as well—you need to be rewarded for what you've done here the last few days," Brigham says.

"That's really not necessary," Darren says as he rubs his forearm.

"Yes, it is," Brigham says as he shifts his stance, making himself look larger.

"You'll come, won't you?" I ask, gripping Darren's arm. "You're free now!"

Darren looks at Embry and Renard. Renard nods enthusiastically and Embry gives a slight nod but looks sad at the same time. I don't understand why he is reacting this way. Did he really want to stay in this place?

"We will of course come—thank you so much both of you. It might take us a few days to get things in order here first," Darren says, and Embry looks relieved by Darren's words. My curiosity is peaked.

"Great!" Brigham says and claps Darren on the shoulder hard, making him flinch. "When you get into town, let us know straight away."

"We will, Brigham, thank you," Embry says and Brigham pats Embry's back a little too hard and turns to Forseti.

"Forseti, I'm going to take Butterfly home now," Brigham says.

"You won't make it there by sunrise," Forseti says, looking at his watch.

"What time is it now?" I ask.

"Three o'clock in the morning."

"Damn," Brigham says and rubs his chin. He loops his arm around me and asks, "Is there anywhere else we can stay? I don't think Butterfly wants to sleep here tonight."

"Absolutely not!" I say, shaking my head.

"I have a cottage nearby—Anton knows where it is, he can take you." Forseti looks around the room. "Where is Anton?"

"He's running an errand for me. He is going to meet us upstairs."

"You're not being mean to him again, are you?" I ask and Brigham lets out a low laugh.

"No."

I lift an eyebrow at him in, he smiles widely, I roll my eyes and turn towards Forseti. "Thank you for letting us use your house, Forseti. I need to get as far away from these pictures as fast as I can," I say and hug him. He squeezes me back and my tears well again. *I'm a complete mess!*

"Not at all, my dear," Forseti says. "We're family." I choke down a sob and Forseti squeezes me tighter. I wasn't expecting this sort of love and family support when I decided to become a vampire. It is so unexpected and I am overwhelmed with emotion.

I let Forseti go and turn towards Brigham and stumble towards him feeling my adrenaline wearing off. I am getting very tired and am starting to fall over my feet. Brigham picks me up in his arms and carries me to the elevator.

"I can walk," I whisper into his ear.

"I know, but I want to hold you," he says softly.

"I'm tired."

"I know, rest now. I'll take care of everything." I close my eyes and lean my head against his shoulder, breathing him in. He smells like sandalwood today and I relax into his familiar scent.

As we ride the elevator up, Brigham rubs my back. It feels like a dream. I still can hardly believe I survived.

"I think I need to feed," I say as my throat starts to burn. "If I don't do it every day, I get so weak."

"Anton's finding someone for you as we speak."

"He is?"

"Yes."

"Is that the errand you sent him on?""

"Yes."

"You're always taking care of me," I say and bite my lip as the tears start to well.

"It's my job," he says in a low voice.

"What's my job?"

"To take care of me."

"Is that it?" I ask.

Brigham laughs. "That's it."

"But you don't get into as much trouble as I do, I mean, you *could*..." I smile at him suggestively.

"I guess your job will be easier than mine," Brigham teases and pulls me in close to him.

"Doesn't seem quite fair that I should have it so easy." I trace his jaw slowly with my finger.

"It is." Brigham kisses me and leans me against the elevator wall. "I'm sorry we can't go home tonight," he says, running his hand against my cheek and looking at me. His eyes have changed to the shade of the lightest blue I've ever seen, almost translucent.

"I shouldn't have taken so long in the cave. It'll be enough getting out of here."

"Can I ask something of you?" he asks, his eyes darting across my face.

"What is it?"

"Can I see in your mind?" Brigham asks, and I notice the slightest tremble in his lips. "I want to see what happened to you the last few days."

"You haven't done that already?" I swallow hard, thinking about him in my mind.

"No."

"I thought you would have."

"I wouldn't do that without asking," he says, looking deeply into my eyes. I ran my hand across his cheek, and his eyes turn to a stormy grey color.

"Will it hurt?" I rub my head, remembering Darren's anguish.

"Not if you let me do it," he says and that fact makes me swallow hard.

"Do I need to do anything to let you in?" I blink rapidly, bracing myself.

"Just relax." I nod and try to relax my body and mind, but it is hard to do.

"Okay," I say and bite my lip, anticipating pain.

Brigham looks deeply into my eyes, and I feel him moving inside of my mind. My head feels cloudy for a minute and then very full. I can feel him shifting through my memories quickly and I try to relax further, not really liking the way it feels but hoping that by relaxing it will feel less invasive. I find myself falling into his mind and am startled as his memories flood me. I see his anger unleashing on Anton, him talking to the Vampire Guild, him standing outside in the dark with his eyes closed sniffing at the air, the panic and fear he feels as he drives the dark streets searching for me, and the image of me in Darren's arms covered in his blood. I feel his passion for me under the calm exterior he projects, and it surprises me. It runs deeper than I thought. I feel Brigham rubbing my ear and I fall out of him, back into my mind.

"You've had quite an experience," he says softly.

"So have you. You were really worried about me…weren't you?"

"I was."

"Did you see all that the guys did for me?"

"I did—I owe them more than I could ever repay."

"They're very nice, and I think Darren has a crush on Forseti."

"I saw that too."

I look him up and down. "So, your secret ability is having an enhanced olfactory sense? You smell me to find me?"

Brigham laughs. "Yes."

"Do I smell funny?" I ask and I try to smell myself, but I can't smell anything abnormal.

"No, you smell good," Brigham says with a feral smile.

"It's kind of a creepy superpower," I tease.

"I don't know—it's come in handy."

"Especially with me?"

"Especially."

"Hmmm…I never thought about covering up my smell. I can't smell myself—I don't smell human anymore, and I guess I thought I didn't have a smell."

"It's a good thing you didn't try and cover up your smell."

"Yeah, I'm glad I didn't figure it out. Things could have ended very differently," I say, my voice falling flat.

The elevator doors open and Anton is waiting in a large room with a young human man standing beside him wearing worn out jeans and a ballcap.

"That was quick," Brigham says, not hiding his admiration.

"I didn't want to get strangled again," Anton says cooly.

"I am sorry about all of that, Anton—I will make it up to you," Brigham says sincerely.

"I like expensive cars and cologne," Anton says dryly and looks at his manicured hand, grimacing while noticing the blood and ash covering it.

"Done."

"Here, Butterfly," Anton says gently, pushing the young man towards me. "He likes to run over animals on the road."

"That's reaching a bit," I say, but my fangs snap out at the smell of this human.

"It's what I could find in a pinch. I'm sure he's done more things—bite him and find out."

Brigham lifts me up to the man's neck and I bite into him hard. His life flashes and I see the pregnant girlfriend he has at home with a black eye as I bite down harder, ripping a large hole in his neck. I drink him until his heart almost stops then pause when he was a breath away from death and whisper into his ear, "See you in hell." I let him hit the floor, his head making a loud, cracking sound.

Anton laughs and claps his hands together. "God, I missed you doing that!" He looks at me expectantly. "So?"

"He has a girl at home he knocks around—she's pregnant."

"I hate people," Anton says disgustedly and nudges the man's leg with a foot.

My shoulders sag. "Me too…"

"Unfortunately, that was only another drop in the bucket," Anton says, looking down at the man.

"Some days, I feel like I could suck the world dry and it still wouldn't be enough," I say dejectedly.

Brigham rubs my shoulder and asks, "How do you feel?"

I roll my shoulder and hold my arms out in front of me. "Much better," I say, wiping my mouth. "Thank you, Anton, for finding him. I really needed that."

"No problem. Are you guys leaving now?" Anton asks.

"Forseti is letting us use his house nearby—he said you might be able to show us the way," Brigham says.

"Why didn't he just show you in your head?" Anton asks Brigham.

"He thinks it's rude to jump into my mind like that, does he do that to you?"

"No, never."

"Do you mind showing us the way?" Brigham asks.

"No problem, the sooner we can get out of here the better—this whole place gives me the creeps," Anton says and shudders.

CHAPTER NINETEEN

Outside, we climb into Anton's car. I snuggle into Brigham's arms in the front seat and we drive away fast from Shawn's compound. I never want to see this place ever again.

After driving for an hour, Anton pulls into a long driveway leading to a cute, brown-and-white cottage on top of a hilltop surrounded by pine trees, and I step out and breathe the mountain air. The air is crisp and clean and so much better than the foul-smelling air of Shawn's compound.

"Where are we?" I ask, looking out over the hill down at all the trees.

"Colorado," Brigham says, looking up at the beautiful pine trees.

"It's going to be a long drive home," I say and rub my throat, still thirsty after draining the dirtbag.

"I'll get a plane lined up for tomorrow," Brigham says, putting his arm around me.

Anton unlocks the cottage door and leads us inside. The cottage is filled with rustic wood furniture and is very different from Forseti's usual style. It is cozy with huge throw pillows on the couches and quilted blankets. It is a perfect place to try and get the images of Shawn's compound out of my head.

"I'll leave you guys here. The bedrooms are upstairs. Take whatever one you like. There's probably a bottle of blood around here somewhere." Anton moves to a cupboard and pulls out a bottle of blood and uncorks it and hands it to me.

"Thank you, Anton," I say and give him a hug, my eyes welling up. I quickly wipe them away and take a sip of blood. Anton looks from me to Brigham and puts his hands awkwardly in his pockets.

"I'm going to go and check on Forseti."

"Are you coming back?" I ask.

Anton looks at Brigham and a sly smile crept over his face. "No, I'll find a hotel somewhere and will make sure everyone stays away." He turns and leaves. "Don't do anything I wouldn't do," he yells over his shoulder, and I roll my eyes.

"He thinks we're going to have sex."

"He's right."

"Maybe…"

"Maybe?" Brigham reaches out and caresses my hip, pulling me towards him. "I rescued you from a psychotic vampire. I think I deserve some form of lovemaking."

"I don't know," I say, leaning into his touch. "Now that I've recovered from my near-death experience, I'm a little mad at you."

"Why is that?" he asks and kisses my neck, and I arch into him and then grab the back of his head, fisting his hair and pulling him away from me.

"If you would have told me about what happened with Shawn and Jacqueline, I wouldn't have met Darren at the coffee shop."

"I was going to tell you—"

"Not until after the new moon."

Brigham hesitates to deny it, but the look in my eyes stops him. "You knew that?"

"You fucking asshole!" I hit him hard in the shoulder and he flinches. I gasp. *He actually flinched!* I am so much stronger now! "I knew it! You gaslighting prick!" I hit him hard in the chest, making him stumble back and my mouth drops open. *I love being a full-strength vampire!*

Brigham rolls his shoulders and squares up to me, his eyes changing to an azure blue. "I didn't want to lose you."

"Why would you lose me?"

"I was worried after you learned what I had done, or let happen, you might not see me in the same light anymore."

"Because you let Jacqueline kill herself?"

"Yes," Brigham says grimly and pushes his hair back from his face.

"But it's what she wanted."

"It was, but I don't know if it was the right thing to do."

"Why do you think that?"

"When Jacqueline came to me, she was different—a changed person. It was like someone punched a hole out of her. She was so empty. It took her a month sitting in her room alone before she was able to talk about what she had been doing the last ten years. When she started to tell the stories, I was appalled. The things she had done, and enjoyed doing, were horrific—the most disturbing thing about her past was how much she enjoyed participating in the cruel acts with Shawn. Can you imagine being in a position where you were expected to torture someone, something you always thought was uncontestable, and then when you did it, it excited you?"

I shudder. "No."

Brigham held his head in his hands. "She told me once that her favorite people to torture were young girls between the ages of twelve and sixteen because they had the best screams."

I cover my mouth with my hand. "Jesus!"

Brigham turns and looks out the window. "Shawn had awakened a part of herself she never knew existed and I don't think she could turn it off."

"But she stayed here with you for three years."

"Yes, but there were instances…let's just say the Vampire Guild was very forgiving with her rehabilitation."

I swallow hard. "How did you ever fall in love with her?"

"It was very easy." I look at Brigham in shock, and he gives me an apologetic look. He rubs his chin, trying to find the words to explain. "Jacqueline was trying, struggling with her desires every day to be a better person. It took a lot of courage—most people wouldn't bother and would give into the addiction, but she chose not to. I admired her strength and endurance. I still do."

"But she killed herself in the end."

"Because she realized she couldn't stop it, and she chose death over making more mayhem. She thought she was a burden on me, even though I told her she wasn't."

"Wasn't she? You had to constantly monitor her, waiting for the madness to break."

"Yes, but it wasn't anything I couldn't handle. I'd do the same for you."

"You wouldn't have to do that for me."

"No, but I've made other allowances." Brigham smiles at me and my body tenses. *Is he serious right now?*

"My excursions? I hardly think that compares." Unfortunately, in actuality, I did see the similarities between Jacqueline and Brigham's relationship and mine and Brigham's. That thought causes a visceral reaction in my body and I rub at my wrist trying to ease the tension. Did Brigham see me as some sort of charity case? Did he think he was trying to save me from myself? Is *that* his type?

"When you're in love, you love that person at their best and at their worst. This was Jacqueline's worst, and I still loved her."

"Do you miss her?"

"Every day." I flinch at Brigham's admission, and feel a small hollow spot begin to form inside of me. Brigham touches my cheek gently and I pull away, wanting to put some space between us.

"That doesn't take anything away from the way I feel about you," he whispers. I nod, unsure if that was true. "I feel like I failed Jacqueline."

"What else could you have done for her?"

"Maybe if some more time had passed, she would have felt differently. I could have made her wait longer…"

"By holding her prisoner—that's the only way I could see that working."

Brigham lets out a sound of anguish. "I suppose you're right. It was always Jacqeline's choice to end her life, not mine."

"If I wanted to die, would you let me?"

Alarm flashes across Brigham's face. "It is very difficult to watch someone you love die."

"That's not an answer."

"That's the only one I'm going to give you." I stare at him quietly and he asks, "Have I disappointed you now?"

"A little…"

"That's what I feared."

"I'm not disappointed in what you did for Jacqueline. It was the right thing to do," I clarify.

"You think so?"

"Yes."

"Forseti thinks that as well, but I'm glad you don't think I was being weak…selfish."

"Selfish?"

"I can't say that my life wasn't easier after she was gone—some things were much better," he says and sits heavily into a large armchair.

"And you feel guilty about that?"

"Yes."

"Love is complicated, even for vampires," I whisper and cross my arms, moving to a window to look out at the woods.

"It is."

"I wish I would have known this sooner," I say honestly, feeling hollow. There really wasn't a happily ever after.

"I'm sorry."

"It's okay," I say, but was it? "I understand your hesitation." *But did I really?* "But I'm not a flake, even if I do flakey things sometimes."

"I know that."

"I don't think you do," I say sincerely and glance at him.

"I saw into your head, remember?"

"And I saw into yours."

"Why didn't you search for the answers about Jacqueline then?"

"Maybe I did, but I wanted to see what you'd tell me."

"Another experiment?"

"I *am* the vampire scientist."

"Do I need to get you a chemistry set?" Brigham teases, trying to lighten the mood. I look back at him and my eyes trail over his body. Despite his declaration about Jacqueline, I still loved him. *Love is so annoying!*

"Maybe…there are a few things I want to experiment with first though." I move over to Brigham and climb into his lap. I run my fingers across his lips. He opens his mouth slightly and exposes his fangs to me and I run my finger against the pointy edge and the fang enlarges. "I know how old you are."

"I saw that—I was hoping you wouldn't mention it."

"It's hard to forget that *big* of a number," I tease and kiss him softly.

"Is it too big of a number?"

"Nothing about you is too big for me," I say with a chuckle.

"Nothing?" he asks and gives me a wicked smile.

"Nope, can't think of a thing." He grabs my hand and presses it against the front of his pants. I could feel his hard cock underneath the cloth. "That? Now that I've seen some vampire pornography, I've been thinking I might have settled for an inferior vampire specimen."

Brigham laughs loudly. "If that's how you feel, you can always leave me."

"Tempting, but I have many more experiments in store for you."

"Like what?"

"Well, not all the pictures in Shawn's bedroom were bad…"

"How much time did you spend in there?"

"Well Darren, Embry and I—"

"Darren and Embry were in the bedroom with you?" he asks and his eyes laser focus on me.

"What, didn't I let you in to that memory?" I ask innocently.

"No!" his head jerks towards me and his fangs elongate.

"Oh, well, you know, I thought I was about to die and had two strapping vampires at my side—what is a girl to do?" Brigham grabs me roughly and flips me onto one of the couches, pinning me. I laugh and his eyes blaze turning cerulean. "Jealous?" I tease.

"How can you block me so effectively already? I can't see Embry, you, or Darren in the bedroom at all!"

"Really?"

"Yes! How is that possible?" Brigham growls.

"You don't see any vampire orgy images at all?" Brigham eyes flash and he snarls. "You can't be mad—as I said, I thought I was going to die."

"You're maddening, woman! How are you blocking me?" His eyes dart across my face.

I give him a smug smile. "Darren gave me some tips."

"I'm going to strangle that guy!" Brigham growls and his fangs elongate.

"No more strangling!" I yell, rising and pressing my forehead to his.

"But—"

"I didn't sleep with them. I was teasing you."

"How do I know?" Brigham face tenses.

"Alright, search me. I won't block you this time." I look deeply into Brigham's eyes, and I let him penetrate my mind. He searches and searches through my memories of Shawn's bedroom. Satisfied that nothing sexual had happened between me and the vampires, I feel him slide back out. "Feel better?"

"Yes." Brigham's face relaxes.

"Good." I kiss him deeply and he pins my arms back above my head and kisses my neck.

"Oh, Embry, *just like that*," I moan. Brigham growls deeply causing me to explode in laughter.

"Sorry, I couldn't help myself."

"That wasn't funny."

"But it's so much fun rattling you—it takes a lot to get you going, you're usually so calm and collected."

"What are you talking about? You're always rattling me," Brigham growls. "I feel more emotions in a few moments with you than I do in decades."

"Really?"

"Yes, I think it's about time I rattled you," he says and kisses my neck.

"Ohhh," I moan. "Yes, that sounds like fun!"

He bites my lip, and droplets seep out which he sucks in slowly. I grab his head pulling him closer into me and he growls again and grinds himself into me, making me gasp. He releases me and gives me a predatory smile with his canines growing.

"You don't have to be careful with me anymore," I gasp.

Brigham lets out a feral sound and hurls us into a large bathroom, turning on the shower while ripping my dress to shreds. I stand naked before him and he smiles and pulls out his phone and sends a quick text then sets it on the counter.

"You better have not just sent a naked picture of me to someone," I snarl and lunge at him. He catches me and presses me up against the cold tile outside the shower and I fist his hair and pull it back hard.

"I just sent Anton a small fortune to buy us some clothes for tomorrow," he says and strains against me, but I pull his hair back tighter. I reach down and tear his shirt away from his body and reach for his pants and shred the front, ripping the fabric away from him as his cock springs out.

"I could get used to this method of clothes removal," I purr and release him, and his mouth comes crashing into me. I kiss him with every bit of strrength I have, and he meets me pressure for pressure. I slide him into me and roll my hips as he thrusts into me hard, causing the wall to groan.

He's so hard for me and I grip him tightly with my pussy, making him groan. "No holding back," I whisper into his ear and bite hard on his earlobe, sucking the tiny droplet away before his wound closes.

"No holding back," he whispers back to me and grabs my ass tighter as he starts to thrust harder and harder into me and I kiss up his neck while wrapping my arms tightly around him, pressing my breasts to his chest, my nipples peeking and swelling from the friction of our bodies. He holds me with one arm and moves his other to my clit and starts rubbing it vigorously as he continues to pound me up against the wall.

I kiss him hard as I climax and scream, "Brigham!" My pussy throbs, clenching around him. He roars his release, and I feel him fill me. He rests his head against mine for a moment and then swings us around and enters the shower.

The warm water hits my skin, and I moan as he starts to wash me with a floral scented bodywash, still holding me up with one arm. He starts slowly thrusting his hips in me again and I look at this magnificent man before me as he looks at me with such reverence in his gaze. I grab some shampoo and start washing his hair slowly, taking my time to clean the ash and blood from him. I moan as he thrusts deeper into me, and I grab the body wash and slowly wash every part of him I can reach, wanting to feel him fully.

I still can't believe that we are here, that I am safe. It didn't seem possible after being in the house of horrors and going through all the pain of being separated. I try to shift off him so I can wash the rest of him, but he holds me tighter and a look of fear flashes across his face.

"I need to be inside you right now," he says softly, and I look at the emotion on his face, so different than what he usually shows me.

I nod and roll my hip towards him, and he presses his head to my chest and sucks on one of my nipples, flicks it with his tongue, and then moves to the other one. He thrusts slowly into me and backs out completely and I feel the head of his cock rub against my clit before pressing back at my entrance and entering me again. I wrap my legs tighter around him and move my hips at an increased pace and he moves us more into the stream of water, rinsing away all the soap off our bodies. The water cascades down us and I kiss him as it pours down our faces, not needing to breathe. I grind against him harder, finding my release and he grabs my ass and pumps me harder as he shudders, finding his. Wrapping my arms tighter around him, he holds me just as tightly as the warm water falls over us.

We stay there for a while and eventually he turns the water off and steps us outside, still staying in me and holding me tightly. He grabs some towels and robes off a rack and wraps them around us and carries me to a bedroom, both of us still dripping. He lays me down on the bed facing him and pulls the covers up over us and runs his hands through my wet hair. I look up at him, and he looks so tired, more tired than I have ever seen him. I try to slide away from him, but he pulls himself back into me.

"Not yet," he whispers as I cup his cheek.

"You're going to have to come out of me some time," I tease and kiss him tenderly.

"Not tonight," he says and kisses me harder. "Tonight, I want to be as close to you as long as I can."

"It's okay, Brigham, you got me out of there," I say softly and darkness flashes across his face briefly, vanishing away just as fast. He nods and runs his hands down my neck and back, moving to my arms and chest, slowly touching every part of me. I nuzzle into him, loving the way his touch feels.

"I might actually sleep for once," he muses and I reach up to him and massage his shoulders and arm. He moans at my touch, and I feel his cock twitch inside me, and

I roll my hips ever so slightly. "Maybe not," he moans again and I clench his cock with my pussy. "Maybe I will make love to you all through the day." I yawn uncontrollably and I can feel dawn approaching. He rolls over top of me and pushes harder into me and holds my face in his hands. "I almost lost you," he says and thrusts harder into me and I grab his forearms, feeling every ripple of his muscles.

"You can't lose me," I say softly, and he moves his hips and grinds against my clit with every thrust as shockwaves of sensation start to pulse from my core.

"Say that again," he demands and grinds harder against me, and I gasp as more shockwaves of pleasure ripple through my body as he holds me underneath him.

"You can't lose me," I gasp out and I climax fully, and he growls as he releases himself into me, laying his head on my chest and letting his full body weight down on me. He stays there holding me tightly, and I massage his head and run my fingers through his hair. As dawn approaches, I feel my body get heavier and heavier, falling asleep underneath him.

CHAPTER TWENTY

"Do we really have to go out tonight?" I ask Brigham, throwing my hands up in the air. He adjusts his shirt collar in the mirror and looks at me curiously. He's wearing a grey sports jacket and pants with a cream-colored undershirt, and I sigh looking down at myself, still in my pajamas.

"It's your homecoming party—you have to go."

"But I don't want to go. I want to stay here," I moan, crawling onto the bed and covering myself with a pillow.

"Forseti has put a lot of effort into this party. He's given you two weeks to recover, and I can't make him wait any longer. Don't you want to see your friends? You've barely left the house since you've been back," Brigham says and moves to the bed. He tries to find me under the pillows, but I dig myself deeper.

"I don't feel ready," I groan and move out of his reach.

"What do you mean?"

"It's not safe." Brigham finds the pillow that is hiding my face and pulls it away. He gently touches my shoulder, and I scowl at him.

"Nothing's going to happen, Butterfly."

I shrug. "Maybe…"

"I'm not going to let anything happen to you," he says firmly, his jaw set tight.

"You can't keep me safe all the time. Eventually, I'm going to be out by myself, and something will happen," I say as my body starts to shake and I bite my thumb. "I'm the strongest I've ever been in my life and I'm still scared! It's illogical! I know that, but I can't seem to shake it!"

"The abduction seems to have really affected you. I think maybe you should go talk to someone."

"I've never felt so vulnerable before. Not even when I was human and I was with you. I can't shake it," I say, running my fingers through my hair.

"It's going to take time, Butterfly," Brigham says softly and pulls me into his arms.

"Do you have any other enemies I need to worry about?"

"Enemies? Not anyone currently that I know of."

"That's a weird answer. Are you sure there's no one else has that any beef with the Vampire Guild?"

"Not that I can think of."

"No ex-business partners who feel wronged?"

"None that have told me."

"Ex-lovers?"

"No."

"Are you sure?"

"Yes."

"I've asked you that question before and you lied to me."

"I didn't lie exactly—I may have withheld information."

"Same difference."

"You can search my mind if you want to be sure," Brigham says and presses his forehead to mine.

"You'd let me do that?"

"Here," he grabs my hands and pulls me up to him on the bed. "Look into my eyes, you'll fall right in." I do what he says and fall into his mind. I search through years and years of memories, searching for anyone who wanted to do Brigham harm. I find numerous people who were fearful of Brigham's power and strength but none of them dared go against him. Satisfied, I fall back out of his mind. "Find anyone?"

"No, but a lot of people find you intimidating," I reply, not sure if I felt better or not.

"That's not such a bad thing."

"Not in this circumstance, no," I say slowly.

"Do you feel better?"

"Maybe a little." There is still this ball of anxiety inside of me that didn't seem to go away now. This is so unlike me—I usually got over stuff pretty quickly, but being abducted and seeing Shawn's compound had set some fears inside of me that I can't seem to heal.

"Good, because Anton wants you to go shopping and hunting with him tomorrow."

"Tomorrow, as in twenty-four hours from now?" I whine and hit one of the pillows, sending it across the room.

Brigham watches the pillow sail through the air with his eyebrows raised. "Yes."

"Can't I hide up here forever?" I groan and try to escape Brigham's arms. He releases me and I dive back under the pillows.

"No, Anton will find you. I've barely been able to keep him from hounding you as it is."

"That's true. I suppose he is dying to torture me. I did promise him I'd go shopping with him."

"He's been bugging me daily," Brigham says, curling his lip. "He can be such an annoying vampire."

"He's not that bad," I say and groan again and hit another pillows hard. *Fuck!* I had to get up and get ready. I can't avoid this any longer.

I jump off the bed, head into the closet, and look at all the clothes that Anton has bought me and feel instantly overwhelmed. I reach for the first thing I see and pull out a black dress that is made from soft, shiny material and slip it on. Rummaging below the clothes, I find a box that has a pair of black boots in it and slip them on, hoping Anton will approve and move to a mirror.

Looking in the mirror, I marvel at my skin. After the new moon, it has a new sheen to it and reminds me of white opals. I run my fingers through my hair and decide to keep it down for tonight. Brigham comes up behind me and wraps his arms around me, admiring my reflection.

"You're beautiful," he whispers in my ear and kisses my cheek.

"You're not so bad looking yourself," I say, admiring him in the mirror. His sports jacket hugs his muscles snugly, illuminating his form. He brushes his hands through his hair, and it falls back in his face, and I smirk at him. His eyes twinkle at me and are slate blue right now. I still hadn't figured out why he seems to be the only vampire who's eyes change color.

"It'll be good for you to get out tonight. You'll see." I nod and squeeze my eyes shut, not believing him but wanting to get over it with. The sooner it is done, the sooner I can come back home!

"Let's go before I change my mind," I say with a sigh.

Forseti's house appears as a blaze of light from the street and as Brigham pulls up to the door, my anxiety thickens within me. I know I shouldn't feel this way—I know these people, but I still feel this overwhelming anxiety. It isn't logical—I am a full-strength vampire, but I feel the anxiety just the same.

Brigham holds my hand as we walk inside and I might be clutching it a little too hard, but he doesn't let on that he notices. We enter a large ballroom and when Forseti sees us, his face breaks with delight, and I can't help but find myself smiling back at him. I have missed seeing him and Anton. Forseti moves rapidly to us with a smiling Darren trailing along. Forseti is wearing dark jeans and t-shirt with a light-colored sports jacket, and it is a little off-putting. I've never seen him dress so casually before and have never seen him wearing jeans. I wonder how on earth Anton had convinced him to wear this ensemble. Looking at a smiling Darren, who is dressed similarly in black jeans and sports jacket, I think I have my answer.

"Aw, Butterfly! My dear, you look fabulous! The change has done wonders for you!" Forseti beams and kisses my cheeks.

"Thank you, Forseti," I say and give him a little hug. His cologne smells spicy and earthy tonight, and I swear I can smell the same odor coming from Darren.

"So glad you've decided to come out tonight. Anton will be so pleased. He's been terribly worried about you."

"I needed some time to myself," I reply shyly and look at Darren, giving him an embarrassed smile. Darren gives me a knowing nod.

"Oh, of course dear, of course, everyone understands—even Anton, although he may not act like it."

"How have you been, Darren?" I ask, but seeing how much lighter and happier his expression is, I already know my answer.

"Wonderful," he says, touching my arm tenderly and Brigham makes the smallest of growl sounds, causing Darren to quickly remove his arm. I look back at Brigham—his face is stoic, but I know he made that sound.

"Your business went well? The move was, okay?"

"Yes, Forseti has been great—our house is amazing," Darren gushes and I squeeze his arm—*I'm so happy for him!*

"Hopefully you won't be there for very long," Forseti says, flashing Darren a mischievous smile.

"Hopefully not," Daren agrees and gives me an embarrassed smile—it almost looks like he is blushing with just the slightest change in his skin tone.

"Where's Embry?" I ask, looking around the room.

"He's around here somewhere. He brought someone from home with him," Darren says, looking around the room.

"From home?"

"His wife!" Darren says and his eyes dance.

"You're kidding!" I gasp and grab Darren's arm hard. "Are you serious?"

"He went to her that same night that Brigham killed Shawn. She was still in the same house they lived in when Embry was alive."

"That's great!" I say and then my eyebrows knit, thinking about her still being human. "Right?"

"Yes. Embry has hated being unable to be with her for the last ten years. He was really hurting being separated from her," Darren says and his face falls for a moment and then he looks quickly at Forseti.

"That's amazing! I'm so happy for Embry!"

"It's nice to see him so happy."

"And Renard? Where is he?"

"Gambling," Darren says, shaking his head and I frown. Renard didn't have the best poker face. "Shawn never let us in his house. He's been at Forseti's every night, getting his fill."

"He's quite good at it," Forseti says, but something in his face betrays that statement.

"No, he's not," Darren says, laughing.

"He tries really hard. Poor lad, he does not have a good poker face, I'm afraid. He's running through the money you gave him, Brigham, very quickly—" Forseti says and pats Brigham's arm.

"He can have more," Brigham says with a shrug. "Set up an account here for him, Forseti—I'll cover his losses."

"You might regret that, Brigham—Renard is a truly horrible poker player," Darren says and runs his hands through his hair.

"Truly," Forseti agrees as he laughs, patting Darren affectionately on the back.

Out of the corner of my eye I see Anton in the back of the room waving at me, trying to get my attention as he points to two glasses of blood wine he has sitting at a table next to him.

"Excuse me a moment, gentlemen," I say and start to walk away. Brigham holds my hand and doesn't let go. I was still holding him so tightly that I didn't realize he was holding me just as hard. I look at him questioningly and nod my head in Anton's direction. Brigham eyes move to where I am pointing and when he sees Anton, he drops my hand.

"Just don't let him get you abducted again," Brigham says, his voice a little tense and Forseti and Darren exchange a look. I look at Brigham, noticing his clenched jaw and stiff posture. *Maybe I wasn't the only one with some PTSD after the incident with Shawn.*

"I'll try," I say, trying to make my voice light. Brigham looks at me, his eyes turning dark grey as he stares at me intently and then slowly relaxes his gaze, his eyes turning a softer blue color. I turn from him, confused by his behavior. He had wanted me to come to this party after all.

Anton's face lights up as I approach him and as soon as I am close enough, he grabs me in a rough hug, crushing my bones slightly. "Finally!" he squeals, squeezing me even harder.

"Can't breathe!" I moan as my bones make a creaking sound.

"Oh, you're fine!" He releases me and I smile widely at him—I had missed him tremendously. "You don't need to breathe—you're a vampire, remember?"

"How could I forget?" I look back at Brigham and see him watching me and Anton, cautiously pacing slightly.

"I've been so bored since you've been hibernating!" Anton cries, handing me a glass of blood wine.

"I was recovering," I say and take a sip of wine. The blood hits my tongue and a warm sensation moves across my body. "I was *not* hibernating."

"Same difference," Anton says, waving me off and taking a sip of his blood wine. "Did you see Darren?" he whispers, leaning close to me.

"Yes, he looks good."

"He and Forseti have been making googly eyes at each other all week," Anton says and rolls his eyes while doing an exaggerated shudder.

"I thought there might be something going on between them."

"I've had about all I can take. I think I might buy a loft somewhere," Anton says determinedly while rubbing his temple, and I laugh.

"Since when are you prudish?"

"Seeing Forseti in love is very disturbing. He's like a father to me and there's something not right about it—plus, I am *still* trying to get laid. Forseti, doesn't even have to try—guys just fall all over him."

"You'd feel differently if you had someone in your life."

Anton shudders again. "Doubt it."

"We'll find you a nice saleswoman who doesn't mind your glamouring problem and you'll be set."

"I've gotten over that!" he hisses in my ear.

I pat him on the shoulder. "Sure, you have."

"I'll show you tomorrow." Anton sticks his chin up high.

"Tomorrow?" I whine.

"Yeah, did Brigham say it was okay for you to go out shopping with me tomorrow?"

"I don't need his permission to do anything," I remind Anton. He looks at me doubtfully. "I don't!"

"Whatever you say, chica." I feel a slight tightening in my head, and I jerk my head quickly at Brigham and shoot him a dirty look. Seeing my reaction, he turns back to the conversation with Forseti and Darren.

"What is it?" asks Anton as he looks between me and Brigham.

"I think Brigham was in my head," I whisper.

"Get used to it."

"I don't think that will be happening," I say tensely and imagine a large brick wall surrounding me and Anton. "So, where are we shopping?"

"Paris!" Anton squeals and shakes my arm, causing me to spill my drink.

"*Wait! What?*" I hiss at him and glance at Brigham. He is still talking to Darren and Forseti, but I swear he is turned so he can hear what Anton and I are saying.

"They have the best designers!" Anton puts his hand over his heart and sighs.

"Won't we have to take a plane?"

"Yep, I already booked us on one of Forseti's private jets."

"How long will we be gone?" I ask as I feel my anxiety growing and I rub the back of my neck. Did the Vampire Guild have a presence in Paris? How far was their reach?

"A few days," Anton says dismissively and gulps his wine.

"Brigham will be pissed." I glance over at Brigham, and he is still pretending not to be watching Anton and me, and I can see his hands fidgeting nervously.

"I thought you don't have to ask permission to go out," Anton teases and takes a sip of his blood wine and moans. "This is the best!"

"I don't have to ask permission," I say but my voice wavers. Would Brigham be upset if I told him I was going to Paris for a few days? I didn't really think he would be happy. Although I didn't like the thought about being away from my soft comfy pillows, I'd never been to Paris before, and an adventure might get me out of this funk.

"If he won't let you go, I understand—it's hard being a kept woman," Anton says, trying to goad me.

"You're trying to manipulate me into going," I say and pinch his arm.

"Yep! Is it working?" Anton asks, his eyes dancing.

"Yes, damn it!!" I say and finish my wine. I glance at Brigham again. "He's going to be so mad," I say barely above a whisper. The thought of Brigham's face when I didn't return before sunrise makes me erupt in laughter.

"C'mon, it'll be so fun!"

"Are you trying to get me into trouble or get back at Brigham for strangling you?"

"A little of both," Anton says and smooths out his shirt. He is wearing a dark green button up with dark pants and looks immaculate as ever.

"You're bad," I huff and move to a table where more blood wine glasses are sitting and pick one up.

"You're worse," Anton says, his tone light and playful.

I snort. "That's true…okay, I'm in."

"Sweet! I'll pick you up just after sunset." Anton hugs me tightly. "I'm so glad you're back! I'd have died of boredom here with these old guys!"

"I love you too, dork." I say and kiss Anton on his cheek.

"Okay, I'll be right back. I need to make a couple more reservations—I wasn't sure you'd be able to get away." Anton squeezes my arm and practically skips out of the room.

I shake my head and watch the vampires around the room talking as I study their immaculate faces. I was one of them now, *a full-strength vampire.*

An arm wraps around my waist startling me, causing me to jump and I whirl to find Brigham standing behind me.

"Jesus, you scared me!" I say, stepping away from him. I hadn't even heard him sneak up on me and my anxiety hits hard with that fact. I needed to pay better attention to my surroundings.

"Sorry," he says softly and steps closer to me. "How's Anton?"

"Same as ever," I say cautiously, not sure what he all heard about our Paris trip.

"Is he excited to go shopping tomorrow?" Brigham asks and looks at me suspiciously.

"Very excited." Brigham encircles me in his arms and looks at me closely, but I avoid his gaze.

"Are you okay?" he asks, grabbing my chin and tilting it up towards him. I look at him trying not to look guilty and try to focus on the brick wall surrounding Anton's and my conversation.

"Fine."

"You're blocking me," he says, amused, with his lips twitching slightly.

"Uhhh…."

"Interesting." He looks in the direction that Anton has headed, and his face gets hard and stoney. I feel him push against the brick wall in my mind and a few bricks tumble down. Panic rises inside of me as I realize how ineffective I am going to be in blocking him and I throw up stone and metal around the brick trying to reinforce it. It had been a fluke—my ability to block the memory of Shawn's bedroom, at the cottage. From now on, I will not be able to hide a single thought from Brigham, and my loss of control makes my anxiety surge as I try to pull out of Brigham's arms. Suddenly, I feel Brigham pulling back completely out of my mind. I look at him, and he gives me a small smile.

"Do I need to worry?" he asks, searching my face.

"Ummm…probably not."

"Hmmmm…" he says as his face softens a little and he reaches for my cheek, touching it delicately and looking deep into my eyes.

"Do you want me to tell you?" I groan, looking at Brigham and feeling utterly defeated. I really am not fond of this mind control thing Brigham can do now to me.

Brigham looks at me and his face stills as he holds his hand to my cheek. "No…but tell Anton I want you back in one piece."

"You'll let me have my secret?"

"Yes."

"Why?"

"Because it's important for you to have and I don't want to be like Shawn. I want all of you, but I'm not going to force you to give yourself completely to me."

"It's nothing really…we're just—"

Brigham presses his fingers to my lips, stifling my words. "It's okay, I trust you."

"Hmmmmmm…"

"What is it?"

I smile wickedly at him. "You might not after tomorrow night."

Brigham returns my wicked smile. "Okay, now you have to tell me."

"It's too late! You had your chance!" He grabs me roughly, pulling me close to him and traces a line on my neck.

"And I thought Jacqueline was trouble."

"Oh, I'm much worse than she ever was. Maybe it would be better for you if you found a nice, dull, elderly vampire to spend your days with. I really don't think you can handle me—I bet someone around five hundred would be about your speed."

"Not a chance," he says and kisses me deeply. I leap at him, knocking him to the floor pressing my body into him. Several vampires standing around us began to laugh and I stop kissing Brigham. I have totally forgotten for a moment that we are surrounded by vampires and I climb off Brigham awkwardly.

"Uh…sorry, still figuring out how much strength I have," I say to the vampires standing around us. I reach for Brigham and help him stand up. The vampires around us smile at Brigham and return to their conversations. I see Forseti and Darren watching us in amusement across the room and I look away from them, embarrassed. *I am mortified!* Brigham steers me into a secluded corner of the room, and I bury my head into his chest.

"I'm so embarrassed," I whisper and run my hands up his chest.

"What just happened is exactly why I love you so much," he says and leans down and kisses my cheek.

"Because I don't think anything through?"

"No, because you're so full of life. Every moment with you is an adventure. What you want with a relic like me is a mystery," Brigham says, his voice dropping.

"You're not so old," I lie.

"I'm seven hundred and thirty-nine years old."

"Ew!" I tease. "It is a little disturbing when you say that out loud." I laugh and Brigham hugs me close to his body. "I can't believe I've had that ancient of a cock in my mouth."

Brigham laughs loudly. "What am I going to do with you?"

"Bite me, murder me, fuck me, kiss me—"

"I've already done all those things," Brigham says softly, holding me closer.

"They were fun, weren't they?"

"Yes."

"I think the bigger question is, what am I going to do with you?" I tease and run hy hand up his arm, feeling every ripple of his muscles underneath his jacket.

"Me?"

"Yep."

"You don't think you can handle being with a relic like me?"

"Oh, I can handle it, but I'm telling my friends you're only four hundred years old. Otherwise, they might think I'm weird."

"They don't think that already?" Brigham teases.

"Now who's being bad?"

Brigham kisses me and I bite his tongue, sucking a few droplets of his blood. He tastes like wine—*well-aged* wine. The thought of comparing Brigham to wine makes me laugh and I break from his kiss.

"What are you laughing at?" he asks.

"Nothing," I lie and continue laughing. I feel Brigham press into my mind, looking for what I am laughing about. "Sorry, I couldn't help it."

"It could be worse—you could have compared me to aged cheese." Brigham wrinkles his nose in disgust, and I laugh harder. I hadn't thought of that one! "Alright, you have to stop now." Suddenly, I feel Brigham take over my body and my laughter ceases. I look at Brigham in horror, and he looks at me equally horrified.

"I'm sorry, Butterfly, I shouldn't have done that. It was an accident."

"It really does feel like you're a marionette," I say swallowing hard. "I had no control over my body whatsoever."

"I'm sorry, Butterfly..." I look away from Brigham around the room of vampires as my heart goes numb. I can't believe he just did that—accident or not. The vampires have forgotten all about us and are laughing and talking in their own circles. I see Embry standing with a beautiful blonde vampire across the room.

"I'll be right back," I say to Brigham, not looking at him. As I walk away, I feel him slide into my mind. I push back hard against him and keep him on the fringes of my mind.

"Butterfly," I hear Brigham say softly in my head, but I ignore him and keep walking towards Embry. *I can't believe that just happened!* Brigham took ahold of my body! Panic is rising in me, and I want to run out of Forseti's as fast as I can, but I don't want to cause another embarrassing scene. How could Brigham have done that to me? Would he do it again? *Was it really an accident?*

"Butterfly!" Embry exclaims as I near him. He's holding the beautiful blonde vampire's hand in his. "I have someone I want you to meet! This is my wife, Vanessa!" The woman smiles widely at me and embraces me in a tight hug.

"Thank you," Vanessa whispers into my ear and I smile at her, trying not to look like I want to bolt out of here.

"For what?" I ask awkwardly. Vanessa releases me and I see the tears in her eyes.

"For giving me back my Embry," Vanessa says and wipes the tears from her eyes. Embry wraps an arm around her shoulder and squeezes her tightly to his side.

"I'm afraid you're thanking the wrong person. Brigham—" As I mention Brigham's name, I feel him press further into my mind and I visualize throwing a huge rock at him, hoping he will stop. "Brigham was the one who killed Shawn—he's who released Embry."

Vanessa shakes her head. "No, it was you. If you didn't exist, none of this would have been put into motion."

"You're giving me too much credit.'"

"I don't think so," Vanessa says, looking me up and down.

"Well, I'm glad you and Embry are together. Whatever did you think when you saw him after so many years?"

"I knew Embry wasn't dead—or, reanimated—what's the correct term I'm supposed to use?" Vanessa asks Embry, putting her hand lightly on his chest and he shrugs.

"I'm still not sure either. I find it difficult to say I'm dead when I feel so alive." Embry says.

"Yes, it's all very confusing. Anyways, I had a feeling that Embry was still out in the world. The police tried to convince me he had run off with another woman, but I knew my Embry would never do that," she says, staring lovingly at Embry with the most beautiful shade of pale blue eyes I had ever seen.

"Never," Embry agrees venomously and kisses Vanessa on the cheek.

"I knew he would come back to me, and all I had to do was wait. I honestly thought it would be sooner than ten years, but I'd spent so much time waiting already that a little longer didn't seem like that big of a deal."

"And you never sought anyone else?"

"I can't say that there weren't other men in my life during those years, but nothing serious. I was trying to pass the time—I was very lonely," she says, rubbing her earlobe and looking at Embry guiltily.

"I've already told you—there's nothing to feel guilty about," Embry says, looking at her with his face strained.

"I've had moments of doubt over the years and my entire family thought I'd gone crazy, but eventually even they stopped trying to convince me to date. It was so funny when he came to see me—I almost murdered him!" Vanessa laughs and pats Embry's arm.

"It didn't help that I woke her out of a dead sleep," Embry adds.

"I thought I was being burglarized!"

"After Brigham killed Shawn, all I could think about was Vanessa, and as soon as you and Brigham left, I went to find her. I was so excited to see her again that I knocked over her garbage cans on my way to the front door," Embry admits, running his hands through his hair.

"I had my baseball bat, ready to pound someone!" Vanessa laughs.

"You should have called the police and not tried to take on a burglar by yourself," Embry says with concern in his voice.

"I can take care of myself," Vanessa shrugs confidently.

"I know…"

"Anyway, when I first saw him, his back was turned to me because he was picking up the garbage he had spilled, but I knew it was him. I would recognize that ass anywhere!"

"She knocked me to the ground kissing me!"

"Really?" I looked at her, impressed—it was no easy feat for a human to knock down a vampire.

"I was so happy he was back that I lost control completely." Vanessa grins sheepishly.

"When did you realize he was a vampire?" I ask.

"About ten kisses in, I felt the fangs." She blushes and touches her mouth.

"And you didn't care?" I ask, my mouth popping open.

"Nope." She shakes her head and smiles at Embry. "He could have come back as a troll, and I would have reacted the same way."

"You're a lucky man, Embry," I say.

"Oh, I know it," Embry says with a grin and kisses Vanessa on the cheek.

"Did you make her a vampire that night?" I ask.

"Yep."

"WOW!"

"It's been a very exciting few weeks," Vanessa says, gesturing around.

"I bet!"

Vanessa kisses Embry tenderly on the lips and he smiles affectionately back at her. They were so much in love, and I find it so amazing that their love had lasted through the ten-year separation. Will Brigham and I be still together in ten years? Thinking about Brigham causes a small pressure to build in my head. I had forgotten he was in there moving around and had probably just heard my thoughts about him. His new ability is getting annoying.

"Are you worried about the sire connection, Vanessa? Are you worried about what it will be like between you two after the new moon?"

"No, Embry and I have always had a very open line of communication. I doubt very much will change," she shrugs.

"Huh…" I try not to think of anything specific. My reaction will be picked up by Brigham, and I don't want him to infer anything.

"Having trouble with Brigham?" asks Embry, shooting me a coy smile as I feel Brigham bristle at Embry's comment.

"Me? No…I mean—" I feel Brigham's attention focus on my words. "Maybe…"

"I could see where he might be a little invasive of your thoughts," Embry says and I feel Brigham move slightly in my head.

I look behind me and see Brigham hanging back alone and he starts trying to look interested in one of Forseti's paintings. The door next to him opens and Anton blows through with a wide grin and starts to make his way towards us.

"Why do you say that?" I ask, raising at an eyebrow at Embry. Anton reaches us and squeezes my arm excitedly.

"Anton's been telling me stories," Embry says, nodding at Anton. "If I was your sire, I might feel the need to reel you in too."

"That's insulting," I huff and Embry and Anton laugh.

"Sorry, it's the truth. I'm just saying—"

"I'm not that bad!" I say icily. Embry looks at Anton and Anton rolls his eyes at him. "What have you been telling him?" I ask Anton.

"Nothing—nothing," Anton says, holding his hands up in the air. I growl at him, and Embry laughs while Vanessa looks concerned.

Brigham presses deeply into my mind, and I try to close my mind to keep him out. I snap my head in his direction and shoot him an icy stare. He holds my gaze from across the room and stays right where he is in my mind not moving in further, but not leaving either.

"Touchy, touchy Butterfly," Embry teases.

"I don't need a babysitter," I growl between clenched teeth. I am saying it to Brigham as much as I am saying it to Embry.

"Whatever you say, chica," Anton says and rolls his eyes at me again. I contemplate plucking his eyes out of his head, but I'm not sure if I pluck them out of his head if they will grow back or be able to go back in the sockets. Maybe I will save that experiment for another night.

"Alright, stop it now, you two," Vanessa scolds and gives me a kind smile. I smile back at her and try to relax. I know that Embry and Anton are only teasing, but I don't like the accurate assessment of Brigham and my issues.

"What are you and Embry going to do now?" I ask, trying to change the subject. "Are you going to live around here?"

"For a while—until Vanessa adjusts. Then, who knows—maybe we'll travel," Embry says as he looks at Vanessa and she shrugs.

"It doesn't matter to me what we do. I'm happy just being with Embry," she says and hugs him.

"Well, I wish you two the best," I say sincerely. They both deserved to be happy after the ten hellish years they both had been through.

"Butterfly?" I jump at the clear strong voice of Brigham in my head.

Anton, Vanessa, and Embry look at me curiously. I try to give them a reassuring smile and say, "Can you guys excuse me for a moment?"

"Sure, no problem," Embry says as his eyebrows draw together. I smile gratefully at them and make a beeline towards the nearest door. I see Brigham move towards me out of the corner of my eye, but I don't wait for him and continue to walk at an increased speed.

Outside, the night air is cool, and I scan the street searching for somewhere to go so that Brigham can't find me, but with his weird smelling ability, there is no such place in existence. I hear the door open and shut behind me and I panic and begin walking south on the street.

"What are you doing?" Brigham asks me in my head. I ignore him and keep walking, needing to get some distance between us. *"BUTTERFLY!"* he shouts loudly, and my entire head rings as I move my hands to my ears, trying to block it out. I close my eyes against the noise and keep moving. I am not giving in without a fight. I feel Brigham's hands on me, and he spins me around to face him, but I push him hard away from me, sending him sprawling. "Where are you going?" he asks out loud. His stoney face is gone and an angry one is showing now.

"Don't you know?" I ask insolently and cross my arms.

"Why are you so mad?" he asks. The anger in his face is fading and his stoney appearance returns.

"I thought you weren't going to be like Shawn." I say, assaulting him and pushing my finger hard into his chest. He tries to catch me up in his arms, but I shove him hard and turn away from him.

"Like Shawn? What are you talking about?" Brigham asks. He reaches for my hand and I step away from him, keeping a few feet between us.

"I don't like you entering my mind whenever you want," I say, turning towards him.

"But Butterfly—I'm always in there."

If I had a heart, it just would have skipped a beat. "You are?" I ask.

"Yes."

"But Shawn wasn't aware of Darren and Embry's every thought!"

"Yes, but he made more vampires than I have, so the connection between him and those he sired was weaker. I only have you, so the connection is stronger."

"FUCK!" I shout and pull my hair hard. "Go make more vampires!"

"Butterfly—" Brigham moves towards me again and I step out of his reach. I didn't want him to touch me now or ever again.

"I don't like this at all!" I cry. Tears well in my eyes and I brush them away then look at my blood-soaked hands angrily. I didn't want my emotional response to dull the impact of my words. "I feel like I have no privacy! *This is complete bullshit!* I want you out of my head!"

"I can't," Brigham says with a blank expression. I was getting so tired of his unemotional face.

"If you're in there all the time, why do I only feel you some of the time?" I ask, trying to keep my voice even.

Brigham's face falters slightly and he gives me an apologetic look. "That probably happens when I'm more curious about what is going on."

"Stop being curious!" I yell and push him hard in the chest, making him stumble back again. *So much for not coming off as an irrational nut job!*

"I can't," he says quietly.

I growl at him and turn away as more tears well. *Fuck!* I must look awful! I start to walk towards the road, but my feet are glued to the ground I yank and yank at them, but they will not budge. "Let me go," I growl, turning back to look at him with my fangs bared.

"Butterfly," he says gently and reaches for me. He tries to wrap his arms around me, but I shove him away. He pins my arms and wraps me up and I struggle against him. Unable to escape, I began to sob into his shirt. "Please don't cry—let's talk about this."

"There's nothing to talk about—I'm screwed! This is exactly what I feared would happen! *This is utter bullshit!* You lied to me about everything! I have no control over my life now!" I sob, smearing red tears into his sports jacket.

"Yes, you do," he says softly and runs his fingers through my hair.

"No, I don't. I can't even walk away from you." Brigham's arms drop to his sides, and he steps away from me slightly. His face is sad, and I wonder if that's real or if he's trying to show emotion now because he read my mind when I was angered by his emotionless gaze. *Probably the latter— jackass!* "Just leave me alone," I say hollowly and wipe my face, looking at the blood on my hands. "Being a vampire sucks."

Brigham mouth twists as he looks at my bloody hands. "I can't leave you alone," he says, raising his voice an octave. I look at him in surprise. He had never raised his voice in anger at me before like that.

"Try," I say as I wipe more tears from my face. I feel the weight that is holding my legs in place lift, and I take a step back from him.

"Better?" he asks as he rubs his neck. I don't answer him as I try to get a hold of my crying. "Butterfly—"

He reaches for me again and I automatically step away from him. He sighs deeply and crosses his arms over his chest.

"You're being ridiculous," he says as his stoney gaze returns and I imagine ripping his expression right off his face.

He cocks his head at me and smiles. Great, now I was amusing him with my silly thoughts. *Wonderful!*

"This is going to be a little difficult for us, isn't it?"

"Bite me, grandpa," I mumble, looking away from him. He laughs and flashes me in my mind what I look like to him at the moment. I look pathetic standing with my hands across my chest, lips in a pout, with shining eyes and cheeks. I look like a child throwing a tantrum and I try unsuccessfully to keep myself from laughing at the image.

"I want you to have your freedom, Butterfly, I do, but I am finding it difficult not overstepping your boundaries."

"How do you and Forseti handle it?"

"Forseti and I only use the connection to talk to each other," Brigham says softly and takes another step towards me. I don't move away from him this time.

"He hasn't ever controlled your body like you just did to me?"

"No, never," Brigham looks at me ashamed and pulls his hair back from his face.

"Of course—our situation is a little different, isn't it," I huff, crossing my arms across my chest.

"Yes," Brigham says and moves closer to me. "I can't break the connection, Butterfly, I'm sorry. I'm not that powerful."

"I don't want you knowing everything about me," I say quietly.

"Don't I already?" he asks, giving me a small smile, and I scowl at him.

"I need to have a part of my life that you can't touch, Brigham, or this isn't going to work for me."

"You're right, but I don't know how to make it better," Brigham says as his eyes turn navy.

"We need to set up some ground rules," I say firmly.

"I'm listening," he says and touches my arm softly, tracing his fingers along my forearm.

"You can't control my body. Ever! I don't like it," I say sternly.

"What if you're going to get hurt?"

I gesture to my body. "What can hurt me?"

"You could trip and fall onto an axe and decapitate yourself," he points out.

"I'm not that clumsy—but if that is about to happen, by all means—take over my body."

"If you try to walk into sunlight, I'm stopping you," Brigham says, shooting me a hard glare.

"Fine," I say through gritted teeth.

"What about during sex?" He gives a slight smile. "Do these rules apply then as well?"

"Yes!"

"You're no fun," he teases and cautiously pulls me into a hug. I contemplate stepping away from him but the weight of his arms on my body feels so good, so I decide to hold my ground instead.

"You're very close to losing all your privileges anyway, so I wouldn't worry about it," I say seriously.

He looks at me deeply and searches my mind for the truth in my words. Finding I was serious, he says softly, "I'll be good." He leans down and kisses my neck.

"This is serious," I say, trying to resist the way my body was wanting to arch into him.

"Of course," Brigham says, his voice low. He pulls back from me and cups my cheek—his expression changes into his more normal stoney expression. "What else do you want?"

"You have to stop entering my mind whenever you feel like it," I say firmly.

"I told you—I'm always in there."

"Okay, but I don't want to feel you moving around in there," I say while making a swirling motion with my hand towards my head.

"I don't think I can do that. I need to know you're safe. What if we limit my…let's call them, spot checks."

"Okay, one spot check a month."

Brigham shakes his head hard. "That's not nearly enough."

"Twice a month?" I ask hopefully.

"Not even close."

"Once a week?" I suggest hopefully. That is still *much* too often, but I am getting desperate.

"No."

"Come on!" I shout and hit his arm. "This is brutal!"

"How about I check in with you once or twice a day…maybe three."

"Three times a day!" I cry and clench my fists. *My own mother, when she was alive, didn't check in on me that many times a day!*

"I think that's fair," he says, nodding. I growl at him, beginning to pace. It was better than all the time, but it was still more than I wanted.

"Fine, but you can't listen in on *any* of Anton and my conversations. My time with him is off-limits!" Brigham growls and his eyes flash at me with his canines showing. *Good!* I wasn't the only one who was mad! "Give me my time with Anton, or else!"

"Or else what?" he challenges. I look back at him challengingly.

"Or else you're going to have a very miserable afterlife," I say, snarling at him with my canines fully protruded. Brigham studies me and I stick my chin out at him. I imagine myself picking fights with vampires, tearing through cities, and running off across the country. It was all a bluff, but I hope the possibilities of me doing these things will scare Brigham enough to compromise. "Well?"

"I'm thinking," Brigham says slowly.

"Think faster," I warn and tap my wrist, pretending I am wearing a watch. I am not sure how long I could keep my bluff up.

"Why, where are you going with Anton?" he asks, and I shoot him a dirty look. He takes a step towards me, his face changing ever so slightly, looking almost predatory. He knew very well I couldn't go anywhere.

"I'm not telling you," I say while stepping away from him, keeping just out of reach.

"Can I come with?" he asks, stepping even closer.

"No."

"I worry about you, Butterfly, especially after what happened with Shawn. I'm finding it very difficult to grant you the freedom you want...sorry—deserve. I honestly didn't think the sire connection would be this much of a struggle to figure out when you were a human."

"You don't have a choice," I point out to him. "We either compromise, or there's nothing."

"Nothing?" he asks. I nod and send him an image of me sitting in a dark room covered in dust and cobwebs, having not moved for decades. Brigham flinches at the image and his face darkens.

"Nothing," I say, my tone low. Brigham's mouth tenses and his eyes turn a dark blue-almost-black color. I know he finally understands how strongly I feel about this.

"Let's try your rules for a week."

"A month," I counter.

Brigham laughs and rolls his neck, making a loud popping sound. "Okay, a month, then we can reassess our needs. Is that acceptable to you?"

I make a face at him and look at my feet. It wasn't perfect, but it was a start. "No body snatching, no Anton eavesdropping, and only up to three spot checks a day."

"Let's make it five."

"*FIVE!*" I shout.

"You're getting a bargain."

"Hardly! You might as well slap the shackles on me now!"

"It's not that bad."

"Does Forseti have you under such strict controls?" I ask and Brigham lets out a snarl, his eyes turning indigo. I know he doesn't, and I hope this fact will change Brigham's mind.

"No…" he growls. He looks at me, and I smile at him victoriously. I had him on that one. "How about four spot checks a day? That's about how often Forseti and I talk a day."

"Deal," I say and stick my hand out to him to shake on it. Brigham takes my hand tenderly and shakes it, grimacing the entire time. It isn't as good as three, but it is better than five.

"I've gotten robbed," Brigham mutters under his breath.

"Too bad for you."

"Butterfly, these spot checks are me going into your mind. You, on the other hand, can enter mine as much as you want. Whenever you want to talk, go right ahead. I'd like it if you did."

"Why?"

"I love you, Butterfly. I like spending time with you—in whatever form we can."

"You're making me feel bad."

"I don't mean to."

"I like being with you too, Brigham—I really do, but the thought of being tethered to you and under your control makes me want to run. I don't know why I can't be like Embry and Vanessa, but I can't. I think I have a restless spirit or something."

"I know…but I like that about you."

"You're not mad?"

"No, I thought you would have thrown your tantrum last week. I'm surprised you let me in your head as much as you did."

"I didn't notice how much you were in there with me until we were out of the house. That and I didn't mind it so much the last couple of weeks—it was comforting after all that had happened," I admit and bite my lip, thinking back about Shawn's compound and shudder a little. "And *FUCK YOU* for calling it a tantrum. I'm reacting completely rationally given the circumstances."

Brigham sighs and flexes his hands. "I'm sorry." I roll my eyes at him and cross my arms over my chest and bite my thumb. "I'm always here for you, Butterfly."

"I know." He takes a tentative step towards me, and I don't move away from him. I let him wrap his arms around me, and I lean my head against his chest.

"There isn't a happily ever after, is there?" I whisper, my voice catching.

"I don't know, I'm pretty happy."

"I mean, there isn't a point where everything is easy—even vampires have complications in their lives."

"You thought life would be easier as a vampire?"

"Yes."

"Some things are easier," Brigham says and rubs his hand over my hair.

"Yes, but other things are much harder."

"Is it a draw then?"

"I don't know, but if I get to have you forever, that's a plus." *I think...*

"Even with the sire connection?"

"Maybe..."

"It'll get easier, Butterfly."

"Do you think so?"

"I do."

"How do you know?"

"I'm a very old vampire—trust me, the first years are the hardest and then they get better and better."

"I suppose I have to trust you. You are a *VERY OLD* vampire," I say and Brigham lets out a low laugh.

"That I am." He leans down and kisses me, and I kiss him back, letting my body relax into him. I love how he feels against me, and I want to stay in this simple moment of being physically close to him, but my thoughts keep pushing against me.

"You still think we are going to work out?" I question Brigham in my mind. I look up into his eyes hoping to find reassurance.

"I have no doubts," he says, answering me back through my mind. He strokes my hair again and I lean my head heavily into his palm. I will never get enough of his touch.

"Why is that?" I ask, hoping to gain some insight into his confidence.

"We have an eternity to perfect our relationship."

"Some people are able to do that in a lifetime." I thought about my grandparents who were married for fifty years. It was very rare to last that long in a relationship these days, but it did happen. Although, now that I think about it—it might have been in part due to the fact that women couldn't have their own bank accounts, have credit cards, or own homes…

"Time can be a great benefit."

"I believe it will be like that for us," I say hopefully. I really wanted to believe that. Otherwise, what will we become?

"Good choice," Brigham whispers and pulls me tight against him.

THE END

…for now

ABOUT THE AUTHOR

Katie Gabbert Downey is a Minnesota-born midwestern multigenre author. She loves hiking, dark chocolate, and drinking copious amounts of coffee. When she is not writing, she is going on adventures with her family, trying to wrangle her kids, and taking care of her menagerie of pets.

To explore more of Katie Gabbert Downey's works and stay up to date, please visit:

www.katiegabbertdowney.com